Jonathan Smith was educated in Wales and at St John's College, Cambridge. As well as his acclaimed memoir, *The Learning Game*, he has written six novels and many plays for radio. A feature film of *Summer in February*, for which he wrote the screenplay, will be released in 2013. It stars Dominic Cooper, Dan Stevens and Emily Browning.

Jonathan Smith lives in Kent with his wife. He has two grown-up children: a daughter, Becky, and a son Ed, who played cricket for Kent, Middlesex and England.

Also by Jonathan Smith

SUMMER *in* FEBRUARY

JONATHAN SMITH

ABACUS

First published in Great Britain by Little, Brown and Company 1995
This edition published by Abacus 1996

21 23 25 24 22

Copyright © Jonathan Smith 1995

A CIP catalogue record for this book
is available from the British Library.

ISBN 978-0-349-10746-2

Printed and bound in Great Britain by
Clays Ltd, St Ives plc

Papers used by Abacus are from well-managed forests
and other responsible sources.

MIX
Paper from
responsible sources
FSC
www.fsc.org
FSC® C104740

*for David Evans
&
the Evans family*

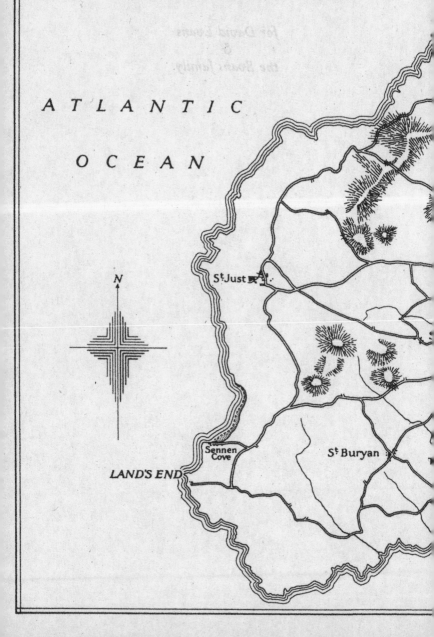

WEST CORNWALL

ATLANTIC

OCEAN

N

St Just

Sennen
Cove

LAND'S END

St Buryan

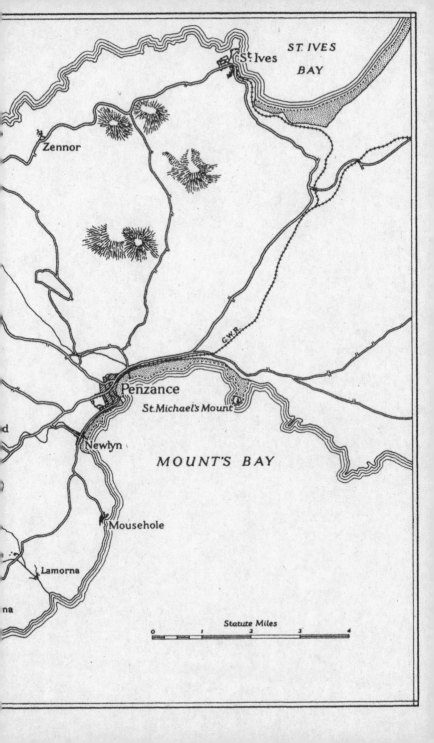

Part One

Part One

That morning, sitting in his spacious study in Castle House, Dedham, Sir Alfred Munnings opened a letter. It was from his old friend, Dame Laura Knight.

16, Langford Place,
St John's Wood,
London
27th April 1949

Dear A.J.,

So you're really really going to do it tomorrow? Is it wise? Is it for the best? And why at the banquet? Won't it open up old wounds?

Whatever, I'll be listening.

With love,

Laura.

Pray Silence for the President, 1949

It was time for the President's big speech. The tapping, the call to order, was pretty close to his right ear so he had no problem hearing it, and it was clear and crisp enough for everyone sitting at the top table. But then those about to speak in public – as you'll know if you've ever done it – are always on the edge of their seats, waiting for the moment to arrive, picking at their food, wanting the lavatory, as dry-mouthed as jockeys lining up for the start at Newmarket, all tensed up and ready for the off, and conscious that the eyes of the world are about to be on them.

And, in the President's case, thousands of ears.

Not that he was nervous. Not a bit of it. If he had been nervous he would have written the whole speech out, wouldn't he, instead of just jotting down a couple of phrases on the back of his menu while enjoying his dinner to the full. Food and drink, the President always maintained, were there to be enjoyed, and the truth was he was looking forward to this speech, to his swansong: he knew what needed to be said to the assembled company and, by God, he was going to say it.

He was under starter's orders.

But!

But, the table-tapping, while loud enough for him, was little match for that large gallery full of all-male banter, and no match at all for the distant, well-oiled laughter which rose to the ceiling with the cigar smoke. The younger academicians on the far tables, who had half heard the toastmaster tapping, pretended, in the time-honoured way, that they had not; and when he was sitting in their place many years ago, the President used to do the same thing, employ the same delaying tactics, only a damn sight worse. So, seeing the distant diners were not going to shut up for that genteel top table tapping, he turned round and told the toastmaster to try again, only this time to 'put a bit of beef into it'. And the toastmaster, a man of solid muscle and bone, took the President at his word and fairly hammered the gavel. He hammered it slowly and loudly, with more than a bit of come-on-gentle-men-now-please.

And that, the extra volume plus the emphatic pauses, did the trick. Even the rowdiest table fell silent; and once the lull was established, the toastmaster, resplendent in red, puffed out his barrel chest and projected his voice full blast over everyone's heads, past the paintings hanging two or three deep on the walls, through the mahogany doors and out into Piccadilly itself.

'Your Royal Highness,' he intoned – and that word 'Highness' helped to do the trick, bringing a respectful hush – 'Your Excellencies, Your Graces, My Lords and Gentlemen – Pray Silence for the President of the Royal Academy, Sir Alfred Munnings.'

Yes, that's him!

Pray Silence for the second son of a Suffolk miller, a son of the soil, but then Constable, the great Constable, was the son of a Suffolk miller too, and who wouldn't be as proud as Punch to follow in *his* footsteps?

There was, too, something about the toastmaster's style that the President liked. Good toastmastering, he always maintained, was like gunnery practice: you cleaned the barrels, you slammed in the shells, you got the trajectory right, and then you discharged a deafening salvo at the enemy. Take aim, fire! and the enemy were brought down. Enemy? At a banquet in Burlington House?

What enemy?

But the enemy were there all right, and in numbers.

As the toastmaster intoned his phrases, the President savoured each and every word. He enjoyed each e-nun-ci-ated syllable. Now *that*, he said to himself, is how to introduce a chap, straight from the shoulder, no mumbling, no beating about the bush.

'Your Royal Highness' – and there indeed was the Duke of Gloucester on his right, more or less upright if rather the worse for wear—

'Your Excellencies' – and there were ambassadors from God knows which country at every table, including some Turk or other, Mr Aki-Cacky, on Top Table—

'Your Graces' – yes, including the Archbishop of Canterbury himself who'd just been up on his feet wittering away – mixed up with the odd Admiral and Field Marshal, he could see old Monty at the end of the table. Not to mention loads of lords and plenty of gents, plenty of boiled shirts and stuffed shirts, plus a sprinkling of pansies who couldn't tell a decent painting from a pool of horse piss.

No, steady on now, Alfred, he said to himself, careful, old boy, you're not in The Coach and Horses now, you're in civilised company, surrounded by The Great and The Good, and they're here for a slap-up do and they're also here, Alfred, to hear your Retiring President's speech and, by God, they're going to get it!

On the toastmaster's final words 'Sir Alfred Munnings' there was some kind of welcoming applause, mostly from Winston and those close by on top table, but enough in all conscience to suggest some kind of recognition of all he had done as President. As the applause died down, Sir Alfred took one more gulp of wine, a bloody good claret he'd selected himself, and checked his flies. All secure there, he stood up.

The banquet was in Gallery Three, Burlington House, Piccadilly, and the place was jam-packed with one hundred and eighty diners. The President ran his eye around the candle-lit tables, then placed both his fists, knuckles down, on the white tablecloth. It was a position he liked to adopt when speaking. Not only did it take some weight off his dicky leg, but the stance also (he felt) suited his attacking style.

So, here he was.

And there they were.

The President faced the Academy; he would not be presumptuous enough to say 'his' Academy. And he faced them with the nation listening on the wireless, thousands of good people from John O'Groats to Land's End had turned on their sets, ordinary folk who liked to hear the simple truth spoken in simple plain English.

So, the truth it was to be.

'Your Royal Highness,' he began slowly, 'My Lords and Gentlemen.' As was his wont, he took his time over each syllable. After a good evening he always maintained it was only sensible to take your time; it was always best to walk your horse home nice and slowly through the lanes. Hurry along, as he'd found to his cost, and you could go arse over tip. The trouble was, though, not only was he slow, he was *too* slow, and without meaning to, his voice caught some of the toastmaster's tone.

'I am,' he began, 'gett-ing some-what dis-tressed. Through some extra-ordin-ary arrange-ment these toasts have all been put upon the Pres-i-dent.'

In amongst that lot there were too many *r*s and too many *p*s. *R*s and *p*s could, the President knew, be a ruddy problem and if he didn't watch it he'd soon be reciting Poe's 'Raven' or running round the ragged rock with the rugged rascals or whichever way round it was.

Pause, he said to himself. Pause, Alfred!

He paused. There was time now to take a quick look down at the notes he'd been jotting down on the menu card, so he lifted it up close to his eye and saw

Casserole of Sole Chablis
Rose Duckling with Olives
Garden Peas
New Potatoes
Asparagus
Gateau St Honoré
Ices
Petits Fois
Dessert
& Coffee

and there was not a lot of help there if you were already stuck on your feet, but there also was a rather good pencil drawing of Winston smoking his cigar, done not ten minutes ago. Damned good likeness it was too. It looked like Winston, his heavily hunched shoulders, his wrinkled forehead, his big cigar, the old boy to a T., and that's what a drawing should do, shouldn't it, look like the subject?

Pleased with this thought, emboldened by this convic-
tion, the President launched himself again, only this time
at a canter, so to speak, pushing the horse on a bit.

'I know what it is, and have known what it is, to sit at
the tables when there has been a much more company' –
what? a much more company, what does *that* mean? Never
mind, no time, keep going – 'ca-rousing and drinking, little
thinking of the poor President there at his table, regardless
of all he had to go through, and to get away with, to put
it in a common turn of speech.'

He breathed out. That sentence, while something of a
mish-mash, went a lot better, though there was a nasty
moment after 'ca-rousing and drinking, little thinking',
when he felt a touch of panic in his palms that he might
be slipping into that familiar, bouncy metre and that
familiar rhyme, slipping in fact into one of his impromptu
ballads.

But, dammit, he wasn't in some snug pub or artists'
party reciting Edgar Allan Poe, he was the President of
the Royal Academy and all dressed up like a toff. He
was the most famous figure in British Art, and the main
thing was, he had to make sense! He had to speak simple
English!

'Now here I am, responding for The Academy. Now
the Archbishop of Canter-bury has talked' . . . a load of
complete . . . 'in a very accomplished way about this body
. . . but what *of* the body?'

The body of men, he meant, the collective body of
English Art, the packed tables laid out in front of him in
Burlington House. And he glared from table to table; he
glared left, and he glared right, and he glared ahead; and he
had to say he did not like much of what he saw. He did not
like it one little bit. It was high time a question was put to
the collective body of English Art, and put bluntly in front

of the nation on the wireless. Then they couldn't say they hadn't heard it, could they?

Are they worthy? Yes, that's it—

'Are they worthy of this building in which they are housed? Are we all doing the great work which we should do? Well, it is not for me to stand here on my head' – *head*? You're standing on your feet, Alfred – 'here tonight and find fault with the Academy.'

At this there were some murmurs of approval, murmurs from posh people trying to warn him off, stuffed shirts trying to divert the President into their polite, diplomatic channels. He could sense them saying under their breaths, 'No, Munnings, you are right, it is not for *you*, the second son of a Suffolk miller, to criticise *us*.'

This only incensed him further. Oh, *wasn't* it! If they thought for one moment they could stop him going on with his plan they couldn't be more wrong. In for a penny, in for a pound, the President said to himself.

'But, BUT I find myself a President of a body of men who are what I'd call shilly-shallying.'

He stressed 'shilly' and he stressed 'shally', and on 'shilly-shallying' a sizeable number of wobbly chins hit the table. There was a sideways flickering of half-pickled eyes, a communal rolling of eyeballs. There was a fearful sense running around the room that he was going to do it, and what was more he was going to do it with millions listening on the wireless. Damn right he was. I told you I would, Laura.

He watched a white, manicured hand reach out in silence for the port.

Shilly-shallying. Monty, for one, liked that. Far too many soldiers, Monty always said, shilly-shallied. Winston, for another, liked it. Far too many politicians, Winston said, and 'so-called statesmen' shilly-shallied. In the expanding silence the President once more glared round the room, not focusing his eye on any particular place, merely allowing the accusation to sink in and hurt. The shilly-shalliers knew who they were, and *he* knew who they were, and he was going to blow them to pieces.

'They!'

His voice rose.

'They feel that there is something in this so-called MODERN ART.'

When he said the fatal words 'Modern Art' there was a gasp, an audible gulp. Yes, Reynard the Fox was now out into the open and running. Now it was clear the hunt was on. Suddenly – it also happened sometimes when he was painting – suddenly he felt an extraordinary power, a quick pump of adrenalin, as if he was going full tilt along the Cornish coast or full split across the flat Norfolk fields, whip in hand and cap askew, full tilt and fearless at a wide-open ditch. There wasn't any point shying away, you had to go for the jump.

His voice rose to a sharper, more competitive level.

'Well, I myself would rather have – ah' – if he was going to blaspheme he realised he had better be civilised, he really should do the decent thing and turn and bow slightly to the Archbishop of Canterbury – 'ah, excuse me, my Lord Archbishop – I would rather have a damned bad failure, a bad dusty old picture where somebody had tried to do something, to set down something what they have seen and felt, than all this affected juggling, this following of . . . well, shall we call it the School of *Paris*?'

That Paris crack, the way he put such contempt into '*Paris*', just came out, he was enjoying himself so much. He was loving it. So he put his hands on his hips, exactly as Charlie Chaplin did in *The Great Dictator*, and pretended to scour the tables for any offending French diplomats.

'I hope the French ambassador is not here tonight.'

It has to be said he timed that aside rather well. In response, there was warm laughter, with-him laughter, and the aside went down best of all with Winston, whose shoulders were going up and down. Good old Winnie, the President smiled, never a great one for effete frogs and their new-fangled fashions. He looked at them all, and went strongly on.

'Not so long ago, I spoke in this very room to the students, the boys and girls, and they were receiving all sorts of gratuities from the Government. For what? *For what?*'

No one answered. No one dared.

'To learn art. And to become what? Not artists. Well now, I said to those students, "If you paint a tree, for God's sake try and paint it to look like a tree, and if you paint a sky, try and make it look like a sky."' Winston, as sure as eggs were eggs, was enjoying every word of all this: the President could feel his warm approval, there was absolutely no need to check. Had they not discussed the textures of trees and the skyishness of skies often enough in recent months?

On he went:

'Only this last two days I have been motoring from my home in Dedham to Newmarket and back. On Sunday I motored through Suffolk, and I was looking at skies all the time . . . on Monday what skies they were! And still, in spite of all these men who have painted skies, *we* should be painting skies still better!'

Skies! Not kittens with as many legs as a centipede. Skies! Not Picasso portraits, not females with two noses and three tits and a set of shark's teeth coming out of their earholes!

Yes, he was into his stride now.

'But there has been this foolish inter-ruption to all effort in Art, helped by foolish men writing in the press encouraging all this damned nonsense' – and this time there was no apology to the Archbishop for 'damned' – 'putting all the younger men out of their stride. I am right . . . I have the Lord Mayor on my side . . . I am sure he is behind me . . . and on my left I have our newly elected extra-ordinary member of the Academy, Mr Winston Churchill—'

—elected by me, that is, because he can paint a tree to look like a tree and he can paint a sky to look like a sky

—Winston Churchill elected by the second son of a Suffolk miller—

'and I know Winston is behind me, because once he said to me, "Alfred, if you met Pee-cass-O coming down the street would you join with me in kicking his something-something-something?" and I said, "Yes, Sir, I would."'

Well, that *was it*! There was uproar. Uproar, no less. Alfred felt he'd done the trick, he had really and truly loosened up the whole show. Gallery Three of Burlington House rocked. Waves of laughter rolled towards him from the back to the top tables. Down at his end Monty was cackling away.

So that was fine. So far so good. But how was it going down with the pansies? What about the Blunts of this world, with their manicured nails and their modulated voices and their porcelain expressions? What did they make of Winston and the President lying in wait in some doorway for Pablo to come down Piccadilly in his beret so that they could jump out and kick him up the arse? Eh?

The President was feeling in terrific form; he had never felt better.

'Now,' he went on, 'we have all sorts of high-brows here tonight, *ex*-perts who think they know more about Art than the men who had to paint the pictures, even those poor devils who sit out and try to paint a landscape and fail.'

Because that, the President maintained, was how you should paint a picture, *en plein air*, as Bastien-Lepage said. It was as simple and as difficult as that. You needed all your colours, your white, your turps, painting umbrella, rags, beautiful brushes, and with your hat over your eyes and your brushes in your mouth, you picked up your easel and palette and canvas and went out into the open air in all weathers, wind, rain or shine, in Norfolk or Cornwall or Hampshire, in peace or in war, you got outside and worked, that's what he and Laura used to say to each other in Lamorna. 'Get outside and work till you drop.'

And *what* did you paint?

Paint the real world, paint ordinary men and women, the land, the sea and the sky, not the sick world of some tortured spirit, not the surreal world of some diseased and malformed imagination. But could you imagine those critics out in the open air? Just imagine Anthony Blunt out in a field, with his eyes watering, his hands blue and with some dark storm clouds coming up. Just imagine him covered in sultry summer flies. What would he do? He'd shut up shop and be back to his boys in his Chelsea boudoir, well, bugger that lot if you'll excuse the pun, because the President would prefer a basket-covered stone jar of ale and an oak-ribbed bar, let's say The Red Lion, some soup, fish and pheasant, or sausage and mash and briar pipes – that was good enough for him, before the slow walk home.

Everyone could see he was enjoying himself. Any mention of the critics always brought the best out in Alfred.

The *cri-tics*.

'They are so – if I may use a common expression – so fed up to the teeth in pictures, they move among pictures, they see so many pictures that their . . . they . . . their judgement becomes . . .'

At this point, as luck would have it, the President saw the offending article. His sight might not be too good these days but he was sure the offending article was there, third table along at the far end, the Surveyor of the King's Pictures. The President didn't plan it. He just said, 'because their judgement becomes blunt, they, yes, blunt. And that reminds me, is he here tonight? Anthony Blunt, is he here tonight?'

Oh, he's here tonight all right and staring at his polished fingernails.

'Who once stood in this room with me, when the King's Pictures were here, and there was a Reynolds hanging there, and he said "That Reynolds isn't as great as a Pee-cass-O". Believe me, what an extraordinary thing for a man to say! Well, perhaps one should not mention names, but I do not care, since I am resigning at the end of the year.'

'Good riddance!' someone said.

The President's blood jumped. His fists clenched. Who said that? Someone had, quite clearly, uttered the words 'Good riddance'. It wasn't loud but he heard the words all right. His eyesight might be poor – and who could be surprised at that? – but his ears were still damned good. 'Good riddance', eh? He could feel his knuckles grinding away into the tablecloth. He moved the weight off his painful foot. His head started to beat, but he fought back.

'I do not wish to go on with an Academy that says, "Well, there must be something in this modern art, we must give these jugglers a show."'

And what about that 'woman'? Woman, my foot! Ask them about that monstrosity.

'Here we are in this Academy, and you gentlemen assembled in the Octagon Room, and there was a woman cut out there in wood, and God help us if all the race of women looked like *that*!'

Yes, they enjoyed that, the diners did enjoy that. And the President enjoyed listening to their laughter, waves of it, good, warm, male laughter, and they were laughing because they were all men together, and they all knew what a woman looked like, and they all knew what they wanted a woman to look like, they wanted a woman to look *paintable*, but . . . did the pansies? *Did the pansies?* Come on, be honest, did the critics? No! What did the modern critics fancy? They fancied Modigliani's models and Henry Moore's holes, Henry Moore's modern heavyweight holes.

'The sculptors today . . . are sinking away into a fashion of bloated, heavyweight, monstrous nudes.'

Blots on the landscape, bloated females, bloated, blote . . .

Blote—

Oh, Alfred, why did you say that?

His left hand started to tremble, then shake. He didn't mean to use that word. It was a word he always avoided. He clenched the tabletop to steady his hand, but the trembling would not stop. It was so easy to be put off one's stride, wasn't it, even when things were going so well. Bloated. He had to blot out all bloated things. But he couldn't. He could see her face, her pale face. It was such a silly name, the very last name you would give a beautiful, paintable, elusive girl, but it clung to her and it clung to him, like anemones to rocks.

There was silence and cigar smoke. But you couldn't have silence in a speech, could you? If he didn't speak soon they would think he'd suffered a stroke. He *had* to keep talking. He could feel the room changing, he could sense a shiver in the subsoil, and the next thing he knew he was on to 'Battersea', another B, oh bloody hell, and

he gabbled on, but his heart was no longer in it. He was
thrown, thrown off his horse, and he heard himself saying
these sentences:

'You saw those . . . *things* exhibited in Battersea Park?
Did you? Things put there by the London County Council.
We are spending millions every year on Art Education,
and yet we exhibit all these foolish drolleries to the
public. And yet I have stood in that park, and I have
been with the public who've been there, I've asked them
questions, and they were disgusted and angered, just as
they were to see this Madonna and Child in a church at
Northampton.'

Henry Moore's monstrosity, they all knew what he
meant, Moore's monstrously modern holes.

'Because . . . I would like to ask everybody here to travel
up to Northampton to see this statue of the Madonna and
Child at this church. I am speaking plainly because my
horses may all be wrong, but I'm damned sure that statue
isn't right!'

At this point there was a kerfuffle at the far end of the
gallery. Three or four chairs were being pushed back. Was
it a protest against the President and what he was saying
or a brace of weak bladders? The President could not be
sure, but it further sapped his strength.

Stop now, Alfred, he said to himself, you've said enough,
probably more than enough.

'Well, I'm not going on too long, Sirs . . . I would not
go on any longer because I know a greater man than I is
going to follow me.'

Mr Winston Churchill, no less. And you cannot get
greater than that.

But he didn't sit down, because he had not yet mentioned
Mr Matisse. He had to get Mr Matisse off his chest.

'But I would like to say that this afternoon I went to the

Tate Gallery, the Tate, the second room on the right with white walls, which is nothing but walls, and you will see this picture by Ma-tisse. It is called *Le Foret* . . . the . . . forest.'

And damn me if it didn't happen again, and in much the same part of the room, only louder this time. More chairs moved. Mentioning Matisse had done it. This time their voices were louder. The critical geese were gobbling and honking and stretching out their long white necks.

'Best thing in the Tate!'

'Wonderful!'

'Lovely work!'

'A beautiful work of art!'

The President glared.

Beautiful, my backside!

'I hope,' he shouted, 'I hope you hear these other members interrupting me . . . As I am President and I have the right of the chair, allow me to speak. I shall not be here next year, thank God.'

'Thank God indeed,' he heard.

But no, no, he was not going to bite back, not this time. No, let it go, let it all go. What was it all for, art, all that toil, all that effort in the wind and rain – and we're gone. And what did *they* know, what do the critics know about skies and a countryman's soul, about the head-work and the hand-work, the steady movement of the scythe, the dance of raindrops? He was trying to explain all that the other day to . . . forgotten his name . . . that Old England was gone, that you couldn't see the barley ears for thistledown, cottages had given way to villas, sleeved waistcoats to boiler suits, horses to tractors, fences to barbed wire, and Sargent to Salvador Dali, and what was *his* art, Salvador Dali's, glutinous watches and sagging pianos, that's all.

The President held up his hand, like a tired conductor on his very last night on the rostrum.

'In the *Telegraph* I was reported as having said "Let a tree look like a tree"' because trees look like trees, don't they, and women look like women. Or *should*! We all know a paintable girl when we see one, and we all know how difficult it is to choose between the demands of a paintable girl and the demands of paint.

'Well,' he pointed a thin, bent finger at the packed, silent room, 'you go and look at that spirit of a tree ... by Matisse. But hear what Robert Louis Stevenson said ... He spoke of the sound of "innumerable thousands and thousands of treetops and—"'

and why-oh-*why* did he ever risk that difficult word again—

'"innun ... immuner ... imminumer"'

He couldn't even speak now. His hands shook. He told himself to take the horse slowly home along the lanes, very slowly. Try again, Alfred, very slowly.

'"in-num-er-able millions of green leaves that were abroad in the air".'

'The fellow's tight!'

'Of course he's tight. Always is.'

'Just a country bumpkin.'

'Disgraceful!'

The President looked at Winston. But the Great Warrior was looking down at his cigar, at the moist black end of his fat cigar. On his left, the President felt well-bred withdrawal; to his right, he sensed stares of admonition. He was as drained as he had ever been. It was time to sit down, long past time. Someone passed the port. It looked blue red purple, like ... damsons.

He put his hand over his eyes. Above all else he had to blot out all damsons. If he didn't blot out damsons he could not go on.

'Gentlemen,' he said, trying to smile but feeling his lips

stuck firmly to his teeth, 'as President, and resigning President, I thank you all for drinking the health of the Royal Academy as you have done. I thank the Archbishop of Canterbury for what he has said tonight, and I wish you all well.'

With these words, with his head spinning, with his right hand a shambles, and with the cat well and truly among the pigeons, he sat down.

The buzz, the reaction, the clapping, the outrage, was much the loudest it had been all evening, though no one spoke directly to the President. The Duke of Gloucester looked glazed and the Archbishop stared steadfastly at the ceiling. Still, the main thing was he'd got the horse home, hadn't he?

It was time to move on. It was time now for The Great Man. The President turned to the toastmaster and nodded. This time the toastmaster, who needed no second invitation, hit the gavel as hard as he could.

He puffed out his chest and bellowed:

'Your Royal Highness, Your Ex-cellencies, Your Graces ... My Lords and Gentle-men, Pray Silence for Mr Winston Chur-chill.'

Even as Winston Churchill was speaking on the air, the BBC switchboard was jammed with telephone calls. Over the next few days and weeks Sir Alfred Munnings received thousands of letters from home and abroad, sacks and sacks full of support.

One letter was from his old friend, Dame Laura Knight:

16, Langford Place,
St John's Wood,
London
28th April 1949

Dear A.J.,

Yes, you mad old thing, you did it. And now you've done it!

Love,
Laura.

Lamorna Cove, Cornwall, 1949

Listening to the Royal Academy speeches on his new Regentone Radiogram, Major Gilbert Evans thought he was alone. Once Winston Churchill had finished his reply, Gilbert sat for a moment in quiet thought, lost in the past, the distant past, then eased himself up out of his fireside chair and turned off the wireless.

Munnings.

Gilbert stood there, cigarette in hand, shaking his head.

Life was a funny business.

Munnings and Churchill.

And still that same Suffolk accent. Or was it Norfolk?

Gilbert stood there, smoking, looking out across the sea to the Lizard. Listening to the speeches, he had become so bound up with the broadcast that he did not notice his younger son, David, slipping into the room. Once *Twenty Questions* was finished Joan had gone off towards the cliffs for her evening walk with Pedro, their dog, leaving Gilbert still settled in his chair. As for Gilbert, he assumed Timothy and David were down at the cove. And what better last night of the Easter holidays could they wish to have? That last night of freedom was very special to a boy before he returned to boarding-school – Gilbert remembered them so well, a boy's precious hours of freedom, though for him they were fifty years ago, or more.

But in fact David was sitting cross-legged on the drawing-room carpet not five feet away, and sitting very still. What on earth had captivated the child? Was it Churchill's style and delivery that transfixed him, that measured resonance, that witty balance? Gilbert hoped so. 'It is a good thing,' Winston said at one point in his speech, 'that art should be above parties, though parties are not above art.' How many people these days could turn a sentence like that? Perhaps if more of them studied Tacitus they could do so; perhaps if more of them studied Churchill's speeches they could.

As for A.J.'s speech ... Well, Gilbert hadn't seen Munnings for years, they had lost touch long long ago, but his forceful, angry, sincere and vehement style was unchanged. Quite frankly, A.J. was not an educated man, never had been. At the best of times he was inarticulate, and listening to him tonight on the wireless it showed. In a way it was rather embarrassing; one was somehow embarrassed *for* him. Yet to hear his country voice was to be grabbed again by the lapels, to be button-holed again, to see his rosy face again one inch from your nose, with drink on his breath, 'Listen, Ev, *lis*-ten to me, will you,' he would say and, of course, Gilbert would listen. With Munnings there wasn't much choice, was there?

Oh, yes, the man on the wireless, President or no President, was the same old controversial A.J. they all knew and loved – well, not *all* loved, but the same old A.J., only older. Although white-haired and famous, if not infamous, Sir Alfred Munnings still sounded like a river about to burst its banks, or – what did Harold Knight say, how did Harold put it? – rather like an agitated bookie.

If you had been mad enough to ask Gilbert before the First World War what odds he would give on Alfred Munnings ever becoming President of the Royal Academy he would have said it was too absurd to contemplate – but then, in 1945, just after we had won the Second World War, it was equally impossible to contemplate the suggestion that Winston Churchill would lose the General Election, which he duly did.

It was a good thing for the banquet, though, that Winston *had* spoken next. As usual he struck just the right note. Gilbert could tell A.J. had comfortably overstepped the mark, but Winston nicely defused it all. 'No one can doubt that the President, whom I rise to support, has some strong views.' Gilbert admired that kind of understated, mature wit. It smoothed ruffled feathers. It put everything back into perspective.

'Who was that, Daddy?' David suddenly piped.

'Winston Churchill,' Gilbert said, 'you must have recognised his voice.'

'No, the man before.'

'That was Sir Alfred Munnings.'

Though he never could, to be honest, quite see him as 'Sir Alfred'.

'Haven't I heard you talk about him before?'

'Perhaps.'

'Didn't he live in Lamorna?'

'Yes, he lived in the hotel. He had rooms there.'

'When, before the war?'

'Before *both* the wars. This is thirty, no, forty years ago we are talking about. Lots of artists lived here then. Lots. Quite the place, it was.'

Gilbert glanced up at the portrait.

'Did she?'

He was so taken aback by the boy's question he was

not sure he had heard David correctly. Rising to his feet, he said:

'Sorry, old chap?'

'Did she?'

'Who?'

'You *know*, Daddy. Did the woman in the painting live in the hotel?'

Gilbert flicked through the pages of the *Radio Times*, trying to collect himself. His young son was staring, eyes concentrated, at the painting.

'Yes, she did. A number . . . of us did.'

'*You* lived in the hotel as well?'

'Oh yes, for quite a while. I'm sure I've told you all that.'

'Did you know her well, Daddy?'

Half armed though he was, that question hit Gilbert like a bullet, and for one who had been hit by a bullet this was no mere figure of speech. He almost staggered. David was such a percipient boy. Perhaps those months when he was so ill last year, those worrying months, had given him – as illnesses often do – special insights into adult devices.

Gilbert took a pace or two towards the painting, glad the light was now fading so quickly that David could not see his face. At various times of day the painting looked so different, depending on the light, and now it took on its most sombre tones.

'Oh yes,' he replied, 'she was a very great friend.'

He could feel David's eyes now on him. Then the boy quickly got to his feet, pulled his long socks up to his knees, turned the tops down, and said:

'Did you know there are adders in the vegetable garden?'

'Yes – yes, I did.'

'I'm meeting the gang at the cove.'

'All right, old chap.'
'I'll be back soon.'
'You won't be late, will you, there's a good fellow. Remember, you're off to school tomorrow.'
And David shot out of the room.

A bit restless, Gilbert pottered around the house and then pottered around the garden. When Joan got back from her walk he told her a bit, in a roundabout way, about the Academy speeches, but of course the whole business with A.J. was years and years before they met, many years before Joan came to Lamorna, and given all that had happened he felt he couldn't very well go into the details with his wife. Nor did he mention to her the conversation with David. That was a private affair, too, and Gilbert rather doubted either of them would ever allude to it again.

As was usual, Joan went to bed before Gilbert. He sat up for a while and read *The Field*, a bit dreamy in his chair, slowly turning the pages, before he was distracted by a bumblebee which had worked itself into something of a state, and once he'd released him out into the night air and he was up on his pins Gilbert thought he might as well go upstairs himself.

But he knew, even before he started to climb the staircase, that he wouldn't sleep. He knew it long before he lowered his head on to the pillow.

What are the best games to play, Gilbert wondered, while trying to switch off an over-active mind, when thoughts speed up and down like restless swallows over a stream? He ran through the little jobs that needed doing in the greenhouse, the seeds that needed sowing in the little meadow, the miles per gallon the Armstrong Siddeley managed, and if these mundane reflections failed he recalled the home matches Wales played in their great days, The Golden Age, before the Great War: he saw some wonderful games, once travelling back on the overnight train from Penzance, changing at Bristol. That was 1911. Or was it 19*12*? Whichever, Wales beat Ireland 16–0. The Arms Park! The gates were closed over an hour before the kick off. But the crowds burst through and then scaled the walls. There were deaths and terrible injuries, and Gilbert saw all the bodies laid out, so *that* didn't work, that didn't help his mind settle.

Nothing worked. He couldn't sleep. So he tried trying to remember the earliest they had ever picked daffodils at Boskenna, picturing daffodils with double centres, trying to remember the names of all the boys in his house at Rugby, the names of the men in his regiment, but that jumped sideways to those friends he lost in the Boer War – and *that* didn't help.

Damn you, Munnings!

Damn you, A.J.! A.J., as was his wont, had stirred him up again. A.J., Alfred, Sir Alfred Munnings, damned Munnings, everywhere he went he stirred people up. Could nothing ever be left alone? Couldn't even the oldest wounds be allowed to heal?

Gilbert leant up on his elbow and slipped out of bed as quietly as he could, careful not to disturb Joan. He went into his dressing-room. There's nothing worse than unnecessarily waking up others, dreadfully selfish, such a precious thing, sleep, especially as we get older, and, feeling older, he pulled on his big cardigan. It was late April and still a touch chilly at nights. Mind you, late April often saw Lamorna at its very best – it's when Gilbert pulls his first potatoes, the summer birds return, the dry heath on the cliffs begins to show a little pink and

'Are you all right, Gilbert?'

'Yes, I'm so sorry, Joan, I'm afraid I've woken you.'

'What is it?'

'Just a bit of indigestion.'

'The milk of magnesia's on the shelf in the kitchen. On the left.'

'You go back to sleep, I'll be all right.'

His problems, that moonlit night, were far beyond milk of magnesia's reach, but all his life he'd had something of a dicky tummy and he was quite happy for Joan to think it was no more than that. A nurse herself, she'd been wonderful to him, quite wonderful; twenty-two years younger and to some that may seem quite an age gap, but they had two splendid boys, and much though he'd miss them when they were back at school, he was a lucky chap to be so on in years and blessed with such young sons.

He went downstairs as quietly as he could.

Unused to his master's midnight wanderings, Pedro leapt up from his basket, and out they went together for a breath of air, Pedro shaking himself, Gilbert pulling his cardigan a little tighter. Round to the right, and past the garages, which reminded him to check the gearbox oil in the spare Armstrong, and across the sloping meadow, until he could see the hotel, or at least its outline.

The hotel.

In the moonlight it was completely black, like one of those huge cardboard cut-outs David enjoyed making with scissors on the kitchen table. If you then cut out a white circle for the moon and hung it above the black card you would catch the reality and unreality of that moment. So quiet was the sea in the cove he could hear almost nothing, and that was rare.

He shivered. He told himself to be sensible. To be practical. It was much better to look to the future, to the boys' future, they're such promising lads, yes, look for new buds appearing, that's the ticket, be sensible, forget the past, that's the only way, Gilbert, no point looking back, come on, Pedro, let's both go back in, shall we, and get some sleep, shall we? Good dog, good dog.

And, being sensible now, he slept.

At seven o'clock prompt, Lilly, the maid, brought him up his cup of tea and his apple. He peeled the apple. When Lilly appeared again, with his mug of piping-hot shaving water, Gilbert got up, feeling very sensible and very practical as he shaved. But at breakfast *The Times* was full of Sir Alfred Munnings. There were columns and columns about the Retiring President uncorking his long-bottled emotions at the banquet. Oh, no, Munnings wasn't going to go away that easily! Try as hard as you could to be sensible you still ended up drinking half the night away with A.J., listening to his dirty songs and, of course, his quite awful poems.

'Where are you going, Ev?' he'd shout as Gilbert tried to slip away at two in the morning. '*Sit down* next to Laura and have another drink.'

You never could escape him, never.

And now, with every column in the papers telling you the whole world was in a most awful, most precarious state (Berlin, the Yangtse, Israel, India, and Communist China), here was an incoherent speech about modern art becoming a sensation. Once again, A.J. took a central-stage position, insisting all eyes stayed on him.

'Twas always thus, Gilbert grunted to himself.

In 1911 it used to be Munnings against Roger Fry (or Rogering Fry as Munnings preferred to put it); and now, in 1949, it was The President versus Picasso, Munnings versus Moore, Burlington House battling against Bloomsbury, with the pink coats on the left wing about to attack that conservative Chamber of Horrors, the Royal Academy, led by Sir Alfred and his blue-blooded hunters.

Gilbert carefully folded *The Times*, left his kippers half eaten and went up to the boxroom at the very top of the house. He had taken the first steps up there last night but thought better of it, thinking he might in doing so disturb Lilly or the boys. He knew exactly where in the boxroom he was heading, though it was years since he last looked. The trunk, a dark brown one with Captain C.G. Evans boldly printed on it, he bought to go to West Africa in 1914. He knew exactly where in the trunk they were. He knew which pages he would open first.

Trembling, he sat on top of the trunk.

Do you realise what you have done, A.J.?

Do you, you old scoundrel?

Part Two

I fear love making and painting don't go together.
                              Alice Forbes, letter to Ethel, 1886

History with its flickering lamp stumbles along the trail of the past, trying to reconstruct its scenes, to revive its echoes, and kindle with pale gleams the passions of former days.
                              Winston Churchill, 1940

The Stranger in the Lane

From the moment they met, Laura could not take her eyes off him. Married woman though she was, she freely admitted as much to herself. And to others. She had never before in her life felt herself in the company of so powerful and challenging a spirit, of so wild and unsettling a nature.

She had been down on the rocks all day with Dolly, working on a big canvas. Since coming to Cornwall her canvases had become bigger and bigger, bolder and bolder, and Harold had very kindly left his own work, as he so often did, and walked down through the village to the cove to help her carry the six-foot canvas, poles and general clobber back up the hill. It's a steep pull up from Lamorna Cove, very steep at first, as it curves round past 'Lamorna' Birch's house, where the water on the other side comes down the valley gathering speed as it runs through a narrow runnel. Going up those first few hundred yards, before it eases a little, you need all the help you can find, and Laura knew she was lucky to have a kind, attentive husband. Sometimes, preoccupied with his own thoughts, Harold went on ahead, keen to return to his own studio, letting her stroll back at will, letting her smell the flowers or eat blackberries while she chatted to Gilbert Evans outside his office.

'Thank you, Harold,' she would often say back in the cottage, 'what would I do without you?'

'Get someone else to help, no doubt.'

Harold always preferred to paint indoors. He was a slow, painstaking perfectionist, and they had worked in separate studios ever since the day ten years ago on York station when Laura punched out their names on one of those penny slot machines: LAURA KNIGHT, and then HAROLD KNIGHT. With a smile Harold took the tin strips from her hand as if that had decided the matter, two separate names, two separate people. He nailed one on his studio door and one on Laura's, though Laura's was often unused because her real studio was the open air.

Everyone in Lamorna noticed how different in every way the Knights were. Laura was all fast hands and full of dash, big canvases, big effort, squeezing paint out of the tube, letting the pencil and brush speak before she could interrupt them; she felt she could run in the playground and not get touched, she was a stormy scatterbrain, she didn't mind, she would show everyone her work – you could stand behind and watch, if you liked.

Not so Harold. He was as still and white as his studio wall; he kept his paintings turned away from prying eyes and woe betide anyone who looked at them until he was good and ready. 'Because we live together,' he said to Laura, 'we must not influence each other too much.' Yes, he was a wise old bird, and there he was going up the hill in his stiff-backed way, just ahead of Laura, on a hot early September evening, a bonus day, a windfall day, when—

When—

By a gate halfway up the lane, just up from where Gilbert

Evans had his office, Harold could see – no, he could not yet see, but he could *hear* a very noisy crowd. For a moment he wondered if it was Gilbert and Joey Carter-Wood, but then Gilbert and Joey weren't noisy types and anyway this noise was very female. Peaceful though it could be, Lamorna was also quite used to its fair share of noise. If it wasn't stormy weather coming in off the Atlantic or the quarry blasting granite by day it was the artists blasting away at a party by night, but by any standards this was raucous, a fusillade of laughter, a real racket.

Harold and Laura came round the bend. Standing in the centre of a circle of girls was a stranger. The girls were all laughing and cheering. It occurred to Harold that the joker in the middle of the pack might well be a travelling performer. They did have the occasional tramp in those parts, attracted perhaps by the easy pickings offered by a painting fraternity, and eccentrics attracted more eccentrics, but even at a glance, this loud young man was the oddest yet.

Harold could not get past him quickly enough. Laura, however, slowed. The centre of attention had light brown hair combed forward with deliberate style, and her first thought was that here was the spitting image of the Robbie Burns portrait she had seen on her last visit to Edinburgh. He was a slim, animated figure; he was expressive with his hands, but in an entirely manly fashion, and his shoulders were broad.

Could Laura take in so much at a glance? Yes she could, and more! He had slim hips, very slim hips. As for his clothes? Well, it had to be said, his clothes were the main point of his strangeness. You would never expect to come across such a figure in a Cornish lane: he wore a shepherd's plaid suit with close-fitting trousers that belled out at the bottom – and he wore it with such style as if to say 'And do I not look the part?' Where on earth did this strange being come from, what was he doing here, and who were all these silly sycophantic girls surrounding him?

They must, she guessed, be Stanhope Forbes's pupils from Newlyn, or they might be models, or both. But some of them looked too sharp to be painters and the others looked too horsy to be models. The first clear words Laura heard spoken among the excitable babble was a high-pitched urging:

'Oh, go on, Alfred, do, please!'

'Yes, Alfred, come on!'

'We want to know!'

This was followed by more cheering and clapping. They were all clearly agreed on what it was they wanted Alfred to do.

Harold Knight, silent and absorbed, forged ahead, but as Laura made to follow her husband up the lane, the stranger looked at her right over the heads of all the girls, and looked at her with a shrewd scan, a look used to judging distances and assessing dangers. More than that, there was a laughing note in his glance.

Laura did not imagine this, she made none of this up. She had a penetrating eye herself and she saw what she saw and she missed nothing. As if to prove this, he half waved at her, almost as if he knew her and knew what she had been up to on the rocks and knew exactly where she was going – back home with her taciturn partner. This sense that the stranger already knew her shocked her. Were her senses that afternoon particularly heightened? She asked herself this because she could, at ten paces, clearly smell the face-cream on the silly girls and clearly see the make-up on their lips and eyelashes.

Thirty yards or so up the road Laura stopped to rest her tired legs. Some wild roses stirred the hedgerows and the late afternoon sun felt hotter than ever on the back of her neck. Sweating, she looked down at her arms, her forearms, and her fingers. It was as if she had never looked at them before. They weren't her arms. They were someone else's arms, they were the arms of a washerwoman. They were blistered red, badly blistered, and as for her face, she did not have to look at her face: that, she knew only too well, would be as red as a beetroot. Even after the shortest of walks her skin took on a strawberry hue, and the day with Dolly on the rocks, with the reflection from the ocean, had been one of unrelieved sunshine.

But why all this worry?

For years she had not given a thought to her colouring. Thank goodness she was past all that young misery, that self-consciousness, such as the terrible anxiety she felt before they were married that, on one of his visits, Harold would suddenly bend down on his knees and see the chamberpot in her bedroom. A visible chamberpot was bad enough but hers was delicately painted with crimson roses and green leaves, surrounded by the immortal words 'For a kiss you may use this'. That chamberpot, she was convinced, would put the kibosh on her chances of marrying Harold.

Oh, the agonies she had been through! She first met Harold when she was a very young fourteen; he was a very old seventeen and so pale and so elegant and so distinguished, and she used to suck her red cheeks in to try to look like Harold, that is, pale and elegant and distinguished. Then her sister asked, 'What are you pulling those faces for?' so Laura reluctantly settled for the round-faced girl she then was and still was now. After all, she might be raggle-taggle, might be red in the face, might have crinkly hair, but she had talent as well.

She knew she had talent.

Then, as she stood in the Lamorna lane, she suddenly looked down at her shoes – at her boots, rather. Ah, that was it, that was what the stranger was laughing at: her hobnailed boots.

When Laura got back to her low cottage her husband was already shut away up in his studio. To cool down she flopped into the deep basket chair by the open door, her feet bare on the flagstones. Once cooled down, but still thinking of that cocky, tanned face and the mocking smile, she put the kettle on the hob.

The only reference Harold made to the incident in the lane came two weeks later. He spoke without looking up from his book.

'I've found out who the bookie is.'

'What do you mean?'

'The bookie with the bevy of damsels.'

'Oh, him.'

'He's called Munnings. Taken that place near the mill.'

'Is he a painter?'

'Of sorts. Apparently. If you can believe it.'

'I can, yes.'

'Invited us to a party.'

'Has he, how nice!'

'You go.'

'What about you?'

'I've got toothache.'

Poor Harold. He'd always had terrible trouble with his teeth.

Suddenly There Came a Knocking

'There are so many artist chappies on my land now, Gilbert,' Colonel Paynter said (more than once) as they walked side by side round the estate, 'you'll soon be taking a roll call at sundown.' This was one of the Colonel's better little jokes. Since Gilbert had arrived down in Lamorna, as the Colonel's land agent, some new artist or other, or artist's model, had appeared almost every month in one cottage or studio or outhouse. Newlyn, of course, had been packed tight with them for many years, but now it was Lamorna's turn (as later it was to be St Ives'). The trouble was, with these artist chappies, someone was always joining the ranks unannounced or jumping ship, so Gilbert decided there would be very little point in trying to keep track of them all.

Tramps, gypsies, coastal walkers and artists, it was not (frankly) always easy to discriminate one from the other. One month they were as penniless as the mice in the church or borrowing off each other; then the news went round that someone had sold a couple of pictures in Bond Street or had an exhibition lining up in Penzance and they all somehow made ends meet – or, more likely, they went mad on the proceeds. So life was never dull. That was what felt so very good about being down here in that far-flung corner of England, a place people came to punt away their previous existence, rather appropriately (Gilbert thought), as the tip of Cornwall was like the boot at the end of a long leg.

For many years Newlyn had been the focal point. Stanhope Forbes ('the Professor') and his wife Elizabeth had attracted a large number of young art students from London, indeed from all parts of England. Then Samuel John Birch (soon to be called 'Lamorna' Birch) settled four miles away from Newlyn in Lamorna, in his house just up from the cove – and what a view he had! Other artists followed. One, two, three . . . became a trickle, then a small stream, and now (as the Colonel implied) the floodgates were open.

'Lots of painters,' the Colonel said, 'but not a decent carpenter in sight.'

That was another of his little jokes.

Apart from the locals, Gilbert Evans was just about the only one who wasn't an artist. Down at The Wink playing skittles the other night he heard a man grumbling away that Lamorna 'weren't Cornwall any more'. The trouble with comments of that nature, quite apart from the fact that they made Gilbert feel unwelcome, was that he was not entirely sure what was meant by 'Cornwall'. By 'Cornwall' did those in The Wink mean windswept, deprived inland farms and poor fishermen risking their lives? Did they mean people who spoke with impossible accents? Maybe they did. But was there not room enough in that strange vast county for all of them, artists and writers and fishermen, even for the occasional army officer turned land agent?

Laura Knight put it rather well over supper. Gilbert, a regular guest up in their long low cottage, was lighting their paraffin lamp and Laura, as usual, was talking.

'Cornwall isn't like anywhere else, you see, so it's no use trying to compare it to your previous experiences. Take Nottingham, take Yorkshire, take Holland, take Paris, they're all so different. Isn't that right, Harold? We've always found that, haven't we? . . . Harold?'

Harold went on reading, his glasses on the end of his nose.

'Harold, isn't it?'

'What?'

'What I just said.'

'Yes.'

'Is that all you have to say?'

'Yes.'

'Oh, honestly.'

'You haven't stopped for half an hour. You're as bad as the bookie. Why don't you let Gilbert say something?'

Laura laughed a nervous, vulnerable laugh. Gilbert turned from the lamp to face Harold.

'Who is the bookie?'

'Laura's new friend, down at the mill. Mr Modesty.'

'Oh? Oh, Munnings, you mean?'

Laura smiled bravely and encouragingly.

'Gilbert's been helping him settle in, haven't you?'

'Not only me,' Gilbert said. 'The place was a shambles, it really was, so we all rallied round, the Colonel gave me a day off . . . well, half a day.'

'Jolly . . . good,' Harold added slowly, after a pause.

'He's a tremendous painter,' Gilbert said, 'not that I'm any judge.'

'Turns out a lot, the bookie, does he?' Harold asked.

'Stacks,' Gilbert nodded approvingly. 'He's always out and about, I see him everywhere. In all weathers.'

Harold stirred with distaste but remained looking at his book, and only at his book.

'Gilbert sees the best in people,' Laura said, 'don't you, Gilbert?'

Though she often added that Gilbert should not try *quite* so hard to be decent, nor try *quite* so hard to make everyone like everyone, because marriages were marriages and life was life, wasn't it, and some people preferred Sennen Cove to Lamorna and some preferred Lamorna to Sennen Cove, and what could you do about *that*? She filled Gilbert's glass to the brim.

'So tell us what *you* think of Alfred Munnings, Gilbert. We all know what Harold thinks; when he doesn't call him the bookie he calls him the ostler. Don't you, Harold?'

Harold exhaled, just loudly enough for it to rate as more than an unconsciously necessary function, slowly put down his book on the side table, made a steeple of his fingers and looked into the grate. There was a silence, which Gilbert did not fill.

'For example,' Laura said, 'do you like him?'

'I don't really know him yet,' Gilbert said. 'I wouldn't like to say . . . just yet. Ask me when I know him better.'

Laura whooped and clapped her hands.

'Marvellous! You are the soul of tact. Isn't he, Harold?'

'Have you been invited to his party?' Gilbert asked. 'On Friday?'

'Who hasn't?' Harold said gloomily.

Laura stood up.

'*Everybody* has, the whole village, Joey, Dolly. The Birches. He's planning to have a party every week, every week, think of that, he's so generous, isn't he? And let's face it, not everyone would invite Dolly, would they? I mean you wouldn't, Harold, would you? . . . Harold?'

Lieutenant-Colonel Camborne Haweis Paynter, JP, or Curl-and-Painter as the local lads called him, owned most

of the land on the harbour side of the cove, that is west of
the little stream which divides the Lamorna valley – all the
land from there right over to Boskenna and a bit beyond.
On the other side, the east side of the steep valley, strewn
with huge chunks of overspilt granite, you have the quarry.
The quarry side of the valley was owned by Lord St Levan.
The footpath to the east runs round from the cove past Half
Tide rock, Carn Du and Kemyel Point, with the sea always
in sight, to Mousehole. Keep going and you reach Newlyn
(and the painting school, where Joey Carter-Wood was a
gifted, if reluctant pupil) and then the wide promenade to
Penzance.

Gilbert was responsible, then, for a sizeable area of
sloping fields dotted with farms and outbuildings, sloping
fields full of flowers and vegetables, and for the rent and
upkeep of all the properties. You could say he 'ran' the
place. If a roof was damaged in a gale, if the water failed,
if there was a crisis, 'The Captain' was called. Gilbert liked
to feel he was 'responsible'. 'What I am not responsible for,'
he said with a smile in The Wink, 'is the behaviour of the
artists.'

'Why don't you arrange a place of your own?' Laura
asked Gilbert. 'You deserve one.'

'Because I'm happy enough where I am. Thank you.
Quite spoilt, as a matter of fact.'

Gilbert had rooms in the hotel: a bedroom – the bed
narrow but well sprung – and quite a cosy little sitting-
room which, with the kind help of Mrs Paynter, he was
beginning to furnish. For the time being it looked rather
spartan, the sort of room a sapper officer might settle
on, with a small carpet, a chair and some curtains, a
small writing desk and a small chest of drawers. There
was nothing small, though, about the views from his
window.

The wide, wide sea: from the Lizard round to Land's End.

The hotel itself was something of an enigma. First of all the name needs clearing up. Cliff House, built in 1870, was not put up as a hotel, which explained why some of the older men in The Wink still referred to it as Cliff House. Then it became Cliff House Temperance Hotel, then Jory's Temperance Hotel, or Jory's Hotel, or simply Jory's.

The name Jory's was, however, anything but simple. That name introduced a range of complications because Mr and Mrs Jory ran rival establishments: Jory's Hotel (let us settle for that), where Gilbert had his rooms on the first floor, was run on a tightish rein and with the firmest and kindest of hands by Mrs Jory. Or, as she advertised it, 'Mrs Jessie Jory, proprietress, furnished apartments (bathrooms), sea view and south aspect'. Mrs Jory prided herself on providing a splendid breakfast and supper to which Gilbert could, and frequently did, invite guests (Joey Carter-Wood and Munnings, to name but two).

A hundred yards or so lower down in the village was The Wink. This inn was run on the loosest possible rein by Mr Jory, or 'Mr Nicholas Jory, beer retailer'. The hotel and the inn were chalk and cheese, control and indulgence, thrift and forgetfulness. When he was returning on his bicycle from a long day at Boskenna, Gilbert could often tell his mood by sensing towards which place his wheels were drawn.

Mr and Mrs Jory were not on speaking terms. 'As long as she do stay up there,' Jory said with his pendulous bottom lip in his beer, and with his elbow on the bar, 'and I do stay down here, it do suit. But if she do come down 'ere, I'll be off faster 'n a fox and that's a fact.'

Marriages, marriages, Gilbert thought.

When Jory did venture up the steep slope to the hotel in

his pony and jingle trap – he was often hired to take guests or residents in and out of Penzance for trains and shopping expeditions – the husband and wife did not so much as look at one another. As Bess, the pony, clip-clopped off Mrs Jory would hiss, teeth clamped, point her indelibly inked finger at his back and say, 'And good riddance.' For his part, once out of sight, Jory would lift his left buttock and fart. This he could do to order.

Marriages, marriages, Gilbert thought: imagine not loving your wife, imagine not talking to her. 'May God protect me from such a union,' he said in his prayers.

After being thrown out of his temporary lodgings in Newlyn for excesses which his landlady did not wish to discuss and which he could not even remember, A.J. Munnings took the damp and deserted dwelling, a sort of studio and stable, not a stone's throw from the mill. He had tried to find a place in Paul and Mousehole and Trewoofe before coming by chance to Lamorna, and as soon as he saw the mill nearby and watched the shutter being released so that the wheel could grind, as soon as he heard there had been a mill of sorts working there since the fourteenth century, he knew he was, in a sense, 'at home'. Bowered in trees, near a mill. Here he would stay. Head bowed, he stood in front of the millstone wheel, a huge circle of local granite; then raised his eyes up at the water, diverted there from the stream at the top of the valley. All this, the drowsy sound of mill and plash, was in his family's veins. The steady flow of water and the familiar sound of the cogs convinced Munnings that here was the hub of the village. Here he could paint! He must have it! And within a week, with Gilbert Evans's practical help, it was more or less habitable. Then the parties began. By day Munnings worked outdoors till he dropped, and by night he roistered. His horses, Grey Tick and Merrilegs, were stabled beneath his studio. When he slept (if he slept) it was upstairs, on a mattress in his studio, or below in the hay with the horses, while Taffy, his terrier, travelled hopefully (sometimes fearfully) between his two beds.

During the long hours of roistering his studio was blue with smoke, blue with everything, some of it belching back down the chimney, which badly needed a good sweeping, but mostly from a variety of pipes and cigarettes. It was crammed tight with young people (including some of the faces seen by Laura in the lane) and anyone else A.J. had just bumped into. And they all brought candles, musical instruments, cakes, bottles and bits and pieces to make his cramped place more comfortable – cushions, for example, went down well.

'Yes, yes, yes,' he shouted at all and sundry, 'in you come, whoever you are!'

His weekly parties started when the sun went down and only ended, according to the watching sabbatarians, when the sin ended. Everyone talked. Everyone drank. Most sang. Most talked art. They laughed, danced, swallowed punch, ate sausages and saw who could wear the most colourful clothes and use the most colourful language – seeing who could, in Laura's phrase, 'Be the wildest of the wild' and 'Something tells me,' Munnings added, 'it won't be your husband Harold.' Usually who-was-the-wildest-of-the-wild boiled down to a straight contest between A.J. Munnings and Laura Knight, although they were amongst the oldest.

The second Munnings party Gilbert attended, and the one which changed their lives, came at the end of an awful day. From dawn to dusk it had rained non-stop, as only Cornwall can, and to make matters worse Gilbert's bicycle had a bad puncture at St Buryan, so he had to push the thing two miles in a steady downpour, encouraged only by the occasional lulls and respites. With the sky a regatta of fast storm clouds, only for those respites to be followed by sustained horizontal sheets of grey rain coming in from the Atlantic – well, such days left Gilbert looking forward more than ever to a party and the smack of drink.

By the time he turned down past the mill, just before nine, his socks wet, and the mill race a torrent, it was gusting a gale. So loud, however, was the din within the smoky blue studio that no one noticed the windows rattling, the downpipe gurgling, the roof groaning and Colonel Paynter's responsible land agent standing there dripping on the edge of the circle of light.

Gilbert watched.

He had never seen a party like it.

He watched A.J. Munnings, this much talked-about life-force, rapidly moving around the room, loving it all, the world of laughter he had created, the bustle and the storm within so great the storm without passed by.

Gilbert watched.

Had he ever, at school or in the army, in Wales or in the Boer War, ever met a man like this? Had he ever heard a man who spoke such sentences?

No.

Suddenly seeing Gilbert Evans dripping at the door, Munnings threw his arms triumphantly in the air in celebration, pushed his way over, shouting his helpful friend's name at the top of his voice:

'Ev!'

'Hullo, A.J., quite a night.'

'Come here, man, come here, you look drowned.'

'I'm all right, really, I'll dry out in a—'

'Come and meet Everyone. Every-one,' he bawled,

'meet Captain Evans, soldier and gentleman. Ev, meet Every-one.'

'Yes, thank you, A.J., but I do—'

'The chimney needs sweeping! It needs sweeping badly.'

'I know, I did tell you, and the downpipes need clearing.'

'Can you arrange it, my friend? Can you?'

'I've already told you I—'

'Amazing chap' – here A.J.'s volume increased to include all those within earshot – 'he fixes *every*thing for me, don't you? Now *that* is what I call a friend. A friend.'

'Ev' was something of a new one, but if A.J. started to use it there was little doubt that 'Ev' would soon be his current name. On the matter of loud general introductions, Gilbert tried to explain quietly to A.J. not to bother, because he knew enough people in the room to be getting on with, thank you, and that once he had dried out a little by the fire he would be quite all right, but he might as well be bidding the ocean to cease because A.J. told him not to move a muscle, not a muscle, mind, until he brought him back a glass, a full glass of something guaranteed to warm the cockles of his soldier's heart.

Gilbert peered through the blue smoke. 'Lamorna' Birch, with his clay pipe, nodded a greeting. A scantily dressed London model (he did not remember her name, though he remembered her smile) half turned and half smiled. A.J. was now heading back, elbows right out, with a jug of steaming punch, holding it in front of his face and shouting out above the hubbub:

'Special Norfolk recipe, this, Ev, got it in The Swan at Harleston . . . or was it the Maid's Head in Norwich, can't remember for the life of me, who cares, whichever, it's bloody good stuff so drink it.'

'Your very good health, A.J.'

'"A.J.'s Special" it's called all over Norfolk, rum, brandy, sherry, shimmered – no, I'll say that again – simmered cloves, lemon rind, lots of fruit and whatever else I feel like throwing in.'

And on his way Munnings went, leaning over shoulders with his steaming brew, nudging the young models, topping them up, encouraging more excess, dropping a filthy limerick here and a filthy limerick there. It was hard for Gilbert to believe that this man had only been in Lamorna a few weeks: he behaved as if he, not Colonel Paynter, owned the place, if not the county of Cornwall.

Gilbert moved to join Laura and Joey Carter-Wood but within seconds of being with them A.J. was back there again, elbowing Laura.

'More, yes, come on, Good God, Laura woman, don't argue, lift it higher, I can't reach down to your boots, can I?'

'You're a wicked man, Alfred Munnings.'

'Of course I am, so lift your glass up.'

As she did so, Gilbert noticed Laura's wide strong lips were already stained blue-red with the wine. Her eyes bulged.

'Lovely, Alfred, that's plenty, thanks, I said that's *plenty*.'

'Don't thank me, Laura, thank the Leicester Gallery, thank the clients, thank all the buyers!'

'I know, wonderful news, well done.'

'Talent, Laura, talent, that's all it is, and you and I have it.'

'You have, Alfred, that's clear.'

Munnings looked round the room.

'Where's your husband, he needs some of this, put a bit of life into him.'

'He's at home, I'm afraid.'

'At home?'

'Yes, still working.'

'What's wrong with the fellow, last time he had tooth-ache.'

'Well, you know Harold.'

'Gilbert, you're a man at least, have some more!'

'No, I still haven't—'

But Gilbert moved his hand just a fraction too late. His glass was brimful again.

'That's it, give me a man who can enjoy life, a man and a soldier.'

'But not an artist, I'm afraid.'

'Listen, Gilbert Evans, there are too many bloody artists in this room, too many in Newlyn, too many in Lamorna, too many in London, far far too many, they need stamping out. Stamping out!'

'I wouldn't know about that.'

Alfred put his arm firmly round Gilbert's shoulder.

'Of course you wouldn't, my brave, and that's why I'm telling you. And that's why you need me!'

Alfred now took up his performing stance. As he did so, Joey Carter-Wood, sensing a poem was on the way, smiled. Alfred began:

> 'Steadily, shoulder to shoulder,
> Steadily, blade by blade,
> Ready and strong,
> Marching along,
> Like the boys of the Old Brigade'

'Eh, isn't that right, Ev?'

'Yes, that's how it goes, A.J.'

A.J. released Gilbert, moving towards Joey.

'Joey, Joey Carter Hyphen Wood, don't be so coy, man,

even if you are a toff. Get your hands dirty for once, there's a good chap, put some more coal on the fire, would you, that's good Welsh coal, Monmouth's Wales isn't it, Ev, well near enough, we need more fire, we need more punch, we need more life in here.'

Joey knelt down by the coal scuttle.

'And where's your sister, Joey, thought she was coming?'

Joey started to put some pieces on the fire, a task at which he showed no skill at all. The tongs slipped off the damp coal.

'No, it's tomorrow she's coming.'

'Staying long?'

'Depends.'

'What?'

Joey turned his flushed face up from the fire.

'I said it depends.'

'Depends on what?'

'On how she gets on down here. Generally, I mean. All round.'

A.J. shouted at him:

'Generally, all round? What does that mean? Talk straight, man.'

'I'm sorry, A.J., I'm not in the mood for this.'

'I mean, she paints, doesn't she, your sister, and she's coming down to learn from the Professor in Newlyn, so what's the problem?'

Whatever the problem was Joey was not suddenly about to unburden himself. Instead he rose to his feet and joined, a little shyly, Dolly and a group of models. Alfred suddenly found himself spun round in a masculine grip. It was Laura Knight, her aquiline nose next to his. He tried to pull back but she held him tight.

'Laura, God, what a drinker, you're back for more already.'

'No, I want you to leave Joey alone, he's far too sensitive for you, and I want you to do what you promised.'

Alfred laughed uncertainly.

'What promise? What are you talking about?'

'You know perfectly well what promise, and it's the perfect moment for you to deliver it.'

Discountenanced, Alfred pulled himself away from Laura's grip.

'It's the perfect moment for drinking, I know that.'

'No, you're not getting away with this, you're always changing the subject when it doesn't suit you, and Gilbert and I heard you promise, down at the cove yesterday, oh yes we did, you promised you'd do it tonight, yes, yes you did, *and* with make-up, and that's why we're all here, well, one of the reasons.'

'Oh, I thought you were escaping Harold.'

'But of course if you haven't the courage, Alfred, if you're only a braggart—'

'Anyway, you're wrong, Laura, I wasn't at the cove yesterday.'

'Yes you were!'

'No, I wasn't, I was riding with the Western Hounds over at Zennor, all day as a matter of fact, and something quite remarkable happened there.'

'All right, the day before then, this silly drink of yours is doing it, but that's not the point, the point is we were all sitting on the rocks watching that big steamer go towards the Lizard, weren't we, Gilbert?'

'Laura's right,' Gilbert said. 'I heard it loud and clear, then you started talking about Roger Fry.'

'Shut up, Ev, what the hell do you know about Roger Fry!'

Gilbert was the first to admit he knew nothing at all about Roger Fry, except that he was a painter against whom

Alfred Munnings spent half an hour each day fulminating, so he poked a circle of lemon down under the surface of his tumbler, then watched it float slowly back up the punch to join the other fragments of fruit. Alfred's sudden irascibility embarrassed rather than nettled Gilbert. Besides, Laura had resumed her attack with fresh vigour, smiling, with her long teeth showing.

'Anyway, we're not talking about Roger Fry now, we're talking about the importance of poetry, but if you can't do something, Alfred, please don't tell everyone you can do it, it's so paltry, if you want to know what it reminds me of, it reminds me of the village louts in Yorkshire, they were the sort who claimed they could hit flying birds with their catapults.'

Alfred pushed angrily away. She followed. He swivelled back towards Laura.

'Look, I *can* do it, I just don't *want* to.'

'That's *exactly* what bragging little boys say, when they're about nine or ten.'

'Little boys do, do they?'

'Yes, bragging little boys, and a lot of men promise a lot of things too, and I'm disappointed that you are one of them, so I think, if you'll excuse me, I'll be going.'

'What, back to Harold?'

'Yes, he's not very well.'

'He's never very well.'

Laura moved her nose close to his.

'Don't be rude about Harold, that's the third time tonight, I won't have it.'

'It's a fact, statement of fact, Harold, your husband, is never very well.'

'And to drag him along to an evening like this would have made him worse, so I'll go back now.'

Gilbert put his drink on the windowsill.

'I'll walk up the hill with you, Laura, it really is a filthy night.'

'Oh, *all* right,' Alfred said, 'I'll do it.'

Laura, as was her way, whooped and kissed Alfred, and in doing so she threw some punch over Gilbert.

'I knew you would, I *knew* it, I was just saying to Gilbert you were a man and not a mouse.'

She had been saying no such thing and she pressed Gilbert's arm to acknowledge her lie before clapping her hands. To get the attention of the whole room she clapped her hands again, and kept clapping.

'Quiet, everyone. *Qui-et* please! Right, there is to be a very special event, so find a seat on the floor, please, wherever you can, any spot will do, but mind the bookcase, it fell over last week, yes, squeeze up . . . yes, sit on each other's knees if you like . . . not so fast, Joey! I want *you* to turn down one of the lamps. And Gilbert, my dear, would you do the other, thanks!'

'Look, Laura,' Alfred said, 'it's my bloody studio, not yours.'

'Not strictly speaking, you're only renting it, and we do surely need a little less light, for atmosphere, yes? You agree? Just a bit lower, Joey, would you, yes that's it, like Gilbert's, yes, stop! Now isn't that . . . Vermeer? Isn't that Frans Hals?'

'Do shut up, Laura,' Alfred said with a storm in his eyes, 'you know damn all about Frans Hals.'

'And wouldn't Rembrandt relish this scene? Oh he *would*!'

After Joey's feeding, the fire was now beginning to pick up again. The flames and the lamps in their globes threw three flickering pools of light. For the first time in the evening the sound of the rain on the studio roof was becoming clear. The wind hustled round the cornices.

Gilbert, unable to find a spot to sit, leant back against the front door; on which move, the cold draught coming underneath made his clinging wet socks feel still colder. In a further sudden assault the rain drenched the window to his right.

'Silence!' Laura boomed.

They listened to the rain.

'No, it's not quiet enough yet,' Laura said bossily. 'I'm going to throw this piece of lemon on the fire' (she held the slice up) 'and when I hear it *hiss* – then I shall call upon . . . Him. Let us listen for the hiss.'

And she lowered herself dramatically, eyes popping, to the floor, kneeling at Alfred's feet. Was this really Laura Knight kneeling at the feet of Alfred Munnings? Gilbert had never seen a grown woman change as much as Laura had this last month. Since A.J.'s arrival in Lamorna she seemed to have lost all semblance of self-control.

All eyes were now on Alfred Munnings. And for the first time Gilbert studied him very closely: his sharp, intelligent face, sharp in bone structure and in expression, the kind of face a shepherd has; Gilbert sometimes encountered such faces when walking in the Black Mountains, the faces of men whistling their dogs to round up distant sheep, faces full of native cunning. No, Gilbert thought, I've got it, it's not a shepherd's face, not quite, it's the face of an outside half in rugger, that's it, the face of a man who lives on his wits, who relies on natural physique and instinct to see him through whatever defences are lined up against him.

As for Alfred's clothes, the clothes Laura first noticed in the lane – well, they changed as regularly as his moods. How many wardrobes did he have? (Looking round, Gilbert could see none.) Tonight the centre of attention wore a check suit with a black velvet collar, black velvet cuffs and pocket flaps, with broad black braiding trimming his trousers. Everything had a distinct, raffish cut. The man, Gilbert admitted to himself as he stood by the door in his wet socks, had style.

There was something else, too, about Munnings which Gilbert, as a soldier, had spotted quite early on, less obvious than his clothes and less obvious than his clipped tones but possibly more central: the way Alfred looked at you. If Alfred looked at you, really looked at you, you did not forget it. More often than not, with his Panama modishly tilted, he did not engage your eyes, but when the piercing glance came you needed courage (as Gilbert had) to look steadily back.

'All right, you buggers,' Alfred said at last, 'you win.'

Far from being troubled by this abuse, his semi-circular audience seated on the floor glowed, drinking punch and expectation, sensing the plot was afoot, and sensing the game was going to be very good. His erratic mood was over, the storm had passed from his eyes; once again he felt he was the main artery.

'You've run me to ground,' he went on, looking at Laura and then Joey (squeezed tight between Dolly and Prudence), 'and I don't mind telling you I feel as cornered as a fox . . . we cornered a fox yesterday, but that's another story, another time, and I feel as baited as . . . as John Clare's Badger, with the whole village baying for his blood. So I must turn to keep the dogs at bay . . . I . . . I'm . . . I feel like Macbeth . . . you remember the final bit . . . bearlike I must stand the course . . . but if I fail you won't chop my head off, eh, you won't be Macduffs?'

'No' and 'Yes' came in equal measure as they encouraged Alfred the Fox, Alfred the Badger and Alfred the Scottish Hero-Villain. Sensing their readiness, he tilted back his head, his bloodshot eyes squinting open, and raised his hand. He wagged a finger for the final depth of calculated, concentrated silence, a conductor holding them before the opening chords were sounded, a mower before he brought down his scythe.

On the fire Laura could hear the lemon slice hissing.

'"The Raven"' he said into the silence, 'by Edgar Allan Poe.'

It was, of course, not silence. The silence merely brought out the strength of the wind, the power of the rain, and the unappeasable storm off West Cornwall that night. Before Alfred began the poem Gilbert, with the storm pounding the door at his back, had the prosaic thought that he was glad he was not walking alone on the cliff path back from Boskenna, let alone on a ship far out at sea.

Alfred started the poem at a whisper, very slowly, allowing the beat of the long lines to weave its spell. Each mesmeric line lulled you, as if you were coming out of or going in to sleep and unsure which was which. Each line was delivered with just the right emphasis to hold the crowded room:

'Once upon a midnight dreary, whilst I pondered
    weak and weary,
Over many a quaint and curious volume of forgot-
    ten lore,
Whilst I nodded, nearly napping, suddenly there came
    a tapping—'

And at that very second, as true as Gilbert was standing there, there *was* a tapping at the door, a tapping which seemed to go right through Gilbert's shoulder blades as they leant back against the door.

Gilbert's heart jumped. The room jumped. Dolly and Prudence grabbed Joey. The colour left Alfred's face. His mouth twitched. His mouth moved again but he did not speak. His first clear thought, which quickly leapt to fury, was that someone, some fool, had gone outside to sabotage the whole effect of his performance, but there was only one door out of his studio and Gilbert had been pressed hard up against it.

Then there was another, louder, knocking. Alfred grabbed the poker and moved towards the door, but Gilbert had already lifted the latch and opened it, and so strong was the wind he felt as if someone had shoulder-barged the panels. Flurries of rain hit the floorboards at his feet.

A man in black, a stout figure in a tarpaulin sou'wester and oilskins, stood framed in the door, with large raindrops running off his moustache. In the lane below stood a horse and wagonette. The horse, head down between the shafts, steamed and glistened.

'Mr Munnings, sir?'

'Yes.'

'I'm led to believe a Mr Carter-Wood is here?'

Joey, looking embarrassed and younger than ever, stepped forward over Dolly's outstretched legs, apologising for the interruption.

'Sorry, what is it?'

'Your sister, sir.'

'Florence? Florence!'

Gilbert watched Joey hurry out into the storm, clatter down the outside wooden steps, and embrace the advancing girl.

'At this time of night?' Alfred said to the man in the oilskin.

'The young lady paid me proper, sir, that's all right.'

'No, the horse, what about the *horse*!'

'That's all right, he don't mind.'

But Alfred did mind and he dug into his pocket and put some coins in the man's hand.

'Give him a bit of something extra from me.'

While this was going on Laura was still inside encouraging everyone to carry on as normal, to enjoy themselves, an order immediately countermanded by the returning Munnings who told them all to resume their seats and told Joey and his sister, still talking outside in the rain, to bloody well come in if they were coming in or bloody well stay out if they were staying out. Joey and his sister were, however, not only bloody well coming in but willy-nilly now the centre of attraction.

'This is Florence, my sister. Down from London. She's a painter too. Much better than me. Not difficult, I know.'

'Hullo, Florence Carter-Wood!' came from all quarters.

Hands took off her long black coat; a gap opened up to the fire; a glass of punch was offered, and a cushion was placed for her on the floor. Before he would let his sister sit down, however, Joey explained to Dolly that Florence would be living in the cottage with him, that is next door to Harold and Laura Knight, and next door, of course, to Dolly, 'or in between you all, if you prefer'. When Dolly shook Florence's cold hand and said, 'Oh, oh, we'll all be nice and cosy then,' Florence's eyes widened and she looked in a puzzled way at Joey because she had never met anyone before in society who ever spoke like *that*. Evidently things were going to be very different in Cornwall.

There had, it transpired, been a misunderstanding over dates, and the train to Penzance was delayed three hours, and there had been a nasty—

'Oh, it's far too long a story,' Florence said, 'but when I arrived in Lamorna . . . Mr Knight told me you were down here, so of course I came.'

'I'm so glad you did,' Joey said. 'It's so wonderful to see you.'

She sat down, whispering:

'So, Joey, this . . . is one of your famous parties?'

'Yes.'

'What fun!'

She wrapped her hands round the warm punch, then inclining her head slightly towards Dolly but keeping her eyes on Joey she privately asked:

'And who is . . . *she*?'

'Dolly . . . You'll like her.'

Florence, amazed at this remark, looked up instead at Munnings, standing above her with his hands on his hips. Meanwhile, Gilbert stopped looking at Munnings and started looking at Florence.

The length of her fingers, the delicacy of her hands, was the first thing he remembered as he sat over his diary, on the edge of his narrow bed, at three o'clock the next morning. And her dark hair, though it wasn't dark, that was the point: as it dried imperceptibly in front of the fire, it turned lightish or auburny brown. Her fingers, her voice, her hair, and the way she walked across the room were the most striking first impressions, and her very upright position, and as for her face – her face was not unlike one he had seen – not in the street, not anywhere in real life, but in a famous painting, but as he knew very little about art he couldn't for the life of him remember it. It was Harold Knight a few days later who provided the answer. Botticelli's Venus.

'That's exactly what I mean,' Gilbert said. 'That's the one.'

'I agree, I've never seen such a likeness,' Harold added, with unusual warmth, 'and to think she's living next door to us.'

Alfred Munnings was standing in the middle of his studio, hands on hips, with little doubt in his posture that he had been seriously interrupted and had waited long enough. He glared. Once again the assembled revellers slowly subsided. He glared again. Dolly, giggling to Joey, was the last to fall silent. For the second time that evening the silence deepened. For the second time Alfred tensed his face and half closed his eyes. Once again he raised his finger ... but then with consummate skill swept up Florence Carter-Wood's black cape from the fender, showering fine drops of rain on his listeners, before settling it high over his shoulders. Now he was a sharply pointed, stagey raven, hovering over the packed room of artists. And now he began:

'Once upon a midnight dreary, whilst I pondered weak and weary,
Over many a quaint and curious volume of forgotten lore,
Whilst I nodded, nearly napping, suddenly there came a tapping,
As of someone gently rapping, rapping at my chamber door.'

He recited the whole poem, all eighteen stanzas, without one hesitation or one loss of total control.

All Gilbert, his heart a slow hammer, wrote in his diary that evening was:

Horribly wet. Studio party. Stayed late. Munnings rather stole the show.

Sammy's Birds' Eggs

After only a few hours of restless half-sleep, punctuated by some terrible dreams, Gilbert was up at 6.30 the next morning. He was up early every morning, except on Sundays, and even then he always tried to make the early service at St Buryan.

Already obsessed, he opened the curtains in his little bedroom and looked down the valley towards the cove. The sea was slate grey and the sky streaky bacon. The violence of the storm had blown itself to bits, the land was swept bare, and at the side of the hotel the sodden grass was trying to shine in the watery light, but the light was not quite strong enough to help. Still, it wasn't raining, which was something, so Gilbert ducked down and put his head out of the bedroom window, leaning right out, to see if all was well underneath his sill. Good, the house-martin's nest was still securely there. All was well.

Next he checked to see if his trousers, hanging up behind his bedroom door, had dried out. They had, more or less. Good. He pulled them on, and as he pulled them on, he thought of Florence.

He usually took his breakfast downstairs alone, well

before anyone else, because he liked to be properly organised and on site at Boskenna before the first of the workmen
arrived in the yard. That was part of his army discipline,
part of what a decent officer should do, and it also suited
him to eat early because he liked to be fed, not fussed over.
After a plate of bacon, egg and sausage he cleaned his teeth
and prepared to leave.

Before he did so (and it was the very last thing he did
each morning before leaving) he opened the small drawer
full of birds' eggs, displayed carefully on cotton wool. Each
morning he opened this drawer and each morning his heart
clenched, then sank. These eggs belonged to Sammy. He
touched the eggs with his fingertips, very lightly. 'Sammy',
as his younger brother Basil was nicknamed, died last year.
On the fateful Friday, Friday the 13th of August, he was
bitten on the lip by an insect. It all looked innocuous
enough at first, just a hard little red dot, but on the
Monday he suddenly developed a fever and started to
wander in his mind. Gilbert sat up all night with him,
talking to him, telling him about the best tries the Welsh
three-quarters had scored, telling him everything would be
all right in the morning, Sammy, very much better in the
morning; but on the Tuesday afternoon Sammy died.

Gilbert resettled the eggs and closed his eyes. How could
such things happen to such a lovely boy? Who 'allowed'
them to happen? Who? What explanation or comfort could
there be? Gilbert remembered sitting through a hopelessly
inadequate sermon on this subject at Rugby. To him it
was an inexplicable grief. Each day Gilbert asked himself
'Who?' and 'Why?' and each day, unable to answer these
questions, he opened the drawer and took out the birds'
eggs as his tribute to Sammy, a private ceremony to
remind himself how fragile life was, how vulnerable not
only Sammy was but all mankind, how precious a gift life

was (and here he thought of Florence) and how much he would try to be worthy of it.

Strangely enough, leaving Cardiff and coming down to Cornwall, which was partly done to overcome the pain, had only intensified the loss. One of the reasons for this, strangely enough again, was Joey Carter-Wood, because Joey bore more than a passing resemblance to Sammy. Sometimes, indeed, it was uncanny: there was the same shy look in his eye with girls, the same walk, the same generous laugh, the same optimistic spirit and the same love of the countryside. Both Sammy and Joey enjoyed clambering, rucksacks on backs, over slippery rocks and steep hills. No doubt, had he lived to be a man, Sammy would have turned into just the sort of splendid fellow Joey was.

Thinking of Joey made Gilbert think again of Joey's sister, now asleep up in the middle one of the low cottages, made him think of her fingers and her face, her black cape, and her drying hair. On what pretext could he call on her? He was not sure. But call he would. And every morning from now on, merely seeing the birds' eggs, feeling their almost weightless bodily presence and the oblique access they gave to Sammy's life, would open the same happy-sad sequence of circular thoughts in Gilbert:

Sammy, Joey, Florence,

Florence, Joey, Sammy.

He decided, all being well at Boskenna, he would bicycle across after lunch to see the carpenter (for Laura) and then contact the chimney sweep (for A.J.) and then, perhaps for tea, to the Carter-Woods, why not, and if they weren't in, he could easily and naturally drop in next door on Laura. Having them all so conveniently placed at the top of the lane was a bonus. And, if they were out, no matter, it was good exercise. If you had something gnawing away at your heart and mind exercise was the thing.

He put away the birds' eggs.

Yes.

The world was once again a fine place as Gilbert set off from the hotel, high on the saddle, riding his bicycle up the lane, and he cut a fine, upright figure. To everyone in the village he was very much 'Captain Evans riding over to Boskenna'. There was not much in the whole district he did not pass his eye over, and everyone, in return, waved to him.

Laura Knight and Alfred Munnings were up early, too. Among the artists they were always the first risers. However late their night, however unsteady Alfred's hand was on his razor, they pushed themselves out into the elements.

Her hobnails ringing on the road, her overcoat buttoned up to her neck, Laura strode down from Oakhill Cottages to the cove, turning sharp right at the bottom. Today was another challenge for Laura. Today she would try to capture the grandeur of that overhanging rock, the sort of rock she imagined frightened the young Wordsworth as he rowed across the dark lake. As she strode down she sometimes smiled to herself, a bit shocked, reliving some of the fun of the night before. And how magnificent Alfred's recitation of 'The Raven' had been.

What a man Munnings was!

Meanwhile, having climbed the uncarpeted stairs to his studio, her husband Harold, clear-headed, austere and immaculate, was drinking his first cup of tea. He sat in front of the easel. And sipped his tea. He eyed one corner of his painting. That corner was not right. It required more careful work. He moved his heavy-lidded eyes closer to the small particles of paint. He would, once he had finished his tea, give it that work. As far as Harold was concerned it was perfectly possible to paint a good picture without having to go out in all weathers and catch your death of cold in doing so. He could not, somehow, see Vermeer or Pieter de Hooch clambering over wet rocks or keeping going in a gale.

Second out of the stalls, banging the door behind him, came Alfred Munnings. He was incompetently shaven and unable to face any kind of food. He also had a stabbing pain, a volcano of blood vessels, in his left eye. If his left eye hurt that much, Alfred worried. He did not look up at the sky or breathe in deeply or do anything to suggest how good and bracing it was to be alive that morning. Instead, head down, he berated himself for his excesses, thrust his hands and sketch pad into his pocket and set off down to the cove. Knowing his master's moods in the early morning only too well, Taffy, his terrier, trotted along just out of kicking distance.

At the bottom Alfred turned left, in the opposite direction from Laura, across a small patch of worm-riddled sand to climb past the quarry and meet the footpath to Mousehole. Riding with the Western Hounds the other day had given him an idea for a painting, a setting near the coastguard lookout, which would combine various aspects – part real, part imaginary, part Cornwall, part Norfolk – into which he would later fit the many figures of dogs and horses and huntsmen. Well, that was the idea, anyway. But having ideas was one thing: doing the bloody thing was quite another.

If his head cleared by lunchtime he might have a sleep on the rocks, or he might ride Grey Tick in the afternoon, depending on how he got on this morning – he might even go over to see Evans at Boskenna, good bloke, Evans – then again he might not. The wind stabbed him in the eyes. He almost stumbled on a stone. This was not the moment to ask Munnings what his plans for the later part of the day were. At the moment he had the energy of a slackened drum.

He crossed the small stream which, after the prolonged storm, was now a milky spate, and his feet hit the bottom of the wet dirt path. As they did so there was a great explosive roar and rumble from the quarry. Alfred coughed up more of last night's smoky mucus from his lungs and spat into the bracken.

Over at Boskenna Gilbert worked hard all morning. From eight until ten he supervised the men hauling the stones, some large, some small, which would improve the surface around the yard and so allow easier access for the flow of carts on their way in and out. When the daffodil packing began in earnest it was like Piccadilly Circus. He took off his jacket and joined in with the men, lifting, carrying, glistening with sweat, his veins bulged and the harder he worked the better he felt.

From ten until noon he attended to the Colonel's correspondence. There was a heavy batch. While he was sorting through all this with the shorthand clerk, Mrs Paynter popped in to ask him for lunch (cold lamb, followed by baked Bramleys) and over lunch with the Colonel the conversation soon took the turn which was now fast becoming the norm in Lamorna.

'What's all this I hear about the Munnings chappie?' the Colonel asked. Gilbert took the opportunity of a full mouth to consider his reply. What exactly had the Colonel heard about A.J.? Given the wide range of possibilities it was probably best to play a straight, defensive bat. Gilbert wiped his mouth on his napkin.

'I'm afraid I don't follow, Colonel.'

'Got into trouble over in Newlyn, I understand. Quite considerable trouble.'

'Really?' Mrs P. was now interested. 'What sort of trouble?'

'That, my dear, is what I'm asking Gilbert.'

'Well, there are always rumours, aren't there?' Gilbert said. 'You know what the village is like.'

They ate for a while in silence. Then the Colonel asked:

'D'you know him well?'

'Not well, not yet.'

'But you like him?'

'Yes, I like him.'

'So there's nothing in the rumours? Nothing a bit "off" with the fella?'

The Colonel looked at his wife and let the sentence hang. With his spoon and fork Gilbert split open his white, puffy Bramley; it oozed sultanas and cream, as the Colonel continued:

'Don't want a cad on my land, d'you see? Not if I can help it. Not a cad, is he?'

'He's . . . unusual, I'd say. But not a cad, Colonel, no.'

'Fancies himself as a comic, I've heard, but impresses as a buffoon.'

'I think that's rather harsh, sir.'

'Bit of a painter too, isn't he?'

'They say he's a genius.'

'Oh, a genius, is he?'

And Colonel Paynter's sniff suggested some considerable reservations over geniuses. Gilbert kept eating, but all that splendid lunch, the cold lamb and the Bramleys, nearly came up again five minutes later because a servant girl half ran in to the dining-room, apologised and said Flirt, Mrs Paynter's favourite terrier, had eaten some rat poison and was dying.

Gilbert hurried over to the stables, while Mrs Paynter and the servants gathered to watch from a distance. Gilbert held the dog as it retched all over his shoes.

The smell!

He felt his stomach churn and he only just choked back in time. The dog writhed and gasped, its shanks sucking themselves in. After a few failed attempts Gilbert managed to spoon some warm milk into Flirt's mouth, not the easiest of operations with the dog grinding her teeth and biting the spoon, but Gilbert kept at it. Butter and mustard followed. Fraction by fraction Gilbert somehow slipped some morsels of that down. The dog writhed on, her eyes rolling, her breathing uncertain.

After an airless and emetic hour, with chubby maids whispering just out of sight, with Flirt's heart bumping fast in Gilbert's hand, her breathing gradually settled into a more steady beat. It seemed the storm had passed. Gilbert stayed on, then laid her, hot and exhausted, in her basket. Exhausted but alive. She looked up at Gilbert with droopy eyes.

He mopped up.

'So kind of you,' Mrs Paynter said, 'so kind.'

'She'll live, I think,' Gilbert said. 'That's the main thing, isn't it?'

White-faced and needing some fresh air, Gilbert bicycled as fast as his legs would take him all the way back to Lamorna swallowing and gulping harsh wonderful gulps of air, but the smell of the poison and the sickness seemed to have seeped deep into his own skin and clothes; and even though he had thoroughly washed his hands and his shoes he wished he had some eau-de-Cologne. The taste was on his tongue, too. He tried to spit it out into the thorny furze and the bramble sprays, but only smeared his mouth with saliva, and when he propped his bicycle against the low wall outside the Carter-Woods' cottage he felt his nerve nearly fail. Next cottage along, he could see Harold Knight's back bent, still working upstairs in his studio, and he considered going instead down the Knights' front path for a harmless social hour, but Joey was sitting in his front room and waved excitedly to Gilbert, motioning him to come in. The door was thrown open. The brother and sister stood side by side, arms open wide in welcome: Florence and Joey, smiling at him.

'How good of you to visit us!' Joey said.

'I hope I'm not intruding?'

'No, couldn't be better, we've just this minute come in from the rocks, haven't we, Blote?'

'Captain Evans,' Florence said, her eyes steadily on Gilbert.

'Gilbert,' Joey corrected.

'We've been collecting anemones,' Florence added, shaking Gilbert's hand, 'and Joey is very excited with his findings.'

'In a minute you can help us classify them,' Joey said, taking Gilbert's arm and leading him into the small sitting-room, 'you're just the man we need.' There was, as usual, a sharp, salty smell permeating the house. Joey had one tank set up down near the shore line, and an aquarium round at the back of the cottage to which he carried his specimens. On most days he could be seen staggering back up the hill, with buckets yoked over his shoulders.

'So you're interested in marine biology too?' Florence asked.

'Your brother's the expert,' Gilbert said, 'I just double-check on the details. He's opened up another world for me.'

'Has he?'

Dressed in silver-grey, she looked younger, less composed, more vulnerable, more lovely, more everything.

'Did you enjoy last night?' Joey wanted to know of Gilbert, with a conspiratorial grin.

'Oh, very much.'

'Is that ... typical?' Florence asked. 'What went on, I mean? Later.'

'Sit down, sit down,' Joey moved some of his things, 'pretty wild, wasn't it?'

'Yes, I suppose it was.'

'And the poem,' Florence said, widening her eyes with meaning, 'what was your opinion of *that*?'

'Extraordinary, wasn't it?' Joey said. 'Quite extraordinary.'

'I asked Captain Evans, Joey. I know what you think about everything.'

'Gilbert,' Gilbert corrected, 'please.'

'Gilbert, then.'

She looked at him, waiting. He felt himself being assessed. He moved his feet. What did he think of the poem? Well, it certainly went on a long time.

'I simply don't know how anyone could learn all that. I know I couldn't.'

'Quite so,' Joey said, 'extraordinary, but then he is, isn't he!'

'Mind you, your entry was even more dramatic,' Gilbert said to Florence.

'Was it?'

'And did you *see* A.J.'s face!' Joey laughed. 'If looks could kill.'

'What about his face?' Florence asked her brother.

'Well, spoiling his moment like that, I mean one doesn't lightly interrupt A.J., does one, Gilbert? No, one does *not*!'

'Really?' Florence said. 'Is he so very important?'

'More than one's life is worth to interrupt A.J.,' Joey went on. 'Still, come on, can't wait to show you what I've just got out the back. *And* the little devil stung me for my pains.'

'Stung you?'

'Yes!'

'Badly?' Gilbert asked.

'Very,' Florence said. 'Is all this worth it?'

Joey looked at his hand.

'Bit of a jolt, just as I pulled it off the rock, but it's a beauty, the best snakelocks I've seen, lovely purples and greens, she's going to draw it for me later, aren't you? Do you want to see my little poisoner?'

'Oh, do let Captain Evans sit for a moment, he's only just arrived.'

Once again Gilbert felt her eyes on his face. He looked steadily at Joey and asked:

'What does the sting feel like now?'

'Oh, prickly torture, nothing more,' Joey said. 'Lots of little explosions, that's all, lots of invisible barbs. Mind you, I've just been reading in Gosse about the Dr Waller experiment, you won't see me doing *that*, Gilbert, not in a month of Sundays.'

'Doing what?' Florence asked.

'Well, it seems this Dr Waller deliberately allowed the anemone's tentacles to touch the tip of his tongue, because he wanted to know the full effect. That was a snakelocks, too.'

'His tongue!' Florence's voice was a low whisper. 'Did you say his . . . tongue? He allowed one of those . . . *things* to touch his tongue?'

'Yes, and the anemone seized it very hard and it took him about a minute or more to claw it off. Imagine that, a snakelocks clamped on your tongue.'

If Joey found all this quite funny, Florence did not.

'But why did he do it?'

'To see the effect, as I said. And it was extremely distressing. Hardly surprising as it pumps poison into you. They may be very beautiful, but they're also very aggressive.'

'The man's a fool,' Gilbert muttered.

'Apparently his tongue felt very swollen, though it did not *appear* any larger, so he dipped it alternately in hot and cold water. Can't you see him doing it?'

'Sounds an even bigger fool,' Gilbert exclaimed.

'And the ulceration of his tongue only disappeared when he applied some nitrate of silver, drastic though that is.'

Florence waved her hands in the air, calling for an urgent halt to all this, shaking her head in a speechlessly urgent request.

'Yes,' Gilbert said, 'enough's enough, I think.'

'Can we go back,' Florence asked quietly, 'to the poetry?'

'The poetry?' Joey looked blank.

'Yes, does he take it all *that* seriously?' Florence asked.

'What?'

'His recitation, his Rook.'

'Oh, the Raven you mean.'

'Raven, then.'

'Good question, isn't it,' Joey admitted. 'I suppose he must. After all it takes a devil of a lot of learning, and I suspect he's got others up his sleeve.'

But Florence had turned her attention, full face and very pale, to her visitor. It was an attention her visitor could not ignore.

'So, what have you been doing today . . . Gilbert?'

'Me?'

Gilbert could not see much of interest for this beautiful girl in the stone-hauling around the Boskenna yard or the Colonel's correspondence, while the incident with Mrs Paynter's half-dead dog might well be most inappropriate in mixed company. But he felt he really had to say something or seem insufferably dull, so he gave a fairly comic and very heavily edited version of Flirt, Her-Almost-Final-Moments. Joey loved every minute of it, so Gilbert relaxed and elaborated a bit, until he saw Florence's face.

'But,' he added with an encouraging smile, 'it all ended happily, that's the main thing, as I said to Mrs Paynter, Flirt will be fine tomorrow, probably already is.'

Her voice, when it came, was intensely considered and not to be denied.

'What sort of poison did you say it was?'

Before Gilbert could answer the question Joey stood up and rubbed his hands.

'Aquarium time, I think, our ocean in miniature, our very own sea floor.'

Joey led the way, followed by Florence, but Gilbert could no longer concentrate on the business of identification. His Flirt story had spoilt the atmosphere, that was evident, and as they walked through to the cluttered back parlour all he could do was to ask her some sensible questions, more or less anything, on more or less any topic, as long as it was sensible.

'So, you've been to your first class ... with Stanhope Forbes?'

'No, we're going tomorrow, I'm afraid I was too tired, I woke so late.'

'I'm not surprised, it's a long way from London.'

In the back parlour, Joey's marble-topped table was covered with small pails and china bowls and various hoop nets and prods.

'Gilbert's always up with the lark, aren't you, Gilbert?'

'I have to be.'

'From now on Joey will be coming with me every day I go to Newlyn, won't you, Joey?'

Joey settled on his haunches in front of the aquarium, slipping a thermometer slowly into the water. Florence spoke to his back.

'Won't you? We've *agreed*!'

Joey wrinkled his nose and shrugged. His eyes were lost in his small marine world of green weed and shells and tiny rocks, with submerged sea anemones half retracting their tentacles. He lightly tapped the glass with his pencil, causing a tiny rhythmic stirring of growths.

'There she is, Gilbert!'

Gilbert's face was only a few inches from Florence's, only a few inches from the glass. He asked:

'Does he run art classes in Newlyn every day?'

'Yes, but we're going three days a week. We can comfortably manage that, and Papa insists on a progress report on both of us, you see, at the end of each month, and if Joey backslides—'

'Look at the stem, Gilbert, and the colour . . . ever seen anything so *mauve*?'

Joey pointed into the gleaming stillness. Florence moved on to her knees. Joey tapped the glass again.

'That's the column . . . and the mouth . . . and the disc . . . but look at the beadlet, it's very like the strawberry, see the difference, and you can see it's much smaller than the snakelocks . . . and that one . . . there . . . is the plumose . . . come on, open your . . . there . . . now look at those reds and greens. Do you think the world of art offers any greater mystery or any greater beauty? Do you?'

Florence stared at Gilbert's reflection and watched his mouth as he asked:

'So you'll be here in Lamorna some months then?'

It took her a few seconds to react, to stop staring at his reflected mouth, and then she saw the strawberry and the reds and the mauves and the anemones opening and closing their mouths. She gulped and turned slowly to Gilbert.

'That's what I plan, but if Joey lets me down, if Papa thinks for one moment his son is wasting his time and his money on these poisonous blobs of jelly which attack you, neither of us will be happy and neither of us will be allowed to keep this cottage or stay down here, I promise you that's true, Joey, and you know it, and all your precious anemones won't save us.'

'Yes, yes,' he said mechanically, 'I know all that.'

Florence's eyes appealed to Gilbert. Gilbert nodded and turned to his young friend.

'You really must,' Gilbert said. 'We *all* want you both to stay.'

'Yes – yes,' Joey mumbled, 'don't *you* start as well, Gilbert. I've come here to show you the snakelocks, not be given a sermon, so if you don't mind . . . I'll just check the salinity.'

'You really want to be a painter, then?' Gilbert asked Florence, straightening up, feeling a bit like the piggy in the middle. She laughed abruptly.

'Why else do you think I'm here? And we have every opportunity to improve, we've got the Knights as neighbours, imagine that, imagine what I can learn from Laura and Harold Knight. Imagine what *he* could learn from them, if he *wanted* to.'

'She's awfully good,' Joey said, nodding at his sister, 'do show Gilbert your latest—'

She shook her head at her brother's praise and stood up.

'Some other time, I think. We've only just met.'

'I'd love to,' Gilbert said. 'Whenever. I really would.'

All three of them turned away from the aquarium.

'The best thing you can do for me, Gilbert, if you really want to help, is to encourage *him*' – she poked Joey's arm with her long fingers – 'to take his lessons seriously. *Don't* smile at me, Joey! I hate it when you do that, it is so superior, and so infuriating. You see, let's be honest, dear brother, Papa already considers art little more than daubing, and if you let me down I shall be dreadfully annoyed.'

Having spoken so sharply, with a sudden softening she kissed her recalcitrant brother and kept her arms wrapped around him. Gilbert could now see the outline of her backbone through her dress, and the way her long hair fell. Joey looked over his sister's shoulder, winking slowly at Gilbert.

'You can rely on Gilbert to keep me up to the mark, can't you, Gilbert?'

'Yes you can, you can indeed.'

Back in the sitting-room Gilbert slumped in his chair, suddenly hit by the afternoon wave of tiredness that comes after too little sleep. His eyes itched and he rubbed them.

'You must have had enough of us squabbling,' Florence said, disengaging her arm from Joey's, 'so we will now have some tea.'

'I'd love some tea.'

'And then you must tell me about South Africa. All about it.'

'Not *now*, Blote! Honestly.'

Joey looked a little shy and a little crestfallen.

'But have I got it wrong? Joey did tell me you fought in the war?'

'Yes, yes I did.'

'But he doesn't like talking about it? All right? Sorry, Gilbert.'

'That's nothing, nothing at all.'

'Now, look, we must arrange our next time for billiards. We play at Jory's,' he explained to his sister. 'When we can.'

'Can I watch?' Florence asked. 'Or is it terribly private? You never know with men's games. No. No, I can see it *is* private.'

'Of course you can watch,' Gilbert said.

'If you like,' Joey mumbled.

'Are you an expert at billiards, Gilbert, as well as rock pools?'

'I've told you, I really know very little about the seashore, I'm a beginner.'

'Well,' Joey answered for both men, 'there is still some dispute as to who is the outright billiards champion of Lamorna and the surrounding parishes, Captain Gilbert Evans of the Monmouthshire Militia or me, but I intend to establish my mastery.'

Gilbert smiled and stared at his feet. Her eyes, he could feel her eyes clamped on him.

Going slowly back to the hotel on his bicycle, at barely more than walking pace, Gilbert relived everything from the moment he arrived at the Carter-Woods' cottage. From tea with Florence and Joey he had returned to Boskenna to do three more hours' work and now looked forward to his evening meal. Whatever his reservations beforehand he had surely been right to call on them. Apart from that one sticky patch it had all gone so well. Then he heard a horse's hooves approaching on the other side of the wall, coming up quickly in the field behind him. He turned to see a rider silhouetted against the grey sky. He stopped his bicycle to watch as the rider leant back in the saddle to make a perfect leap over some tangle bushes. It was Munnings.

'Evans!' he shouted going past, wheeling and coming back to join him.

'Hullo, A.J.'

'Easy, Tick, easy.' He pulled up his horse, stroked and patted him. 'Glad I caught you. Heard you were out and about on your funny machine.'

He smiled in a way Gilbert could not follow, and the purplish tint in his cheeks creased as he smiled.

'Most enjoyable party last night,' Gilbert said, 'it really was.'

Munnings waved a dismissal, as if all that thank-you-guff was taken for granted.

'But you like "The Raven", that's the point, you liked Poe's stuff?'

'Yes, I did.'

'D'you know it?'

'I'd read some at school, of course, but not—'

'Thought you would, thought you'd like it, so I've brought this. For you.'

From his pocket he took out a small, red leather book of Poe's poetry, but immediately pointed at the gatepost by Gilbert's elbow.

'Look at the rust stain on that post ... same colour as the book, almost, but that rust was dark brown yesterday, sorrel red today, bit of rain, different day and it's a different colour, different world depending on the sky, you've got to use your eyes if you're an artist.'

'Thank you for the book. It's most—'

Alfred bent closer to Gilbert.

'So, what a-bout this Miss C. Hyphen Wood, eh, what d'you make of her?'

'I don't really know, I've hardly met her.'

'Yes, yes, no need for all that, but you were drawn, eh,

you smelt her, you spotted her as she went past, you were
not *un*-a-ware of her presence.'

'She strikes me as very—'

'Paintable, exactly, ex-actly, very paintable indeed.'

Alfred sat upright again, as if they were obviously in as
close accord on her paintability as on everything else.

'Yes,' Gilbert said, 'I can see that she would be. To
an artist.'

'Like coffee, though, always remember that.'

Gilbert said he had not quite caught what Alfred had just
said. It sounded like 'coffee'.

'That's right, coffee. A girl. Like coffee. Never tastes as
good as it smells. Don't know why.'

Gilbert looked at his handlebars. Did people really have
to talk like that? Was it necessary to be so hopelessly
inappropriate in one's comparisons?

'I wouldn't know about that, I haven't had enough
experience. I haven't, you know ... known enough to
say.'

A.J. nodded and winked, as if Gilbert should nevertheless
commit this shared coffee secret to memory, a secret that
would help him through his inexperienced life, until he *did*
meet enough girls.

'But it's true, Ev, believe me ... however refined or
sensitive they seem. Still, she can draw a bit, she *can* draw, if
nothing else. Bastien-Lepage would have been quite proud
of her. Yes, Stanhope Forbes has a winner in her, all right.
Or a runner-up at least.'

'So Joey said. It's very exciting, isn't it?'

'Just seen 'em, she's no fool ... she can handle a pencil
and a brush ... needs to be bolder, of course, her pencil's
too polite, needs to burst out, needs to tell the world who
she is, doesn't she, Tick?'

He stroked his horse.

'Oh, you've already seen her art?'

'Yes, just called in, not long after you, funny we should both call there today, isn't it, something of a stalking party, still, must get on. Right, Tick, we'd better be off.'

He turned the huge animal towards his studio.

'*No*,' he stopped himself, '*knew* there was something else! That bicycle of yours, no good at all, from what I can hear, bloody hopeless in fact, so I've come up with a plan.'

Gilbert bridled.

'What nonsense! This bicycle is top-hole, it's a wonderful machine, it's made the most marvellous difference to my days here.'

'Top-hole, is it?' A.J. laughed. '*I* heard all the holes were in the tyres.'

'I've just bought new tyres in Penzance, the very best.'

'Yes, yes, no doubt, but there's not much point having a bicycle with a record like yours, is there, like a boat that leaks, so tell you what I'm going to do, Ev, you can have my pony, borrow Merrilegs whenever you like, I mean it, no charge, my pleasure, and it'll make all the difference, all the difference, you'll see, you'll catch everyone's eye.'

Gilbert disliked all this, both the man's substance and the man's tone.

'I am interested only in going from A to B, not catching anyone's eye!'

'Do it quicker on a horse, then! Do it much quicker!'

'Colonel Paynter always lends me a hunter if I need one. In fact, he's offered me one many times.'

'Even so, easier if you take my offer, no favours and closer to home, get my drift, then we can ride to the hounds together, chase foxes together, after all we're friends, aren't we, Ev, and what are friends for?'

Gilbert pushed his bicycle a few yards, his eyes on the

front tyre. He wanted Munnings to go away, and go away now.

'That's very generous of you, Alfred, but I doubt I'll have the time.'

'You're missing the point! God, you're so slow!'

'Oh, am I?'

'Yes! Merrilegs will *save* you time on your missions of mercy, that's the point, you idiot! You'll see, you can go all over the Colonel's estate in half the time, even stop for a rest to read a few poems, don't fancy that funny machine's much use in a field or on a rocky path, do you, and on Merrilegs you'll be Lord and Master of all you survey, a *master* surveyor, she's a real treat, you'll love her, paintable as a girl and quiet as a lamb, she really is, you're made for each other, you and Merrilegs.'

And with this assertion he leant over and stretched his hand down to Gilbert to confirm the offer and to settle the deal. Gilbert felt he was in a stronger presence. A.J. gripped Gilbert's right hand firmly and looked sharply into his eyes.

'And remember, Ev, whatever I do or say, even when I lash out, I'm your friend. Do you hear? D'you hear?'

'Yes.'

'Even when I'm a silly bugger. And Merrilegs is yours, I mean it, whenever you want her, whenever you want the little beauty, she's yours. Right, I'm off.'

And off he struck, his big horse kicking up the turf, and soon boldly into his stride. Troubled, Gilbert stood by his bicycle, motionless, watching the horse and rider until they disappeared.

Bastien-Lepage

When Joey also mentioned Bastien-Lepage, over their next game of billiards in Jory's hotel, Gilbert fibbed by saying he had 'half heard' of him. To Gilbert's ears Bastien-Lepage sounded like one of those obscure French generals who made a frightful mess of things in the Franco-Prussian war. The name came up partly by way of Joey explaining how all these artists, the Carter-Woods included, came to be down there in West Cornwall in the first place and how they came to be doing the kind of work they were doing.

(Gilbert, by the way, was not playing at all well. The very stillness of Florence's concentration on his shots made him unusually nervous.)

For many of the Newlyn painters and students over the last twenty years, it seemed Bastien-Lepage was the original inspiration. More than that, it appeared he was the cult. When his canvases, so full of uncompromising realism, so full of peasants and drunks and truth to the Lorraine countryside, were shown in London there was a spontaneous wave of feeling for him. Bastien-Lepage was, so Joey went on, 'the man', he was the creed of the day. Listening to all this, while playing a cannon, Gilbert found it far too close to worship: sometimes, he felt, artists dangerously confused God and Art.

Stanhope Forbes, now Florence's teacher, had also visited Brittany back in 1881. For him the Frenchman's figures seemed to live in paint as they had lived in life, in the countryside and in their natural surroundings; Bastien-Lepage's men and women breathed air not linseed oil, his skies were skies you could reach up and touch. (Gilbert liked that phrase.) His skies threatened you, inspired you, leapt out at you, Florence said, and why on earth could not English painters do the same? Especially in Cornwall. The Cornish air and the Cornish coastline beckoned you to leave London and leave the galleries and go outside and see the world of nature for yourself.

'Bastien-Lepage was so closely in sympathy with his subjects you felt you became part of the world he painted.'

That was Joey's view.

Florence wasn't so sure.

She said the perspective from which Bastien-Lepage viewed his subjects was often quite high, just above the figures, rather than on the same level, as if he was highlighting them.

'Like Rodin, you mean?' Joey asked.

Florence's point had reminded Joey of Rodin, a famous story about Rodin, the greatest sculptor since Michelangelo, who was theatrical as well as realistic, because hadn't Rodin – to get the unusual perspective he wanted – climbed a stepladder before beginning his sculpture of the Pope? And the Pope, of course, did not particularly approve of Rodin going up a stepladder in the presence of His Holiness.

'No, no, no, Pope above,' the Pope said, 'Monsieur Rodin below.'

'All right,' Rodin growled, 'you go up the ladder then.'

Florence laughed, while Gilbert (feeling all this was a bit

over his head) compiled a steady break of twenty-three. Even so, he now knew that when Laura Knight and Alfred Munnings, come rain or come shine, strode down to the cove to attack their canvases, they carried with them the spirit of a Frenchman from Lorraine called Jules Bastien-Lepage.

'And he died very young,' Florence said.

'Your shot,' Gilbert said to Joey, pointing at the cue ball.

While Joey studied the options and played, Gilbert sat next to Florence, so close to her hands and her face, only inches away, which was a perspective he greatly liked.

Skies you could reach up and touch.

Reynard on the Rocks

When Joey and Florence arrived, in high spirits, at Jory's hotel for this game of billiards, Gilbert was lying on his bed up in his room. Tired as a rag from a stomach upset he was feeling more than a bit sorry for himself, but the news that Florence was waiting downstairs made him leap off his bed, clean his teeth and make the effort.

Gilbert could never be down in the dumps for long, and there was his young friend Joey refilling his pipe from the humidor, there was Joey so civilised and charming even when losing, and there was his wonderful sister, Florence. 'One day,' Gilbert thought, listening to the Bastien-Lepage art lesson, 'I'll tell them both about Sammy.' He had never spoken about his young brother, had never been able to, not to anyone, and oh, it would be so good to share his loss, perhaps on a Sunday walk to Mousehole or on a picnic, with the hamper open at their side and the ocean behind her back, with Florence listening, and if she listened that would help him so much to bear it, when who should pop up again like a jack-in-the-box?

'Have you heard about Munnings?' Joey asked, striking a match and sucking hard on his pipe.

'What about Munnings?' Florence said.

'That he's offended Harold Knight again?' Gilbert offered.

'No.'

'That he's burnt down his studio?' Florence suggested.

'I wouldn't be surprised if he had,' Gilbert laughed.

'No,' Joey said, aware his audience was nicely hooked, 'no, I'm talking about the business with the fox.'

'What fox business?'

'Well, they're all talking about it down in The Wink. Some farmers were in there when I called, they saw it all, from start to finish, and quite full of it all they were. Amazing business!'

'Amaze us,' Florence said, sitting very still in her seat. And she listened to the fox story at much the same time as A.J. Munnings, the man himself and dressed to kill, was walking into The Wink to an admiring bar, where he ordered drinks for all. As usual there was a small problem (he had no money) but he mentioned that little detail somewhat later and 'paid' for his drinks with a series of drawings done there and then on the spot, plus a promise to Jory that he would come back within the week and paint a full-size picture of the premises which would sell for a fortune. (It did.) The landlord and the painter shook hands on the bargain, while the locals gathered like a swarm of bees around the man himself.

'Tell us about the fox,' Mr Jory asked, putting his first pint in front of Alfred.

'Yes, go on, Mr Munnin's.'

'Tom Mollard's bin in, so we do know a bit.'

'Tom Mollard!' the painter barked. 'Don't mention Mollard to me!'

'We'm 'eard a bit, that's all; just enough to wet the whistle.'

Munnings raised his hands.

'No, no . . . not now, not in good drinking time.'

While they all protested he drained half his drink.

'But it's true, what we'm 'eard? 'Tis true?'

'Depends what you heard,' Munnings said, smacking his lips.

'Easier if you tell us. Get'n from the 'osse's mouth then, don't us?'

'Go on, Mr Munnin's.'

To the click of billiard balls Florence listened; to the click of dominoes and the suck of pipes, the bar listened.

A large turnout of the Western Foxhounds had been running towards Morvah. With Munnings among the front runners, they were moving fast from parish to parish, hugging headlands, sailing over stubble, running across the granite country, all across the undulating moor, not far from Zennor. The fox was well in their sights. The front riders, in high spirits and sure of a kill, leapt a low wall. A.J. was riding hard just behind the huntsman, Tom Mollard, and stride for stride with Jack Stone, the whip.

Their quarry was tiring. That was clear. Unable to reach cover, the fox suddenly turned right in desperation and ran down to the cliff, where Munnings spotted him way below, small and brown, crouched into a ball on some jutting rocks which hung over the sea.

The leaders dismounted. Munnings was first off his horse, then Jack the Whip, a tall man with a black beard, and the two of them very slowly and very carefully crawled down the cliff face, holding on to deep-rooted tufts until they were just above the curled-up fox. All Munnings could see below him was the fox, the rocks and the boiling foam.

Just as Munnings turned to tell Jack that enough was

enough and they should call it a day, Jack suddenly stretched his arm right down and flicked the fox sharply with the lash of his whip. The fox barked and jumped right out into the sea. Munnings stumbled to his feet and swore bloody murder and nearly fell into the boiling foam himself.

By now the whole hunt was standing above them on the clifftop: all the hounds, all the riders dismounted, all were looking down on A.J. and Jack and the little fox swimming for dear life, the little fox lifted up and thrown back by the swell, its brown fur now black. For five minutes or more the fox took on the elements, an unbearable tension for Munnings, who was kneeling on a rock calling out encouragement, 'Keep fighting,' he roared, 'keep fighting, Reynard, you little blighter, God bless you,' when a large wave suddenly picked up the fox and seemed to place him with a careful hand on a wide, safe rock. Munnings rose to his feet, arms aloft, and cheered.

The fox rested a moment. Then, head down, shanks sucked in, sodden and reduced to a small greyhound, he shook himself and started very slowly to climb or clamber up, ledge by ledge, until, too weary to be wary, he once again was trapped in a narrowing crevice. This time his eyes went blank and his nose went slowly down. The fight had gone out of him.

The whip saw his chance.

'Come on, Mr Munnin's, let's get him.'

'No!'

'But he's trapped, he's done in.'

'No,' Munnings roared at Jack and the waves and the assembled hunt above. 'No, *leave* him, for God's sake *leave* him.'

'We must get him, or what'll Tom say?'

The whip pointed up at the scarlet coat and the black cap of Tom Mollard silhouetted against the sky.

Munnings teetered, lost his balance, and fell but just held on to the edge of the rock face. Bruised and still stretched out on the rock, he shouted he didn't give a bugger what Tom said, the fox had run for his life, saved himself, swum for it, climbed for it, damn near died for it, and that was good enough for anyone – let alone Tom Mollard.

Munnings rose to his feet and stood defiantly between the fox and Jack.

'And,' he roared, '*you're* not going to get him out!'

The whip climbed back to the top and, panting for breath, told Tom Mollard the full story. Tom heard him out, stony-faced, then said that was the last time, the very last time, Mr Munnings of Suffolk would ride with the Western hounds. And off they trooped home without him.

'That's quite a story,' Gilbert said, 'it really is.'

'Isn't it!' Joey added. 'And so typical of A.J. from start to finish.'

'You mean it isn't quite true?' Florence asked evenly. When she said this, Gilbert felt a slight shock in his hands, and Joey coloured, blurting out, 'Of course it's true, Blote, ask the huntsmen who were there, it's as true as we're playing billiards.'

'I'm sure it's true,' Gilbert said, 'why would anyone make it all up?'

Florence smiled an unruffled smile.

'So Captain Evans and Mr Munnings both save animals?'

Gilbert was not sure if he himself was now being mocked, yet he could see no mockery at all on her face.

'Oh, mine was small beer by comparison. And I must apologise again for ever mentioning it.'

'No, I'm glad you mentioned it, death by drowning and death by poison are both terribly dramatic, don't you agree?'

Unable to frame a response, the men played inconsequentially in constrained silence. When Joey broke the long silence it was with an exaggerated, overcompensating heartiness:

'Look, Gilbert, we'd like you to join us for supper soon, wouldn't we?'

'Very much,' Florence said. 'As soon as possible.'

'The sooner the better!' Joey exclaimed.

'And I'd very much like to come, thank you.'

'And let's ask A.J. as well, shall we?' Joey went on. 'Then it'll be even more fun, and Florence can question him further over the fox.'

'Why on earth should I do that? I merely wanted to know if you both believed the story.'

What no one knew was what happened in the hours after the hunt had deserted Munnings on the rocks near Morvah.

He sat alone in the same place, with the wind bending the bracken and his shirt drying on his back. He sat there, fighting his anger, until the rioting behind his eyes abated. Above all, foxes should be respected. Who on earth did these ignorant sods think they were? And did these ignorant sods never think, in the vain glory of their chase, why there were so many legends and stories and fables about foxes? What about Reynard the Fox, and what about other foxes' encounters with Chauntecleer the Cock, Tibert the Cat, Bruin the Bear and Tsengrin the Wolf? Why did they think there were figures of foxes carved in churches all over East Anglia, not that these ignorant sods even knew where East Anglia was? The fox was a hunter and he was hunted; he was a beast and a king, real and fabulous, and that was why he, Alfred Munnings, second son of a Suffolk miller, had kept this particular Reynard alive – Reynard the Triumphant – because that little fellow stuck out there on the rock a moment ago was a triumph of the spirit. An inspiration.

Feeling much better after his reflection on ignorant sods and fearless foxes, A.J. started to ride home, talking to Grey Tick about fools and foxes, and stopping as and when on the way for hot gin hollands. In one pub named, as luck would have it, The Fox and Grapes he hunched by the fire lost in thought about a paintable girl until he overheard some youngsters, mere boys, well, undergraduates by the sound of them, talking about Omar Khayyam.

Omar Khayyam?

There were three undergraduates in the pub: a ginger-haired one, a bearded one with a pipe, and, lastly, a pale exhumation. They all talked with heated warmth about Omar Khayyam's merits. A.J. listened to this for a while then uncoiled his legs, stretched back on the settle and called over to them.

'Who's this Omar you keep talking about, then, an Arab horse thief?'

The undergraduates looked at each other, then looked at the rough mud-bespattered rider, and decided they had not quite heard the question. So Alfred glared at the three of them in turn and repeated the question more loudly. Unable to ignore him now, the ginger-haired one coughed and said politely, 'Um, no, he's not, no.' He glanced at his colleagues. 'He's . . . not an Arab horse thief.'

This was followed by some laughter. Munnings decided he would enjoy himself as well.

'So who is he? I couldn't help hearing, and I don't know who he is.'

'It's . . . it's the title of a work, a translation in point of fact, a version by Edward Fitzgerald. From the Persian.'

'Sorry, never heard of him either,' Alfred said. 'Who's he? The Persian?'

Dear-God smiles escaped from the undergraduates; small smiles of complete complicity flitted from face to face.

'Fitzgerald,' the bearded one spoke even more carefully, as if a dangerous animal was out on the loose, 'Fitzgerald is a poet . . . a great poet. The Rubaiyat is an allegory.'

'Oh, poet, is he?' Munnings was pleased. 'Landlord, fill the young gentlemen's pots, there's a good chap, thank you, and do draw yourself another, and then the young gentlemen can recite for us some of Omar by Edward Whoever and I must say I'm looking forward to hearing a bit of great poetry by a great poet, even if he is a Persian.'

Munnings settled himself down as an overattentive audience would, and his overattentive pause and the panic it created all around him was quite delightful.

'I'm . . . we've . . .' began the pale one. 'I'm afraid we haven't brought a copy of his work.'

A.J. forgivingly spread his hands, as if he would be the very last person in the world to criticise anyone for that.

'Doesn't matter, does it, just recite me some, give me what you might call a taster of old Omar. In English. Or Persian, if you prefer.'

At this, they looked cornered and went into a whispering huddle. For his part, A.J. patiently waited a while and then said:

'But if it's great stuff you can, surely? No? You can't? Ah well. Does it rhyme? Can't stand stuff that doesn't!'

The remark about rhyme somewhat released the pressure

on them and they reverted to their lighter tones; they may well have been unable to remember a line of poetry in English or Persian but at the very least they could all be critics.

'Well, that's rather bad luck on *Paradise Lost*,' said the ginger-haired one.

'And a bit of a pity about Shakespeare's plays,' said the pale one.

And these supposed put-downs led to some Oxford chortling.

'Good stuff, rhyme,' A.J. reasserted, 'rhyme is the thing.'

While the landlord placed out another round of drinks there was something of a lull in which A.J. wiped off their ironic smiles by reciting the first fifty-two lines of Gray's *Elegy*, and before the pale one could say Gosh that is actually quite something of a feat I must say, A.J. followed it up by giving them his favourite passages of prose, verbatim, from Surtees, and standing (ale in hand) with his back to the fire and with the landlord's mouth agape, he finished 'By way of a finale' with a handsome swathe of *Hiawatha*,

'By Henry Wadsworth Longfellow,' he added, with a patronising smile, 'and he's a fucking good poet too. From Portland, Maine, not Persia.'

They all ended the evening in tremendous fettle, all singing together, arms around each other's shoulders, before A.J. (by way of payment) covered the black blinds in the bar with some chalk drawings of horses and young people drinking and the three young people in the drawings all had muzzy faces very like their own and were depicted toppling backwards in their chairs towards the floor, laughing as they fell, and they all loved that, and they all thought him one helluva fellow.

A.J. saluted them at the door before taking his big-stepping horse home very slowly to Lamorna.

'Call me a sentimental sod, but all in all,' he said to Grey Tick, stroking his horse's powerful neck, 'not too bad a day, Tick. All in all, eh?'

Botticelli's Venus

Before she left her London home for Lamorna, Florence Carter-Wood went into her father's library, stretched right up on tiptoe and took down their large, leather-bound Atlas of Great Britain. She opened it out on her knees and sat very upright – it was a habit of hers to sit very still and very upright, a habit which immediately attracted Gilbert Evans, was noted by Harold Knight and copied, as the days went by, by Dolly – with the landscape of England beneath her hands. She turned and stroked each page, sliding her fingers over the western counties.

The West. The western counties felt so far away they might as well have been the Bahamas. Florence had, it is true, already travelled a good deal, but as far back as she could remember it had always been the same journey: from London to Carlisle and from Carlisle to London, from town to country house and back, and these journeys to the Cumbrian coast were always taken at much the same time of the year in much the same company. Until twenty she had led, she now realised, a well-guarded life.

To her, each page of the Atlas now seemed an open road, a possibility if not a temptation. She had money, and with

Papa's generous allowance where could she not go and what could she not do?

She stroked the map. Her fingers soon found the south-west tip of Cornwall, then traced a line down the map south from Penzance, along Mount's Bay, to Newlyn, and then on to Paul and Mousehole, where the road seemed to wind and twist and turn. Mouse-hole? That sounded a strange place. It made her laugh. As for Lamorna, that did not sound English at all. La-mor-na could easily be a beach in the Bahamas, which Mousehole could not. But it was in Lamorna, Joey said, that the most wonderful and the most extraordinary people in the world were living.

'Where did you say this painting school was, my dear, Mouse-hole or Newlyn?'

'Newlyn, Mother.'

'Oh good, that sounds so much better, much more congenial, though I fail to see why you have to travel quite so far to sketch something.'

'Why does she have to sketch anything at all?' her father said, forking a kidney.

This was familiar territory for Florence. Embroidery and quilts her father could understand, that was the right kind of thing for a woman. But daubing! Facing her father and his kidney, Florence spoke with icy control.

'Because Mr Stanhope Forbes – oh, we have discussed this *so* often – because Mr Stanhope Forbes teaches in Newlyn and because Mr Wilks who is teaching me here at home cannot teach.'

Mother and daughter listened to Mr Carter-Wood crunch his kidney. This took some time. Mr Carter-Wood ate slowly. What Florence could not understand was how a man who ate so much and so often could remain so thin. He wiped his mouth and spoke as he slowly lowered his napkin.

'Mr Wilks is considered a good enough painting master for most families. Don't get too many fancy notions, my girl, or you'll soon be brought back here.' He pushed back his chair to curtail the conversation. Even as he did so, even as the maid cleared the plates, Florence fancied she could smell the longed-for Atlantic. Her face took on a fresh, childlike excitement, she felt the wind on her cheeks, the excitement you feel when you come round a bend in the road and for the first time on your journey your eye hits a sunburst on the sea or you lean over a gate and admire the view and talk freely or walk arm in arm with brilliant and unconventional artists.

So she was not as sad as she might have been when she said goodbye to Papa (kissing his dry cheek at Paddington) and boarded the Cornish Riviera Express, nor quite as sad as she might have been when she said goodbye to her mother in the drawing-room, her mother in tears and holding Florence's hands a little longer than Florence wished them to be held. Certainly Lucy, her elder cousin who had kindly agreed to accompany her on the journey, thought she might have made rather more of an effort all round. After all, she was leaving home for the first time.

'Exactly,' Florence said, as she settled into her carriage and took out her new sketchbook. And did this other England, did the West, look as she imagined it would when she sat in the library with the Atlas in front of her? In something of a trance she sketched these swift intrusions, glancing out of the window, looking up and down from passing landscape to the pad on her knees, listening to the tiresomely voluble Lucy as she had to do, but the landscape went past all too quickly for her to form impressions beyond Elizabethan gables, oaks and elms, pillared porticos, slow rivers, warm and trim red-brick towns, calves at the edge of a pond and horses in a field

... and the further west she went (no, no, she really did not want sandwiches or scones, thank you, but you do, please), the further west she went the England of oaks and elms and slow, wide rivers gave way to undulating moors, faster streams, plain villages and windswept stone-walled country.

'Have you noticed, Lucy, there are fewer people?'

'Quite a lot got off at Plymouth.'

'No, silly, fewer people out *there*, I mean, fewer houses, more gorse, haven't you noticed, more slate.'

'If you say so,' Lucy said, spreading the damson jam on to her bread. 'How long will it be to Penzance?'

It should have been no more than twenty minutes to Penzance but it took them two and a half hours. It was beginning to rain quite steadily when, for no apparent reason, the express suddenly went into a convulsive shiver, then a violent series of judders and clanks, pitchforking Florence off her seat. The train grunted and shrieked in spasms, taking a long time to slow and grind to a halt. For a moment or two everything was very quiet, then there was the sound of running feet and loud shouts.

Dusk was falling and the rain started to come on in full strength. Through the rain men ran back up the line. Three guards gathered at the side of the track and were later joined by a policeman in a shiny cap. Observing all this, Florence sat very still, only her eyes moving. As she wiped the window with her handkerchief she watched the racing raindrops compete with the condensation and with a murky reflection of herself.

Lucy exhaled. Then exhaled again, as if Florence had not heard the first exhalation, and then stomped out of the carriage in a huff to see if she could find out what on earth was causing this dreadful delay. Florence took the opportunity of her cousin's absence to slip her hand into her pocket to read, yet again, the crumpled letter.

Dearest Blote,

I have decided I will brook no denial. If you are as dismayed at your lack of progress with Mr Wilks as you say you are, and, dear sister, you have always been one to tell the truth, and if you are as keen to improve as I believe you to be, you are to join me here. There is room enough in the cottage. By the same post I am writing to Papa to urge him to permit this. To be admitted into the company of artists here is far more to be desired, is it not, than to be presented at court?

As for your neighbours, on the right-hand side, as I have previously told you, you will have Harold and Laura Knight, two quite wonderful artists, and on your left, as I have not previously told you since their arrival here from Bermondsey is quite recent, are Dolly and Prudence, two most beautiful models. Did God ever make elsewhere such perfect forms?

In the six months I have been here – is it six months already? – I have learnt far more about the human and the animal world than I ever learnt in London. Another stroke of good fortune has been making the acquaintance of Captain Gilbert Evans. He is older than I by some five years but when was age any barrier to true friendship?

If my findings on the sea coast so far are any guide I think, in time, I might well be able to astonish the world. For the moment I will say no more, beyond assuring you that the anemones, and rock pools in general, also offer endless possibilities for the artist.

Do ensure you bring the appropriate clothes.

Your loving brother,

Joey.

'The human and the animal world!' Florence smiled to herself as she folded up the longest letter she had ever received from her loving brother and placed it in the pocket of what she hoped would prove an appropriate coat. She placed it there just as Lucy came back into the carriage with the news that there had been an accident, but as no one would tell Lucy its exact nature Florence herself stood up and walked, in her most composed way, through to the back of the train. As she arrived there she looked out of the open carriage door to see a man's trunk being placed on a brown leather stretcher. Both his legs and one of his hands had been cut off.

That delay, with a confusion over the date which Joey later admitted was his own fault, explained why he was talking to Dolly and Prudence at the studio party and did not meet her at Penzance station, and explained why she arrived at the most annoying possible moment for Alfred Munnings.

Florence was now sitting in her neighbours' cottage, at the plain wooden table set by the Knights, while Laura was telling Florence her version of the story of Alfred and the Fox, in which Alfred was even braver than he was in Joey's account.

Harold looked at Florence's profile: Botticelli's Venus, no more, no less.

Laura rattled on about Alfred Munnings, no more, no less.

Harold had, quite early in the piece, switched off the Munnings story, suspecting many and various embellishments from Laura, and switched on his forensic stare, as if he was measuring Florence for a frame, gathering the lines of her features in his clear mind's eye. It was clear. Florence was perfect for his purposes, the perfect accompaniment to his art. She was as poised and as pale as Munnings was red-nosed and foul-mouthed (Florence stayed still, whereas Munnings threw his arms about like a windmill) and as soon as the extremely tedious fox saga drew to its long-awaited conclusion Harold would ask her how her classes with Stanhope Forbes were progressing.

'Oh, not as well as I had hoped, I have to say.'

'But . . . quite well?' Harold liked her understatement. It offered a blessed relief from the obligatory superlatives of the fresh-air brigade.

'Oh yes, *quite* well.'

'What is . . . disappointing? If that is the case?'

'Joey and his tanks and aquarium! Will you do all you can to ensure he attends the classes with me? Please. It's a matter of life and death. Well, it . . . could be.'

Harold pushed his glasses up a little on his nose.

'I'm not sure he pays that much attention to me. He's more likely to listen to Laura.'

'But you can *try*. He's here to study art, not the lowest order of animals to be found in a muddy pool.'

'And I will try of course. But your brother lives very much – how shall I put it? – his own life down here. And I am told a young man must have his head.'

'Har-old!' Laura said, with a warning emphasis.

'And what kind of subjects do you favour?' Harold quickly asked.

Florence looked from Harold to Laura to Harold, trying to understand the nature of the warning, then said:

'At the moment I am simply trying to improve my drawing. That is all, and, for the moment, that is enough.'

She spoke, she invested, each ordinary word with care and precision.

'That's practice, that's all,' Laura broke into the conversation, 'you keep at it, Florence, just hammer away at it, page after page, sketch pad after sketch pad, believe me, I've got piles of them on the shelf there, look at mine for yourself if you like, and before you can say anemone you'll find—'

'But *take your time*,' Harold countered, with quiet emphasis, pushing his glasses up the bridge of his nose again. 'Art is not a race, art is not a matter of who can cover the most paper!'

Laura clapped her hands and stood up and made some tea. She knew only too well that Harold was criticising her as much as talking to Florence, so she cut some chunks of bread and listened through the open kitchen door. Had Florence Carter-Wood ever, in her pampered days, seen *chunks* of bread? Laura doubted it. There was, however, no doubting her husband Harold's interest.

Come to think of it, Laura Knight thought, Florence looked exactly right for one of Harold's interiors, with the tone and quality of a quiet sitting-room, with a place prearranged for the picture in the quiet corner of a gallery; she even spoke in the same finely balanced tones as Harold painted.

Laura carried in the chunks of bread, even chunkier than they need have been, and told Florence to help herself. Florence did not. As for Harold, he did not even notice Laura's return into the room. He was staring at Botticelli's Venus sitting there opposite him, anticipating his painting, absorbing her in his hands and eyes. In a sad way, Laura found it all rather funny. He looked like a bird of prey eyeing a field mouse, an old buzzard mesmerically circling a young, unguarded prey . . .

No, no, stop it, Laura, stop it now.

But the staring was, in all conscience, enough to put the Carter-Wood girl off. Not that she looked at all discomfited by his scrutiny, quite the reverse. She sat with her hands on her lap (having again refused the bread) and waited for the next question. It was inevitable. After some preliminary clearing of Harold's throat, followed by a very thorough cleaning of his spectacles with a large blue handkerchief, it duly came.

'I would like to ask you a favour, Florence, if I may . . .'

'Of course.'

'It is quite a substantial favour. I would like to paint you . . . if I may.'

'Paint me?'

'If you have the time, that is. But then you are only next door, which is a blessing.'

He closed his eyes and waited for the confirmation.

'That might be difficult, I'm afraid. At the moment.'

Harold opened his eyes.

'Oh, I quite understand, you are over at your class in Newlyn three days a week, and your work must come first. Of course, of course. As you said, that is why you have joined us here.'

'No, it's not simply my work, important though that is. It is that I have already promised to sit on a horse for Mr Munnings.'

'On a . . . horse?'

Harold seemed to find difficulty with the concept.

'He asked me today . . . he called on us again this morning. Somehow I could not refuse.'

'Oh, he didn't come here,' Laura said with some sharpness. 'What time exactly did he call?'

'He wishes to paint you on a horse?' Harold blinked.

'Yes, it seems so. Outside his studio.'

'Oh, ah, oh, I, yes, I see. On a . . . horse. Yes.'

Harold nodded sadly to himself, and to their tortoiseshell cat by his feet. Munnings, he thought. Munnings, the procurer of models.

'You do ride, do you?' Laura asked, as if willing to be surprised.

'Yes, I do.'

'A.J. is a great rider, the best in the district, I'm told, better than anyone else.'

'So we hear,' Harold said. 'So we hear.'

'There's nothing wrong with exercise, Harold. Some people rather enjoy it.'

Harold focused on his thin knees, trying to recover his equilibrium, and trying to imagine what in God's name could be achieved by placing a person of Florence's exquisite beauty on the back of an animal.

'You could ask Dolly to sit for you, or Prudence,' Laura went on, 'I'm sure they'll be keen.'

'I think . . . perhaps . . . not. Not quite . . . my . . .'

'Cup of tea?' Laura offered.

'No, not quite,' he said to himself.

And as soon as he could Harold excused himself to finish a, well not to finish exactly, it had not reached that point, but to . . . return to . . . to continue with . . . his work upstairs.

'So,' Laura took over, watching her husband leave, 'what exactly were you doing before you came down here?'

'In London?'

'Yes.'

'Nothing,' Florence smiled, 'nothing at all. Just waiting.'

'Waiting for what?'

'Just waiting.'

Florence stared at Laura as if 'waiting' were self-evident.

'Oh,' Laura said.

Then Florence laughed, and laughed in a way which quite

worried Laura, as if Laura's question were quite absurd. As quickly as Florence had laughed she was serious again.

'May I ask *you* something, Laura?'

'Of course,' Laura beamed.

'Do you like Alfred Munnings?'

'Now there's a question! There *is* a question.'

'I hope you don't mind my asking, I mean I can see he's crude and loud and unpolished and Joey says he cuts his toenails at picnics but I wanted to know if that stops you liking him. You are quite sure you don't mind the question?'

'No, I don't mind the question.' Laura felt her face flush, transfusing from strawberry to raspberry, a colouring which reminded Florence of a sight in Joey's aquarium.

'I think Alfred is quite splendid, yes, he's one in a million, a breath of fresh air, and he's frank and fearless, which is always a fine thing. He has a rare quality, he seems to seize life, to *seize* it, and not many of us do that, do we?'

'You do like him!'

'Yes, I do.'

There was more defiance than warmth in Laura's toothy smile. There was a pause. And then Florence asked:

'And do you like Captain Evans?'

'Gilbert!'

'Yes.'

'Gilbert? Of course I do. Good God, who doesn't! Any more questions?'

It seemed there were not. Then it seemed there was just one more.

'If you don't mind? But I fear I am going too far.'

'Anything, anything, why not?'

Laura laughed. Then Florence stood up.

'No, I think I should go. I have clearly overstayed.'

Laura followed her to the front door.

'Why, don't go, no, I was enjoying our talk, there's no need to rush off like this, just as we are getting to know one another.'

'There is. Will you excuse me? And please tell your husband I will indeed sit for him . . . I answered him very clumsily, didn't I? Very stupidly. Especially as I had asked for his kind help and support over Joey. Sometimes I am very selfish.'

They shook hands rather formally, even though Florence had merely to walk down the garden path one way only to walk back up it the other side of the wall. Laura watched through the window as Florence opened and closed the gate behind her. There was nothing clumsy about that. Nor about the way Florence looked back at the watcher at the window and nodded.

Laura coloured once again, from strawberry to raspberry.

The Girl on Horseback

'Did I hear your brother call you "Bloat"?'

'Yes.'

'How do you spell that?'

'B-l-o-t-e.'

'And what sort of bloody silly name is that?'

'I wish I knew.'

Her absence of curiosity over her name intrigued him. He painted. She sat. And then she said, without any change in her position or tone of voice:

'And do you have to swear all the time?'

'Where does it come from? This B-l-o-t-e business?'

'I have to say I don't know. It's just a word.'

Florence's eyes were steadily trained on the middle branch, exactly as A.J. had bidden them to be. Her expression was thoughtful, her skin pale and faultless, exactly as he wished them to be. He also liked the odd way her mind worked and the little unexpected jerks her answers gave his hands. His brush touched the canvas, no, bugger, it was meant to be only a touch of the brush but, hell and high water, he hit the canvas far too hard. Blast his vision! *That* was a sodding *splodge* he'd just put on the canvas, not a touch. Don't tell me this girl was already affecting his skill? He scraped some of the paint off, which only made everything even worse. He burst out:

'You must have *some* idea!'

'My Uncle John in Carlisle was the first to use it, I'm told.'

'Well, I'd want to know why I was called something, so ask him.'

'That would be difficult, he's dead.'

She waved away a fly, a winning wave.

'Oh, I'm sorry.'

'Quite a nasty death, I understand.'

Tilting the brim of his Panama Alfred looked up to check the expression on her face. He could not quite tell: a filter of bright light behind her head left the eyes and mouth, the seats of mockery, in shadow.

She, Florence/Blote, was sitting as still as a statue, sitting side-saddle on Merrilegs, wearing her ankle-length coat and cream hat. That afternoon it hit Alfred again and again that Miss Carter Hyphen Wood was as paintable a girl as he had ever seen. No, *more* paintable! And what a bewitching poster she would make! No one in Norwich, in his Caley's poster days, no one in London, not even the buxom nudes in his Paris atelier caused more stir in his fingers than this Aloof Florence Female.

And was this aloofness of hers genuine or was it false aplomb?

Good question, A.J.!

Either way, how very different she was from the strapping and sturdy fishermen's wives in Newlyn, standing together outside their houses in their black hats and aprons; how different from the masculine Laura Knight who was always making eyes at him in her hobnails. This girl was delectable, without a doubt, de-lect-able, and as for that small bunch of sweet peas hanging from her waist, was that a sweet disorder, a careless random decision, or a studied effect?

Good question, A.J.!

But there was no question she had the best-cut nose he'd ever seen, lovely chin too. Perfect hands as well, while we're at it. But . . . the question was, when hot nights were scented with roses, did she have a tempestuous petticoat? Did . . . she?

He put down his brush. It was time for a little Herrick. Yes, he felt a little Herrick coming on. He stepped away from the canvas, flexing his stiff fingers and loosening his rigid lower back a little, before announcing to the empty clearing:

'Robert Herrick.'

She turned to look through the trees.

'Is someone arriving? You might have mentioned it.'

'No, I said "Robert Herrick". He was a poet.'

'Oh.'

'Kept a pet pig too, Herrick did.'

'Did he?'

'*And* taught it to drink from a tankard. His father committed suicide.'

'I can't say I'm surprised.'

'No, the suicide came just after Herrick was born, before the pig, that is. But listen to this. Listen, and you won't find anything finer.'

'Shall I get down?'

'No, it won't take long. Just listen. Stay exactly where you are and listen to every word.

'A sweet disorder in the dress
Kindles in clothes a wantonness:
A lawn about the shoulders thrown

Into a fine distraction:
An erring lace which here and there
Enthralls the crimson stomacher.
A cuff neglectful, and thereby
Ribbons to flow confusedly:
A winning wave, deserving note
In the tempestuous petticoat:
A careless shoe string, in whose tie
I see a wild civility:
Do more bewitch me than when art
Is too precise in every part.'

'You spoke that beautifully,' she said. 'And I do like the final lines. Would you please say them again?'

He did so and she thanked him.

'No, thank *you* for listening. More to the point, the lines are true. You prove them true in every particular.' She smiled and nodded her acknowledgement of the compliment.

'You obviously like poetry a great deal?'

'I write poems as well, I'll write one for you if you like.'

'Would you? You really write poems?'

'Painting is a kind of poetry too, poems are paintings I keep in my mind. And this painting is a poem, the best poem I've ever written.'

He looked at Florence on horseback, unable to assess her, then rubbed his hands in anticipation.

'*So* . . . back to work. Back to the girl on a horse with a name no one understands.'

'I thought you said the horse was called Merrilegs.'

He stopped.

For a moment he was confused by her remark, then worked it out.

'What? Oh, I see . . . Never could sort out my syntax.'

Merrilegs was standing at the edge of the wood, in a clearing close to Munnings' studio, and from the clearing, looking the other way, you could see part of the mill, and before he went to bed most nights Alfred liked to wander along there with Taffy to listen to the plash of the water. That sound made all the difference, it made a man feel he belonged.

Florence adjusted her hat.

'Don't move!' he barked.

The leaves above her head had caught the sun, and the light was running down to her hat, making it almost white, that light must be caught and caught now, he mustn't miss that, the way it ran down to her hat, his eye moved up and down, from her neck to her cuff, back and forth, from point of light to point of light. He made fast moves, using greens, yellow, white, ochre, more blue, just a . . . that's *enough*, not too much, lighter touch, *barely* touch . . . and the brown behind her hat, that helped if he whitened the . . . and the stronger and the mellower . . . it was vital he . . .

On he muttered to himself.

Then, without taking his eyes off his work, he asked:

'And is Joey being a good boy?'

'Do you mean is he attending his classes?'

'Amongst other things. Tilt your head back a bit more.'

'Like that?'

'Yes. Yes!'

'You've obviously heard about Joey's truancy.'

'Yes . . . And his billiards. He . . . enjoys life, your brother. What's he up to at the moment? Out in the exploding foam? Looking at his beauties, is he? Out with his chisel and oyster knife?'

She disliked this knowing tone.

'I really don't know. Oh, he's so annoying, he'll ruin everything.'

'In what way?'

'He'll sacrifice me, I know he will, he'll sacrifice me to dredge up something the tide brings in!'

'Well, we can't have that, can we? Can't have you being sacrificed . . . lower your hand a little . . . the cuff's not quite right.'

Even the horse seemed now to have caught some of his sitter's stylish stillness. Alfred knew he must not lose this moment, this was a flying start, though he might need to whip her a bit coming round the bend.

'Tell me about your family. Then yourself.'

'My father owned a brewery in London.'

'A brewery?'

'And our home is in Chelsea.'

'A brewery? You'd better keep me away from it then.'

'Why?'

'Why!' he snorted back.

'Because you drink too much? Is that what you mean?'

A.J. put the brush between his teeth for a second, like a pirate pausing for a breather during an attack, and put his hands defiantly on his hips. She was some girl, this one. A girl who seemed to know her power. Feeling his colour rise up the back of his neck he took the brush out of his mouth.

'Yes, that *is* what I mean. I drink too much. All right?'

'But that is no concern of mine, surely? Men do as they choose.'

Part of him wanted to attack her hard, but he needed her to stay exactly where she was, so he nodded a rueful recognition of her point.

'No, no, you're right.'

'And we have a house in Silloth.'

'Never heard of it.'

'Well, it is there, nevertheless, on the Solway Firth.'

'Never heard of it.'

'Would Carlisle help? Have you perhaps heard of the Lakes? The Lake District?'

'Wordsworth, good man. So, you're rich? You strike me as rich.'

'Yes, we are. It is no disgrace, I hope?'

'No, no.'

'Good.'

He started to paint again. Then he felt a competitive pride welling up in his chest, until his pride burst out.

'I'm not rich, but I'm coining it and soon will be. I've sold ten paintings this year, twice as many as anyone else down here, including Laura, *and* I've got an exhibition coming up in less than a month.'

'So I've heard.'

'From Laura? You heard about it from her? Was it from Laura?'

'Of course. She's always talking about you, but then one finds everyone is, Laura, Joey, Gilbert, everyone.'

'But not Harold?'

'Yes, even Harold.'

He was now painting very quickly. He was Constable.

'At the Leicester Gallery. That's where I'm exhibiting. In Leicester Square.'

'Really? I know the gallery quite well. I've been there with Joey.'

'Well, go there next month and you'll see the works of Alfred Munnings.'

'You'll be famous, I can tell, there's absolutely no doubt of that.'

He needed the whip.

'Oh, do sit *still*! You were doing so well . . . Yes, that's better. *Still!* I said. So . . . so . . . your father sent you both down here, getting you off his hands?'

'My father? No, I came of my own accord, I wanted to.'

'But he allowed you to? Must have! Can't have a girl like you wandering around here. Unless . . . that is . . . no, you're not one of those advanced girls, are you?'

'I do have to have Papa's permission on everything, of course. So, for me, it is a matter of persuasion. But I do not intend ever to be . . . swallowed up, if that is what you mean?'

'Can't hear you,' he said. 'Wallowing in what?'

'It doesn't matter. It wasn't important.'

The clearing was now very still, and the sky was woolly and soft. They could hear the mill grinding.

'So you're *not* one of those advanced girls . . . flowing silks, reading books you can't understand, soft in the head, paintings by Rogering Fry, that sort of caper. No? *Good!* You're not.'

'Evidently not.'

Her hat was making the picture glow. It was coming to life, keep going, Alfred, keep going. She was as alive on the canvas as she was on Merrilegs. He had the light running down her coat, transmitting, he was doing exactly what he wanted, today, in this clearing, he was Constable, didn't Constable say landscape painting at its best was a branch of natural philosophy, and these trees were a presence rather than an instance, and wasn't a picture an experiment in philosophy, your whole body alive to the world and its rhythms, his body taut yet malleable, alive with the work, a tumult of energy, he knew this was his art at its best, a conflagration. And that was no surprise because – well—

Because had any woman ever looked better on a horse? And had there ever, in the history of women and the history of horses, ever been a less horsy woman who looked so at home on a horse? They were *as one*. They were made for each other.

'But he allowed you to come to Cornwall because down here you'd be safe and sound?'

'Yes.'

A.J. looked up at her, his eyes screwed against the sun.

'And to keep you away from the undesirables?'

'I suppose that could be right, yes.'

He grinned and said:

'But that plan hasn't worked, has it?'

'Why not? Who here is undesirable, apart from Mr Knight?'

That was sharp! That was sharp indeed. A.J. hadn't laughed so much in . . . well, in a good while, not since he saw those undergraduates' faces in The Fox and Grapes. Poor old Harold! Yes, this girl took some beating, this one sitting for him now was a champion filly all right, a complete stunner, but his laughter was cut short because at that moment Taffy, his damned dog, overexcited by his master's loud laughter, escaped from the stables and ran barking and yapping up the lane. This unsettled Merrilegs. More important, it upset the picture. A.J. dropped his brush and chased Taffy and if he'd caught the little terrier he would have beaten him to within an inch of his life only he realised he'd better behave himself as he was being closely watched by his sharp sitter. Taffy eluded him like a mad hoop. Each time A.J. dived at the dog, it swerved.

Unperturbed by the chase Florence dismounted and spent the time looking closely at the unfinished painting. She studied the stippling, the intersection of lines, the form, the techniques pointed out to her only the day before by Stanhope Forbes. She could perhaps learn even more from Alfred Munnings than she could from

Stanhope Forbes. Or would it not be better to learn from them both? Or should *this* be where she spent all her days?

'Taffy! Come here! Heel. Heel! You little bastard.'

After a humiliating five minutes chasing this fugitive itch Munnings grabbed the dog, and brought him back, half pulling, half smacking him.

'Just settle down . . . you little ruffian . . . you little killer.'

Florence turned slowly from the painting and looked at the dog. He did not look a killer.

'He's not a killer, is he? He's far too lovely to be a killer.'

'He's a killer all right. Look at his eyes. That's how you tell. Look into his eyes.'

'What about them?'

'Like bits of coloured glass. The eyes tell you everything.'

She bent down and patted the dog. She looked into his eyes.

'I don't believe you. His eyes are very gentle.'

'Believe what you bloody like,' Munnings said, still panting a little from the chase.

'You make most things up, I'm sure of that.'

His eyes were ready to leap at her but he controlled himself.

Being corrected by her, even being shamed by her, felt special.

'Twenty-seven chickens before breakfast last January. All dead, every one, cost me a terrible packet, Taffy, didn't you?'

'Is that true?' she asked the dog.

'Well, seventeen chickens. Is seventeen all right? Are you always such a deflater?'

She walked two paces away.

'And was the fox story true? *Did* the fox survive?'

He took out his big coloured handkerchief and wiped the sweat from his forehead.

'Ah, you've heard!'

'I was so glad you saved the fox, so very very glad.'

'So was the fox.'

She laughed.

Yes, she was delectable, *and* sharp *and* she looked so composed in her gloves, in the clearing, standing there before him. Art was art, humans were humans, but art was best when it was human.

'I killed a rat once,' he said, turning away to light a cigarette.

'With rat poison?'

'No, blew it to bits among the bullrushes. Spread it everywhere. Boom!'

'And you regretted it? You did regret it, do tell me you regretted it.'

'Yes, it was terrible. Terrible. But only because I was so close to it, no other reason.'

'Tell me something else.'

He picked up his brush and looked at her.

'Mmm.'

'Do you think Gilbert Evans has ever killed anyone?'

'Gilbert!' He laughed.

'Do you?'

'Gilbert? He's the gentlest man on earth, nicest person going, wouldn't harm a living creature.'

'But he fought in South Africa, so he might have done, mightn't he?'

'That's different, that's not the same. War's war.'

'Oh? So that's that, is it?'

'Would you like it if he had killed someone?'

He looked at the canvas, taking stock, reminding himself exactly where he was, and preparing to resume. Florence meanwhile was walking away, straightening her gloves.

'I'm sorry, but I have to leave now.'

'*Leave? Now?*

'Yes.'

'But you can't. Not now! Do something useful and sit on the horse!'

'I have pins and needles and I have my own work to do. I can't be both sides of the easel, can I?'

Desolate, he opened his hands, pleading. He could hear his voice stumbling, he could hear his words falling over each other.

'But you see ... I'm on the edge of it ... I'm just beginning to grapple ... dammit you CAN'T go!'

But she could. She was off.

She was away down the rutted track towards the mill, walking at an unhurried pace.

He came up again to her and spoke to her shoulder.

'Is tomorrow ... a possibility? Is it? Or next week? Say yes.'

'Yes.'

'When?'

'Next week.'

'Good, good, next ... Tuesday then? Tuesday? Or Wednesday? How about Thursday?'

'Tuesday.' She turned to face him. 'In the afternoon. If it's fine, Tuesday afternoon will be all right.'

'Shall I ride up to your cottage, or meet you here? Yes, that's it, I'll come up on Merrilegs and collect you! You'll enjoy that!'

He noticed his voice did not sound quite the same, though hers did.

'There's no need, thank you. I will walk down with Joey.

Then he can watch you and he can learn. Yes, that's exactly what he can do.'

'Bet he won't stay! He'll have something else up his sleeve.'

Her face was briefly petulant, then cleared. She quickly shook his hand and was gone through the trees, a retreating cream coat disappearing into the green.

God Almighty!

Alfred turned on Taffy.

'That is your fault, you bloody silly stupid animal! Did-you-hear-me?'

The dog backed carefully away from his fistshake.

Stanhope Forbes

'Tout le monde peint tellement aujourd'hui comme M. Bastien-Lepage que M. Bastien-Lepage a l'air de peindre comme tout le monde.'

If Paris did not know whether to follow Manet or Bastien-Lepage, Newlyn had no doubt about their leader: Stanhope Forbes. Respected by artist and fisherman alike, Stanhope Forbes was the centre, rallying point and anchor of the Newlyn Group from 1884, and he founded his audacious school there in 1899. By that time the town was almost an English Concarneau, crammed with painters of every age.

'The Professor' taught his pupils in three wooden studios. All three huts were full with easels and standing students, and Florence Carter-Wood was often the first to arrive there, with rainbows of dew on her feet as she came down Paul Hill. She was also amongst the last to leave.

She walked briskly along the cobbled streets, with every corner a picture, up steep narrow cuttings that led to the studios, with their commanding views of the wide and busy bay beneath. As she walked up there early in the morning heads turned. Old men took their pipes out of their mouths and followed her footsteps with their pale blue watery eyes. They didn't see many like her, not in Newlyn. Not with a walk like that. Not with hair like that.

Inside the crowded studio, however tight the squeeze, Florence established her stillness and space, a circle of concentration, a moat of silence. Arriving mid-morning, the Professor, now in his fifties, soon found himself standing behind her. One word from Stanhope Forbes could, she knew, raise her to the skies. Equally, one word could crush her. Often he said nothing, unsettling her with his restless activity and tuneless humming. On Saturdays, for those who were bold enough to face it, he delivered his 'Crit'.

The first hut he set aside for beginners, drawing from plaster casts. Some went no further than this, and unless he pulled his worsted stockings up, this fate could well face Joey. In the second hut, where Florence was, were the living models (clothed) who took the opportunity to sit out of doors when the weather allowed. 'Out of doors, outside, come on,' the Professor urged, sometimes invoking the name of Bastien-Lepage. 'What does a bit of dust in your eye matter when destiny calls?'

As for the nudes they were in the third of his studios. The pretty local girls were too shy to pose so most of the nudes came down from London. Only the most talented and most assiduous students reached this third studio. After a few weeks of moving back and forth behind his new pupil, of admiring her work (and the nape of her neck and the colour of her hair), the Professor had no doubts that Miss Carter-Wood was sufficiently talented and assiduous. Aware that he might, however, be more than usually susceptible, he asked his wife Elizabeth for a second opinion on the work of Miss Carter-Wood. It was quickly agreed: Florence had passed The Crit with flying colours.

At the moment the Professor told her of her promotion to the third studio Florence felt very honoured but also very anxious. Except for her own in the mirror she had never seen a naked body.

Bloodshot Eyes

Alfred looked at the picture and tried to reanimate the feelings he had felt not five minutes before. Five minutes ago he was Constable working on a masterpiece, he was John Sell Cotman, he was God. But the music had gone from his fingers. Now he was a sullen bull. It was difficult, so difficult, to recover the mood, to move back inside his painting. How *could* she swan off like that, his star turn, with her gloves and her airs and graces? How *dare* she! Anger leapt up inside him. No, anger grabbed him. He would hack the blasted picture into thousands of pieces. He picked up his sharpest knife. He moved. He hesitated. He threw down the knife and punched himself. He ran at the dog to kick it, but again the dog was just too quick for him, so he kicked the earth instead.

It was impossible to go on.

He put his head in his hands.

No, it was not impossible. Only weak people gave up. You're only beaten for a day, never for ever. He strode up and down the clearing, his eyes glaring into the green, trying to throw off his anger. He wanted his paintings to be heard all over the world, didn't he, like poems, like Poe, like Herrick, like Hiawatha, the songs to be sung in every gallery, and for that to happen he had to be strong, he had to be insatiable.

So stop piddling about.

After a quarter of an hour he picked up his brush and worked on the muscle and bone of the background trees. She might not be there but the trees were, these English trees, and they always would be.

Taffy lay, happy and safe, at his master's feet.

Alfred had his reward. It was a fine Tuesday and, as agreed, Florence and Joey turned up on time at his studio. Fat chance she'll bother, he'd been saying to himself only moments before their voices came along the clearing. He leapt up and ran down the outside wooden steps, arms open wide in greeting.

The brother and sister were bright-faced and healthy from their walk. Joey had on his haversack, while she (Alfred was delighted to note) was wearing the same coat and the same hat, which showed she wasn't just another stupid woman, she could think as well as sit on a horse. Even her hair was set up in the same style. Oh, yes, she'd *thought* about it all right.

He led them up the steps.

'Come in, come in, let me take your coat, for a moment, just for a moment, Joey, excuse the mess . . . you know what I'm like, find a seat, move those.'

Joey moved some drawings from the chair, noticing that Alfred had carefully combed his hair forward and had polished his boots. Not only that: he was in his most expansive mood, offering food and drink, ginger beer, wine, everything. Indeed he almost force-fed them. Fortunately, being blown about on the cliff path had made them both hungry.

'Has Gilbert been away?' Joey asked. 'I haven't seen him recently.'

'Busy man, our Gilbert,' Alfred said. 'And I'm off soon myself.'

'To London, for your exhibition, so I've heard,' Joey said. 'How wonderful!'

'No, before that, the next fortnight. On the road. On my own.'

Florence now spoke for the first time.

'You go off on your own? To paint?'

He looked directly at her. She noticed his eyes were bloodshot. He noticed she was annoyed.

'All the time,' he said. 'I have to.'

'Oh.'

'Always have done. Well, not on my own exactly. With Tick and Taffy, you never feel alone with them, they're all I need. And my paints. And some sunshine.'

'But not Merrilegs?' she asked, sipping her ginger beer.

'No. Not even Merrilegs,' he said, with a laugh.

'Where do you stay?' Joey mumbled, his mouth half full with cake.

'Anywhere . . . in a pub. In a barn, if need be. My bed's the least of my worries.'

'So you're bored already with Lamorna?'

'Blote! Really!' Joey gave her a disapproving glance.

'No, fair question. Yes, I'm often bored, but who's got half a brain and doesn't get bored? Some days I retch with boredom, don't you? Come on, be honest!'

Florence turned her glass in her hands. There was a small silence in which Joey stood up and crossed to the window, his walking shoes clipping the wooden floor. Below all was ready: Merrilegs was tethered and the paint-smeared easel was placed, waiting for the canvas. There was a pail of water by the easel.

The painting itself rested inside, against the studio wall. Looking at it again, from where she sat, gave Florence a shock. There was something wrong. Surely she was already fully painted, yet here she was no more than an outline. Last week her hat and coat were perfectly realised. Yet now she could see no hat or coat at all, merely the line of her shoulders. She had all but disappeared.

A.J. saw her start.

'Yes, I changed it all. Wasn't good enough, not up to the mark, worked all night on it, well, yes, all right, not *all night*, but most of it, until five and that does not mean I am exaggerating, it means I went to bed *at five!*'

He ended his sentence sounding angry.

'Beautiful sky though,' he went on, 'and that was something, the sky, that was my windfall, my extra payment you might say. The sky.'

Florence went closer to the picture, still amazed at the ruthless and irreversible decisions he had taken. As well as her missing self, some densely worked areas of the background trees were now blank.

'Can you work on a painting, then, without the model?'

'Once I have it all in my mind, yes, once I've done enough drawings, but I have to do plenty.'

He pointed. With a second, deeper shock, she saw eight or ten drawings of herself, drawings of her face from every angle, her walk, her stance, her neck and shoulders as they turned.

'But I couldn't do it for ages. That took years, that skill, but I don't have to tell you, you're an artist yourself.'

'So I'm not needed today?' Florence asked with a balanced smile.

A.J. blurted out of a dry throat:

'Of course you're needed, my dear girl.'

'But you've clearly committed me to memory?'

He jumped up.

'Look, I hate talking about art!' He stamped around. 'Anyone can *talk* about art, Rogering Fry's always talking about art, let's cut the cackle and get on with it or, God help us, we'll all end up critics!'

A.J. picked up the canvas and as much clobber as he could and went outside. Joey, pulling his haversack back on, picked up the rest, then watched as the open-air scene was carefully reset. He watched him help her, with great courtesy, on to Merrilegs. He saw him give the horse a sweet then settle the fall of Florence's coat exactly as he wished it. He watched Munnings very attentively reach up and tilt her hat a touch, then tell her to look at exactly the same branch of exactly the same tree. Only when he was perfectly satisfied with every particular did Munnings take up his stance, the fencer, sizing her up, flexing his elbow . . . and begin to work.

'I'll be off then,' Joey said.

Neither his sister nor the painter acknowledged his remark or his departure. The only move Florence made was to wave away some flies. A crow settled on a fence to watch.

Feeling dissatisfied with himself and with all this, Joey left, rather at a loose end, hoping he would find Gilbert in his office.

Joey walked slowly along, pausing to watch the ducks on the mill pond. Some children, let loose from school, ran past him. He loitered, smoking his pipe. What was it exactly that niggled him about his sister, the sister he loved so much and so longed to join him down here? Could the difference in her behaviour, a difference he found it difficult to put his finger on, be simply that she was, for the first time, away from home, far away from Papa's scrutiny and the constraints of family life, and suddenly in the company of some pretty rum characters, for example A.J. up there in the clearing?

It was tempting to see it as no more than that. Tempting to say they were both adjusting and settling into a new stage of their lives – tempting but to be resisted. He could not, for example, forget the way she described the accident on the railway line. Of course, on one level, one could do absolutely nothing in the face of such an appalling event, that was true, and he certainly did not want little doses of sentiment from her, but the way she responded to such an accident, the manner and the words with which one addressed or spoke of such horror, surely suggested something about one's view of life?

And what did she say? He tried to recover the extreme silentness of her face and her exact words.

'But how terrible for you,' he had said.

'Not really,' she replied, 'I just waited for the train to move on.'

That sentence came to Joey when he was half asleep. It came to him as he watched the ducks. It disturbed him. It missed the point. He flicked a match into the pond and watched the match move, a trembling longboat, as the ducks slipped away.

Again, when he was wild about A.J.'s feat in reciting 'The Raven' that first night, Blote quietly asked if he thought such a strange poem worth making 'all that effort' to commit to memory. All right, A.J. was a bit of a backslapping windbag and sometimes he tried the patience of Job, but he had a heart like a bucket and this kind of comment wasn't worthy of the Blote he knew and loved.

Joey moved on down to the cove. Sensing a thunderstorm was working its way around the Lizard, he put his haversack on the sea wall and watched the swell.

To make it all the more odd, on the way over to meet A.J. just now, she had never been more animated. With more than a touch of pride she told him about her move to the third studio, which had temporarily softened her annoyance with his own lack of progress, and yet as soon as she was back in A.J.'s company she changed. Was it affectation? Or was it something she could not help? He asked an incoming wave, could she not help herself?

Was that it?

'Jo-ey! Jo-ey!'

It was Gilbert Evans riding down the hill, riding too fast too, and waving a warm greeting. If he wasn't careful his front tyre would hit the small open drain at the bottom and throw him over the handlebars. Roused in a second, Joey leapt down from the wall.

'Gil-bert! Hullo! Stead-y!'

The coat was now right. The hat was right. The horse was right, with good lighting on the back, loins and mane. He had to admit, he really was very pleased with the horse. The slim tree trunk, the line of her glance, Merrilegs' pricked ears, the dash of sunlight on her hindquarters, all these 'worked' too, as did the alternating light and shade of the tree-flecked planes. 'Whoever said there are no short cuts,' Alfred said to himself, 'never said a truer word.' The tension between the gentle touch and the dense solidity of texture was as he had conceived it just before dawn; the interlacing branches and foliage gave the picture the spontaneous feel which he loved.

Cotman, Crome, Constable, and . . . Munnings.

He was fit to stand with them.

He was now very tired. His eyes throbbed and his back ached. His gout was the worst he had known it. Perhaps the jumping-powder breakfast he'd given himself of champagne and game pie had not helped and to have gout so young was certainly a private shame but, for the moment, he was elated at a job well done. Moving slowly back from the easel he half missed his footing and reeled. He just steadied himself. Florence was sure, watching him scrutinise the picture yet again, that he had been drinking. He took another half-step back and looked again; then a small step to the left and a step to the right. He tilted his head one way, then half inclined it the other.

So.

Now, Alfred—

Now for the nasty question, the nastiest question of them all. What *wasn't* right with the picture? What would the critic in him say? Perhaps the bottom left-hand corner needed a little more detail. It was a touch muddy. Perhaps her right hand was not exactly caught. Well, those could easily be corrected.

'Easily, my arse!' he snorted aloud.

Nothing was easy, and nothing's easier than botching a good job with a final bit of overfussiness. But the main point was: the total effect was there, a beau-ti-ful woman riding on a beautiful horse in a beautiful setting. And that was what art was meant to be, wasn't it, real life captured on canvas and captured beautifully. *And* he'd got the title. *Morning Ride.* Yes, that was the title!

'Could have been made for each other,' he said without looking at her.

Did he mean the painter and the sitter, or the sitter and the horse?

She would not ask.

'I'm so glad . . . it pleases you.'

'You're perfect together.'

Ah, so that was it. The sitter and the horse. Mild irritation touched her voice.

'If it's finished, may I dismount?'

'Dis-mount? Yes yes, you may, you may.'

He helped her down, placing his hands round her waist and landing her lightly on her feet. How easy that was, the first touch. And she felt so light. She stroked out her coat. He smelt her scent. With her back to him she rearranged her hair. Sensing the game would end in his favour, he stood behind her. She could hear his breathing. Standing there, he sounded and felt different from Stanhope Forbes humming away behind her. Very different. When he spoke next it was with a self-mocking, defensive tone.

'Bravely done, is it not?'

For a while she did not reply. Her eyes stayed on the painting, though her spine felt his presence. She was looking at herself, only at herself; and she knew she was being looked at looking at herself. When she turned to face him and his bloodshot eyes, her lips had a bluish tint.

'Yes, I like it very much.'

'Are you all right?'

'Yes.'

'You're not, you don't look well, do go inside and sit down. Please.'

'In a moment. If you don't mind I would like to look at it a little longer. I can learn so much from you. Unless you mind?'

'Mind? Mind? Why should I? It's all over now. Now it's up to the critics.'

Clumsily, his eyes smarting and feeling his collar tighten, he gathered up his brushes. He patted Merrilegs, good girl, he patted Taffy, good boy, good girl, good boy.

By the time Florence joined him upstairs he was stretched right out in his low chair, legs wide apart, eyes closed. He was fast asleep. She tiptoed to the spare seat, barely making a rustle. He moved uneasily in his chair, his head tilted back at an awkward angle, his face turned to the ceiling. She looked at his sharp Adam's apple and the patches of unshaven stubble on his neck. She looked at his boots and his tight trousers and his long slim legs spread wide. She tried not to look at the bulge but it seemed the focal point of his position. She had never seen Papa or Joey, even at their most relaxed, sit quite like that, not once, not quite so . . . openly. Still, soon she must learn to face and to study the nude figure. It would be worse even than this!

She felt a tumble of emotions in her stomach. She glanced from her hands to his bulge, then back to his paintings and drawings which lined the floor and walls.

'Not asleep,' he said, causing her to jump a little, 'just resting my eyes.'

'I hope I didn't wake you.'

'No one could sleep in your company.'

'I'm sorry if I did wake you.'

'No – no . . . So, here we are . . .' His eyes were still closed. 'At the end of the day.'

'Yes, here we are.'

'Two painters and one critic.'

From where she was sitting she could see seven studies of herself, a sequence on the floorboards, seven faces of Florence.

'I wouldn't say I was a critic.'

'So you like it? The picture, I mean? The portrait of . . . Blote on Merrilegs. *The Morning Ride* passes the test?'

'*The Morning Ride*?'

'A possible title.'

'Titles don't matter, do they? It's the painting . . . and the painting is wonderful.'

'Is it?'

He opened his eyes.

'Truly.'

Her voice was round with warmth, rounder than he had heard it before.

He moved a bit more, slightly restless. His chair creaked and groaned. She felt a little fear. He waved his right hand airily, then ran it across his face in an exhausted gesture.

'Tell you what, Blote?'

'What can you tell me?'

'I can show a lot of things I can't say, can your expert eye tell you that?'

'I'm not an expert.'

'Bugger being an expert, use your eyes, bugger the experts, forget I used the word.'

He sat up just a little, but stayed leaning back, resting on his elbow, with his legs still in the same position, asking:

'So, what other good paintings have you seen?'

'I'm very keen on Reynolds and Gainsborough.'

He roused and slapped himself.

'Reynolds and Gainsborough! You're keen on them? So am I! So you *are* an expert all right, you're a first-class judge.'

'What makes me one?'

'Gainsborough was a Suffolk man too.'

'And that is important?'

'Yes, *yes* . . . and your aim must be to be as good as Gainsborough. Or better!'

'It is.'

'Good! Now . . . tell me something else.'

They looked uneasily at each other. He tapped his boots.

'Is Joey calling back for you?'

'I really don't know . . . we didn't make any plans.'

'Left rather abruptly, didn't he? Probably had an appointment . . . so to speak.'

'How do you mean?'

'Nothing.' He grinned. 'Didn't mean anything.'

'Shall we go for a walk?' Florence suggested, and stood up to reinforce it.

He stayed where he was, waving his arms in all directions, as if to encompass all the footpaths and cliffs and rock pools of Cornwall.

'Out and about, you mean ... If you like. If that *is* what you want? Never can tell what women want. Never could.'

'But you're exhausted,' she said, 'you stay where you are ... I'll go now. I think I should.'

'Nonsense.'

He rose immediately to his feet, almost stumbling, rubbing his face, then saw out of the window two village children swagger down the lane and start to throw some small stones at Merrilegs. He bawled at them and leapt down the steps two at a time to give chase. With a small smile of passive acceptance Florence buttoned up her coat, as if to say that-could-have-been-worse.

He was waiting at the bottom of the outside steps. Going down to meet him she said:

'There is something I want to ask you.'

He smiled up at her.

'It's not by any ghastly chance about my drinking or swearing?'

'No, nothing like that.'

'And you're not going to pry into the fox business?'

'No, it's not that either. It's that when you're painting you ... sometimes you ...'

He stood waiting, eyebrows raised.

'Yes?'

'Sometimes you become very angry and scrape bits off. And, well ... I couldn't help noticing it.'

'I do, yes, because that bit is bad, too much or too little paint, it's as simple as that. Why d'you ask?'

'Because Stanhope Forbes says we should hold the brush very lightly as if we were holding a tiny bird, and it's often when you hit the canvas hard, and I wondered why you took . . . or employed that approach? It's so different from anything I've ever seen before.'

He had gone white. The muscles in his face stiffened. She stopped. He pointed to the wicker seat by the easel. The two boys who threw the stones were watching at the end of the lane.

'Sit down.'

'I'd rather walk, if you still want to, you must be ready for a—'

'Sit down!'

Some alarmist rooks took off from the treetops.

He grabbed her arm and pushed her fiercely into the chair. He stood above her, then bent down so that his face was at her level. Panic came near her. His nose was up against hers.

'So you couldn't help noticing, eh, and you wanted to know why I *bang* into the canvas? And why I put too much paint on? So you'd better look, hadn't you? Look!'

She averted her eyes, only to see the two boys watching all this. She looked at the trees. But he took hold of her face and wrenched it hard so that she had nowhere left to look but into his eyes. He held her face in a lock. He was crushing her cheekbones together. They were going to crack.

'And . . . you can see a mismatch. One looks quite clear . . . no . . . in fact it might be a bit bloodshot. The other is a bit like a smoky marble . . . but it's not a smoky marble. Look! I said, LOOK!'

'I'm looking,' she whispered, and she looked from

right eye to left to right. The pain in her face was intense.

'And the reason, my ... beautiful Florence, my dear ... Blote, my lovely Miss Carter-Wood ... is that I am completely blind in my right eye.'

She uttered a small sound.

'Yes,' he said, 'blind.'

She wanted to put her hands over her face because she could not hold his gaze any longer, but the way he had positioned his elbows prevented this. She could not bear this assault, his breathing, the reddish-brown bristles on his cheeks, the hairs in his nostrils.

'And that is why this,' he removed his right hand, 'bumps into that.'

And on 'that' he lifted his right hand as if to smash her face but he only moved two fingers slowly towards her, and they jabbed into her soft cheek with a force which he neither controlled nor she expected.

Her heart pumped hard. Sweat mixed with her scent.

'And *that* happened, because I do not have bi-noc-ular vision.'

'I see,' she said.

'Do you? Oh, *good*!'

He was only twenty then, ten years or more ago, and staying with his Aunt Polly on her farm at Mulbarton, not all that far from Norwich. Only twenty but already drinking too much and working too hard; only twenty but he had already won plenty of prizes and been catapulted out of plenty of pubs. But it was a good day to be out with Aunt Polly's dogs, crossing the wide fields, his mouth full of banter and oaths and, to crown a good day as good days should be crowned, the prospect on his return of pushing through a black oak door to sausages and mash and good beer.

With him there were two dogs and a puppy and Alfred never could resist a puppy. He loved the silly things. He rolled around in the barn or in the fields with the puppy, a boy at heart, a kid letting the puppy lick him, a bit of a young puppy himself, when suddenly the two dogs spotted a hare and the chase was on, and Alfred himself always loved a chase and no lively puppy likes to be left behind when there's fun in the air. Across one bumpy field they chased, across another, with Alfred and the puppy doing their level best to keep in touch with the front runners.

Alfred made hunting horn sounds as they came to a hedge and a stile. Over went one dog. Over went the second dog, but the puppy couldn't climb it or quite get a footing or quite squirm under it either, so Alfred picked the little fellow up and held back the hawthorn with his right elbow, and dropped the puppy on the other side.

Keen to keep going with the dogs he tried to take the stile too quickly himself, the bent hawthorn spray rebounded from his elbow and he felt as if someone had fired a needle into his right eye. He stumbled back, swearing, rubbing his eyeball, with water now coming out of both wincing eyes. He reeled around in a small circle, treading in cow pats, with a dirty yellow handkerchief over his right eye. He cursed the bloody stupid bush and tore off the spray, cutting his hand a little as he did so.

When he took the handkerchief away, and wiped off the tears, there was a fog falling. He stood still. He looked at an oak tree with his left eye, covering his right eye with his hand. All right, more or less. If he put his hand over his left eye, however, the world was white-grey with a red edge. And the oak tree? What oak tree? He could only hear the dogs yapping and church bells on the wind. By the time he stumbled back half an hour later into the farmyard the fog was red.

That evening, in Mulbarton Village Hall, with a patch over his eye and introducing himself as Alfred the Pirate, he held himself steady on the back of a wooden chair, and led the choruses and sang two acceptably clean songs. By popular request he then recited some Surtees and some Longfellow. He made no mention of the accident but drank too much in a forlorn attempt to ease the pain. 'My stupid fault' was as far as he would go. By the time, bandaged, he arrived at Moorfields Eye Hospital in London, some weeks later, it was far too late.

So that was that. Still, as he sometimes said over a pint, 'In the land of the blind the one-eyed man is king.'

Over the years Alfred made a point of collecting the names of other artists who were afflicted with eye problems: Durer, El Greco, Reynolds, Turner, Constable, Whistler, Degas, Monet . . . 'and' (he added with a self-punishing bark) 'Munnings'.

The Water Diviner

Gilbert stepped off his Waverley and offered the handlebars to Joey.

'Would you like to ride it?'

'I would, yes.'

'Well, do. I'm sure you'll have no problem.'

Joey settled himself on the saddle, with the tip of his toes just touching the ground. Grinning apologetically at Gilbert he did a tentative, wobbly circuit around the cove, narrowly missing the pile of large granite blocks which were waiting to be carted away to London, and then shaving the sea wall. Gilbert lit a cigarette and watched Joey's uncertain, lively progress. There was something about Joey which reminded him not only of Sammy (and Florence) but also of a keen young subaltern arriving to join his regiment, open, fresh-faced and full of hope.

'Keep going, Joey,' he called out.

'Just another minute, may I?'

'As long as you like, but keep up the momentum, don't ease off, press hard, harder, that's it!'

Joey shouted:

'How far up the hill can you go, Gilbert, without getting off?'

'Farther than you!'

'Bet you can't.'

'Go on then, let's see how strong your legs are.'

Both men knew they were talking to each other like boys and they both liked it. Joey made a big run at the slope and reached the bend just above 'Lamorna' Birch's house, then, having done the hard part, gave up much earlier than he need have done. Gilbert was disappointed, but still managed to say, 'Good effort,' as Joey returned with a diagonal skid, 'and do borrow it whenever you'd like.'

'Let's go and see Alfred, shall we?'

'Yes.'

'Blote's up there too.'

'Is she? Oh well, another time would do equally well.'

'Don't be silly, Gilbert, she was asking after you only this morning.'

Gilbert stubbed out his Capstan on the sea wall.

'I don't want to interrupt anything.'

'What's there to interrupt, he's just painting her, that's all. You do annoy me when you talk like that!'

'We could go to the rock pools. Why don't we?'

Joey placed Gilbert's bicycle carefully against the sea wall, holding it there a second to ensure it did not topple over.

'I mean,' Joey said, 'the man's a genius, isn't he, let's face it, he's one in a million.'

Quite so, Gilbert nodded, a man in a million, so what is the point? He kicked some clay off his boots.

'And how is your painting progressing, Joey?'

'Let's talk about what *you*'ve been doing, Gilbert. If you wouldn't mind. Blote's always asking, "Exactly what does Gilbert do?"'

'Me? Exactly? Oh, usual things, old chap, visiting the tenant farmers, collecting rents, mostly on the move, basic jobs you know, coming and going. You know, there are over thirty small farms on the Colonel's land, over thirty, so I might take up A.J.'s kind offer of his second horse sometime. So many of them are off the beaten track, miles from each other, and that will test the Waverley to the limit.'

To show that there was no lack of respect in the comment Gilbert patted his bicycle.

'Are you a good horseman, Gilbert?'

'I've always ridden, yes.'

'Do you ride with the hounds?'

'No, used to as a boy, but I've lost interest. Tell you what though, I'm just off to see the water diviner, over at Tregiffian . . . It's the third meeting I've had with her this month, and I think we're getting somewhere.'

'With *her*?' Joey's voice was a scattering of exclamation marks.

'Yes. I've always been deeply suspicious of the type, but after spending an hour with her last Monday I'm convinced she's rather a good sort. She could help Lamorna.'

Gilbert was noted for his broad categories of human-kind: poor type, good sort, very good sort. Joey saw the opportunity to tease.

'And what turned her from a poor type to a good sort?'

'She found three sources of water.'

'Is that good?'

Gilbert affectionately punched Joey.

'You artists! Heads in the clouds! You chaps drink and wash, don't you, at least let's hope so, so you must know how important water is going to be for this whole community. Have you thought of that? The number of

people living here in Lamorna is rising every month. I
can hardly keep up with you all, and we have to provide
good water for the farmers, for the artists, for every home
in fact.' He pointed at the sea. 'That's no help, is it?'

'Never really thought about it, Gilbert, sorry.'

'Well, do think about it, old chap. Life's not all canvases
and aquariums.'

And they leant shoulder to shoulder, looking out to the
Lizard, while Gilbert described his daily work at Boskenna.
He was i/c the men who packed the flowers, i/c rent
collection, and now entrusted with the whole question of
the estate's water supply.

'We're in safe hands with you,' Joey said with his
open smile.

'So you keep telling me.'

The truth was Gilbert worried over the problem of
potential building sites for the new houses to be built
on the cliffs, worried where exactly the land needed to
be levelled, wondered if improvements could be made to
outbuildings and whether or not there was any conceivable
use for the various sheds dotted here and there, apparently
at random, around the fields and coastal slopes. Colonel
Paynter saw very little value to man, woman or beast in
this rickety hut or that derelict shed, but Gilbert wanted
to see more artists' studios. He saw potential. Surely every
building could, with a little effort, be cleaned up, made safe
and used? At the moment the Colonel was unconvinced
but had promised a thorough review once Gilbert had a
complete inventory.

'So that's it,' Gilbert said, 'for what it's worth . . . My
average day.'

'I'll tell Blote, she'll be fascinated.'

Gilbert grinned sheepishly.

'Will she? Sounds pretty mundane to me.'

'No, not a bit of it. Portrait of a man in the open air. Right up her street.'

'Not always the open air, I'm afraid.'

'All right ... Gilbert among the daffodils then ... Gilbert up the ladder.'

Gilbert climbing dusty ladders made dangerous by missing rungs, poking his head through cobwebs and out of holes in the roof; checking flues, testing the butts for rainwater, cycling along lanes, pressing plaster to see if it crumbled, helping the men push carts clogged with mud, packing flowers into boxes, Gilbert at the very top of a house, then Gilbert ducking into cellars, into the world of cold stone, of slugs and frogs and slither.

It was though, Joey sensed, only a half insight, a privileged momentariness. There was so much of Gilbert one was not allowed to know. He was that kind of man, the courteous sensitive man it was not done to press.

'Promise me something, though, Gilbert?'

'If I can.'

'You'll come roller-skating with us one Saturday in Penzance. Please. I've promised Blote I'll round everyone up.'

Gilbert moved away from the wall, seeing the rain closing towards them from round the point. They would be lucky to escape. Joey tightened the straps on his haversack.

'If I can get away,' Gilbert said.

'On a Saturday? Oh, come along, you can't work all the time, it's the most terrific fun, you'll see, especially if everyone comes.'

'Everyone?'

'Yes, so let's go and see Blote and A.J. They'll persuade you if I can't.'

Joey put his arm round Gilbert and shoulder to shoulder they pushed the bicycle up the steep slope. On the way

Joey also persuaded him to join them that evening for supper. The Knights would be there, and Dolly and Prudence. Gilbert was, Joey insisted, Laura Knight's absolutely favourite man.

'After A.J.?'

'Oh, of course, but it's an absolute fact you are, and she makes a particular point of saying so to all and sundry. Dolly is also . . . intrigued.'

'Oh Dolly is, is she?'

'Yes.'

Just before they turned down to the mill it started to pour, which cooled Gilbert's blushes. They sheltered under a canopy of trees, by a padlocked gate. Gilbert noticed a dead jackdaw at his feet: his chattering, fluttering days were now over.

'Gilbert?'

'Yes.'

The rain poured and Joey's voice sounded different, though his face was a picture of innocence.

'Do you mind telling me what you think of my sister?'

There was a perplexing pause.

He had to be careful.

Gilbert watched the rain fall, a scene of desolate beauty.

He could not say oh I go to sleep with her on my mind, oh yes, I sleep next to her, in freshly starched sheets with a hint of drying lavender, I wake with her in my narrow bed, I show her the birds' eggs, I tell her (only her) about the night we were surrounded by the Boers and lost eleven men, I ride with her on Merrilegs, with the scent of carted corn in the air and poppies still blooming, she holds me round my waist, her cheek pressed to my shoulder, I play long games of croquet with her and allow her to win, I interweave my fingers with hers on our walks up Rocky Lane, we look at patches of charlock and circle the Merry

Maidens hand in hand and find a place out of the wind just over from Tregiffian and she tells me she—

'Your sister? I think she is . . . really very splendid.'

'Anything else?'

'In what sense?'

'Anything you've . . . noticed?'

Gilbert inhaled, wondering whether there could be anything about her he had *not* noticed! Did everything depend on his answer, which might well be reported back from brother to sister?

'Only . . . that I've never met a more beautiful person.'

Joey smiled at Gilbert's nervous reply.

'Yes – yes, I know all that, *everyone* says *that*, Harold Knight says that, even *I* can see that, but you're such a perceptive sort of chap and I wondered, you know, don't you ever, be honest, think she's—'

'What?' Gilbert asked.

Above them some leaves, weighed down with the rain, shed their drops, one of them spluttering Gilbert's cigarette. He had to suck hard to keep it going, the heat fighting the damp.

'Well, Gilbert, what do *you* think of her?'

'I think she's . . . extraordinary.'

'*Extra*-ordinary?' Joey asked.

'Oh, yes. Very much so.'

'As simple as that?'

'Yes! She is extraordinary. Absolutely extraordinary.'

'But not extraordinarily odd?'

'No, not even fairly odd, to tell you the absolute truth.'

And by now they were both laughing, laughing like boys, like very young and very close school friends, and they left their den and walked on in the pouring rain, and a dog ran past with one hind leg in the air and they laughed in the rain (arm in arm) like a couple of absolutely extraordinary idiots.

That night, before he once again snuggled up with Florence, all men and women elsewhere, Gilbert wrote the following words in his diary.

> Had supper with Joey and Miss C.-W. The Knights there too. Dolly and Prudence not, though expected. Most enjoyable.

He slowly closed his diary and pulled back the bed-clothes. He would read for a while. After some page-turning, from which he absorbed nothing at all, he got out of bed and opened the diary again. He picked up his pen. 'Most enjoyable,' he said sharply to himself. Then he suddenly felt very sad and very alone. Words really were useless. His feelings contending, he picked up his paper knife, turning it over in his hands, looking at it very closely but seeing no more than he saw when he turned the pages of the book in bed.

Could he not add a little to that entry?

Such as—

> Most enjoyable . . . mostly. If a little disconcerting.

No, that would not help.

Should he not keep a fuller diary, a journal, fill an exercise book with all he thought and felt?

No, not at the moment. Too much was happening, inside him.

He slipped back into his starched sheets, faced the wall and closed his eyes. She was not with him. He was determined that when next he opened his eyes it would be a bright fresh morning full of work and hope. It was quite simple. All he had to do was tell himself to do it, to focus on her shoulders as he did at supper, and her mouth, her wide mouth as she turned to ask him a question, but as he opened his eyes, superimposed, there was Sammy's swollen mouth the night before he died.

No!

To cheer himself up:

He would see her mouth instead, widening in a slight smile, as she asked a friendly question, her mouth making a simple, everyday teasing remark because any remark she made, about her art or his work, was made memorable because she made it. She spoke first to him just as Laura offered him more potatoes and leeks. He could see the whole scene so clearly, the blue plate, the white potatoes, the long pale green leeks, her long fingers resetting a hair pin just above the nape of her neck. He loved the way her hair swept up from her neck, to be pinned higher, and her necklace, the way it fell. He looked her up, he looked her down, and both secretly, so secretly.

'Captain Evans, I saw you the other day. Just above the mill.'

'Blote, it's "Gilbert", we've already settled on that.'

His heart bumped. Where? Just above the mill? He had not seen her. His mouth dried. How on earth could he have missed seeing her?

'I'm so sorry, I did not see you. Where was I?'

'I was walking with a friend and you went past, *swept* past I should say.'

He was none the wiser. He had no reason to be where she said she saw him. He felt bewildered. There was an unheard moan in his heart. He had no recollection at all of the scene. She put her hand on his arm.

'And you were looking very serious. As you are at the moment.'

'Was I? Am I?'

'Yes.'

'I'm afraid I often do, or so I'm told.'

'But I like people who look serious, Stanhope Forbes looks serious as well and I so want to know what is in the minds of serious people, what's making them so melancholy. A preoccupied face is worth a penny of anyone's money, don't you agree?'

Gilbert was determined to move on to something else by bringing in Laura, but before he could do so Florence smiled and tapped her napkin as if to say that little topic, the question of his seriousness, unresolved though it was, was over for the time being and now she wanted to ask him something important. She spoke to him as if no one else was at the table. She did not want Joey butting in.

'How long have you been an officer? I do want to know that.'

'Eight, no, nine years now. In the Militia.'

'And you fought in South Africa, at a very young age then?'

Gilbert sensed Joey was trying to hear their conversation.

'Yes. I was nineteen when I went out there.'

'Nineteen! To think of you younger than I am, out there, and fighting in a dreadful war.'

'Many did,' Gilbert said. 'It was not unusual.'

'Did you kill anyone? That would be unusual, wouldn't it?'

Gilbert felt both his arms knot. His mind locked. He did not know what to do. In a split second Laura came in; Joey may not have heard all this but Laura certainly did.

'I think, my dear, that men do not ... enjoy this kind of discussion. More wine, Gilbert?'

'Oh? In which case I shall never refer to it again.'

'No, I don't mind all that—' Gilbert stuttered.

'No, Laura is right, I'm sure.'

'You've heard Alfred's off soon?' Laura said breezily.

'Off where?' Joey asked, equally breezily, from the other side of the table.

'Captain Evans,' Florence said, putting down her knife and fork, 'I apologise, but Joey assured me when I arrived in Lamorna that you all talked about everything, and *that* was what made this place so special, that sense of frank discussion. Let us return to the water divining.'

At the Water's Edge

She saw him standing alone at the water's edge. He was trying to kick something. From her distance it might have been a pebble, and he was trying to kick it as far as he could. She moved closer, though still unseen. It was a pebble. The next one he caught only a glancing blow. He picked up another. This time he missed it completely, stubbing his toe. So he kicked the sand instead and attacked it with both feet, hoofed it, kicked it violently like a small boy whose sandcastle had been destroyed by a warring tribe and was now getting his own back on whatever lay in sight: it was a terrible, random tantrum and very prolonged. Watching it made her want to laugh. It also made her want to put her arms round him. Only when he turned from attacking the sand to attacking his dog (that little killer who was leaping around and loving every second of it) did she button up her overcoat and hurry, calling to him, as she ran down the slipway to the beach. Her face ached with cold. She called. He did not turn, though he must have heard her.

'Alfred! *Alfred!*'

'Oh, it's you.'

'You must have heard me.'

'Quite a night,' he said.

'Yes, I was hoping your roof stayed on.'

'I wasn't at home.'

'Oh, where were you?'

He ignored her. The sea pounded down, undulating, lifting itself up in big long surges of grey lit by a multitude of white dots. The sucking and pushing and retreating was competing only a few feet from them. He walked along the foam's edge.

'I'm having a terrible time,' he said.

'Why?'

'I can't paint. Can't do it any more.'

'Oh don't be so silly.'

'Just done a bloody awful one, the rocks look like sponges and the hounds look like statues, I just can't get it right, it's worse than beginners' rubbish, it's worse than the stuff they do in Forbes' first hut.'

'Even you can have an off day.'

'No, it's not that, don't you see?'

'No, I don't.'

'You're not playing bloody games, are you? It's . . . it's that I can't paint anything except you.'

'That can't be so.'

'It *is* so. Without you I can't work.'

'But you had a whole exhibition of work before I met you.'

'Look, go *away* if you're going to argue about it.'

He picked up another stone, and punted it cleanly. This success seemed to cheer him.

She drew level with him. For the first time she felt, with a curious stab of understanding, that she was in a sense the older person. But that was quite ridiculous. He was at least ten years her senior. Seeing her at his shoulder he accelerated away. She kept up with him, but made heavy weather of it, her feet sinking deeply into the soft sand. All along the beach there were smashed things, piles of seaweed and driftwood covered in white, decomposing froth. Where on earth could he have slept on such a night?

He spoke sharply, without looking at her.

'Why are you alone?'

'Joey's out on the rocks by Carn Barges. But I enjoy my own company . . .'

'And what have you been doing with your own company?'

'Painting all day, eight or ten hours at a time. And sitting for Harold next door, when I can.'

'And entertaining, I hear. Gilbert Evans. With dances.'

'Yes, that too.'

'Unburdening his soul to you, was he? Was he?'

'No, why would he do that? I enjoy his company very much.'

He suddenly put his hands to his head in self-recrimination.

'I made a fool of myself with you . . . last week. Why did I do it? A terrible exhibition.' Then he savagely added, 'Pleb!' and punched himself.

'When?'

'Don't "when" me, you stupid woman!'

He pointed to his right eye with his forefinger.

'Oh, yes.'

'Yes, said too much, usual trouble, bloody fool, no brain.'

'You do exaggerate. Anyway I'm glad you felt you could tell me, I'd much rather know.'

'I didn't "feel I could tell you", I lost my temper.'

'Even so, I prefer it when people tell the truth, so much talk is so empty, isn't it, even down here? And to have achieved all you have . . . is all the more—' Her voice tailed off.

The dog looked at them both, from one to the other, as if to say 'Let's go' and they walked off the beach and up a sodden track, bordered by cigar-brown heather. As they climbed she noticed Alfred had some difficulty in moving freely. She wanted to ask him what was wrong, but dared not. At the top of the track, limping and panting a little with the exertion, he said quickly:

'I'm going away soon.'

'I know.'

'I have to.'

'So you said the other day. Where?'

'Don't know, just know I'm going or I'll burst. Thought I might visit your house in London, see if you're as rich as you say you are.'

'Our home in London, but—'

'But I won't, don't worry. I'd like to go to Norfolk, or Suffolk, but I may not.'

'How long will you be away?'

He shook his head and shrugged and moved on. She had no idea where he was heading, nor why his moods affected her so much. She tried to imagine her mother's expression as he was announced. She tried to imagine him pacing about in her London drawing-room, dressed in his strange clothes. She tried to imagine her father sitting next to him. She found herself smiling at the contrasts and the shock waves, his country accent and his unavoidable oaths.

'I need to paint you again before I go, so when's it to be?'

'I've just told you, at the moment I can't, I've promised Harold Knight I will be avail—'

'I *have* to! That's the point.'

'All right, but only if I can paint you as well.'

He turned to her, his colour high, his eyes piercing.

'*You* paint *me*?'

'Yes ... I thought I would start with you, what better practice?'

'Well, you can't.'

'In which case I shall have to disappoint you.'

'Is that how you behave?'

'Isn't that a question you should be asking yourself?'

'Oh, do as you wish.'

'Where are you going?'

'I'm going for a drink, then I'm going off to be with people I can be with.'

And with that he turned on his heel and plunged deep into the high wet ferns. Taffy leapt after him.

'But why,' she called, '*why* do you drink so much?'

Whether he heard that question or not she was not sure. A little angry with herself and very angry with him she was soon retracing her steps down the path and back along the water's edge. Sharp and clear in the sand, going in the opposite direction, were the footprints they had made not fifteen minutes before.

Mr Money

                                          A caravan:
                                          By the light
                                          Of the silvery
                                          Hamp-shire moon

Dear Ev,

A surprise!

A letter from your friend and so very soon, barely a week after we parted. That's what friends do, isn't it? They think about each other!

What an evening we had in The Wink! And those splendid crabs from Jeffery, I've never tasted better, but I must apologise for the spirit in which I first greeted you, what a foul day I'd had, and what a foul impression I must have made, I felt like an old buck rabbit stamping in his hutch, but we certainly got into our stride in The Wink, you and I. Never have I seen you so animated! Early next morning did you have a head? No! For was there ever in God's world a more organised man or (I do not flatter) a more reliable one? It occurs to me some of us can only be truly prankish if some people are truly sane. Perhaps we all have our own spheres?

How intelligent I feel tonight! In the rain yesterday I imagined you giving instructions in your gaiters, sloshing around that big cobbled yard at Boskenna. And at night are you still enjoying hippety-hops and beanos and dances (but not, I hope, enjoying them as much without me)?

Where was I?

Yes, what a contrast the thought of you, sitting in your room, makes with the fellow in the next caravan to me. He is wearing earrings (can I see you wearing earrings?), a deep red scarf, a black felt hat, sleeved waistcoat and tight trousers. He is sitting in a – no, he is not in his caravan, I lie in my teeth, he is in a yellow-wheeled gypsy cart. The horse is covered with brass-mounted harness. What a splendid sight! And here is something else for you to think about as you check the water levels and collect your dues and circumnavigate your farms and properties, think about this – soon there will be no coachmen, they are being pushed out by chauffers (spelling?), God help us, show-furs, and is that what you want, my engineer, my sapper friend, lots of hoots and horns all over England and not a moo to be heard?

I think of you because all around me are tents, old Army bell-tents, and being a bit of a villain myself (set a thief to catch a thief) I smell stolen stock, and if they are stolen I only hope they do not belong to the Royal Monmouthshire Engineers . . . or Militia or whichever lot you are a big shot in or with – all the more reason for you to stay there and not carry out one of your famous inventories on the Romany estates!

How is Florence? How is Laura? How is Joey

behaving? No, let us be honest, eh, Ev? HOW IS FLORENCE? The pipe dream renders it bearable for us?

You are sitting – I hazard a guess – in your comfortable rooms being waited on hand and foot by Mrs Jory, or perhaps you are taking your time over lunch – what a cosy place you have, or is it that wherever you are you do make other people feel at home, because you draw them out with your quiet attentiveness? – while all around me here in the cold fields are white wood ash fires on the ground, one in front of each wagon. Underneath each vehicle is a lurcher and a greyhound. To my left a stiff breeze belabours the breeches on a makeshift washing line, and to my right a man with a big bowl is throwing faggots down to hungry families. Children fight for them. Dogs are barking. Hens are thrilling. Chicks are panicking. Horses are having kicking matches.

Life. LIFE, eh?

Further to my left is a mission hut. The man in there plans to lead these good Romanies into the paths of righteousness, plans to take them off to God. Well! Have to say my money is on the status quo. So far at least our mission man has had very little effect on their language. Theirs makes mine seem pure driven snow. The air is as blue as the camp fire.

'Do that again and I'll kick your bleeding shins.' (This from a man.)

'Do that again and I'll pull your bleeding lights out.' (This from a woman.) Would she really blind her child? A Romany Regan? She looks capable of it.

I am filled with the desire to work. It burns. It consumes. I have so many models here, all related to each other (so who knows what goes on under their painted roofs? Better not ask). How shall I describe them to you, Ev? Let us take a touchstone, known to us both, Miss F. C.-W. Well, the women here are dressy women, real dressy women (whereas Florence is dressy but does not wish you to know she is. Am I right?). One here is my favourite. She wears a black silk apron over a full, pleated skirt, a pink blouse showing off a tough, lithe little body. (You'll be seeing more of her, Ev, my boy, in my pictures, so see if I'm not right! See the contrast with Blote; and, by the by, is not 'Blote' a bloody silly name?)

She wears strings of red beads, wonderful earrings (do they compete with the men on earrings?) under the most wonderful blue-black hair, oh, the Romany hair, a large black hat complete with ostrich feather, and when she walks SHE WALKS. You can feel the life BEATING in her. How about that for a woman? Can you see her? Can you smell her? Is she not paintable?

'D'ye want me ter-morrer, Mr Money?' she asks. MR MONEY!

Yes, she thinks that is my name, or perhaps it is her joke (never never underestimate a Romany woman) and if it is, the joke will not be lost on you. Mr Munnings pays a gypsy woman a shilling an hour, ten shillings a day, to make enough money to dazzle the world (and other women?). In this way the lower and the higher orders are conjoined!

What a model she is! She is alive and happy in her skin. With bodies like hers, every day here is a gala day.

'Yes, my lady,' I say, 'I would like you tomorrow, please.'

'Or would ye be wantin' to do a 'orse instead?'

'No, my lady,' I say, 'only you. I do not want any horse. I want only my lady on a horse.'

She loves me saying 'My lady' and gives me such a look, glancing back at her caravan (does anyone in Lamorna give such a look?) but watching us there is a fellow sharpening sticks with a knife, and it's not my canvas that concerns him. His knife looks extremely keen. My marvellous model, her body touching mine, washes my brushes for me and keeps popping round the easel to see how she is coming on.

'Cor!' she says, and 'Cor!' is her greatest praise. 'That me? Is it, Mr Money? You's the Champ and no doubt!'

And she brushes my arm again with her fingers as she moves off.

And tomorrow I shall paint her, as she leans out of the half-door, holding the reins. Children – hers? who knows? – with cheeky faces will be poking their noses over the door. Others will be sitting on the shafts, dangling their legs. Poultry will be slung in crates or cages from the wheels. A blackbird will go by like running ink. And all this, my friend, you will see for yourself, captured for ever by the magnificent Munnings – or maybe not, BECAUSE (dammit) I've got to sell them, haven't I, and does one paint with one eye on the guinea? Does one write with one eye on the guinea? I suspect people do, you know.

Anyway, if all goes well, I shall paint a picture every three or four days and leave you to control things your end. Mind you, it could go wrong. My hands are blue, my left thumb has gone dead under the weight of the palette, my right foot feels the size of a horse's thigh with gout (didn't ever tell you about the gout I've got which I don't deserve,

but do I deserve your friendship? I would say YES
to both).

So there you are in Jory's, there you are in Lamorna.
And what did you eat last night? I know, I know,
soup, cold mutton with mint sauce (very little of), cold
rhubarb and cream, with Florence and Joey as guests,
with Joey for billiards and Florence for admiration?
If I am right, smile!

Perhaps I should stay here? Perhaps this is the
MILIEU for a man with my restlessness? Am I a
gypsy at heart?

And how's old Laura? Still bumping along like a
balloon?

And how's Joey? Still looking for blennies in the
rock pools?

And how's you? Don't simmer too much inside,
will you? You must let off steam, and not make a
masterpiece of self-effacement. Don't be ashamed to
be different, or it's a rather chained fate you choose.

By the way, how is the Dolly gel? Dolly is, I
suspect, rather more than meets the eye, and plenty
enough meets the eye, take my meaning?

And I wish you all health, Ev, and I send this letter
along earth tracks and deep culverts and open ditches
and rain-polished roads and green fields to you (but,
God, what else are fields BUT green?).

Yours,

A.J.

Underneath his signature, and all over the envelope, were
quick witty drawings, a whiff of A.J.'s world.

Cézanne's Apples

In the weeks while Mr Money was away with his black-haired gypsies, the foundations were being dug for a handsome new house on the cliff. The site was not far from Jory's Hotel and Gilbert, of course, was deputed by the Colonel to supervise the early stages. He did so happily. Very happily, as it meant less time sloshing around the big cobbled yard at Boskenna and more planning chance meetings with Florence. From the site it took him less than ten minutes to cycle over to her cottage, he overtook her on walks (Joey was vital for intermediary hints), he waved to her as she sat upstairs in Harold Knight's studio and one wonderful evening, a pipe dream come true, he rode over to Newlyn and brought her back from her art class on Merrilegs. Every step of the way his heart unfurled and sang.

It soon became clear, too, that Gilbert was the only one who had received a letter from Alfred. This distinction surprised him. He asked Laura. He sounded out Florence. Laura was somewhat put out to hear all this rhapsodising over the Romanies but Florence, at her most assured, only said, 'Why no,' no, she had never expected a letter or anything of the sort, why should she? To ride Merrilegs, to receive letters, to see so much of Florence, to sense her measured distance diminish, to look high over hedges, to see gulls following a plough, to spot a different ground swell in the ocean and enjoy the wide panoramas of a bigger busier world, all this experience seemed to be coming Gilbert's way with an abrupt rush.

His confidence grew.

His world expanded.

He rode into Penzance for some shopping, and to greet Gilbert and his private thoughts the church bells chimed as he trotted along the promenade towards the centre of town. These last few days Gilbert sensed he was noticing things he rarely noticed; today, for example, on entering Penzance, the bird droppings on a statue's head. He saw them so clearly. Passing Morrab Gardens he noticed the palms and myrtles, the geraniums and camellias.

Mother's birthday was coming up next week, with brother Lionel's only four days later. Never very original over such matters, Gilbert knew he would buy a new book for Mother, he always did, and a new pipe (a rather pukka Loewe with an amber stem) for Lionel. And at the bottom of his list (or the top) was a visit to the Morrab Library. That was the item he was moving towards.

Everything went perfectly. He completed all his business calls; he bought the book and the pipe in Chapel Street; he saw the surveyor and had a ginger beer at a small shop, and that left only the library before he put his foot back in the stirrups. Never before had the prospect of a visit to any library excited Gilbert, but in the last week the word, the words, had been niggling away in his mind, and the only thing for it was to go to the source of words, the dictionary. Coming back down Morrab Road towards the Promenade, he turned left into Morrab Gardens. He sat in the sun for a moment, a stone's throw from the sea, and listened to the gulls cry, and the palms rustle.

Liddell and Scott, he remembered that big black tome at Rugby, and he also recalled how difficult he had found it to grasp Greek grammar. He followed the librarian through the high, quiet rooms, not to Liddell and Scott, but to the large Oxford English Dictionary. He took down the volume he needed. How could a dictionary cause his hands to tremble and the muscles in his arms to tighten like a rope? He placed the weathered spine on a reading-table and turned the pages, trying to make as little noise as possible.

black
blanch
bloom
blossom
blot

Surprisingly, there was a good deal on 'blot'.

blotchy

Must be soon, or is there no such word, don't say there is no such—

blote

His finger stopped. It was easily the shortest entry on the page, almost as if there were some doubt amongst the world's lexicographers as to its existence. He read:

blote obs. [? connected with blow in blow-fly, fly-
       blown. (The sense can hardly be explained from
       OE. blat, 'livid, pale' to which the form
       answers)]
       The egg or larva of flies and other insects.

This was not at all what Gilbert wanted to find. He had not followed this trail to encounter larva and flies and other insects. He wiped Sammy away. He wiped out of his mind the sight, and particularly the sound of fly-blown bodies and the heat of the South African sun, the sight of his friend's face covered in flies and the horse with a burst stomach and barrel chest and flies walking on its teeth.

Livid? No. But . . . pale, yes, she was pale. He looked down again at the page.

bloten

bloten . . . to soften or moisten . . . anoint. Moistening, yielding.

He looked up and across the room. Soften, moisten, anoint, yield. He saw nothing, then he saw Florence standing at her easel in Newlyn, and with that softening sight and with those yielding words he was comfortable, with those words he could face and handle the future.

Florence was not standing at her easel in the third studio in Newlyn, though she should have been. She was sitting, with her hands in her lap, on the creaky chair which Alfred Munnings had once again placed twenty yards from his studio. The chair was placed against a perfect background of foliage. Her oval face was pale. Her bracelet shone in the sun. She had a headache which worsened by the minute as she sat full face in the glare.

Alfred had returned at breakfast time, his trap full of gypsy paintings, and called on her unannounced; and before she knew what was going on, before she could say 'No' she was on the way down the slope with him. Unusually, he was sitting down to work. Usually he was too restless, moving around like a dancer or an angry fly, but here he was, tired from travelling all night, the taste of beer still on his tongue, sitting on a low milking stool, his long holland painting coat plastered yellow, his sleeves rolled up to the elbow and his Panama hat tilted over one eye. She could not see his eyes, nor had she dared look directly at him since his terrible explosion.

He drew her, also making pencil notes on the side of his pad, his thoughts over possible colours.

'Been seeing a fair bit of Ev?'

'We've met a few times.'

'Good . . . good. Thought so. Thought you would.'

'They're building a new house, didn't you know?'

She looked at his hands. They were tanned brown. She looked at the little hairs on his forearms. She hadn't noticed those before.

'Don't move!'

'Don't shout at me!' she shouted back. 'I already have a headache.'

'I can't work if you keep on moving.'

'I haven't been shouted at while you've been away, not once. It has been a most pleasant fortnight.'

The sun glared. She blinked. He was glad she shouted back.

'You're my apples, you see. Cézanne. Heard of Cézanne?'

'Of course I've heard of Cézanne. I suspect I may know as much about him as you do.'

'Point being,' he stood up to resettle himself and sat down again, 'point being, Cézanne painted the same bowl of apples countless times – there's always something new, you see, to say about a bowl of apples, the same bowl, so he kept painting them until they were perfect, that's dedication, Blote, that's art, and remember you're my apples. Same with horses. Most people can't paint horses, can't make 'em shine.'

'But you can?'

'Yes, I can.'

'You've returned at your most modest, Mr Munnings.'

'Most modest people haven't a clue,' he yawned, and

stroked his unshaven chin, 'sorry, bit tired, and . . . horses, yes, horses shine, you see, you look at them when I take you to the races, you really look at them and you'll see I'm right, and making them shine is the challenge.'

'I'll remember that. At the moment I find the human form enough of a challenge.'

'I prefer cows though.'

'Cows?'

'Cows, I said.'

She started to tremble.

'So ridiculous, you really are, I don't know why I'm here. I should be at my class.'

'Best one I ever had was a cross between a Friesian and a Jersey bull, with white markings. Marvellous! What a model! I've just bought a cow, by the way.'

'Don't be ridiculous! You will say anything, anything.'

She had to stand up to stop laughing but that only made it worse.

'No doubt about it, give me a cow. They stand still, they have no ambition, they don't want to be petted or patted, you don't have to say "poor thing" or "thank you", they don't require any knowledge of their character, they're not disdainful like some people I know, they don't want intimacy, you don't pay homage to a cow, they never complain of headaches, yes, they're my models, oh bloody hell, the sodding sun's gone in so you might as well have a proper rest. Is my bow tie straight?'

'Not quite.'

'Straighten it, please.'

She did so, her shoulders still shaking, her hands trembling on his tie. His face was red-brown. She stepped back.

'Is that right?'

He felt his collar.

'Yes. But you heard what I was saying about apples?'

'Yes, I heard you, Alfred. I expect people in Penzance heard you.'

'Ah, see what I mean? Now no cow I know would say a thing like that. Or horse. Now look at Tick. Come on . . . let's look at Grey Tick. Now you probably think Grey Tick is a world away from us, but look at it this way . . . his hocks are your ankles, his knees are your wrists, he walks on his fingers and his toes, the stifle joint is your—'

blotless came next. Blotter. His school blotter. Gilbert remembered how its perfect, pristine texture was slowly spoiled with spreading pen marks, filled with wonderfully interesting spiders' webs or outlines of Africa or the shape of a leaf or the central nervous system. His finger moved on. No, he must go back, as blote was an obsolete form of bloat. He moved a few pages back.

black

blithe, that was a word he'd always liked, blithe, a pleasurable word

blizzard

bloat, brought him up sharp

But puffy, swollen and puffed were not words he liked. Nor was that the spelling, Joey was quite clear on that point. At least they were all agreed on the spelling.

He replaced the dictionary, just as the sun hit the top of the bookcase.

Now for Sandro Botticelli. From another shelf, in the darkest corner of the library, he gathered three histories of art, each with a helpful entry on Botticelli of Florence. (And what a happy accident it was that Botticelli came from Florence; it was as if the gods had conspired to make the parallels between the two women perfect in every respect.) In the third book he found exactly what he wanted, a

coloured engraving of *The Birth of Venus*. Here before
him was Botticelli's Venus.

Venus stood there on the page before him naked. Almost
naked. Florence stood there. Gilbert studied her.

He looked at her as closely as he could.

In the clear morning air beauty came into the world with
Venus, and it was the mystery of her arrival, the moment
of her arrival, which Botticelli caught. She came naked
from the sea (a sea such as there never was in Cornwall),
perfectly balanced yet somehow tilting forward on the
daintily lipped cockle shell. The air slipped around her.
Calm though the sea was, an unreal flat calm of grey water,
Venus seemed to sway gracefully on the shell. It should
have been precarious – there were such risks! – but she was
balanced and confident and self-assured she would not fall.
This Venus made a nonsense of gravity.

Gilbert borrowed a magnifying glass from the librarian,
and then turned his back so that it could not be seen over
which picture he was poring. He moved the glass slowly
across the page. Two winged zephyrs, flying past, blew
her on to the shore with jets of lustful air, their breath
warm and the air full of floating petals, petals which hung
and hovered. On closer inspection Gilbert saw they were
a shower of roses, cut short at the stalk. Cutting flowers
was something Gilbert often did. 'Another sign,' he said to
himself. 'It all fits together. Everything.'

On the shore stood Time, a nymph in a white dress,
with a wreath of myrtle around her neck, waiting with
a beautifully embroidered purple cloak, patterned with
daisies. Was this a cloak to veil her, a cloak to cover
her nakedness? There was surely no need for a cloak
and certainly no request in Venus's eyes for one. This
woman, this goddess, did not seem embarrassed by her
state. Indeed she challenged you to look her in the eye.

Gilbert bent over and studied her again. No, perhaps her eyes were sad and accepting. Oh, it was *so* difficult to read people's eyes, wasn't it?

With a steady hand he looked, through the glass, slowly down her body. Her right hand screened her bosom, covering her round high right breast. In her left hand she held some of the very long tresses of honeyed, auburn hair in front of her lower nakedness. To cover it, Gilbert felt, was also to draw one's attention to it, to imagine more fully what could not be seen. Was it Botticelli's purpose to excite such thoughts?

No.

Botticelli's Venus was as delicate and as tender as Florence. Her skin was cool, and cool in the same way. She was a gift from Paradise, a gift from the gods, and she walked towards him out of the sea in Cornwall, tapping the door against which he stood. She came out of the sea towards him, and the orange trees and the grassy dunes ran down to the sea in welcome.

She came towards him as he waited. He held out his hands.

Botticelli's Venus.

Botticelli, Painter of Florence.

He closed the book. He must go back on Merrilegs to Boskenna.

There was so much to do. He left the Morrab Library.

'You're not listening!'

'I am.'

'You're not, you're just nodding.'

'I *am* listening, and I can see exactly what you mean about the horse. Put like that, it *is* almost human.'

'More human than some humans I've met. Have some more wine.'

He lifted the bottle.

'No . . . I really mustn't. My head is thumping quite badly.'

He filled his own glass, spilling some on to his left shoe.

'And,' he pointed his glass at her, 'I'll tell you something else.'

She knew he was waiting for her to say 'What?' She said nothing.

'I've painted some winners in my time, but you're the best. Blote . . . is . . . best.'

'Apart from the cows?'

He looked round the clearing.

'Yes, of course, apart from the cows.'

They were sitting on the grass not far from the mill. Behind them a peacock strutted. She felt so tired and giddy, and she hardly knew why she asked the next question, it just came out, in a tired and giddy way.

'Will you be coming roller-skating next Saturday?'

'Roller-skating? Next Saturday?'

A flicker of fear touched her. Did his blindness affect his balance? Had she offended him again?

'Do come, please, it'll be more fun with you.'

'Probably won't, it depends.'

'Depends on what?'

'A number of things. For example, who else?'

He suddenly slumped and lay full out on his back, with the bottle crooked in his elbow.

'Well, Joey and I are.'

'Sit here.' He tapped the grass, next to him, looking across at her.

He saw her mouth tighten, her frown caught in an axe of sunlight.

'I'm quite comfortable, thank you.'

He drank. She heard the gulps go down. If he had to drink surely he could do so less noisily?

'Fine. That's all right. Stay where you are. Fine. Do everything with Joey, do you?'

'Whenever possible. But he goes off on his own more and more.'

'Does he now? But, deep down, we're a devoted brother and sister, are we?'

'You might say so. He doesn't know anything about me, of course, but yes, we are very devoted. Underneath.'

'Underneath? Underneath what?'

'I suspect you know what I mean.'

'And another thing . . . How d'you know Joey knows nothing about you?'

She picked at the longer stalks of grass, then very carefully took the heads off some daisies.

'Boys don't know much about girls. Girls know considerably more about boys. If you listen and if you watch, as girls have to do, it's not so very surprising, is it? Look, I can see you're very tired so I think I'll draw you lying there, just as you are now, and you can rest.'

'You're determined to get your way, aren't you, to do only what you want?'

'You don't have to move at all. Stay exactly where you are. In that position.'

'Anyway you can't draw me now, you've got a headache.'

'You paint every morning with a headache, the amount you drink you must have one at least until midday. I have one very rarely.'

'Women!' he mumbled.

'I'm sorry?'

'If you insist on this, *I* insist on a chair.'

*

He was twisting and turning in his seat, the same seat she had been sitting in earlier. A tense hour passed. She looked him up and down. He looked left, right, at his feet, at the sky. He rubbed his chin. While he twisted and turned she did not move a muscle.

'Bloody hell, I hate this . . . I haven't even shaved.'

'What's so difficult about sitting for me?'

'I don't want to do it, it's the last thing I want to do.'

'I didn't want to this morning either but then you called.'

'You weren't travelling all night.'

'That's true. But that's not the point. You *wanted* to travel all night.'

'What *is* the point, then?'

'The point is . . . you've never been much good at accepting any kind of discipline.'

'Oh all right, get on with it. I've been here bloody hours already.'

'I doubt we've been here one.'

'Haven't done this since art school . . . must be twelve years or more.'

He settled down a little more.

'Where was your art school?'

'Norwich . . . Evening classes . . . after a full day's work. Every night of the week.'

'You paid for yourself, even then?'

'With what I earned in the day. Who else was going to pay? For six years I was apprenticed to a printer.'

'It's not every day I have an opportunity to draw you . . . so . . . would you please put that coloured handkerchief in your pocket?'

'This one? In the breast pocket?'

'If you wouldn't mind.'

'Like that?'

'Yes . . . that's it, and if you'd look there . . . as if you choose to look past me . . . at the mill.'

He ran his hand over his face. She could hear the bristles rasp.

'Orders, orders . . . Joey must have had to listen to you a fair bit in his time. I feel sorry for him. Very sorry.'

'That's it. Over my shoulder . . . with your chin up a little. More . . . up more . . .'

'Just because you put on a smock doesn't make you an artist!'

It was a difficult position to hold and she knew it, but that position precisely expressed his arrogance and power. And his petulance. After looking at him very steadily she resumed drawing in a careful, deliberate way. He could not see her at all.

'And put your knees together please.'

'My knees!'

'No one wants to be looking . . . there.'

She spoke quietly, as much to herself as to him. She went on:

'Laura Knight tells me you will be the most famous painter in England. She said that to me twice . . . in front of Harold, too.'

'How is Laura? Off with Dolly, is she? Haven't seen her for a while.'

'Please don't move . . . with your eyes to the left . . . yes . . . and knees together. And I believe her. You will be, I can tell. You will be very famous. I cannot imagine there is anyone like you.'

She said this as if she wished to establish a neutral fact. There was no particular admiration in her sentences. When next he spoke he was serious, his voice stone-cold sober.

'Laura's more likely to be famous than me. I make more noise, but Laura will be the famous one.'

'But Laura is a woman.'

'More or less.'

She laughed, then immediately wished she had not.

'That was very rude,' she said.

'You shouldn't have laughed then. How's our Harold? Still knitting away in his nightie?'

'I call round whenever I can. Their house is lovely and cool, and it doesn't smell of salt water. And they're always very kind to me. And kindness is important.'

For quite a while only the leaves moved. Her pencil made its defined edge. She looked at him with searching eyes. His chair creaked. She noticed his swollen eyelids. She thought of his blindness, and blushed. No one spoke, until almost slurring with sleep, his voice said:

'You said, about an hour ago, about Joey, that boys don't know much about girls. Did you mean men and women too?'

'Oh yes.'

'Whereas you know so much about men and women, do you?'

She did not answer.

'Do you?'

She was trying to capture the way his left eyebrow went up and the sharp edge at the corner of his mouth. More than any part of his body the corners of his mouth expressed his irregular moods.

'Whenever my father and mother entertained at home, I watched people, the way men and women manoeuvred. The way they . . . circled each other.'

'And men have said things? Said things to you?'

'Yes.'

'And done things, no doubt?' Which made the corners of his mouth go up. She waited until they went down again.

'Or tried to. Once. Things I'd never allow.'

She saw his swollen eyelids jerk. She made some connecting lines between his eyes and mouth. She did this confidently. Each morning this week, rising early, she had been drawing herself in her bedroom – for an hour or more before Joey got up. She looked hard in the mirror, looking hard at herself as she had never done before, and the more she looked at herself, the stronger her grasp of her features became, the underlying structure, the way her hair fell; and if she moved further back from the mirror, the way her head sat on her shoulders. And further back still, her top half framed, as it were in a picture. Recently she had been taking off her nightdress. At first she looked only at her face, or looked away. Then she looked at herself in a new, open way. Use your eyes, she said to herself. Don't look away. And what about Dolly? Does Dolly next door look at all like this? At all as I do? Don't look away. Do all women? Or is it just me?

She looked at his collar and bow tie . . . and his neck, so red and brown.

'And as for your . . . bow tie . . .'

She mused only to herself, but he picked it up.

'The wrong colour? Is it?'

'No, I was going to say it's perfect for you. Most men look silly in bow ties.'

'Does your father wear one? I'm trying to picture him.'

'Yes.'

'Perhaps I'll meet him soon.'

He felt more relaxed. He eased back in the chair. He was going to ask her if her father looked silly, very tall and very thin and very silly, but he met her eyes and dropped the idea. He was annoyed at her unspoken coerciveness, and at himself for buckling under. Who the hell did this girl think she was! And why the hell was he playing second fiddle to her? To put her in her place he needed some help, and help suddenly came from a surprising source. Just when he was despairing of his next stratagem, Charlotte, his cow, walked heavily into view. Alfred said nothing. Florence could not see it. He waited until the cow was chewing the cud only ten yards or so behind her back then he stood bolt upright and said in a breezy, social voice:

'I'm so very sorry, do let me introduce you to my favourite model.'

She turned and screamed.

'So you'll be coming roller-skating?' she asked.

'You know damn well I will.'

'Why should I know that?'

'Because you're going, that's why.'

She paused and smiled and said she was glad, very glad. She had decided to forgive him for the cow, he had been silly, that's all; but he had decided it was time she was further ruffled, high time he brought even more colour to those usually pale cheeks.

'Have you heard about Gail?'

'Gail? Is she one of your gypsies who Gilbert told me about?'

'No, she's not. Told you about my gypsies, did he?'

'I'm afraid I don't know anyone at all called Gail.'

'Well there is one. And she's quite a girl!'

'Are you pulling my leg? Is Gail your name for the cow?' He laughed.

'No . . . Gail's quite a girl, but she's not a cow.

'There was a young lady called Gail
On whose chest was the price of her tail,
While on her behind,
For the sake of the blind,
Was the same information in Braille.'

And that, coming on top of everything else, was the last straw.

At about the same time as Alfred's limerick was bringing an end to the sitting, Gilbert was knocking on the door at Oakhill Cottages. He found no one in.

No Florence. No Laura. No Dolly.

Only Harold Knight patiently at work upstairs. Harold opened the window and leant out. His glasses nearly slipped off his beaked nose.

'Oh, Gilbert,' Harold said, 'bad luck all round, I'm afraid.'

'What's happened?'

'Munnings is back,' he called glumly down, then withdrew his head.

Dolly on the Rocks

Each day that week, a week of unbroken sunshine, Laura was down on the rocks with Dolly. These were the big rocks round to the right from Lamorna Cove. When the tide draws out there you're left with the most wonderful range of natural pools, better pools than any on the West Cornwall coast, deep enough to swim in, as well as providing perfectly flat rocks to picnic on. It was, Laura said to Gilbert, as if God had put them there not only for the marine biologists but also for the Lamorna artists, huge cubes of rock, to sweeten life, to please those who had troubled to find this sheltered place with the light every artist needs.

From early each morning Laura had been painting Dolly, studying the line of her shoulders, the way the light fell on her full breasts, and the soft turn of her arms. Dolly was the most beautiful form Laura had ever seen. She sat on the rock naked and unselfconscious. Laura looked at her shoulder blades and her ribs and the shape of her back. She was a goddess, a Tanagra Greek, a daughter of the sun, and every time she looked at Dolly's smooth form and tapering legs she was glad she was paying her rent.

Looking back, or looking out to the Lizard, it was infuriating for Laura to realise how many wasted years it had taken her to find the confidence to paint a nude even indoors, let alone out of doors, out here in the open air on the rocks by Carn Barges. What was it about the naked body? Was one more real or less real when unclothed? By the time she was twenty Laura had drawn plenty of art school statues, but sooner or later she had to work from life. (Sooner or later, as she complained to Harold, Discobulus had to throw his disc.) Well, now, here, at long last, on the rocks near Lamorna and looking out to the Lizard, she was.

'Are you all right, Dolly?'

'Me? Yes.'

'Still comfortable?'

'Couldn't be better.'

'You wouldn't like another rug underneath?'

'No, this is the life.'

Laura smiled at Dolly's London accent, and her satisfied sighs.

'Tell me when you're hungry, won't you?'

'No, got me apples, don't mind me.'

But Laura did mind about her models, especially Dolly.

'Are you enjoying it down here with us? You're not too bored?'

'Best day's work I ever did, coming down here.'

'Could you move your right knee a little . . . outwards.'

Effortlessly Dolly did.

'Like that?'

'Lovely. How long can you stay?'

'Till Christmas, if you like.'

'No . . . today, I mean.'

'Till four . . . I'm meeting someone at four.'

'Oh good, I'm glad you're making friends. Very glad.'

'So am I.'

It wasn't as if Laura had a priggish upbringing like Florence. (How strange it was, she thought, how very strange, to have Florence Carter-Wood, all la-di-da and top drawer, living on one side, and Dolly on the other.) As for herself, Laura had felt the pinch, she'd seen plenty of deaths, they spoke freely as a family, but for years she simply lacked the insight, she now realised, to grasp that the best subjects were always right there under your nose. Take her sister, Eva. If a sense of propriety had not interfered Laura would have painted Sis taking her bath in the round tin in front of the fire, right there in their Nottingham kitchen, her cuddly little form topped by a head of golden hair (the same gold as Dolly's). But propriety did interfere. It often did. In Harold's family, for example, propriety had a stranglehold, as strong a one (she was willing to bet) as it did in the Carter-Wood family. How many lives, Laura wondered, were chilled to the bone by civility, stunted and darkened prematurely by propriety? As many, she was prepared to believe, as there were Cornish trees bent double by the prevailing wind.

Eventually Laura did draw her first nude indoors, a male, surprisingly: Jack Price he was called, a blind young man with a fine body who modelled at the Nottingham Art School. At first she was afraid to look at him, choosing a position from which she could not see his penis. But when his hourly rest became due he would often turn round in her direction, his face tilted up, his hand stretched out and ask for 'Laura' to come and help him down from his model's throne. He could, she felt, just as easily have asked Harold or one of the other life class students, but he didn't, he always made a point of asking for 'Laura'. And before he did step down he also asked her to mark with a piece of chalk the position of his feet so that after his rest he could resume the exact pose. With the piece of chalk in her hand, and her face quite close to his private parts, she blushed and drew the marks. It was a terrible ordeal.

Anyway, Harold (who, by way of contrast, had never shown his penis much) had raised no objection to the undressed developments with Dolly as long as he was allowed to pursue his own work at his own pace upstairs in his own studio. Harold even enjoyed the bizarre conversations he had with the Bermondsey girl. Dolly, believe it or not, did not have the least idea before she arrived in Lamorna what a cow looked like, and she thought cabbages grew on trees.

After a few nights' proper sleep and a few long walks with Florence, Alfred was back on top form. He told everyone in The Wink about his cow and his time with the gypsies and he galloped around the area on Grey Tick, rustling up friends for his next party, and high on his list was his good friend, his very good friend, Gilbert Evans. But Gilbert was not over at Boskenna, he was up at the new building site on the cliff above the cove, so Alfred rode back across Rosemodress, keeping the ocean and the coastal path to his right, shouting out loud with the exhilaration and the joy of it all, whooping and roaring across Rosemodress, as mad as they come.

About half a mile from Carn Barges he slowed his horse. He could see two women walking along the path side by side, and walking towards him with a determined stride. There was a sense of mission in their manner, unusual in Cornwall, especially on so hot a day. If ever there was one, this was a day for a gentle stroll, a picnic on the rocks, a doze in the sun. He stopped.

He touched his cap with his whip.

'Good afternoon, ladies. Lovely day.'

They were dressed for serious walking, and their serious faces matched their practical clothes.

'Good afternoon,' said the taller one. 'Do you know whose land this is?'

'We need to know very urgently,' said the shorter one.

'Yes, as a matter of fact I do. Can I help?'

'It's not your land, is it?' the shorter one went on.

'Mine? No, I wish it was. No, it's Colonel Paynter's, I've just come from there.'

The ladies looked at each other, as if to confirm an unspoken decision, and asked Alfred for directions to Boskenna. Some instinct encouraged him to delay them a little while.

'Is there something wrong?'

'Wrong! There is something very wrong indeed. But this is not something we wish to discuss in any shape or form.'

The shorter one looked over her shoulder, shuddered, and walked away, staring at the sea. The taller one, with a prominent nose, suggested Alfred kept well away from the rocks for the next stretch, kept as far away as possible.

'But I know this area quite well, what's so dangerous?'

The taller one started a sentence, then closed her eyes. When she eventually spoke it was with a ferociously frozen smile.

'If you would be so very kind as to direct us to . . . Colonel . . .?'

'Colonel Paynter's place, right, you cut across this field, and the next, then keep to the wall on your right, beyond that hut, d'you see, then there's a path, and careful with the brambles, keep straight on and you – but, look, my dear lady, if it's *that* urgent, may I take you there? Tick can manage me and a lady of your figure, can't you, Tick?'

Grey Tick snorted but they were adamant. There was not

the slightest call for that. Munnings insisted with a smile. Without a smile they stood their ground.

'No, no, thank you, but no.'

And there they were, striding away from him across the first field, their eyes on their goal.

'Well, good afternoon, ladies.'

Amused, Alfred watched them hurry into the distance, then trotted on towards Lamorna. So what on earth is all this, eh, Tick? Approaching the rock pools he slowed, stopped and dismounted. Let's have a look at whatever the fuss is, let's have a scout, shall we, he said, tethering Grey Tick to part of an old broken fence. A rabbit bobbed out and bobbed back. Alfred climbed to the top, scanning the ocean below. My God, what a view! Ye gods, what a day! He drew in the Atlantic air. Beat that!

But . . . hang on a minute, yes, ah, yes.

Oh yes.

Yes, ladies, he could see now what the fuss was about. There was another view altogether. His riding boots had slippy soles so he moved carefully to his left, to the grassy part, and eased or half slid down the first part on his bottom, using his hands and heels as brakes. It was risky stuff because the slope was very dry. He inched along and just before he was visible from the rocks he held on hard and crouched right down, while keeping the scene below him in sight.

He felt a hunter. Now he was about thirty feet above Laura and Dolly. He watched.

Then, stealthy as a fox, he stalked a little further. His right foot dislodged a small stone but he just managed to hold it in position before it rolled down. Now he was very close indeed, almost in breathing distance, a bird of prey sighting a morsel of flesh. He lay on his stomach, just above them, his brown hair and sunburnt face camouflaged in the rough grass and heather. But the dusty earth affected his nostrils and his eyes itched and he had the devil's own job not sneezing. Making the smallest movement possible he wiped his forehead with his large coloured handkerchief and slowly loosened his bow tie and collar. This close to the ground it was very hot.

He pressed his body hard into the earth. He kept as still as he could and stared. The sweat shone on the hairs on the back of his hands and glistened on the back of his neck. One of Dolly's knees was raised, the other leg stretched straight out. Her hair, loosened over her shoulders, was slightly fairer than Florence's. Or perhaps the strong light made it seem so.

Here was a picture!

Could he memorise it?

Should he memorise it?

In Florence's hair there was more auburn, which he had tried to catch, but he had never seen her hair flowing like this. Never. But he must. He must!

Dolly was a touch taller than Florence. No, how on earth could he tell? If only she would stand up, but if she stood up, she would see him. His body shocked with panic at the very thought of that, at the position he was now in, and the shame of being apprehended.

A snooper.

Her legs were in some ways like Florence's. How could he say that? He had not fully seen Florence's legs, not as he was seeing these, so carelessly splayed. Trickles of sweat started to run off his eyebrows. He brushed them away, and the sweat ran instead off his nose and the back of his hand.

Dolly gazed out to sea. He could *hear* her eating her apple! He was looking over her back, almost above her, hovering over her like a kestrel. He could hear her lick the juice off her lips. He looked at her, from her breasts down to her feet. His mouth felt as parched as the ground on which his chin rested. He looked between her legs. And stayed looking. He very nearly sneezed.

Dolly, I have seen you. And it is good. Does Florence look like you? Does she look like *this*? He gazed. Does Blote look so good? He had to get back to his horse, but he had to stay. A seagull swooped and shrieked, sending his heart into an even crazier beat.

'Noisy things!' Dolly laughed, and then imitated the seagull, 'Squawk, squawk.'

Crawling back up the slippery slope would be more difficult, much more difficult, than coming down, and he might so easily dislodge some stones.

What would Laura say? What would Laura say if she turned and saw him? His heart pumped against the earth.

The heat was intense, his body damp with sweat, the sight below him a branding iron.

He stayed where he was.

Taking Partners

They all agreed to go to Penzance, and they all arranged to meet: Promenade Roller-Skating Rink at two, Laura, we're all going, Blote, you too, Dolly, no excuses, Gilbert, you're not that busy, we'll see you there, Alfred, and don't be late, we want you there.

The weather had turned nasty again, the waves thrashing, the sea a broth, its moods even more volatile than Munnings, forcing the fishermen's wives closer together in their black hats and aprons, huddled together against the cut of the wind. Setting off in good time Joey and Florence took Jory's pony and trap. On the way Joey played Scottish airs on a penny whistle, with Florence singing the occasional verse. To be seen bowling along with his sister, to be seen with such a beauty, made Joey feel proud. The fishermen's wives glared.

Joey had skated a few times before; Florence had not. He helped his sister on with her skates, lacing these preliminaries with technical hints and cautionary stories. She absorbed his do's and don'ts, then waited while he put on his skates, still talking away nineteen to the dozen, and then, hand in hand, they stepped out on to the rink.

As soon as they started to skate the others seemed to turn up and watch. Even worse, and much to Joey's annoyance, he was far less skilful in keeping his feet than his sister. He half ran, half pushed his feet across the centre of the rink, arcing and curving, pushing his skates till the soles of his shoes burned, running as if trying to establish an early lead in the cross-country, only to stub his toe just in front of Dolly, sway forward, then rock helplessly back on his heels and slide feet first, backside next, into the surrounding boards. He refused Dolly's help. He stumbled, red-faced, to his feet.

For her part, keeping initially to the outward fringes, Florence eased her way into the skating, taking tentative waltz steps, humming Joey's little Scottish air to herself as if dancing with an unwelcome partner at one of the more tedious balls she had endured, as self-contained as they come, like loose silk hanging free. Soon she built up a steady, flowing, easy rhythm, avoiding the crush of other bodies and warmed by the measured exercise.

When Joey, after a while and some adjustments to his technique, had achieved a level of competence and sorted out his bruised pride, he skated round hoping to join his sister. But too late. She had already been asked by another man.

Then another.

Then another.

When had it been otherwise?

Alfred set out from his studio on Grey Tick at much the same time as Florence and Joey. We're off to Penzance, he said to his horse, and I'm in fine fettle. And shall I tell you why, Tick, shall I? Because ... be-cause I was up at the sparrow's crack and working and I have to tell you I did some damn good stuff, not a break till noon. It's the girl, you know, Tick, she's the secret, she's the ticket, Tick. Well, the girls, plural, as a matter of fact.

At seven in the morning, however – this he did not tell his horse – he was very grumpy. He felt there was a critical man, an unwelcome collaborator, a critic leaning over his shoulder and making scornful comments about his latest work. Well, he saw him off, and by noon not only had his breeches dried on the line but he felt more at one with himself. By noon the hounds in the picture were looking like living hounds not statues, and the rocks looked like rocks not pieces of black sponge. And do you know how I did this, Tick?

Tell you a secret, shall I?

Today, whenever I felt a bit low, or a bit down, I thought about that Dolly on the rocks, that girl, and suddenly I was alive, amazing, I was *alive* in the picture, and that's when I know I'm doing well, when I'm living in the picture, I can feel it in my balance, in my feet, I even feel I've got my binocular vision back (though there's bugger-all chance of that), I feel it in my hands, and they were both with me, d'you see, both of them in a thunder of plunging, the one on the rocks was in Florence's dress and watching, and Florence was there . . . her legs on the rocks, lying in the same way as Dolly, Florence undressed, and Dolly came back with me in Florence's dress, because she wanted to, and they both stood in front of me undressed, both lay down in the studio, both lay on my bed and they were both paintable, Tick, they were so paintable, one clothed and one watching, then the other wore the other's clothes and the power poured into my painting, sometimes I may be tired, Tick, but you see they both wanted to be painted on the floor, they wanted to be painted every colour of the rainbow, all over, they both wanted to stay, they wouldn't go, they begged me to go on painting them as they lay or walked barefoot on the floor, and I painted them as they went past, I painted their backs and their fronts and we rolled in the paint and laughed at Harold Knight who only pieces bits of a picture together like embroidery, that's no good, no good at all, so I painted them, they were painted, no fooling, it's got to be dramatic and virile and direct and that's art,

THAT IS ART.

Alfred pressed on, thrusting his horse on, towards Penzance, he and Grey Tick at one together, sensing each other's bodies, like a painter and his model, until they came to The Star Inn. Here, on the outskirts of Newlyn, Alfred pronounced himself 'parched'. He said so to Grey Tick. His mouth was as dry as it had been face down above Dolly.

'Parched,' he said to the landlord, plonking himself down, legs apart, on the low wooden settle with a window view of Mounts Bay and a big ship passing. In three steady pulls he drained the first pint. He smacked his lips and belched. He was, he proclaimed to himself, still parched.

'Still parched,' he said with a challenging smile, as if to suggest that the landlord with the pock-marked face could surely draw off a bigger and better pint than the last.

'And you'll have one yourself to join me, I hope?'

Surprised to find such a good mixer at lunchtime, the landlord fumbled with his match, left his pipe unlit and returned to the barrel.

'Thank you, sir, I will.'

And with that, while Florence was a mile away, and skating along like loose silk hanging free, they fell to talking, man to man, the landlord and Mr Munnings, elbows and shoulders together, and found they had mutual friends in the hunt, and found the fox story was still running, and Alfred arranged to have a ton of hay sent to his stables, before they moved on to the vagaries of the weather and the sea, which led naturally enough to horses and women and life, and how some women looked good without trying while others, however hard they tried, always looked like lumps, and how men who knew about horses and women and life knew the pleasure of riding home with a frost beginning and a young moon in the sky and puddles crisping over.

For a moment A.J. was distracted in full flow by the fly bottle, because the flies in the bar were being attracted to the beer in a bottle and they fell through the hole and got tight and were drowned. Alfred jabbed his finger at the bottle.

'And *that* is life, too.'

'And death,' the landlord said. At which both philosophers laughed.

After four pints Alfred, feeling increasingly at one, paid up, did a quick drawing on a piece of card and presented it to the landlord, bade him a fond farewell, wrapped his lemon-yellow muffler round his neck, went out into the wind and smacked his wide, shiny old stuffed saddle, asking Grey Tick a few questions as they went on the last leg to the rink, asking for example, why:

Why is it I feel at one with a pub, *in* a pub, eh, as with a painting, as with a good chat with a stranger over a drink and sausages and mash, as with a horse, the sweet, curious smell of a horse in a lane, the smell of pastures coming through the pores of their skin, and as he asked Grey Tick these questions he scratched his neck and stroked his long curly mane.

Augereau, Anarchist, Rufus, Cherry Bounce, Winter Rose, Red Prince, Fanny, Merrilegs and Grey Tick.

Merely to memorise the names of the horses he'd had was to see the sheen of a clipped coat, a warrior of a pony,

a mare with long black legs and dappled quarters, a white
mare with an Arab-looking countenance . . .

What horses!

What friends!

And *another* thing, how articulate he was today! Today
he could explain everything. Quite often Alfred found,
when put on the spot by Laura Knight or some critic
in a gallery, that he could not say much in the presence
of a painting. Words frequently failed him. He became
tongue-tied. The whole assessing and comparing business
made him bang his feet around on the floor, it made him
so churned up inside that he couldn't trust his arse with
a fart, but as he strode out of the pub he knew exactly
what he thought about horses and women and art and
narrow-minded Methodists and bloody Sabbatarians and
he could spell out what he thought to all and sundry.
At length.

Everything that day, by contrast, seemed to conspire
against Gilbert. By lunchtime he despaired of ever arriving
at the skating rink at all. Not only had he woken feverish
with cold but Colonel Paynter called at Jory's to ask
him over to Boskenna at around ten to discuss possible
improvements and developments to Gilbert's new office
in Lamorna. As he was spending an increasing amount
of time in and around the village supervising the new
building, Gilbert could see the merits of the plan. It
would save him time, it was sensible, it would make the
estate more efficient, it was all very well for the Colonel to
consider it, but they were standing in a chill wind and the
minutes and the hours of the long-awaited Saturday were
steadily being gnawed away. If he looked at the ground
long enough, however, he felt the Colonel would eventually
grasp the point.

Eventually he did.

'Anyway, Gilbert, I mustn't keep you, it is Saturday after all, and you young chaps need to relax.'

'That's quite all right, Colonel.'

'But you're optimistic about the water source? In the pipeline, so to speak?'

'I am, yes, very optimistic. Lamorna is quite a spot on the map now.'

'And the foundations on the new property, all going to plan?'

'Very much to plan. It'll be a handsome place when it's finished.'

'Sort of place you might consider yourself one day, no doubt? All being well?'

'If I ever get married, sir, and my pocket reaches that far.'

'And before you go, Mrs Paynter's most keen you come over to dinner soon, you quite won her heart with the dog business, went straight to the mark.'

'I'm glad it all ended so well. I saw Flirt just now and she looked full of beans.'

'Thought we might ask along Miss Carter-Wood. Quite a looker, eh?'

'I'm sure she'd be delighted to come.'

'*Very* taken with her, we are!'

'So are we all.'

'Good, good. We'll set all that in train then. And, by the way, Gilbert, you're doing a first-rate job, first-rate, don't know how we ever got along without you.'

'Thank you, Colonel.'

'And the men know you're fair. That's how it should be. Good man!'

Hot with this praise, Gilbert bicycled back as fast as his legs would carry him, he tore around the lanes to the hotel and bolted the lunch Mrs Jory had ensured was kept warm for him. While on his way back from Boskenna he was aiming to cut lunch altogether but the look in Mrs Jory's eye as he rushed in immediately reversed that strategy. He sat. He ate the soup and pie. A gentleman, Mrs Jory held, had to eat properly. He looked at the clock on the sideboard, sure he would now miss everything that was good about a Saturday afternoon in Penzance. Thanking Mrs Jory he ran up to his room where he spent an unnecessary ten minutes trying on three different ties, a blue one, a red one and his green regimental tie, until his hands were damp with the bother of it all and his collar stud began to chafe. He had never in his life been so put out over something so unimportant as a tie. This was not like him at all. Nor was his mood improved by his involuntary memory replaying one of A.J.'s silly songs.

> You can only wear one tie
> Have one eyeglass in your eye
> One coffin when you die
> Don't you know!

Damn A.J., always butting in.

Even then, delayed as he was, he had a quick look at the tray of birds' eggs, and another visit to the lavatory, before toiling up the long hill, pumping his legs as hard as he could to make up some of the lost minutes. But he was delayed by a herd of cows, and by the time it was downhill into Penzance he was back angrily on foot. Yes, another puncture, and another puncture meant yet another opportunity for the jaunty A.J. to laugh.

By three o'clock, when he placed his damaged machine next to the long iron railing, the skating rink was packed, so packed he was at first sure all his friends must have left. She must have left. There was no Florence. Never mind.

What do you mean, *never mind*?

Mind you, he did not quite know what he was expecting to find. In his mind's eye, while pushing his bicycle, he had seen her and perhaps twenty others on the rink. In fact there must have been over a hundred. There was a roar of noise, and the roar of the skates; there were excited cries and anguished warnings, near misses and exuberant twists and turns. He could recognise no one.

Then he saw A.J., lemon-yellow muffler flying behind him, A.J. with his boyishly high parting and port-wine complexion, whoosh, he went past like an ostler being chased by the furies, only he was taking someone to hell with him. Dolly! He was holding her round the waist with one hand, and holding her waist as if he did not give a damn who saw him holding her waist. He whooshed past again, showing the cut of his jacket, his dark grey Melton jacket, and wasn't *he* the thing, and wasn't he holding her so tight and wasn't she enjoying it!

Spotting Gilbert he raised both arms in a salute and nearly lost his balance.

'Gilbert! Thank God, you're here at last!' A.J. shouted, his eye as hard as a sparrow's, then he swerved and nearly caused a collision. With his arm round Dolly's waist he came over.

'Where have you been?'

'Working, I'm afraid. Dolly, how well you skate!'

'Working?' Dolly said. 'On a Saturday?'

'D'you mean *I* don't skate well?' A.J. asked.

'Gilbert!'

It was Laura, bouncing over like a balloon.

'Laura!'

'We all thought you'd deserted us, where have you *been*,

no, don't tell me, the speed machine, I can see it in your face, disaster strikes again?'

'Yes, I'm afraid so.'

Gilbert felt he was a symbol of silliness. Laura laughed like a trooper.

'You poor boy, trust these,' Laura said, pointing down at her shod feet.

'I've got news for you, Laura. Very good news.'

'Yes?'

'Following the business with . . . the two ladies.'

'What business?'

'Haven't you heard about Colonel Paynter and the complaint? You must have.'

'No.'

So Gilbert told her, shouting to make himself heard above the roar of the rollers. She was aghast.

'Oh, Lord. Really? No! I didn't realise. How typical of me.'

'No, do listen, please, the Colonel didn't mind one jot, he sent them off with a flea in their ears, you'd have loved every second of it, they walked in, and the Colonel heard them out, looked them in the eye and said, "Mrs Knight is on my land, and Mrs Knight is a very remarkable artist and Mrs Knight can paint who or what she likes and now if you would both be so kind I am extremely busy."'

'The Colonel said *that*? You were there?'

'No, he gave me a verbatim account. He's obviously very proud of himself.'

'So he should be,' she clapped, 'so he should be.'

And Laura jumped up and down, her face red, her ragged skirt whirling, her unruly thatch of hair bouncing.

'And there's more to come . . . Just before I left he said he would very much like you to have a studio on his land.'

'But I can't afford one, my pictures don't fetch A.J.'s prices, you know!'

'This is rent-free for you to have as long as you like, I promise, rent-free, it's only a little shed, but I went to check it yesterday afternoon, and with a little work—'

'It's not that one on the way to Tregiffian, the one we walked past?'

It was dry, with a view of the ocean, with a sound roof, a foursquare place with room enough for a table, easels, and a chair: set up in there and an artist's hours would fly by.

'Yes, that's the one.'

Laura hugged him hard, then kissed him loud smacks on both cheeks. Smack, smack. 'Gilbert Evans, you're my saviour!'

Gilbert was very pleased for her, if a bit uncomfortable with the length and power of the hug. Laura's noise level went up as the news went round and in no time Gilbert was The Saviour, surrounded by A.J., Dolly, Florence and Joey. A.J. handed over a hip flask of whisky in celebration and Laura (to Dolly's evident delight) retold the story to Alfred. Dolly's eyes widened and she clapped her hand to her mouth and kept on saying, 'No! No, *really*?'

Florence stared hard at Dolly, then hard at Gilbert. Feeling he had to release himself, and without knowing quite how he managed it – he felt automatic as he moved – Gilbert found he had taken Florence's elbow, though saying not a word, and soon he was skating away in the middle of the rink with her. She seemed pleased. He did not speak but he had somehow disentangled himself from the crowd and was alone with her: that was the point, that was all that mattered, he had done what he most wanted to do, he was with her, he was holding her hand.

'You skate very well,' she said.

'So do you.'

As they came round past the noisy group again, A.J. bawled something and pointed at Dolly. Gilbert did not hear it, but he did see Dolly's head go back with her loud laugh.

'Did you hear that?' Florence asked, suggesting she had.

'No, what was it?'

'Only one of his awful rhymes.'

With a small shake of the head she finished the topic and smiled at Gilbert.

After a few more circuits, with Gilbert enjoying it more each minute, she came off the rink at the opposite side from the others. She led the way to a wooden bench, indicating he should sit next to her. She unbuttoned her coat, looking steadily across the rink.

'Gilbert?'

'Yes.'

'Did you feel impelled to rescue me?'

'No, I wanted to skate with you.'

'Laura is very smitten with Alfred, isn't she? It's rather obvious.'

'I think it's more that they are two of a kind,' Gilbert said.

'Two of a kind?'

'She is very devoted to Harold. That is clear.'

'Is it? I'm sure you're right. How lovely . . . to be so devoted. But in what way are Laura and Alfred two of a kind?'

'Perhaps she should have been a boy, who knows, but she obviously cannot abide stuck-up men.'

'And who could be less stuck-up than A.J.?'

'Exactly.'

'And he perhaps cannot abide . . . stuck-up women, as you call them?'

'I think that's likely, yes.'

'Hence Dolly.'

'I'm sorry?'

'This is all very reassuring, it really is.'

She leant over and touched his arm. He felt his body go taut with her touch.

'And tell me another thing, if you would. Something quite different. Do you think the only people who can understand artists are other artists? I've heard Joey say that, and as you're not an artist, I thought I'd ask Captain Evans.'

As she finished on 'Captain Evans' she smiled, so here he was sitting far away from the others and having an intimate talk with the most beautiful woman in the world, a beauty worthy of Botticelli's genius.

'No, I don't think that. It's true I'm not an artist, but the main thing is to imagine what it's like to be someone else, to stand in their shoes. If you do that you've made a big start to understanding A.J. or Laura, or whoever.'

'And Laura loves vulgar things?'

'Does she?'

'Yes, of course she does, and I must try to remember that, because it has always seemed to me difficult to despise and desire at the same time.'

Gilbert was baffled by all this.

'She loves a good time,' he said, 'that's all. That's a healthy thing, isn't it?'

'And Alfred Munnings is a good time?'

'Yes.'

'Because he breaks the rules? Whereas you do not?'

'Yes, you must know that as well as I do. He does what he likes. And he's changed everything down here, hasn't he? I've never met anyone like him.'

'I seem to hear that every day of the week!'

'Well, have you? Have you met anyone like him?'
Her eyes widened.

'No, of course I haven't. Where *would* I have done? Before you got here, by the way, Laura said something very disgusting. Something very disgusting indeed.'

'Did she? What was that?'

'Do you really want to know?'

'If it would help to tell me.'

'What she said was, she disliked being red in the face so much, that when she was young and wanting Harold to marry her she used to go into her family's back kitchen, would you believe, and touch the bullock's heart that was there . . . It was on a plate. She said it was red and bloody and slippery and to touch it, to look closely at it and then touch it, made her feel sick and go white . . . So that when she went back into the room to see Harold she was as pale as she wanted to be.'

Gilbert smiled. Florence, who had gone very pale herself, turned and looked at him.

'That is disgusting, isn't it?'

'I don't take it that seriously,' Gilbert said. 'Quite a lot of what Laura says, and what A.J. says for that matter, is really for effect. For fun. They're looking for attention, for applause, I had friends like that at school and in the army, people are always trying to show off . . . It's fairly harmless, it's circus entertainment. Believe me, there are many more disgusting things than touching a bullock's heart.'

'Are there?'

'Oh yes. Many.'

'In which case, I bow to your experience.'

Uncertain what exactly he had transmitted to merit this tone he said:

'There is no need to put it like that.'

'When I said I bow to your experience I meant it.'

'Did you?'

'After all you are the only one Alfred communicates with.'

'You mean when he was staying with the gypsies? Did you hope he would write to you?'

There was a full silence, and it lengthened. Then she stood up very deliberately and walked back towards the skating-rink. At the edge she turned and took Gilbert's arm. Moving slowly, then skilfully together, a tall and elegant couple, they passed Joey and Dolly, then A.J. and Laura going the opposite way round, then it was A.J. and Dolly again, and Joey and Laura, a skating kaleidoscope, but Florence refused pressing invitations from others on the rink. Others could swap partners all they liked all afternoon. She assured Gilbert she was more than happy to continue as she was, skating with him, she was enjoying every moment, and she would look forward to the evening with Colonel and Mrs Paynter, whenever that might be, and seeing the walled garden at Boskenna, very much look forward to it, and to further talks with him. Gilbert felt powerful and powerless. Above the rink he felt there was a shower of roses, cut short at the stalk, hanging and hovering in the air.

Later that night Gilbert took out his diary and dipped his pen in the ink. He wrote quite slowly:

A long day. *The History of the Monmouthshire Militia* arrived in the post. Boskenna with Col. Paynter in the morning. Arrived Penzance p.m., roller-skating. Puncture en route. A.J.M. and Miss C.-W. announce their engagement.

Part Three

Part Three

Sammy's Exercise Book

Last night, just before my supper was served, Laura Knight rushed along the upper landing in Jory's to tell me how everything had gone at the wedding. She had promised she would do so. However, the moment she knocked and hurried into my room, looking paler than I had ever believed she could be, I could see her news was shocking.

In a week or so, when they return here, I will no doubt find out more. Laura told me all she knew and all she could surmise. Then she added:

'And, thank God, they are coming to live here in the hotel.'

'Here!' I said.

'You'll be such a help, Gilbert.'

'*I* will?'

'Yes! Of course, of *course* you will, it's the best possible plan. Surely you can see that?'

Though less shocking, this was (if possible) even more of a jolt to me than her earlier dreadful news. The only rooms that can possibly be allotted to them – the only rooms Mrs Jory has available – are next to mine. They will be my closest neighbours; she will be next door, only a bedroom wall away. When last we spoke, admittedly some weeks ago, Florence assured me they had rented and intended to live in that house on the outskirts of Penzance. We both agreed that was a sensible plan. It couldn't go on, and a few miles would be easier for us both than a few feet. I even went to view the house a number of times to check if it was the most suitable place in the area they could hope to find, with generous studio space for them both, a studio each in fact, and stabling nearby. It was. Yet now I am told, if Laura is correct, that they will be back here, man and wife, here in Lamorna, in this hotel, on this floor – and eating at the same table.

What are they thinking of! And whose idea is it?

Before that happens, however, it is essential during the intervening days that I run through in my mind all that took place in the period between the announcement of their future intentions at the skating rink and Laura's terrible account.

One thing is clear. My diary will not serve this purpose. The cramped, small pages of the Letts diaries I use every year allow only the briefest entry for each day. Normally that is sufficient. That is my army training, and I shall of course continue as usual to record the main events in that way, while seeing this exercise book (an unused one I found in my brother Sammy's bedroom when I tidied up his things – it even has his name on the cover) as the more private account.

In the first few weeks following Florence's engagement to Munnings I felt like a lone swimmer on a surging sea. I saw next to nothing of her and nothing at all of him. This was deliberate. For reasons of pride, and with my stomach a net full of knots, I found myself unable to help Joey with any further exploration of the rock pools, even though I knew he had discovered a dahlia anemone, usually only found on the Yorkshire coast, because to see his face would be to see hers, and how on earth could we avoid the whole question? Equally, I'm afraid, I found myself unable to ride Merrilegs. I could not bring myself to ask Munnings if I could borrow the horse, even though this proved an increasing inconvenience. The daily footslogging and bicycle riding was exhausting, but I settled for that.

So, to compensate for the lost hours, I got up earlier and earlier each morning. Soon I was living in a half-world of unremitting work, a detached and driven wretchedness, a borderland in which I looked into every aspect of the estate's dilapidations. Property after property was examined. I drove the men too hard. I tidied my desk every day and reorganised all the drawers in my Lamorna office. One evening I banged my head so hard on a low beam I was dazed for half an hour but even that did not hurt. I ceased to notice, shame to say, that I was living on the most beautiful coastline in England. The great virtue of all this busyness was that when I undressed I slept and slept the sleep of the dead. Except, of course, when I had my dreadful dreams, as I still do.

She had chosen him. That was the end of the matter. For Florence I had been some moment's dalliance on a skating rink. Perhaps she saw my concern for her, and my approach (if such I had) as solicitude, and for her, perhaps, solicitude seemed a kind of slavery.

It was not difficult to avoid Munnings. He was only in Lamorna for a few very short periods in between his engagement and his wedding day. He went to London (for his Leicester Square exhibition, amongst other necessary meetings), to Hampshire and to Norfolk, from where he wrote to me.

The London exhibition of his paintings, entitled *Horses,
Hunting and Country Life*, was a great triumph. Laura
described it in those words herself and showed me an article
in *The Daily Telegraph* where the critic saw the paintings
as a 'slap in the face of the Royal Academy, as well as a
long-needed change to the landscape of English Art'. For
the opening, Florence and Laura travelled up together on
the Cornish Riviera Express, Alfred having gone on ahead
by himself. This was the first time (Florence later told me)
she had been on a train 'since the day we met', the day she
saw the man dreadfully truncated while successfully trying
to end his life.

Do most men, like me, wonder what women talk about
together, in the privacy of their rooms or in a railway
carriage? I find it difficult to picture what Florence and
Laura talked of from Penzance to Paddington. Did they
discuss the forthcoming marriage? Did they discuss Laura
and Harold's marriage? Did they discuss Alfred, the man
they both – in their doubtless very different ways – loved?
Did they sit in silence? Did they talk about art? Was I
mentioned, with understanding smiles? I have no idea.
Most men in my position and of my background are,
perhaps, rather in the dark where women are concerned.

On that first journey to London, as well as the exhibition,
there was another matter pending. Munnings himself had
to call on Mr Carter-Wood at his home to ask formally for
the hand of Florence. To put it mildly this meeting was not
(according to Laura) a great success. Munnings, it seems,
stormed in, moved through the mahogany and across the
marble, as if he was on his way to sorting out a tiresomely
overdue account with Jory at The Wink – only to be asked
to take a seat.

While sitting down, never Munnings' favourite position
at the best of times, he was informed by a very severe

Mr Carter-Wood that he had never had much confidence in artists as a bunch and saw little evidence before him to alter that view now, that artists usually failed to provide a proper home and standard of life for themselves let alone their wives and families, that his daughter was accustomed to a full allowance of privilege and had always been expected to marry well, that his son and heir, Joseph, had managed so far to waste ten precious months of his young life clambering over cliffs and into rock pools collecting even odder species of multicoloured life than artists and was so little known to Mr Stanhope Forbes of Newlyn (to whom substantial fees were being paid) that the same Mr Stanhope Forbes could not even put a face to the name of Joseph Carter-Wood, and that Mr Munnings, as a token of his serious hopes and honourable intentions of becoming the future husband of his daughter Edith Florence and his son-in-law to boot, would be expected to show willing by earning a thousand guineas before they could even consider the possibility of sitting down to discuss any dates or arrangements for the wedding ceremony.

After this point-by-point lecture Mr Carter-Wood sat back, tall and upright and thin, on his side of the wide mahogany desk, expecting Munnings to answer them point by point. Instead the red-faced Munnings stood up, reached over the desk with his right hand outstretched and said, 'Deal!'

'Deal!' he said, and off he went.

No one can know how much it pains me to record that as a way of talking about a lifelong union with Florence, but even as I write it I feel a grudging respect for the man's theatrical bonhomie, his refusal to be discountenanced and his satirical compliance. Whether, of course, Munnings' account of the interview, relayed to Laura, tallies with the facts I do not know, but at

Lamorna we have seen enough to believe it. More than enough.

'A thousand guineas!' he exclaimed to me, throwing his arms around me in The Wink while going on nineteen to the dozen, his hands and his head waving like a cuckoo clock out of control. 'Is she worth that much, Ev?' he asked, but his laughter, to assure me he was only joking, made it unnecessary to reply: a good thing, as bad blood was beginning to boil up in my veins.

When he was laughing at his own jokes, laughing at the prospect of Florence, and laughing at his own lesser nature, I noticed for the first time how sharply pointed his front teeth were. Insensitive though he usually was, after a while he saw I was tense and untalkative. He had talked himself almost dry, however, and through a yawn he said:

'So, so how's things going, Ev? The Colonel isn't overworking you, how's the house on the hill, any more dramas at the rock pools, any more shocked walkers, seems years since I saw you, when was it?'

'At the skating rink.'

'So it was, so you see I've got to get earning, one thousand no less, do a few potboilers if need be, might even stoop to a few pretty sea anemones, mind you the silly bugger doesn't realise I already have four hundred guineas from one dealer, so give me a month and we're as good as there.'

'Yes, I'm sure you are.'

The sharpness of my tone fell on barren ground.

'We'll have a great party, won't we! There'll never be a wedding like it. Old C.-W. won't believe his eyes! All of us together.'

'Laura showed me the paper, well done.'

'You saw the announcement in *The Times*? Very grand, eh?'

'No, the account of your exhibition, a triumph.'

'Oh, that. The *Telegraph*, wasn't it?'

'The critics certainly liked you this time, Alfred.'

'A pot for porridge and a pot for stew, they don't know the difference.'

I told him I did not understand. He drained his drink and smacked his lips.

'Fooled the lot of them, what do *they* know!'

'But if they *hadn't* liked your paintings you would have called them fools too.'

'Good point, Ev. You might be right.'

'But you would, wouldn't you?'

I noticed my voice was becoming querulous and high. He put his hand on my knee to calm me.

'Yes, of course, sharp point, I'm not a fair chap . . . never was. So, time for another? Yes!'

He left our table. Over in a dim corner, close to the wood fire, my eye caught two old men, regular visitors to The Wink, smoking their pipes and playing dominoes; their faces were like pickled walnuts, darkened by vinegar. They were totally absorbed in their game. Their dominoes held their minds and their hands and I envied them. At the bar two men were haggling over the price of a cow. I envied them, too.

Munnings sat down again, pushing another pot of ale my way. He already had his to his lips.

'Cheerio.'

'Your good health,' I mumbled.

'How's the billiards?' He spoke over the beer as he drank, 'Still the best, still beating all and sundry?'

'I haven't played for a good while.'

'What about Joey?'

'I haven't seen much of him.'

'Bet you were champion in the officers' mess too?'

'As a matter of fact, there wasn't a table in the mess.'

He looked round the bar, belched quietly to himself and rubbed his stomach with affection.

'Too busy, doing too much for too many people, that's your trouble, Ev, you're too good, and that's what makes me feel bad about asking you to do a bit extra for me as well. Makes me feel bad.'

'Does it?'

He wiped his mouth dry with the back of his hand, and turned his penetrating eyes on me.

'I'm off again, I always go about this time of year, sally forth so to speak, it's vital I do. Change of scene.'

'But you've only just come back.'

'That was London. London doesn't count!'

'Are you off to Hampshire and the gypsies again?'

He laughed.

'No, no, not Hampshire this time, this time it's Norfolk.'

'Ah, back to your roots.'

'Well, more or less, Norfolk and Suffolk, and while I'm away, rustling up the money to shut Mr Carter Hyphen Whatsit up, would you do something for me, something very special, which only you can do? Would you, Ev?'

As he said this he gripped my arm and held my eyes. I could hear his breathing and, in the background, the sharp click of the dominoes.

'Of course, if it's in my power.'

I wanted him to take his hand off my arm.

'Keep an eye on Blote, would you, old chap? Just for me.'

This was no bad dream. It was happening. I kept my voice as even as I could.

'But won't she have Joey, they'll have each other, and there's always Laura next door, and Harold's extremely fond of Florence, and she could—'

I interrupted myself to drink. He kept his hand on my arm, saying:

'Joey? Laura and Harold Knight?'

'Yes, they practically live in each other's pockets.'

'Oh, *come on*, Ev!'

'She couldn't ask for better or closer friends.'

'Yes and no, yes and no, but she's a determined girl, you see, does things her own way. Mind of her own. She's started to paint long hours, very long hours, good idea of course, better than thinking she'll learn much from old Forbes, who knows, maybe she's feeling competitive, thinks she has a point to prove to me, strange things, girls, and she won't ask you herself if she gets lonely, not the sort to ask for help, is she, not the easiest girl to grasp, is she, if you get my drift.'

'I'm sure,' I said stiffly, 'we'll all rally round. She's always welcome everywhere.'

He gripped me even more tightly, his nails sharp in my forearm.

'Rally round? You're not listening, Ev, are you? We're *both* . . . very fond of you. *Both* of us. You're the most honest man I know, I'm not talking about her being welcome everywhere, that's bloody waffle, isn't it, just words, you're talking to me now, you're talking to a friend.'

'I suppose I find it a rather odd request.'

'What's odd about it? I'd do the same for you. Lent you my horse, didn't I?'

'Yes, but it isn't quite the—'

'For example you could take her to the races, give her an airing, she'd like that.'

'Would she?'

'Yes, she'd love it!'

I could see this was becoming hopeless, so I agreed, and

as soon as I agreed to 'keep an eye on her' he smiled and quickly released his grip. The tension eased somewhat. Soon we were drinking more freely. We fell to talking of other matters, of the estate, horses, the new house on the cliff, fishing the stream and the news (circulating the bar) that French boats had once again slipped into the cove and stolen Jeffery's crab catch. A.J. said he'd like to fire shells at all frogs.

By midnight I was sitting in his studio, drinking.

Why do I forgive him so quickly?

It was, though, a full week before I began to 'keep an eye on her'. The weather saw to that. It was beastly: if it wasn't a deluge it was a freak gale. I often bicycled off into a morning headwind and arrived at work thoroughly soaked, wet in the foot and wetter still in the collar. There were roofs blown off at Downs Barn and Borah. Even though I also felt rotten with a series of bilious attacks I somehow managed to pull through the days. Strangely I sometimes found the wind and the rain a great comfort. My feelings and the rain fell together.

With the weather better I decided to see her not at home in the cottage but, if possible, outside Stanhope Forbes's painting school. Harold Knight assured me she was there. Suddenly the sea was as smooth as the page I now write on. My new bicycle, a Sable Singer, fairly skimmed along, and apart from a brief tussle with a yapping dog with an aversion to bicycles, the trip was a perfect dream. As I arrived in Newlyn I had a tune playing, mocking me almost, in my left ear. It was the last of the tunes I heard Florence humming to herself as we skated. I am not very good on music, a lamentable lack in my education, but I have since found out it is from Schumann's *Kinderscenen*, Scenes from Childhood. Maddened by the memory of it I hummed it later to Laura. She recognised it immediately and happily pounded it out for me on the piano at Jory's.

I stood on the far side of the road, facing the door from which I expected her to come out. I imagined she would emerge with a folder of drawings under her arm. Above all I did not want to meet her in company, least of all a crocodile of female students. As for myself I hoped I did not look too out of place and cumbrous. If Munnings was right, and she was working all hours on her painting, if she really was competing with him for glory, the chances were she would be late.

I waited and the hands on my watch seemed to stick. A tight swarm of feelings clung to my stomach. Why was I there, when I felt such resentment at the way I had been treated? Why was I there when the way she behaved towards me that Saturday afternoon led me to believe it was my company she most enjoyed? Her happiness was clearly not dependent on my homage.

Was I standing there, no doubt looking a little foolish, with my new bicycle as my only companion, merely because I did not have the strength of character to tell Munnings it was no business of mine or, come to that, of anybody else's to 'keep an eye' on his fiancée, to comply with his wishes while he made his thousand guineas and carried her off?

'Keep an eye on her.' The more I thought of the phrase, it was a damned cheek.

And, anyway, how on earth could I do that? You cannot keep someone else's love warm, you cannot love by proxy. It was far more likely, I thought, that by doing this favour for him I would simply be throwing some nuts on to the fire of my love, brightening its blaze for a brief moment or two, rekindling my hopes which would as quickly dampen the moment he returned triumphant from his

Norfolk and Suffolk sojourn. What on earth was I doing? I was not his manservant, fetching up warm water for his soothing bath!

She was there.

She spoke first.

'Captain Evans, what a surprise!'

'I was going to Penzance to shop, and suddenly realised where this was.'

It did not convince her and it did not convince me. I went on quickly:

'What have you been doing today?'

'Drawings from life . . . But you don't look very well. Have you been ill?'

I have always greatly disliked talking about illnesses, mine especially, and how could I tell her about my stomach and my sleeplessness, when she was their cause?

'Nothing much,' I said, 'a touch of this and that, but how is your life drawing?'

'Are you sure it's nothing serious, you seem to have lost weight. Let me look at you.'

I found myself unable to meet her concerned gaze. I started to walk aimlessly, talking for the sake of talking, with the bicycle between us, but whatever I asked she diverted. Indeed it was as if I had not even asked her the questions at all. Sometimes there seemed little connection between what I asked and the 'reply' she offered. It reminded me of playing tennis with someone who is either not trying or is unaware of the rules, someone who plays on after the ball has dropped out. It was only when I told her I had been prising some damaged corrugated iron off the old hut which Laura Knight was now using as a studio, that she connected with my thoughts, asking if I could find her such a place herself, saying that she wanted such a place all to herself more than anything else on earth and that if

I could provide one she would be eternally grateful to me. There was a note of desperation in her voice.

'But surely,' I said, 'once you're married you'll have everything you need?'

'In what way will I have everything? Do you believe that is likely?'

'I'm sure A.J. will provide you with the best studio anyone could wish, I'm sure he will.'

'But I want a place in the middle of nowhere. Can we search for one together? Please!'

This disturbed and excited me. We walked on.

'It should not be too difficult to find one,' I said. 'Do you know how long he will be away?'

'Alfred, you mean?'

'Yes, of course.'

Who else could I have meant?

'How would I know?'

'But you must.'

'No, I really have no idea, I have not heard a word from him since he left.'

'Oh.'

'He is not a great writer of letters. At least, not to me.'

'I suppose he has so much to do, so much to achieve, but I know how much he will be missing you. I'm sure he'll be tearing back to see you very soon.'

This rather gushed out. She stopped dead in her tracks – we were leaving Newlyn behind us now – and she looked very directly at me. Then, without further comment, she put her arm in mine, and with a small pressure motioned me on.

Her arm in mine.

'How is Joey?' I asked, my mind racing.

'You tell me,' she laughed, 'I rarely see him.'

'Nor do I these days.'

'Really? How odd! He's always "Off to see Gilbert", or that's what he says as he leaves.'

'I was wondering then,' I went on quickly, 'I was hoping rather, that you would like to go to the races, at St Buryan. With me.'

'*Horse* races?'

'Yes, it's a very popular day.'

'Really?'

'Yes, it's next Saturday . . . if you have the time . . . But I expect you haven't.'

'I would like that, yes.'

'You would?'

'Yes. Quite apart from a day out with you I would like to understand what it is about horses that makes them so appealing to some people.'

Some people. I found that phrase odd. Did she mean Alfred, and if so why not say Alfred?

As we walked up the hill, arm in arm, I explained the kind of day it would be, that I would call for her in good time and we would, if she wished, be able to see all six races. The races started after lunch, and it did not matter if she claimed to know nothing about the horses because quite frankly no one else knew much either, least of all me. We stopped to watch some dun-coloured cows bunch and huddle and heave and wallow in a puddle by a gate, nosing each other away. We walked on past some wild rhubarb leaves in full growth.

Everything was now going splendidly. There was a spring in my step and a natural sound to my voice and a wonderful prospect ahead. I could see her gliding around the paddock, I was at the races already and, so to speak, jumping the hedges at the head of the field, when I stumbled.

Looking very directly at me again she asked:

'Have you been before?'

'To St Buryan races? Oh yes.'

In fact I had just been made Vice President, but did not tell her this.

'And whose idea is all this, may I ask?'

'Whose idea?'

I felt my knees go weak as I spoke.

'Yes.'

'That I should accompany you to the races? Well, mine of course, if you want to go, that is.'

She smiled her beautiful, open smile and pressed my arm.

'Oh good, you see I wouldn't really have enjoyed it at all if I felt you were standing in, so to speak. *That* . . . I would resist.'

Standing in. No two words could have hurt me more. Though we were now approaching her cottage on a beautiful evening my chest felt airless and my feet like lead.

'Yes of course . . . I can see that.'

'And when I saw you standing across the street with your bicycle I thought . . . oh dear, he's been sent and he doesn't look at all well.'

'Sent?'

'That was how it looked, at first glance.'

'If you don't wish to go,' I said sharply, 'I quite understand.'

'No, I very much want to go, as it's your idea, very much so. Thank you. And I've been so bored. So very bored.'

'I can't imagine you bored, ever,' I said.

'Oh, I'm so bored I scream out loud.'

I smiled at this.

'You do?'

She did not return my smile.

'Oh yes. One day I'm happy, one day I'm bored, and I can't begin to account for either. It's all . . . unaccountable.'

We walked on.

'And looking back, Gilbert, it's quite a strange feeling, you see, to have given oneself away so lightly.'

'Oh, surely not? I can't believe that's the case.'

'But, then, Alfred is a genius, and there is no one in the world like him.'

I am quite sure those were the exact words she spoke, odd though they look now on the page before me. Even odder, as she said them, I could see Joey scurrying past the tubs of geraniums and into the cottage behind her back, and evidently as keen as he could be not to be spotted by either of us. Florence withdrew her arm from mine, turned to face me and smiled.

'Thank you for walking me home, Gilbert, I enjoyed it so much, and I'll tell Joey we met.' She raised her hand to correct herself. 'If, that is, he returns.'

Barely two days before the races at St Buryan a letter arrived for me at the hotel. I knew the handwriting. Once again it seemed I was the chosen one.

Dear Ev,

Dear boy! What do you say to THIS? Come on, admit it now, you did not expect to hear from me so soon, did you? I may be deemed a difficult chap but here I am, pen poised, no, not with the glorious gypsies in the hop fields of Hampshire, but far away in a rather wintry Norfolk. Back home I travelled, through Essex and Ipswich, and now reside just south of Norwich. Devoted though I am to you all in Lamorna, here is home, here I lay my head. But what specifically – when so much calls me West – brought me here to the East?

Instinct, Hal, instinct: Falstaff's instinct.

Believe me, it happened without my intervention. Suddenly I was carried away, bound upon a course, fancying myself in my Melton jacket and brown-top boots, very natty, and that course led me to a strange, unplanned reunion, yet so strange and so fortuitous it must surely have been planned. And throughout the vicissitudes of this strange reunion I have been happy to know that you are there in Cornwall, KEEPING AN EYE ON HER, as well as everyone else. Oh, you are in-dis-pensa-bull.

What a week it has been, a turbulent week! I might have guessed that Shrimp would be the cause. But, as is my wont, I am rushing headlong ahead, I have not told you about my favourite model – no, I do not mean my cow Charlotte or my paintable girl, my adorable Blote – I refer to one Shrimp.

I ran into Shrimp, fingering his glass and his half-shaven chin, in a snug little bar (where else?), with his small stack of coins placed in front of him like draughts. The very same Shrimp who stood, sat and acted as my model in earlier years until I settled (don't laugh, I am more settled than ever) near my mill in Lamorna. Being a model, is he (you may be asking) astonishingly handsome and graceful, is he a subject fit to set before a king?

No, Ev, he is not! He is rough and tough, small and artful, a villain and a brigand. He lazes with lurchers under the caravan; he haunts with harpies, snatchers and strutters. (Now do notice the alliteration, old boy! It took some minutes of mental agility to marshal those.) He lives on the road. As far as I know he knows no home, or at least he admits to none, and there is something in me that warms to that. He is a swaggerer, a braggart, a Pistol who discharges (if he has his way) upon mine host. Shakespeare would be proud of him. If I say to you he saunters up to me, mouth insolent, wearing a sleeve waistcoat with black pearl buttons, with both his hands stuck in the front pockets of his tight black cord trousers, you may also see the sight for yourself. But what no one (not even you, Ev) can picture is the way he halters the wildest, unruliest colt, or the style with which he sits on an unbroken pony, because no man ever had a more velvet hand with animals or subdued nature so naturally.

Because you are an educated man, Gilbert, and no doubt schooled somewhere posh, AND Vice President of the St Buryan races, and because I am a half-educated artist and nowhere near half a gentleman, I ask you: is it possible to be uneducated and know too much? Let me release you from your misery. The answer is 'Yes, may I introduce you to Shrimp?'

Shrimp is a wild man, no mistake. He has pure blue eyes, as clear and innocent as cornflowers, but red swollen eyelids which – it is no secret, eh? – suggest that this latter-day Pistol, this bareback rider, is partial to pint pots as well as hostesses. He also loves his pipes. Between puffs, leading the horses ahead, he says over his shoulder:

'So, Toff, where you bin?'

The cheek of the fellow! 'Toff' indeed. Where I bin?

'I bin getting myself hitched soon,' I said.

He laughed, a rather insolent laugh, as if to doubt I was the marrying kind, but I let that pass. He can see I am impatient to paint, and he is very paintable; and peacock that he is, he knows that, for males are every

bit as vain as females. He is at ease in his boots, he likes
his look in the mirror, he delights me, he inspires me,
but he is a villain. He enrages me (me, the mildest of
men). He is steeped in cunning and roguery: in fact
he is something of a fox—

Where was I? Yes—

On Monday, towards the end of the day, I told him
to take the blue caravan and horses on ahead to The
Falcon, the pub in Costessey where I planned to take
my supper. He struck up as soon as he could, pausing
only to look at my painting and say, 'That bridle ain't
right.' This made me swear. Who was this ignorant
cowhand and horse-breaker to think himself a critic!
But he was right enough. The bridle wasn't right.
It was very wrong. Still, it was a beautiful winter's
day, Monday, and what a sky there was (and you, I
imagine, were riding Merrilegs along the cliff?), and I
had at most two hours of daylight left to correct the
poorly painted bridle.

As well as a perfect day I had a perfect spot: a track
ran down to the river, and went on over an old cart
bridge, and my eye was carried to marshland with
sloping fields on either side. Between the line of
poplars I could see the tall tower of a windmill. I
worked in silent cold toil, transfixed, close to the
silent river, and I imagined it as summer, tapestried
with leaves, with scarlet fields of poppies shimmering
in the distance. And to my joy I found I could paint
exactly what I imagined! How fast the minutes go,
Gilbert (why should I always call you 'Ev'?), how
fast they go when you are working en plein air with
Bastien-Lepage presiding unseen by your side. And
by the time I set off for the pub, loaded with clobber,
the bridle was right.

Smacking my dry lips in anticipation of a pot I made my way back, arms aching, gouty foot hurting, fit only to drop, through a farmyard full of frightened hens but not too tired to miss a trick of dying sunlight on some lichen. At the inn gate, facing its fine front, I was met by the landlord, all crimson tinge with pebbly eyes, reddish-brown mutton chop whiskers and teeth that showed an inch of gum. And Trouble was brewing in those pebbly eyes!

Shrimp and the caravan had only just arrived. The facts were all too immediately clear, the landlord said, from the moment Shrimp was seen. He stood up, swayed, and fell headlong off the shafts. There he was lying still, and still dead drunk, with the front wheel stopped against his head. It was a miracle he had not brained himself. For a moment I wished the scoundrel had. He's a villain, as I said, and impervious to improvement.

'Let's teach him a lesson!' I said to the landlord.

So we carried him round to the back and put his head under the pump, and while I held the half-drowned little rat the landlord pumped away. Suddenly, shocked by the freezing water, the brigand came to life and fought like a cornered badger, kicking me with great force in the shins and told me if I f———did that again he'd f———kill me, so we pumped some more water into his filthy mouth.

I told him I'd forgiven him and hoped he'd learnt his lesson.

That was punishment enough, you might think, to make him correct his ways. (How would the Army have proceeded?) But no! On Wednesday, only two days later would you believe, he was arrested at

Aldborough Fair for using bad language and committing an assault. While I was peacefully painting
a group of tinkers, a colourful crew, he picked a
fight. Disorderly conduct. Arrest. I could not, though,
allow my model to be so detained. He is vital to my
work (and hence my prospects with Blote). I paid
the inspector a fifty-shilling fine, and all this before
a crowd which had gathered for an unexpectedly free
theatre show.

'He's lucky,' the arresting officer said, 'to have
a gentleman to pay for him.' To accompany the
payment I assured all concerned that this was a most
unusual aberration.

'Ta, Toff,' Shrimp said, raising his hand by way of
thanks when the storm had passed. The shamelessness,
the ease of his self-forgiveness, made me apoplectic.
How I needed some of your military control! If there
was one more such incident or anything of a similar
savour, I told him, that would be the end of his work
with me, and that meant the end of his money, and the
little villain does love money. He rubs his hands over
his florins, giving them his warmth, before parting
with them at an inn.

All the next afternoon he sat head down and
morose, his brow as black as sin, holding the horse
hard with his knees, as motionless as the wintry trees.
I painted as in a dream, with only the blackbird's song
and the sound of my brush, and a winter's sun to
lighten up the loins and brighten up the coat. Three
hours without a murmur Shrimp sat. How much,
would you estimate, is his skill and sympathy with
animals worth? Florins by the score! No horse I have
ever seen stood still so long. And you could smell
the pastures through the pores of the horse's coat,

the very opposite smell to bloody petrol. The long peak of Shrimp's cap covered his insolent mouth, hid those blue eyes and swollen lids, but if I told him to 'Brighten her up a bit' with a touch the mare grew in stature. He is, you see, the most important piece on my chessboard.

'Bin punished, ain't I?' he said afterwards, mooning about, hands in pockets, kicking the ground, or whistling silently. 'Bin punished good an' proper.' This time I could see true penitence. He felt sorry for himself and what he had done and I felt sorry for him.

'Tell you what, Toff,' he went on, 'this is a bloody bore. Me legs is achin' awful.' Bore or not, with his bout of drunkenness and bad language and assault he assuredly had now done his worst. There could be no continuance of his outrages.

What a lot of rot!

As I was sleeping last night in dreamful happiness, sleeping like a happy spinning-top after another successful day, I gradually awoke to the sound of a soft pounding, a thumping. It was a still night, a cold night, a moonlit night. What on earth could it be? Animals, of course, but what were they doing? Some cattle must have strayed on to the grass at the side of the inn. I took up my stick, the one with the heavy knob, and stepped out in my nightshirt. I listened and tiptoed away. Then, realising the sound was fainter, tiptoed back, and found the source, right under my caravan would you believe, and I bent down and there was Shrimp and there was a maid from The Falcon. I pulled him out by his feet, his backside white in the moonlight, and kept pulling. Painful, no doubt, but what a business, Ev, right under my caravan and the two of them under an eiderdown and tarpaulin. In this weather! Brass monkeys!

There was some flustering from the wench, a tall robust girl with a strong figure who started to punch me. I advised her to return to her rightful bed. For her part she was evidently no respecter of persons, for she kicked me as well with her sharp shoe.

'Lor!' she screamed, ''Tis only nature!'

'Nature?' I roared.

'Mind yer own bleedin' business,' she hissed. 'Who be you tellin' us what to do!'

'Off you go,' I shouted at Shrimp, who was buttoning up before belting his trousers, 'get out, you bareback rider!'

They ran off into the bushes.

After that I could not sleep. I communed with the clear night sky but in my mind's eye, I admit, I returned under the caravan and saw Shrimp pinning a well-positioned girl. Only nature? I suppose you could say so, and in the morning I most certainly felt cold porridge.

You could argue he appears a crude little hero, this Shrimp, an ill-bred little hero, and I do think his unreliability would grate on you, Ev, every hour of the day. There is abundant evidence, in this letter alone, that he needs whipping.

Yet.

Yet he has characteristic charm, and indeed leads a charmed life, and when I contemplate how indescribably stuffy, say, Mr Carter-Wood of Carlisle and London is, I wonder will I be stuck with stuffed shirts and hemmed in by stodgy people, am I marrying into a circle in which I will be strangling yawns? And when I start to think like this I warm to my little brigand,

and when I see the white hairs of the old mare on his black breeches I could sob with gratitude.

You see, I NEED HIM. The truth will out, and if that statement makes me unworthy of your friendship I am sorry, but I wish to be given no lectures on it. Too many people, I have found, have no sympathy with or fellow feeling for failure and weakness. You see, I dream of great success, I dream of fame, I dream of being a name on everyone's lips, and Shrimp is a figure in the future I paint. But I ramble, I rant.

How are YOU, Gilbert? Busy, busy, I'll be bound, and thinking of other people, while my mind is restless though my body is loitering in a Norfolk inn. Everywhere I see crossroads with glinting signs pointing me east, west, north and south, and I want to take them all. Difficult business, this life. Still, you are keeping your eye on everyone, I warrant, with your strict impartiality and your unobtrusive dignity.

Sometimes I wonder if people think I rather bagged Blote before – but no, another time for all that, and besides I call to mind your politeness in the face of improper suggestions, and I even wonder if I was wise to include herein my account of Shrimp's nocturnal lechery when you have the bright, unsullied character of a saviour.

Oh yes, I must remember to ask. How is your poor bicycle? Do avoid thorns and nails, won't you, but no . . . I won't banter on. Rather, I ask you to give the enclosed to Blote and assure you that I will see you soon.

Your good and true friend,

A.J.M.

I read his long letter twice. The second time I read it I found more than half my mind was running towards the smaller, enclosed envelope. Soon I found myself opening it very carefully, something I have never done before in my life, and an act I would only admit in the absolute secrecy of these pages. I eased it open with a pumping heart and with all the skill I could manage. BY HAND he had written on the envelope, and it was with a guilty shaking hand that I read his words.

TO BLOTE
The moments fly fast when the artist at last
  Has found himself the right spot
Box, canvases, easel and grub in a bag—
  Not even the bottle forgot!

With the hours passing by, he works on the sky
  And the faraway distance and tone:
Nobody is nigh; not a soul passes by.
  He is working at peace and alone.

But our painter of tone, who sits working alone,
  Is not quite at peace in his mind,
Which all unaware, goes straying elsewhere,
  As thistledown floats on the wind.

  His work on the spot, alas! is forgot,
As his mind strays away from the moat*
To a far different place, where it dwells on a face—
  The face of adorable Blote!

                    A.J.M.
      (Poet Laureate, Painter Laureate)

* In fact it is a valley,
But you are not Sally.
Because you are Blote,
It had to be 'moat'!

PS Essential we meet in London. Essential I take you to Suffolk. Essential I order a suit, and where else but in Southwold? Suggest you and Gilbert make the journey. Suggest it to him. I know a place in London for our Gilbert. Good hotel.

I resealed the envelope. There was no visible sign of tampering, and later that night, I placed it through her front door.

Florence was there, waiting for me.

To my mind she had never looked more lovely.

In the days before our meeting the hands on the clock walked, as it were, with boot-clogging clay. I worked hard on the estate and did extra little jobs in my rooms (new hooks on the back of my bedroom and sitting-room doors), nothing was too trivial if it passed the time, or I stared away minutes looking at the fading rug by my bed, with my fingers fidgeting and my mind racing ahead. The maid scurried out of the ironing-room and cleaned around me as if I were a statue. Would Alfred arrive back, full of his stories, on the very day before the St Buryan races? Or would she wake up unaccountably bored and scream out loud and change her mind at the last moment? I really had little idea what kind of 'mind' she had, so how possibly could I judge? What if his love poem had gone straight to her heart, affecting her in some new way that would ruin the whole enterprise? Would she refer to Alfred's proposal of a visit to London and, if so, how exactly was I supposed to fit in to such a joint venture? I would not be a pawn. Above all it was imperative I gave no indication whatsoever of having read the contents of his note to her. Each time I thought of that I blushed.

The day dawned, Alfred had not returned from Norfolk, and she was waiting for me.

She looked – the words will have to do – so beautiful. Botticelli's Florence, Botticelli's Venus.

Furthermore, there was none of the fashionable delay which some simpering girls favour in such circumstances. Jory, jingling the harness, still smelling of beer and pickled onions, carrying in his clothes what he called a 'whiff of The Wink', drove me up to her cottage in the trap. I could see Florence sitting upright in the little front sitting-room. She stood up and waved gaily. She did not wait for me to knock, but rustled past me as I approached the door, with:

'Good morning, Gilbert . . . Good morning, Mr Jory, thank you for being on time, I am so excited I can barely contain it.'

She smiled confidently and settled beside me. For the expedition to succeed I knew I had to be confident, courteous but confident. Women, I had noticed, do not like ditherers. Women, I had also recently suspected, do not like errand boys. In the stream I have, while fishing, missed many good fish through striking too late; in billiards, fortunately, I strike at the right time. We sat side by side. I had, by the way, hired Jory for the whole day. With me, even when he had a hangover, he was never ratty, indeed he was only too willing to help, partly I suspect to spite his wife – in a sense they vied with each other for my approval. Most men try to soothe their angry wives; Jory provoked his further. The other side of his keenness, of course, was that he greatly fancied a day at the races himself. And there he was driving us, with his large lower lip, his one-sided smile and his one wobbly tooth, grumbling happily, blinking his hangover away, telling Florence which horses he would give the time of day and which only a blind fool would follow. When it came to temptation Jory was both wild and tenacious. Florence listened attentively to him, then turned to me.

'Gilbert, may I ask you a favour?'

'Of course,' I said.

'It's quite a large favour and it may not fit in with your plans.'

'If I can help you, I will.'

'Alfred has asked me to join him in London, and he is wondering if you would accompany me. If you would I would be delighted. It would make all the difference.'

Jory seemed to choose that very moment to drive on more quickly.

'London? I see.' I paused, as if to give myself time to think this over. 'Go with you to London? When would this be?'

'As soon as possible. As soon as you will agree, oh, please *do* agree.'

'And for . . . how long?'

'I don't know . . . a week perhaps. Perhaps less. Would you be able to get away? Wouldn't you enjoy such a break? I'm sure you need one.'

'I could ask the Colonel . . . It could prove difficult, there's a lot on.'

'Would it be a help if I asked him too?'

The suggestion, she could see, rather put me on the spot, so with her hand hovering over my arm, she added:

'Anyway, would you please give it some thought . . . think of London!'

All the way through the narrow lanes to St Buryan she was absorbed and excited, admiring that cleanly cut hedge, pointing out the fuchsias, and did I happen to know where that path or that lane led. My eyes followed her gaze and Jory or I answered as best we could. While she spoke to Jory about the horses I examined her face. Had she done her hair differently? Had she lavished any extra care on herself, or was she natural? She was natural. I then heard her enlisting Jory to persuade me to travel to London with her.

'If *you* won't, sir, I will,' he laughed, revealing his tooth, 'if the young lady do ask me.'

From this familiarity it was, when we arrived, a small step to marking her card. Jory put a small pencil cross next to four horses, his tips. Florence seemed to pay the most serious attention to all this.

Over lunch, an excellent hamper, I tried to ask her about her painting from life but she would have none of it. Nor did she seem at all keen to talk of Alfred or to know the contents of his letter to me, while a question about her brother Joey plainly irritated her. But the sight of the horses, the jockeys carrying their crops and the smell of the animals meant that Alfred's spirit loomed over us; indeed I found his raucous presences were distributed throughout the day. It was as if I kept bumping into him. I looked at Old Jory sitting there, scratching his head, eating bread and cheese and hevva cake, and I looked at Bess, his horse, with her nose in a big hessian bag full of feed, and I thought, 'If Alfred was with us he would be painting them even as we sit talking.'

The damned man was there even when he wasn't!

I said 'loomed over us' but it was not clear to me whether Florence was as aware of his dominating unseen presence as I was, nor if she missed him at all. Surely she had not 'given herself away so lightly' that she now never even thought of him? No. More likely she was so sure of him she felt no need to refer to his name.

As soon as we had finished lunch she left, alone, to study the runners. She insisted on being unaccompanied.

'Please,' she said to me, 'it's *so* good not to be pampered and protected, and I have ample money.'

I was on my feet to accompany her, but she was adamant. She put a restraining hand on mine.

'No, thank you, Gilbert, you really are kind, but I would rather meet at the end of each race. Then I will enjoy your company all the more.'

The next few hours of pounding horses passed in a whirl. She was like an escaped bird, her eyes full of exhilaration, tension, despair and shrieking fun. On one occasion, when her horse seemed for a while about to be overtaken, I thought truly she might go mad. She ignored Jory's advice in every race and gambled the whole hog. Three times I saw her place substantial sums.

'It is essential,' she turned to me with absolute seriousness, 'that the rules do not hold us.'

There was little, too, of her promised conversation at the end of each race because she was either collecting her winnings or having her attention drawn to the next event. Excited myself by her excitement, I trailed her at a close distance, so near and yet so far. Munnings might be the lucky man but as I watched her, so animated in a way I had never seen before, I felt my life too was peppered with good things.

A moment or two before the last race she suddenly said:

'I did not think very much of his poem, did you?'

'What . . . poem?' I managed.

She looked down at her race card.

'Oh, I beg your pardon, what am I thinking of, the races are making me muddled.'

She was a substantial winner. On our way home, her mood uncontrollably elated, she tried to press a considerable proportion of the money she had made into my hands. I could not possibly take it and told her so. She said it was of little consequence to her and it would give her so much pleasure to part with it. I nodded towards Jory's back. For a while he too resisted: no woman, no lady, he said, had ever given him money and he'd been properly paid for his services by Captain Evans but, even though he had lost on every race, he arrived back at The Wink a much richer man, a man who could not believe his luck.

'I'm as loaded as a bee,' he said.

I arrived back at the hotel feeling troubled. For, as we parted, Florence reached up to kiss me on the cheek, saying:

'You will come to London, won't you? Both Alfred and I hope you will.'

'I'll ask the Colonel if I can.'

She moved back a little and looked at me.

'And let's go for a walk tomorrow. You choose which path, Gilbert, and tell me when we meet. There's so much I want to talk about.'

'Is there?'

'And there's no one else in the world, no one else I can count on, no one of your loyalty. And it was a wonderful day at the races, wonderful, and whatever happens in the future, I'll always look back on today with pleasure.'

As I sat, disturbed, on my bed and ran through all that had been said and done, I felt both a winner and a loser.

How many men, I wonder, live their lives with a woman in their minds, and that woman more alive than any reality? And for how many men living in that daily anguish is the woman in their mind another man's wife? Not that Alfred was married yet to Florence, but as good as.

The alacrity with which Colonel Paynter acceded to my request for a few days' leave was gratifying. Indeed he pressed on me the notion of staying up in town for the full week if I so pleased. I declined. Good though the workmen are I had no wish for standards on the estate to slip, although the Colonel added that recently I had looked tired and that he was sure I deserved a rest.

Alfred had booked me a room at Fuller's Hotel, near Hyde Park, and was, by way of a 'thank you' for escorting his fiancée, to pay my bill. Florence was to stay at her family home. As for Alfred's precise plans, Florence was vague, beyond that he would be meeting our train at Paddington.

Mrs Jory handed me a hamper for the journey with a disapproving pout before Jory drove me to collect Florence and be at Penzance station in time for the early train: a pleasant enough spin until some fool came tooling down the middle of the road in his Wolseley and as near as dammit had us all in the ditch. Though it was no fault of Jory's or mine I found myself apologising as I helped Florence back into her seat. Sometimes my attempts at courtesy come out as misplaced apologies.

'Oh, no,' she said, 'it's rather fun to feel one's heart hammering. After all, they're crossing the Channel by aeroplane now.'

'Cars and aeroplanes!' Jory said viciously.

After the spill Jory raced on, scattering some chickens on a bend, and soon had us nicely settled into our carriage. There were four other occupants and one of them, a sullen individual with a red nose, seemed unaccountably disgruntled at our presence and Florence's luggage.

'You and your wife,' he said, 'are not the only pebbles on the beach, you know.'

Florence smiled at me without moving a muscle. I was so flustered by the reference to my wife that I stammered out a rather ineffectual retort along the lines that I lived in Cornwall and knew quite enough about pebbles and beaches, thank you.

I had not been to London for nearly two years, not in fact since I very nearly agreed to go to Peru. Instead of being a fisheries officer in South America, at the last moment I had, however, decided to be a land-agent in West Cornwall; and thank God, otherwise I never would have met Florence nor had those hours close by her side on the train, even though she passed some of them reading Browning. I did not feel excluded or unwanted as her eyes were held on the page, her full lips slightly apart. Instead, I tried to imagine what kind of life she was expecting in her marriage, but when she put her marker in the book all I asked her about was the poem. She was surprised.

'Have you not read *The Ring and the Book*?'

I had not and told her so.

'It's a Roman murder story.'

'It looks very long.'

'Yes . . . yes, it is. But it always takes a long time to arrive at the truth, doesn't it, and in Browning all the characters have their say. Which is as it should be.'

'Is there a hero?'

'There's a heroine.' She smiled, and looked away.

'You'll be seeing Alfred soon,' I said.

'Yes, it's exciting,' she said to the window.

We arrived at Paddington half an hour late and there, pacing around the platform, was Alfred in his pepper and salt covert coat. He was not in the best of form. Furious at the delay he whisked us off towards Piccadilly.

'Is it so important to go this very minute?' Florence asked his back.

'Yes,' he said. 'You must see for yourself.'

'Where are we going?' I asked.

'The Summer Exhibition,' he said snappily. 'Where else?'

I had almost forgotten how abrupt and forceful a fellow

Alfred was. Was this the same man who so recently wrote me such full and engaging letters, letters from Hampshire and Norfolk which evinced considerable affection? Had he, not I, been in that carriage there would surely have been an almighty row even before the train left Penzance. When he is with you there seems little room to breathe. It is as if, like some chemical force, he expands to fill all the space available. Yet he showed no special pleasure in greeting Florence. I had prepared myself and stood well aside on the platform to allow the great reunion. There was none. I do not quite know how to explain it except to say that he treated us as if we were of the same sex.

We hurriedly crossed the cobbled courtyard of Burlington House, and it was on the cobbles that he fired the first shots. The walls of the Academy were packed high with paintings, sometimes three deep, and to my amateur eye they were all splendid but he was of a different mind, and immediately talking at the top of his voice. Whenever Florence spoke to me on the train, asking me about my earlier life, her voice excluded all other listeners, the soul of privacy. With Alfred it was the opposite. Alfred addressed the world.

'Good God, Blote,' he said, 'what would Gainsborough want to do with all *these*? What would Reynolds *do*? And as for Hogarth! The place should be blown up, boom, I'd blow it up, Ev, painted ceiling or no painted ceiling. And to think I have always dreaded rejection by this lot! By some ex-pert, some would-be conno-sieur with a piece of chalk, putting his X on the back of the rejects and his D for doubtful. D for doubt-ful!'

I could see the other visitors looking at Munnings as if to say, 'Who *is* that fellow?'

Perhaps unaware, and certainly unperturbed, he marshalled us this way and that, pitching his voice at just the wrong level, finding an occasional word of praise here, more often a curt dismissal there. From room to irascible room we trooped, his vapourings growing more and more excitable, as he claimed to have seen better art in wayside urinals and asserted that the Royal Academy needed a breath of fresh air more than a French latrine.

Finally, we turned a corner and with a sharp shock stood before three of his own paintings. One was of the Western hounds chasing a fox on Zennor hill. The second, *The Path to the Orchard*, showed a girl in a white linen hat and apron leading a pony along a path. In the foreground were clumps of white and crimson phlox. It was a happy, breathtaking picture. The third was *Morning Ride*. Florence was sitting there on Merrilegs.

'You see why you had to come,' he beamed. 'You see why you're here.'

Florence stood, speechless and pale, before the painting.

'Yes . . . yes I do,' I said. 'Well done, A.J. Very well done.'

He hugged me hard.

'And *you*,' he said to Florence, 'adorn the Royal Academy, and let the world see you!'

We all looked at *Morning Ride*. Florence was right; the man was a genius.

In bed that night, with the sounds of London traffic in my ears, I asked myself for the first time some unthinkable questions. Why should Munnings, genius or no genius, want to marry Florence? Having asked it once I asked myself it again. Of course I do realise that one answer is manifestly simple: any man in his right mind would want to marry her. But as I lay there, sleepless and unwilling to face my dreams, a second, third and fourth possibility occurred. Once I had allowed myself the first thought others raced in behind like waves, a rising tide of disturbing doubts, mounting waves crashing into Lamorna Cove.

That he, a wild drinker and spender, wanted and needed the financial security of her family, a family who could afford to live only in certain rooms.

That a man of his humble beginnings, a miller's son from Suffolk who felt himself at odds with the established order, wished to align himself with a rich and accomplished woman who was not only sympathetic to art but an artist herself.

That he was exacting a kind of revenge on a world that he suspected did not want him, much as he felt and expressed about the Royal Academy.

That he planned to have not so much a wife as a beautiful possession, a self-effacing subject who would not rebel, one to whom he would seem a God or hero; a cheerful welcoming face who would become the mother of jolly children. Did part of his befuddled mind envisage a wife playing bridge and eating ginger biscuits, a life of lacy parasols and sculling boats and flower-trimmed hats? But no! He could not, because Florence was no such woman. And if she was not, what exactly did Florence see in him?

My head was spinning with these analytical reflections. In the months ahead I could see Munnings behaving increasingly irrationally and Florence becoming increasingly crestfallen. I got out of my bed and paced the hot, stuffy room. I wondered what kind of night she was having at her home. I wondered where A.J. was staying.

Surely I was not thinking that all this with A.J. and Florence was only for appearances? Was it not a love match, the simple attraction of opposites? Yes. Things would work out in the long run . . . I lay once again on my bed. After all it was not my affair, it was time for sleep, and I closed my eyes.

Only for another, bigger wave to come crashing in.

Why, no sooner than his proposal of marriage had been accepted, did he go away and go about a great deal? Stay away, in fact? And, when away, why did he write at such length only to me? Again, when we left the Royal Academy that very afternoon, why did he assume the pose of the showman, a glass too much and one glass more, and launch into his pungent stories, when there were the clearest signs of distress etched on Florence's face?

Of course such night thoughts as those might never darken Alfred's door. Maybe he was simply too happy at feeling the fresh wind of success on his back, too preoccupied with the path that opened up before him to notice what he was doing? But if he continued not to attend to Florence's needs, how long would a woman so beautiful and so gifted remain untempted? To put it another way, had she trapped herself for ever by an afternoon of pique on Penzance skating-rink? Or could she, even now, retrace her steps, and if she could, would her steps be directed towards me?

Dangerous thoughts.

I tried to sleep but saw her sitting beside me in the train. I felt the warmth of her shoulder. Did the look she gave me in the carriage, and the same glance again in the Academy, did those pressures and glances encourage me to abandon self-denial and become more than a friend and observer? To become Alfred's rival? After all, it was not unknown for engagements to be broken, even at the very last hour.

No.

I knew I had to silence those threatening thoughts.

I awoke with a headache, unsure where I was, but sure that I had dreamt dreadfully. Usually I have variations of two dreams. By writing them down, who knows, perhaps I may encourage the wretched things to go away, to leave me alone. Laura Knight told me that writing them down often helps to exorcise their power. We shall see. At the moment, however hard I work to ensure an exhausted sleep, I find they come round regularly, swinging like grotesque faces on a roundabout.

Now there is a third.

The first dream: it is a hot day. I have killed someone. I have no recollection of doing the deed, and no reason for committing the act, but the person is dead at my feet. I feel sick but cannot be sick. There is no blood and no evidence. No one saw me do it. I bury him very carefully, taking precise bearings and marking the exact spot. I am, after all, a surveyor. I survey the land and make coded notes in my small pocket diary, in amongst the number of trout I have caught, the number of miles I have bicycled and the size of my breaks in billiards. I can remember no distinguishing feature of the landscape, no trees or undergrowth or footpaths. But I know exactly where I have put it . . . put *him*. When I return to check, to see if it is undisturbed, I can find no trace. It is as if I did not do it. But I did. I know I did.

From this dream I always awake very distressed.

The second dream: there is a blazing sun. I have sunburnt legs. I am in South Africa as an official war artist. I have been commissioned to record, in as much detail and in as authentic a way as possible, what I see in action. This bothers me since I am an officer and no artist at all. I am being asked to sing the leading part in an opera when I have no voice.

The place in South Africa is not specific but that it is South Africa I am clear. I know I am facing the Boers. They are bearded. They carry their rifles across their backs as they ride their Basuto ponies. It is very difficult to draw or paint

horses in full flight but I know there is a famous English
artist who can do so. I cannot remember his name. The
Boers have leather bandoliers slung over their chests. There
is a skirmish. Because I am less confident about the horses
I concentrate on very detailed drawings of the Mauser
Mod 60 rifles and Eighth Field Battery fifteen-pounders.
There are burnt-out wagons and putrefying dead horses,
but (sitting on my hillock) I am absurdly safe from the fire
all around me. The mail has just come in and I read my haul
of letters from a beautiful girl whose face mingles with the
words. Big guns are coughing and smacking. I finish my
bread, sardines and bully and drink my coffee. I sit on
my little hillock, a mound the size of an appropriate seat.
Then, with increasing discomfort and a sudden realisation
of leaping terror, I find I am sitting on an ant hill.

I awake from this one scratching myself.

But the dream I had that night in Fuller's Hotel was in
some ways the worst, and it continues to plague me.

One of my oil paintings is brought back from South
Africa and much admired. It is hung in the Royal Academy,
in a shadowy corner not unlike the place where the elegant
Florence sits on Merrilegs. Entitled *Fight to the Last Man*
it depicts heroic death on a battlefield. A young officer
is lying on the ground, his head cushioned on the hands
and knees of a comrade, and he is being given a drink,
probably his last drink. He is very young. He looks a
little like Joey Carter-Wood. There is no blood visible
and no wound. Around him are poor devils cowering in
filth. The mountains in the background are not unlike
the Drakensburg Mountains, and not unlike the Black
Mountains on the Welsh border, yet this cannot be for
those two ranges could scarcely be more dissimilar.

At the foot of the mountain range I see another figure.
Looking closely I see I have drawn with perfect skill, a skill

I do not possess, the face of my young brother, Sammy.
There is a black insect on his lips. The bite mark swells
into a mound.

From this dream it takes me some time to recover and
compose myself.

It was not easy for me to write those out.

Alfred, Florence and I were not due to meet again until
lunch so I had the morning in London to myself. Alfred
insisted upon an Italian restaurant in Shaftesbury Avenue
because 'For 1/6d. we can eat like kings.'

I shaved, cut breakfast and tubed to Hope Bros where I
got measured for a suit. By then my headache was clearing
and I was in need of coffee and a newspaper, the pages of
which were full of the strikes and of miners marching down
the Rhondda Valley, while there were fears, too, of general
unrest in Liverpool. To sit in the centre of London and
read the newspaper is to feel at the centre of the world,
and I realised how remote from the main events of the
day I had become in Lamorna. It even took me a while
to spot the difference in the noise on the streets: the horse
carriages had largely given way to motor buses, but on the
day before Florence so filled my eyes I had not noticed
this on the journey from Paddington station to Burlington
House.

One minute I was scanning the paper; the next I was
walking. In a trance I found myself pushing past pedes-
trians and going in quite the opposite direction from the
restaurant where we were to meet. I turned left and right
automatically and was through the doors and up the wide
stairs, as if guided and drawn.

There were far fewer people. Less oppressed by the
crowd I could now enjoy the still privacy of the moment.

Without anyone else nearby I could now look at her as hard and for as long as I wished. It held and moved me greatly. In my mind I was in that clearing with her, and mercifully free of Munnings, but would she ever be, that was the point, could she ever be free of the man who had so perfectly captured her in paint? Could I free her?

I heard footsteps, but I did not turn. They came steadily on. I knew whose footsteps they were, I would know them anywhere. They stopped just behind me. Usually I give little credence to outlandish events in everyday life. Indeed I tend to be rather short with people who tell me how abnormal or unearthly some of their experiences are. I spoke first.

'I wanted to come back . . . on my own.'

'I knew you would,' she said.

'But I had no intention of doing so. How could you have known?'

'I knew you would, Gilbert.'

'Because you know me?'

'Yes.'

Still I did not turn. I spoke, as it were, to her portrait.

'Where is . . . he?'

'Talking to my father.'

'Oh, yes.'

'There are so many . . . details. So many arrangements.'

'I'm sure there must be.'

'There has been a change of plan.'

My heart jumped. Was it possible? At the last minute had she stepped back from the brink? A change of plan!

'Has there?'

'We would like you to join us for lunch at home.'

I swallowed hard.

'Would you mind very much if I did not. I have some shopping to do.'

Her voice became a painful whisper.

'As you wish,' she said.

'Do we have time for a walk in the park?'

'I'm afraid not . . . there's no time for anything.'

I looked at her.

'Gilbert,' she went on, 'you mustn't. You mustn't over-rate my virtues.'

'I don't . . . I don't.'

It was as if she was on a secret mission the nature of which, whether serious or bizarre or mysterious, was quite closed to me. We turned our backs on her portrait, and at the foot of the wide staircase we parted, she to her father and future husband, I to the Army and Navy Stores, where I bought two calabash pipes, and then on to an electric bioscope theatre.

'You know I love you, don't you?' I said aloud in the darkness, but by the time I returned to Lamorna I knew, deep down, I would not attend their wedding, and I did not.

It is impossible, I now realise, to see it as anything other than premeditated; and the most careful premeditation at that. I have considered it, mulled it over from every conceivable aspect, or at least from every aspect that I can conceive. Could sudden anger have led to it? Or the onset of despair? And if so where did the despair deepen into such a decision? Was there perhaps a half-hour of unimaginable tension when it did not matter what dreadful crime was committed as long as the desired end was achieved?

No. No!

To do such a thing required precise planning, stealth and concealment, and everything planned to happen in the most intimate setting. For this to succeed there must be no hint to one's partner of what is being contemplated or coming.

There can be no question of mad impulse or rush of blood. The blood that planned this must have been cold.

Her voice shaking, her feet occasionally banging the floorboards in distress, Laura Knight told me the facts. Then, when she had calmed down somewhat, over the tea served at Mrs Jory's insistence, she started to fill in the details of the day. After the service, in St John's, Westminster, in which Florence looked 'quite exceptionally lovely', there was the reception for the guests, an extravagant affair at which Munnings spoke with considerable generosity of spirit and some skill and, reading between Laura's lines, rare self-restraint. In their rather stiff way the Carter-Woods were, Laura said, pleased at the union of their daughter and the much-talked-of artist, or at least managed to seem so. Indeed the whole day, in Laura's opinion, had gone 'well from the start, you couldn't say otherwise'.

I did not ask Laura why or how she came to be staying at the same hotel as A.J. and Blote. The same hotel! That still strikes me as decidedly strange, but then, set beside so much that is appalling, such strangeness pales into nothing.

Laura said she retired to her room in good spirits – in such good spirits that she drew, for half an hour, the curtains, washstand and water jug. Then, while thinking of going to bed, there was a violent knocking on her door. She opened it to see A.J., hollow-eyed and incoherent. She followed him along the corridor and up two flights of stairs.

Florence was lying at the foot of their bed on the carpet. At first Laura thought there had been a terrible fight, that A.J. had throttled her. She was breathing very hard, making a choking and gurgling sound as if being strangled. Her face was grotesquely distorted, the muscles in her neck taut. Then Laura knew it was poison. There was no need for chapter and verse, she had encountered cyanide before, in her younger days in Paris. She had seen its effects. It was poison, she was sure of that, as she fell to her knees at Florence's side.

Part Four

As on a Damson

'I was wondering,' Gilbert whispered, his voice more uncertain than he had ever heard it, 'do you by any chance have any books, any reference books, that is, on poisons?'

The librarian looked over his glasses, and whispered back.

'Poisons? Yes, that would be in the second Reading Room, if you—'

'And their . . . effects.'

'Of course, sir, this way.'

'I'm sorry to bother you.'

'You are not, and I know exactly where it is. Someone else was asking about this only a few weeks ago.'

He was in the Morrab Library again, the place where not many months before, in a state of high excitement, thinking he might well be the man most in her mind, he had scanned the dictionary for the meaning of 'Blote' and then the art shelves for a facsimile of Botticelli's Venus. Once again the librarian was most helpful. Once again Gilbert sat in the same dark corner, guiltily covering the book, but this time as he pulled up his chair he was a shaken man.

Around him, old men dotted the seats, single with their thoughts and their sticks.

He had seen the approach of death before: he had held Sammy's hand as he shivered and sweated. And he had seen violent deaths, but shocking though they were that was part and parcel of his life as an army officer. For that kind of death he was, in a sense, prepared if not trained. Apart, however, from seeing Mrs Paynter's dog and the painting *The Death of Chatterton* he knew next to nothing of the after-effects of taking poison, and his knowledge of his ignorance led him back to the Morrab Library. He had to know. He had to know everything, and everything he read there in the library suggested that the reality of a poisoning was far less pleasant and far less peaceful than the graceful, even elegant position of Chatterton's body in the painting by Henry Wallis led one to suppose.

As he braced himself to look for the entry on cyanide he wondered how on earth Florence had obtained the poison in the first place. He tried to envisage her in the act of purchasing it. With a chill, he realised he could. She would purchase it in a most matter-of-fact manner. But did she know, know in a specific way, what she was going to experience? Did she have any detailed idea of her proposed end?

Cyanide. Heavy though the book was, it fell conveniently open on the page.

Cyanide, he read, starves the body of oxygen, so the result of swallowing it would be much the same as suffocation or even hanging (Gilbert swallowed and nodded). This would go some way towards explaining Florence's red and swollen face, as described by Laura, and her noisy, strangled gasping for breath.

In her final moments she would find her heart beating faster in an effort to force the blood round her system, with her brain pounding from an increased pulse. As her chest heaved rapidly in the fight for breath her limbs would become numb. There would be a roaring, as of wind and waves, in her head.

At the thought of such pain running through her body Gilbert closed his eyes, hoping by doing so to see Venus delicately floating on the shell, coming steadily towards him on water so calm there seemed not the merest breath of wind to ruffle it. This did not work. He opened his eyes to the roaring, which soon gave way to blackness and unconsciousness.

How soon the blackness came depended on the individual. It was a difficult task to describe the time it took to pass from unconsciousness to death. After death, however, the stages were clear. After death all her muscles would relax, including her involuntary muscles, so that her bowels and bladder would be voided. To one entering the victim's room at this juncture the strong smell of faeces and urine would be immediately evident.

Her body would be cyanosed, with all parts of her flesh now bearing a deep purple sheen, as on a damson. Her tongue would be swollen and extended, her eyes open and staring, showing broken blood vessels or *pettachia*, a vital clue for those looking for strangulation.

These *words*, Gilbert gulped.

Pettachia was not a word Gilbert had before encountered. The word stopped him reading. He tried to push back his chair quietly. It squeaked loudly. Head bowed he walked a few paces away from the open book. His brain hammering, he once again asked himself why would a woman so beautiful and so sought-after plan to kill herself on her wedding night and in such a horrible way? Worse still, why would she choose to do so in the bed she would share for the first time with her newly married husband?

Gilbert put his hands over his face to block out the pictures. What did Florence imagine would happen in that bed that justified such a self-inflicted end, and was not to inflict this on herself also, in a sense, to inflict it on Alfred? What blow could be more damaging to the partner left alive? Did it not all smack of revenge?

When his eyes cleared Gilbert resumed his seat. He read on. The next section upset him, if that were possible, even more. With his stomach a hard painful knot, he read that within twenty-four hours of death Florence's skin would shrink, giving the impression to the onlooker – onlooker! Who could look on while this hideousness happened? – that her hair and her nails were continuing to grow after death.

Her long tresses . . . her long fingers.

A day or so later rigor mortis disappears and her body begins to decompose, turning into fluids and gases.

Decomposition.

By the end of a week, and Gilbert realised it was exactly a week now since the day of their wedding, her body would have changed colour to green and purple, the skin so loose it could, with ease, be rubbed off. Another week, and the gases forming in the gut made the stomach swell and swell until stretched balloon-tight, fit almost to bursting.

He had seen such horses, with long teeth and open mouths and bursting stomachs.

He dreaded a fourth dream, a new portrait of Florence and Merrilegs.

By the third or fourth week her body had decayed so much that her hair and her nails, her long hair and her long nails, could easily be pulled out, and her oval face was green and purple and bloated.

Gilbert shut the book and rose unsteadily. He stumbled out of the library, blinking in the sunlight and the tilting

seagulls. He held tightly on to the handlebars of his bicycle,
feeling that the more firmly he held on to the bicycle the
more firmly he held on to life, to the earth. Out on Mounts
Bay the sun reflected sharply off the sea. He cycled along.
He passed Stanhope Forbes's school and looked up at the
three huts. He climbed Paul Hill. His mouth felt dry, his
legs felt weak. After a mile or so of bicycling, his energy
and his teeth-gritting determination would pump his legs up
the slopes no more. By the gate where he often stopped to
admire the view of the sea he retched into the tall nettles.

That evening, for the first time, Alfred and Florence were to
come down for dinner. Mrs Jory, of course, knew nothing
of the wedding night. As far as Gilbert knew, only he and
Laura and Harold Knight did, and even they knew only of
the final act of the drama, not what events or motives led
to it. They could speculate all they liked, and Gilbert and
Laura did, but Florence's face would tell them far more.

'Mr and Mrs Munnings,' Mrs Jory told Gilbert proudly
over his early breakfast, would be arriving in the late
morning. Best to keep well out of the way, Gilbert thought,
while they moved in their possessions, or what few would
fit into such a small set. And while they moved in he would
not come back for lunch but stay over in Boskenna. After
all, presumably the last thing they would want at this stage
would be any kind of reception?

'Such a pleasure they're coming here, isn't it?' Mrs Jory
said, with as close to a purr as she could manage. Then
added:

'And so soon after the wedding, I'm so proud they
changed their minds, aren't you?'

She rolled her eyes and puffed out her bosom.

'Aren't you?' she repeated.

Yes and no, Gilbert thought, nodding into his tea. Whose

decision was it to live in the hotel? Alfred's or Florence's? Perhaps, for entirely different reasons, they now both wanted the setting of a hotel, neutral ground on which they could be served, a place with the distractions of daily comings and goings.

As Gilbert changed nervously for dinner he could hear the new occupants moving around beyond the adjoining wall. He heard chairs and furniture being readjusted, the sound of wardrobes opening and not closing properly, of suits and dresses being put on coat hangers. Florence and Alfred were, after all, both so well dressed. Through the wall he could also smell, or did he imagine it, oil paint and turps; and, or did he imagine this too, the scent on her dresses, the same scent that sat beside him on the train and stood behind him in the gallery.

He listened. He sat very still on his narrow bed and listened. There were mumbles, a low exchange or two, another coat hanger rattling the panel of the wardrobe, an abrupt laugh but no distinguishable words, which suggested Alfred had somewhat modulated his volume levels. His feet, however, continued to clip the floorboards. Hers made far less noise, as if she chose the carpet instead.

In his attendant silence Gilbert looked at Sammy's birds' eggs, even turning a few over with as light a brush as possible. What clothes would she wear at dinner? he asked the eggs. How would she look? Would she be terribly damaged? How would she behave? For her to be at the same table with Alfred and Gilbert would be – but no, that was to suppose he himself was in some sense special or chosen. He put away the eggs, with the exercise book safely beneath it, and hoped he would not hear their bed when they both were in it.

He stood up and checked his hair and his tie. He checked his watch, then went downstairs to await their arrival. It was not a long wait. Gilbert rose to his feet as she came into the dining-room just ahead of Alfred. Dressed in a silk blouse and blue skirt she walked, very upright and poised, with her hand held out in greeting.

'Gilbert.'

The hand he felt in his was steady too, steady and warm. Her skin was as clear and pale as it had ever been, but healthily so. There was nothing he could see in her bearing or her manner to suggest she had so recently been so close to death. Her hair shone, her eyes were clear, there was no sign of . . . what was the word . . . no *pettachia* in sight.

In those split seconds, seconds in which he seemed to live more than in many whole months, with his hand in hers, his mind jammed. Are you feeling better? You look so well. Forgive me for asking, but what did you say to each other when you recovered consciousness, what did you say to each other the next hour, and the next morning, and the next night? How long are you planning to stay here? Sitting next to Alfred, did you read Browning on the train down from London? Are you keeping the studio near the mill? Will you come and see the painting hut I have found for you? Did you come here to the hotel to be next to me? Because you could both appeal to me as a friend, but give me your own side of the story?

Gilbert need not have worried. Alfred, the picture of rosy good living, gripped his hand and elbow.

'So, what's been going on, Ev, and what's for dinner?'

They could have been old friends or officers meeting up for a weekly dinner in a familiar club, which in one sense they were.

'Oh the usual, you know. This and that, this and that.'

Gilbert helped Florence with her seat, bending forward slightly to slide it under her, with his face close to her shoulder. He breathed in, and again, to be sure he wasn't imagining the scent. Yes, it was the same.

'Paynter pushing you too hard, asking too much as usual?'

'No, it's been rather slack at Boskenna, to tell you the truth.'

'Anyway,' Florence said, 'it's wonderful to see you.'

'Slack? Don't believe you!'

'Do tell me about this new house,' Florence went on, 'we saw it this afternoon.'

'Coming on fast, isn't it?' Munnings said. 'Marvellous for seascapes, if it's seascapes you're after.'

'Is it for you?' Florence asked. 'The house?'

'Me? No, no . . . It hasn't been sold yet.'

'I told you, Alfred.'

'Are you interested in it?' Gilbert asked.

'Might be, might be. Doubt it, don't see me settling here, so read us the menu, Blote, there's the girl.'

Florence picked up the menu. A touch of colour came up her throat.

'And since you're in charge of everything, Ev, on the walk we were on just now, never seen so many pieces of paper and orange peel and matchboxes just strewn all over the place . . . see it's cleared up, will you?'

Alfred laughed his only-joking laugh and smacked Gilbert's shoulder.

'Good to see you, really is, good to have a bit of civilised company.'

'Are you keeping on the studio?' Gilbert asked.

'Yes, and the horses. All as before. I'll work down there.'

'Soup,' Florence began, 'cold lamb, mint sauce, rhubarb and cream.'

'What sort of soup?'

'It doesn't say.'

'I'll ask Mrs Jory,' Gilbert said.

'Felt like some roast pork,' Alfred said, drumming the tablecloth with his fingers.

'Do tell her, she'll happily provide that tomorrow. She's only too keen to please.'

Florence turned to Gilbert and spoke in a voice only for him.

'You've heard Joey is to leave?'

'No, no, I had not . . .'

'There's no appeal, I'm afraid, Papa is adamant.'

'That's very sad,' Gilbert said. 'I'll miss him dreadfully, I really will.'

'Never very interested, though, was he?' Alfred said briskly, leaning forward. 'Not really, bit of a dabbler, wasn't he, preferred the seabed.'

'Not originally,' Florence said.

'And his other beds,' Alfred grinned, flicking out his table napkin.

'What . . . other beds?' She looked sharply at her husband.

'No, Ev, never very interested once he'd met Dolly next door. And . . . what's her name, Prudence. Hammer and tongs, I heard.'

Gilbert looked at his fork.

'Hammer?' Florence asked. 'And tongs?'

Alfred stared at Gilbert. Gilbert stared at the table.

'Don't have to spell it out for you, Ev, do I, point being, my biologist brother-in-law has been rogering Dolly for months, and those who don't believe it only have to ask Laura, she should know, and I can't say I blame him, either, can you?'

'We will not involve Gilbert in this!'

Gilbert fervently hoped she would not now ask Alfred

what rogering or hammer and tongs meant. Florence's fingers twisted the wedding ring on her finger.

'And no,' Florence continued in a firm, even voice, 'I won't be asking Laura or anyone else because I don't believe you.'

'Suit yourself, my love,' he said standing up. 'Anyway, I know what I think and I know what Ev thinks, and we think it's long past time for the men to have a drink.'

'But isn't this a temperance hotel?'

'That's what you were hoping, my dear, but it isn't . . . not since we arrived!'

He strode out to find Mrs Jory. Florence waited for his feet to die away then swiftly closed the door.

'Will he succeed?' she asked.

'I expect so. Have you settled in?'

'It's a great comfort for me to have you there.'

'There?'

'Next door along.'

'Oh . . . oh yes. Good.'

He smiled nervously at her. They nodded to each other.

'Florence . . . You look well. Very well.'

'Better than you expected?'

Gilbert swallowed.

'Yes . . . much. But you must . . . you must—'

'Gilbert,' she cut in with slow emphasis, placing her hand on his, 'do not ask what happened.'

'I won't. I wasn't going to . . . not for one moment.'

'Ever!'

'But Laura and I, we can't understand . . . when so many people love you, how—when you have so much ahead of—'

'*Promise* me.'

He looked at her, searching her face.

'I promise. If you promise never to do it again.'

'I promise.'

She smiled as if to close the chapter, but left her hand on his.

'And I am sorry,' she said, 'about the walk in London. Very sorry.'

'It wasn't your fault.'

'I should have been stronger. I knew it at the time.'

'You had no choice.'

'I had a choice ... and I made the wrong one.'

'Did you?'

'And you had a choice. But you didn't feel strongly enough.'

'How can you say that?'

She shook her head.

'You didn't ... not strongly enough.'

They both listened for his returning footsteps. They did not come. Gilbert spoke next.

'But you had made your decision.'

'And I will keep my side of the bargain. That is what I must do. And now we must talk of something else.'

She withdrew her hand. There was a silence.

'Will you return to Newlyn for your classes?'

'No ... I shall paint wherever I can.'

'I have found a place for you ...'

'A place! For me!'

'I'll take you there whenever you wish.'

'How far? Oh do tell me.'

'It's not far, but you could easily miss it, it's sheltered from the wind ... I think you'll like it. I've had the men working on it.'

'What a fool I am!'

She closed her eyes, then opened them as if she had, in that few seconds, taken stock.

'Thank you. Thank you. I'll keep going.'

'I hope it's a spot you can work in, the hut.'

'And we'll see a good deal of each other, Gilbert, won't we?'

'It will be difficult not to.'

His words came out stiffly. She did not deny their force. Instead she started to reach her hand across the table, then stopped. He saw her wedding ring.

'And . . . another favour. What Alfred said about Joey . . . it's not true, it can't be . . . I want you to know that.'

'Does it matter . . . does it matter so much?'

'Matter?' She withdrew her hand to her lap just before the door opened.

'Told you,' Alfred said in his spry way, 'not a problem, bottles coming, bottles plural, Mrs J. said it was the least she could do in the circumstances. "This calls for a celebration," she said, how about that, Ev?'

'Indeed it does.'

'And the soup's tomato.'

When Mr and Mrs Munnings retired to their rooms Gilbert bade them goodnight but he did not follow them up the staircase. Instead he walked slowly up the steep lane, hands on hips, breathing in the night air and the scent of dog roses. He passed the low walls of the unfinished house on the cliff, then cut across through the bracken and fern to the clifftop.

It was a clear night, with a half-moon above the Lizard. He sat for a while on a rock, breathing deeply in and out, hoping the air would refresh his fuddled mind. For a second a white band of surf below suddenly assumed the silhouette of a rearing horse.

'I am not sure,' he said to the moon and the sea and his cigarette, 'I am not at all sure how much I can take of this.'

In the Studio

Some days later, days in which Gilbert had found few chances to speak to Florence beyond the normal courtesies, days in which he had glimpsed little more than her back going along the landing, Mrs Jory beckoned him on the stairs. Asking Gilbert if he wouldn't mind stepping into her room for a minute, she half closed the door and gave him the look of a woman who knew more than she cared at the moment to communicate.

'Wonderful to see, Captain Evans, isn't it?'

'What is, Mrs Jory?'

'Mrs Munnings.'

'Yes, it is.'

'I've never seen a happier woman, not in all my days.'

'Haven't you?'

'I have not, no, have you? It quite restores one's faith, it does.'

'I'm glad to hear it,' Gilbert said, at the beginning of a sidle towards the door.

Mrs Jory smiled and moved an ample upper arm into the opening he had spotted. In moments such as these Gilbert could see why her husband called her 'that there woman'.

'When you see it, Captain Evans, you know it, believe me, sir, I've known the other side of the coin and this woman is close to the man she loves. Close.'

Gilbert found nothing to say either way, which Mrs Jory took as middlingly normal for a man when such weighty issues were under discussion. It could be taken as read from her eyes that this morning she herself had more than a few moments free and she was more than happy and willing to elaborate, and elaborate she would.

'And she's eating so well, that's always a good sign.'

'Is it?'

'Oh yes, that is a good sign, and it's a privilege to spoil her, and why not, it's not often one is in a position to look after a lady of her . . . quality. You weren't in last night but she enjoyed the roast pork, she did that, every mouthful, and the crackling.'

'And the crackling? Oh, that is jolly good.'

Mrs Jory raised an eyebrow to see if Gilbert's last remark was in the appropriate spirit, decided it was, and went strongly ahead.

'It's the second time Mr Munnings has asked for his pork and he fair wolfs it down, does it proper justice, and last night she's glowing next to him, it's the Cornish air of course, because when they first arrived she looked a bit . . . London round the cheeks, didn't you think?'

For 'London' Mrs Jory always reserved an emphasis of special distaste.

'I suppose she did a bit, yes.'

Though Mrs Jory preferred the curtains in the hotel pulled to protect the carpets from the strong Cornish light, she always claimed, in her proprietorial way, that the Lamorna sun and the Lamorna air were bracingly good for one.

'Mind you, when I did see what he's got in their bedroom, well it wouldn't be my—'

At this point, stopping as short as a runaway train could, Mrs Jory inwardly censored further detail, unaware that for the first time in the conversation Gilbert's attention was fully engaged, though he just managed to mask this.

'What . . . what has he then, in . . . the bedroom?'

Mrs Jory closed her eyes and shook both her head and her forefinger.

'No, it's not for me to say, sir, I shouldn't have spoken, to you it might seem quite . . . but there we are, there's no accounting for . . . we're all quite different, but I know I'd be happier without it, and if you'll excuse me, sir . . . oh, and will you be in for supper tonight?'

'No, I'm afraid not.'

'Oh. Oh. Very well.'

'Nor tomorrow night. It's one of those spells at Boskenna, we have them sometimes, working every hour that God gives us.'

'There's no cause for dissatisfaction I hope, sir.'

'No, good heavens, no. You don't happen to know if Mrs Munnings is in at the moment, do you?'

'I really wouldn't know, she has been going up to Mr Knight's most mornings, he's been doing her a fair bit, so she said.'

'Has he?'

'But I do know Mr Munnings is away.'

'Away?'

This time his tone betrayed him.

'Yes. Went off very early this morning. And without his breakfast.'

'For the . . . day, d'you mean?'

'Oh, no, sir . . . Didn't know exactly when he'd be back,

he said. But,' she smiled and closed her eyes and nodded, 'I'd be surprised if it was long, wouldn't you?'

Aware that she offered a gentler, more predictable life, Taffy quickly transferred his affections to his new mistress, and the little dog accompanied Florence and Gilbert on their walks. While Alfred was away (and he was away much longer than Mrs Jory expected) the three of them were often to be seen, with Taffy in the lead, going through the wood to the waterfall, then crossing the road and up Rocky Lane, and weaving around the Merry Maidens, the prehistoric circle of stones; they were spotted together sitting at a discreet distance with their backs against a stone arch, then at the Neolithic burial chamber, then sitting on a stunted, gnarled oak, split with age; some evenings they roamed through the heather or waist-deep in ferns throwing sticks for Taffy to bring back.

The walk Florence most wanted to do with Gilbert was all the way to Mousehole, but crossing the rutted farmyard at Kemyel Gilbert suddenly stopped her. Oblivious of their presence, a man with two buckets of pigs' food swinging from a yoke across his shoulders splashed the rough path close to Florence's shoes.

'I'm sorry,' Gilbert said.

'It's not your fault . . . he didn't see us.'

'Do you want to go on?'

'To Mousehole? Of course I do.'

'We have to go very close to the cliff face, it's quite dangerous.'

'Good!'

'You like danger, don't you?'

'I always feel very safe with you.'

It took them an hour along the coastal path, an hour spent watching their feet and watching the sun and watching the clouds slide across the headland, an hour watching small boats below and the birds skate and strut. They rested for a while at the coastguard lookout, with rabbits hopping in the heather below, and steamers spouting black smoke on the horizon. In the midday heat they heard the tiny snaps of gorse beans, and for long periods they did not speak. They enjoyed this silent companionship, as if there was an underground river they were both instinctively following. Gilbert, though, preferred to keep moving. Simply moving took some of the churning from his body. Because Alfred was away she spent most afternoons painting in his studio by the mill, after mornings sitting for Harold Knight.

'Your hut will be ready tomorrow, you'll have a place all of your own.'

'Tomorrow? Tomorrow! Why didn't you *tell* me!'

'I wanted it to be right for you first.'

'You secretive thing!'

'I'll tell you where it is, exactly, and we can meet there if you like. Around four?'

'Tomorrow at four, I'll be there.'

He made her repeat his instructions and she walked on, as close to skipping as he'd seen her. Because she was Mrs Munnings and everyone in the district knew she was Mrs Munnings, Gilbert made sure he kept his proper distance from her as they went along, except when she crossed stiles or stepped over stones in a stream. If she needed his help then, or to open a broken gate or gingerly to negotiate a sloshy path (or to avoid splashing pigswill) he took her hand, her long fingers firmly pressing his. On one occasion she kept hold of his hand, long after it was needed, and sat on a fallen tree with her shoulder hard against his. The tree sloped down in his direction. She did not adjust her position. The sinews in his neck were taut. He wanted to tell her he loved her, but he could not. He must be content with discontent. He told himself the best apples were always out of reach. He had never known such painful pleasure, such deep-reaching feeling, as he felt on those afternoons. That may sound as if Gilbert's spectrum of pleasure had been narrow but to have known a large number of women was, he suspected, no guarantee of finding what he found on that fallen tree, perched on the edge of a remote, poor farm.

Their silence was broken at last by the sight of a pack of hounds running past the far side of a distant field, followed by some hard-riding huntsmen strung out in a long, tired line.

'Are those,' she said, standing up, and pressing down her skirt, 'the hounds Alfred rides with?'

He leant forward, resting his elbows on his knees.

'That's the Western all right. No one else hunts this district.'

'Shall we go on?'

'What do you think?'

'Perhaps we should go back?'

They looked ahead and they looked back and they looked at each other, and they did not know which to do.

Tap tap tapping on the high high road. Just before tea time, singing at the very top of his voice:

> 'You can only wear one tie,
> Have one eyeglass in your eye,
> One coffin when you die,
> Don't you know!'

Alfred returned triumphant and happy. Panama hat tilted, face tanned like a gypsy, he let his assertive sound echo briefly down the wooded valley, and over the flat water lily leaves, and then he cleared his throat and recited his new one on Titian. The new one on Titian he'd picked up only the other night while passing through Plymouth, and he liked it enough to repeat it aloud to all and sundry or, as in this case, to the privet fence and to the gooseberry bushes and to the currant bushes on the edge of Lamorna:

> 'When Titian mixed his rose madder
> His model he placed on a ladder.
> Her position to Titian suggested fruition
> So he mounted the ladder and had her.'

The village, while not hearing every precise artistic detail, certainly heard his coming. His trap was full of new paintings, carefully strapped down and covered with tarpaulin. The village heard him bursting into song and cursing the flies, flying down the slope and rounding the steep curves, forcing a black Minorcan cockerel to scurry to safety.

Alfred held the reins high. He peered over the hedges, hedges sprinkled high with fine white dust. He was excited, with a thrill of expectancy in his sharp eyes. He had not been at his best, he knew that, but now he would put things right with Blote, put those early weeks of marriage behind him. The last few miles he had been thinking a good deal of his Shrimp and of the dark-haired Hampshire gypsies and of his paintable girl. Painting had its sorrows, he knew that, as did life, but now, now for the joys. He felt his face. His skin was fresh and smooth. His eyes were clear. From now on she would be happy, and he would make her so. It might all have been his fault, but the present state of affairs could not continue, that much was obvious. He checked the knot in his bow tie to see if it was just so. It was, and his blood was full of crescendoes. He waved to the men sitting outside The Wink and he passed the mill pond and turned into his clearing.

Whoa!

On the back, as well as his paintings, he carried a basket-covered stone jar of ale and a cold rabbit pie embedded in sparkling jelly. Just thinking of it made his juices run. And had not Melbourne Art Gallery just offered him five hundred guineas for one painting? 'FIVE HUNDRED!' he shouted to the studio. That made the juices run, too.

FIVE HUNDRED.

Florence stiffened. By the time she heard the hooves and the wheels bumping over the rutted lane she knew it was far too late to leave. She felt a flush of panic on her throat but there was no hope now that she could lock the studio and be gone through the trees without being seen. The only way out was the way he would come in. She must simply continue with her painting. She heard his feet banging up the stairs, heard his sound of bemusement at finding the door open. Heard him stop.

'Oh!' he said, 'Oh ho.'

He could not believe his luck.

'Well, well, well.'

She turned slowly but did not stand to greet him.

'I wasn't expecting you. I'm sorry.'

'My fault,' he beamed, 'my fault. I should have written, my dear, but then I'm never that sure.'

'I hope you don't mind, Alfred.'

He stepped inside the doorway and put down the jar and the pie on the table. He beamed at her.

'Mind? Mind? Why should I? What is mine is yours, and what is yours is mine.'

The aptness of that stole up on him. Sometimes he surprised himself with his aptness.

'You did say I might use your place. It's the last time I will, I promise.'

'You can use it whenever you like. You know that.'

'No, this will be the last time.'

He walked towards her, his riding boots clipping the boards as he came. There was no escape.

'You look well, very well. Better than I have ever seen you.'

'Thank you, Alfred. I feel it.'

'Very well indeed . . . you really do.'

He grinned at her. She looked back at her painting. He took up a position close behind her. His breathing told her he was studying the canvas, studying her painting. She knew the sound of his nostrils so well.

'Where is this?'

'It's the farm . . . over at Kemyel. Towards Mousehole. Do you know it?'

'You've been over there? Good . . . good. And I like it. Fine stuff. Bolder. Yes!'

'Is it?'

'*Much* bolder. And I like the fallen tree . . . the way it lies. A good setting.'

'I am glad you like it.'

'I do. I do like it, Blote. I like it very much.'

He put his hands on her shoulders. Then on her neck. She felt small and she shrank. She swallowed and closed her eyes. He stroked her neck. She stood up, slightly dazed and moved away. He took her shoulders and turned her round to face him.

'I'll have to be careful,' he said, smiling at her.

'Why?'

'Your painting. It's good. It's very good. I'll have to watch you, won't I?'

'Will you?'

He undid the top button of her dress, his fingers jabbing her neck. She shrugged him off. He pushed her arms roughly and undid more of her buttons in one pull.

'Let's see you,' he said. 'Let's see the beautiful Blote. You're . . . better than any painting.'

Florence sidestepped a little towards the front door but he was on her with another light, playful laugh.

'There's no rush! No rush that I can see.'

'I have to go. I must go, I must go *now*.'

'Go? But I've only just arrived!'

He told her she was a beauty. She begged him. He said it was long past time.

'Ask any man,' he said. 'Let's see more of you! What's yours . . . is mine. Let me see . . . more of you!'

She pushed him in the chest. He pushed her back. Half timidly, half insolently he faced her, and rolled up his sleeves and pushed her down on to the floor. She scrambled away, gathering her skirt around her, moving her back to the wall, her knees bent and her feet poised ready to kick him.

'Stay there!' she said.

He raised his eyebrows at the fun of it. He liked her so spirited.

'Oh, really?' He laughed, kneeling above her, unbuttoning his trousers.

She turned her head away. He pulled at her hair to loosen it. He said he loved her, he said it incessantly. There was a brief struggle, in which he laughed as if in horseplay; she scrambled away and tripped on a roll of canvas. He pulled her back and turned her over. He was very red in the face as he forced her down, trying to push open her legs. Her fingers tried to pull away his forearms but she failed. She could see the hairs on his arms. She could smell the warm beer on his breath. He told her to stop whining. With his left hand he pulled at everything he could get hold of, with his right he pulled at the top of her stockings. She bit his left hand. He laughed, and said she could do it again. He put his left hand in her mouth.

'Go on, I liked that! Do we have a little vixen here?'

He knelt above her, pulling at her knees, pulling at her stockings, pulling her towards him and trying to do all these, fumbling and forcing, and staring above her head with piercing eyes and baring his teeth and telling her to do what she bloody well should, because that's what bloody women do, ask Shrimp, ask Shrimp, ask ... and then ... and then ... he seemed to be shot and he very slowly crumpled away, moaning, curling over and folding into himself. She heard him hit the floor. He held himself and half pulled at his trousers. She could not see him but she could hear him, his mouth mumbling close against the floorboards.

'You're useless. Useless ... You ... cow. Worse than useless.'

She heard it as she ran up the clearing, with Taffy chasing after her. She ran and ran.

Useless. Worse than useless.

In the Painting Hut

There was a list of things Gilbert wanted to check before Florence arrived there at four. He was, however, delayed a good while in the walled garden by an irritatingly slow and wandering set of instructions from the Colonel, so he had to hurry along the headland for all he was worth. He did not wish to be rude to the Colonel but he hated keeping anyone waiting, least of all Florence and least of all today. The men watched him running off into the distance. He did not wish to be rude to Laura Knight either, but when he saw her across a field he pretended he had not. There was no time to be lost.

First, the roof: the recent heavy rain proved that it leaked a little in the corner and seeped steadily down the back wall. The damage this could do to her canvases was incalculable. This, he was assured, had been corrected, and he wanted to be absolutely sure. Secondly, he'd told the young carpenter to take down a sturdy table the Colonel had kindly spared. The lad, though, had a memory like a sieve and Gilbert was not convinced this would have been carried out. Thirdly, and above all, the hut needed to be made secure, with a new lock as well as a bolt on the inside. Especially for women in lonely places that sense of security was essential.

He slowed to a walk. His breathing eased. There was no sign of Florence. Kicking away some sheep droppings he took out the new key. It turned easily and satisfyingly back and forwards in the lock (good); there was a firm bolt fixed on the inside (good); the Colonel's table fitted very neatly against the side wall, looking as if it belonged there (good); and the afternoon light came strongly in the wide, generous window. All this made for a warm welcome. (Very good!) Gilbert took out a coat-hook from his pocket. He had time to screw that on before she arrived, and he enjoyed the feeling of the screw biting into the wood. He rubbed the sweat from his forehead, and stepped back. Now she could hang her coat on the back of the door. He looked round from roof to floor.

What else?

What else could he do?

Some cobwebs on the window caught the light. He wiped them away. His eye picked up a dead starling, lying on its side with its beak open; he threw it out. He brushed his jacket sleeve over the windows again to make quite sure all trace of cobwebs had disappeared, then he wiped his jacket sleeve. He peered out. Still no sign of Florence, but the second Gilbert sat on an upturned box to survey a job well done, directly above his head a seagull landed on the roof and scrambled noisily around, a sound soon mixing with a barking, excitable dog and running feet and he pulled open the door to see Florence half running half stumbling her way towards the hut.

'What's happened?' he called. 'What's the matter?'

Taffy leapt around Gilbert, circling him. As Gilbert rushed to meet her she stopped dead, panting, her hands stretched out, but not in greeting, stretched out, palms facing him, warning him to stay away, telling him to keep his distance.

'What's the matter?'

'No!'

She shook her head, gulping and sobbing.

Gilbert moved forward slowly, with the dog still leaping madly up and down at his elbows. His voice was very controlled.

'It's all right,' he said, 'it's all right.'

But Florence did not move. Her eyes threatened him.

'No . . . no . . . no!'

'Whatever it is, it's all right . . . you're all right. Whatever it is.'

Some instinct made him stop. Instead he took hold of the dog, calming and comforting the dog, patting the dog, while keeping his eyes on Florence. She was now on her knees about ten yards away, with her hair all over her face, fumbling with the top buttons on her dress. He allowed another minute to pass. He did not move. He could see smears of paint on her hands.

'Where have you come from? What is this?'

She shook her head violently, unable to do up her buttons.

'No!'

Another minute and she was breathing more normally. She continued struggling with her buttons. He lowered himself on to the grass but moved no closer to her. The dog looked at Gilbert. Gilbert watched the tears dry on her face as she shook her head firmly from side to side in a metronomic way.

Even before the tap on his door Gilbert had heard the upper landing floorboards creak and the feet stop right outside. There was a pause, as if in consideration.

There were two soft, questioning taps.

Tap tap.

'Come in.'

'I saw your light on, I'm sorry, I hope you don't mind.'

'Of course not.'

Gilbert straightened up in bed.

'Can't you sleep?'

'No.'

'Nor can I . . . but then I haven't had a drink. Not one.'

'I've been writing my diary . . . and reading.'

'Ah. Ah, yes.'

A.J. stood just inside Gilbert's room. He was in his purple silk dressing-gown. He had high spots of colour on both cheeks. His voice, when it came, was an apologetic whisper.

'May I . . . sit down?'

Gilbert got out of bed.

'Of course. I'll just move these.'

'You keep a diary? I didn't know. So you jot down your thoughts? Is that . . . what you do?'

'Not always. Only when there's something to say. Often it's very little.'

'Interrupting, aren't I? As usual.'

'No, no . . . Of course not.'

'Reading too? Eh? Improving your mind?'

'No . . . browsing, you know . . . nothing too heavy. When did you get back?'

Alfred's voice and his eyes were suddenly suspicious.

'Blote didn't tell you? She said she bumped into you.'

'No, she didn't tell me.'

'This afternoon . . . yes. This afternoon.'

'Everything go well?'

'What?'

'With your painting trip?'

'Oh? Oh, that . . . Yes . . . very. Lot done . . . Can't complain. Can't complain at all.'

Alfred slowly rubbed his knees with his hands and smiled uncertainly at Gilbert. There was a long pause before he spoke again.

'You weren't in to supper. I was . . . hoping you would be.'

'No, didn't feel like it . . . to tell you the truth my tummy's not been in the best of shape.'

'Anyway, Ev, wanted to thank you for all your help . . . way beyond the call of duty . . . she's delighted.'

'This is to do with?'

'The place . . . the hut. She tells me you're meeting her there tomorrow. To show it her.'

'Tomorrow,' Gilbert said quickly. 'Yes, yes.'

'She's asked me to . . . confirm it's fine . . . She can't wait to see it. Oh, and she said . . . four o'clock is fine. She's . . . as pleased as can be. Good man, Ev, you're a friend!'

'I'm glad.'

'You really are. In so many ways.'

Gilbert's mind clambered over these developments. He felt he was being pulled over a divide into deceit.

'It really was no effort.'

'Really? No effort at all?' Alfred repeated very quietly. Gilbert said nothing.

Alfred tapped the table.

'You're the only one I can talk to, you see. The only one I can trust. Don't mind me saying that, do you?'

'No . . . I'm glad.'

The hotel felt very still. Four o'clock tomorrow? And why, why on earth had she sent Alfred in with this? The silence lengthened. Alfred rubbed his knees.

'Anyway . . . I'm not allowed to go there . . . just been

told . . . that's been made very clear tonight. Crystal clear. That's women, eh? Hut's out of bounds.'

With one eyebrow raised he smiled questioningly at Gilbert. Gilbert did not know what to do. He had to say something.

'Of course she may find it too lonely out there . . . after a while.'

'Oh, lonely spot, is it? Very intriguing . . . but don't tell me where it is, don't, she says it *must* be a secret. Know what women are, over secrets, they live on 'em!'

'Do they?'

'Beyond me, they are.'

'As long as she finds it to her liking.'

'So, what is the Captain reading? Poetry, I hope? Ballads, I trust?'

Alfred leant down and picked up the pile of books from the floor, his eyes on the spines.

'*History of Nigeria . . . Nigeria, Its Story, People and Religion . . . Cambridge Natural History, Vol. IV*. Well, I don't call this lot light reading, Ev, do you? Not exactly *light* now, is it, Ni-jeer-i-a? Where on earth d'you get these dusty tomes?'

'Penzance, from the Morrab. The Morrab Library.'

Alfred opened the cover of each to check. His hands were shaking slightly.

'So you did, so you did . . . But why? That's the point.'

'I'm interested in West Africa.'

'Are you? Are you indeed?'

'I always have been.'

'Have you? Is that your secret, eh? Everyone's got a secret. Did you know that?'

'I suppose I've always liked other peoples and places. Different cultures . . . different races. For a while I considered living in Peru. Very seriously considered it.'

'Peru?'

'Yes.'

'Good God! Peru? Good God. Do you have a cigarette?'

'Of course.'

'Nigeria? Peru? Amazing chap, Ev, you really are.'

'Well, *you* like going off on your own, A.J. You've got the wanderer in you ... riding away on the open road ... you're away more than you're here, aren't you, you disappear for months.'

'Yes, but that's Norfolk, not amongst the nignogs ... not in Peru. I mean, Hampshire's Hampshire, isn't it? You know where you are in Hampshire.'

He laughed quietly, then coughed on the smoke. His face darkened.

'God, Ev, I've just thought. You're not ... leaving us, are you? You're *not*?'

'No, I'm not.'

Munnings coughed and coughed, till the blood vessels swelled full out on his forehead and temples.

'You wouldn't!'

'I have no plans to leave at present.'

'At present! At present?'

'I really haven't, but everything has its natural end.'

'Its natural end!'

Alfred stood up, very agitated, his voice growing louder, his eyes wild. Given what he could hear from their room, Gilbert was sure Florence must be able to hear every word of this as she lay in bed.

'But you mustn't, you'll kill us all, you mustn't go. God, I can see it all now, that's why you're not talking to me, that's why you're not eating with us, God, think what you're going to, Ev, no mulled wine, no beer, no sausages and mash, just savages and tomtoms and tree snakes, I mean France, yes, I can *almost* see you in France, just about, frightful though they are, and Germany, Germany, at a pinch you'd understand the Germans, yes, but you're not cut out for the southern savages, you'll be eaten, picked white to the bone, bag and baggage, get my drift, I'm not joking, Captain, you *must* keep going here, you're indispensable, you've got the perfect job for you, everyone says so, you're the only thing in the world on which Jory and Mrs Jory agree, I'm going to tell Blote about this, I am, and she'll stop this nonsense in its tracks, you'll listen to her if you won't listen to me, and if I'm embarrassing you with this I'll embarrass you all bloody night!'

'Alfred, please, I've just ex—'

'Blote won't *hear* of this! She wouldn't dream of letting you go.'

Gilbert stood up, inches taller than Alfred, and put a restraining hand on his shoulder.

'Alfred, do sit down. You're making quite a noise.'

'Am I?'

'Yes, you really are. Quite a noise. Sorry, but you are.'

To Gilbert's surprise Alfred sat down, and stayed sitting, staring at the rug by his feet. When Gilbert next spoke his voice was so soft no one could have heard his words through the wall, not even a terrified wife.

'Alfred?'

'Yes.'

'When I saw Blote today, she was . . . very distressed.'

'Was she?'

'Yes.'

Alfred, motionless, stared down at the rug, then whispered urgently.

'Don't go, Ev, will you? I beg you not to go.'

'I really don't know what I'll do. Time will tell. That's not the point at the moment.'

'She gets like that . . . Uncorks you might say. Hysterics.'
'For no reason? Are there any . . . warning signs?'
Alfred put his hands over his face, shaking his head.
'Just does. Beats me, the whole business.'
'What business?'
'Women.'

The Letts Diary, 1914

He sat on the upturned box; she sat on the table with her legs dangling, her arms outstretched. Behind her back, the sea was greyer still than the sky.

'And it's all mine?'

'Yes, no rent, and no strings.'

'All, all mine?'

'Of course, courtesy of the Colonel.'

'*And* courtesy of Gilbert. My courteous Gilbert.'

She dropped to her feet, pirouetting around, as if trying to touch all four walls as she turned, stretching out and out into a larger being. She stopped and put her hands out to him.

'You've given me a new life, you do know that?'

'Have I?'

'Yes. Instead of sitting for Harold Knight I can do exactly as I want!'

It was as if yesterday had never happened. Her bright eyes and confident manner made that clear. She did not wish to go into yesterday nor Alfred's late-night visit (if she knew about it) nor anything else, beyond these crisp details:

'I've made an unacceptable marriage, that is obvious. No, please, don't say anything, Gilbert, there is no need to be polite or to soften the truth. Please! You know it. I can see it in your eyes. So there. Now, let's go for a walk . . . it can only be a short walk, I'm afraid, as I must start straight away. *This* will keep me sane.'

She indicated the brushes and the tubes of paint, and Taffy nosed the door. Gilbert stood aside to let her pass.

If Gilbert was not sure, as he looked at the moon and the sea, how much more he could take of this, the answer Time gave him was 'A year, or just over'. Day by day, starting with their brief meeting at the painting hut, week by week, rainy summer and rainy autumn, winter and spring, the days passed, day by day, as days do, until he could bear it no longer.

At first he closed off his conscious mind. He punished himself for his unfulfilled dreams and won golden opinions at work. He told his ears not to hear her too often, his eyes not to see her, and his senses to stay quiescent. For the most part they did as they were told. He cycled and he laboured, and in what little time he found on his hands he walked or fished or shot woodpigeons. On fine days he knew she was painting in her hut so he tried to avoid that high part of the headland, that part where his heart lay. Just occasionally he would hurl a stone into the sea or fire randomly not at a bird but at a rock or give a gratuitous rocket to one of the men. Only his bilious attacks and his dreams told another story.

It was in January 1914 that he began to make some brief and irregular entries in his small Letts diary. This is what he wrote.

Monday 19 January.   Had dinner with Blote
                            and A.J.

Tuesday 17 February.	Blote waved goodbye to me from her bedroom window. Went to London by 10.00 a.m. train for interview at Colonial Office.
Wednesday 18 February.	Had interview, which seemed very hopeful.
Friday 20 February.	Returned to Penzance overnight. Had breakfast with Blote and A.J.
Sunday 22 February.	Had early lunch with Blote in my room, and then for a walk over the cliffs to Penborth where we had tea. Then back by the road in the evening. A summer's day to be remembered.
Saturday 21 March.	While cleaning bike telegram came giving me appointment in W. Africa. Blote walked over to Boskenna with me. Had dinner with Blote.
Sunday 22 March.	Breakfast and dinner with Blote.
Tuesday 24 March.	Blote and I rode into Penzance and lunched.
Wednesday 25 March.	My farewell supper at Jory's.
Thursday 26 March.	Blote helped me pack. Boskenna. Tea with the men. They gave me a silver cigarette case and matchbox.

Friday 27 March.　　　　Left Lamorna. Blote said
　　　　　　　　　　　　goodbye to me.

The night Gilbert announced he had applied for a position
in West Africa, on the night of 19 January, 1914, to be
exact, Alfred was snappily dressed for supper in his new
bow tie, and fresh up from The Wink where he had been
talking nineteen to the dozen. He was in good form. Above
all he was relieved to have a man's company for supper,
especially a friend of whom he saw too little, a friend of
whom he saw far far too—

Gilbert's news stopped Alfred mid sentence. Only
Florence could find a few faltering words.

'Did you say . . . Nigeria?'

'Yes.'

'Nigeria. I see. But, forgive me . . . why?'

Gilbert looked at her.

'Because it feels the right thing to do. I've thought about
it a good deal, believe me. There's not much more I can do
at Boskenna.'

Florence faltered on.

'And for . . . how long? For how long is the
appointment?'

'If I get it!'

'Yes, if you get it.'

He did his utmost to be matter of fact. Being matter of
fact was surely for the best.

'Three years.'

'Three years,' she repeated without expression.

'But I probably won't be offered it. There'll be fierce
competition.'

'So!' Alfred suddenly exploded. 'We're back to the
blackies again, are we? We're jumping off to the jungle,
are we? Have I got this right? Have I!'

'But . . . why?' Florence pleaded again the next day as Gilbert passed her going down the stairs. He looked around and muttered at the banisters. He muttered at the top step and the missing stair-rod.

'Because it can't go on, can it?'

'It . . . can't? What can't?'

'You can understand that, can't you? It can't, can it?'

'No . . .' she said, 'I suppose not.'

'So don't keep asking me why. You know better than to ask me why. You know what it's like.'

Florence looked up and down the staircase.

'Would you meet me, at my hut? Please. Please, Gilbert.'

'When?'

'I don't know.'

'When!'

'Whenever suits you. I'm always there. I'll be there. Waiting.'

Gilbert, sensing the unseen presence of Mrs Jory, nodded and hurried on down.

And so, because it could not go on, it started. He ran full tilt over from Boskenna. She heard him coming. He knew she heard him. She heard his feet pounding the turf. She threw down her brush and ran out to meet him. It started without words. Then the words came.

'Three years,' she said, 'three *years.*'

'Yes. Initially.'

'Don't . . . don't say that.' She stroked the back of his hand, then lifted the back of his hand to her lips.

'You must paint hard every day,' he said, looking round over her shoulders, 'then I'll be able to see you here, so to speak. If I go, that is.'

'I'll write . . . I'll write every day . . . I won't be able to stop writing.'

'I may not get it. I've explained that.'

'But you will.'

'I may not accept it,' he said in a lighter way. 'Not now.'

He held her as tight as he could. How tight could he hold her?

'Oh, you'll go,' she stroked his face as she spoke, 'you'll go, you'll go.'

'How do you know?'

She shook her head slowly.

'I know. I can tell you're going, Gilbert.'

'How? How can you know?'

He tried to read her expression, but she closed her face back into his chest and cried quietly, bumping her head gently into him, her hair brushing his chin as she cried.

'Gilbert.'

'What?'

'It's been endless. Endless. I've tried. I tried to accept it.'

He held her head to his chest with his hand. He felt her tears go through his shirt. She heard his heart going, going, going.

'I know. I know. I've tried, too.'

'That's what I . . . should do, isn't it? Accept my lot. Just accept it. I've tried. I tried and I tried, you don't know how hard, and *don't* say you do because you don't.'

'I do.'

'Did you try as hard? Men don't try as hard, they don't.'

'Just as hard.'

She pulled her face back and looked up at him.

'How did you . . . bear it?'

'How did you?'

'I don't know.'

'People do ... People do. All over the world, I suspect.'

'Don't go! Don't, I beg you.'

It went on. They met and they met. They rushed to meet and to greet and to touch. He told her about Sammy, he told her as they sat on a huge rock and he felt the weight lifting. They talked and walked, as they often did those cold January days, around the circle of stones, around and around, as if mesmerised by the configuration of the stones and their position and their own fates, careless now over prying eyes. He felt her hip against his. He ran his fingers down her spine, up and down, up and down over the ridges.

'Poor Sammy,' she repeated, as she stroked his familiar hand. Then, because she could not lift this weight from her own mind, she sighed. 'Three years. Three years.' Three years. He wanted to say three years would pass quickly, quite quickly anyway, three years can fly by, just think what you were doing three years ago and think how quickly all that has gone, hasn't it gone quickly, but what possible point was there in all that? It was comfortless. In three years' time she would still be Mrs Munnings. And three years after that. The years stretched ahead, and Munnings would *always* be there: that was the blunt truth. So why come back? She knew and he knew. She knew the telegram would come, and he would go.

'The Merry Maidens,' she said, bitterly naming the prehistoric scene they circled.

He touched the cold stones. Lichen-clad, roughly hewn.

'I'll always imagine us here ... together ... When I write.'

'Promise?'

'Promise.'

But writing letters . . . what did that achieve? Waiting from first light, hands shaking, sighing a little aloud, running downstairs, running upstairs, hiding it in your pocket, trembling arms, shutting doors behind you, stomach trembling, sitting in the bathroom, tearing open the letter, trying not to tear it, an illusion of intimacy, reading, eating up the sentences, the distances closing, transported back into each other's arms in the hut with the rain on the roof, you held in your hands the paper on which the one you loved had written these words for you, you saw your lover, pen in hand, you saw your lover at the Merry Maidens, or stopping to kiss you over a gate on Rocky Lane, or running across the wet fields with a wild, strained look in his eyes, standing tall over you, standing behind you, running his hands across your breasts, tracing them around, then his fingers, feeling your knees go weak, feeling—

But he would not be there! She would not be there!

'I can't imagine it!' she cried fiercely. 'I can't.'

'What?'

'Where you're going, so far away, it's so different. If I can't imagine it I can't bear it.'

'I'll show you on a map.'

'What does a *map* tell you!'

'Something. The ship goes from Liverpool to Madeira . . . to Accra . . . and Lagos.'

A doubter's pause, and then:

'And another thing . . . there's another thing, Gilbert, a terrible terrible thing.'

'Yes.'

'I can't imagine a day here without you. With him.'

They held each other close, for warmth, for comfort,

breathing the wild air. The wind was sharp enough to make her bury her face.

With the beer working and the dominoes clicking, the men in The Wink were soon pooling their findings and observations.

'Never seen a better figure on a woman, and that's a fact,' said Jory. '*And* she can pick a horse. Should a' seen her at Buryan!'

'She's a striker, all right.'

'Where's he always off to, then?'

'Who?'

'Munnin's.'

'London and all that. Bigwig, in't he, now? 'Es, he's big now.'

'She'll be big an' all before long too.'

They cackled at that.

'See less of him in 'ere, I do know that. Much less.'

'Always the same, once they do get to be top nobs.'

'See less of the Cap'n, too.'

'Where's he bin then?'

'Seen 'ee and Mrs Munnin's up the Merry Maidens, I did.'

'When was that?'

'An' over to Kemeyl Farm.'

'Keepin' er company, is 'ee?'

'Keepin' er warm, more like.'

''Nough of that!' Jory said. ''Nough of that!' But they cackled on, sucking their beer.

Throughout this time Alfred painted and drank. His gout was now a daily pain, with the weather often beyond a joke – no one, not even Mrs Jory, had known rain like it – but Alfred simply stood there in the clearing, or sat hunched under his umbrella, warming himself with a hip flask of whisky. His coat heavy with damp, his trousers limp, he painted each daylight hour, wandering away from his easel only to piss against a tree or to scrabble around in the straw for another bottle of whatever he could find left from Jory's last delivery. Laura Knight caught him doing precisely that, and for the first time feared that her husband might well be right about Alfred.

But he painted. He painted horses, a beautiful old white mare with a long curly mane; he painted the sheen on a skewbald; he painted stallions silhouetted against a white band of surf, big bays in silver-mounted harness; he caught the light on ponies dozing or stamping, a mare with dappled quarters; he painted early evenings with gathering storm clouds, he saw the light shining on the wet laurel and that same light shone on his canvas.

He travelled and he painted and his paintings sold.

And as he painted he remembered better days, when the marsh dykes were alive with spawning frogs and marigolds, haymaking with the drag rake, the large stacks in the yard and the creaking wagons; he remembered throwing scuppets of maize into the shallows for the ducks and the cry of the corncrake; he remembered better days with his dark-haired gypsies, gypsies with blue-black hair and pheasants and partridges and luxuriant rushes and hares and rabbits, lurchers and swedes, and he remembered better days with sedge-grown banks and marguerites and pink vetch in the breeze and the bare-arsed Shrimp with his fishy eyes and his crafty face, and hop pickers and sandpits and lavender almost purple through the heat haze, the meadowsweet and the red-brick wall pitted with nail holes; and the best days of all, when his dog (now hers) pulled rat after rat out of the stables by the scruffs of their necks and shook them till they snapped.

But Taffy was not there to comfort him. He kicked the ground. Even the bloody dog had buggered off, the little killer hero who slew a thousand chickens and terrified tramps and always always made Alfred happy.

Was there no loyalty left in the whole wide world?

ANSWER ME THAT!

He shouted the question to the dripping trees.

WHAT DO I DO?

Then he brushed raindrops off his red-blue nose and barked at himself and sang:

> 'I've got a little cat
> And I'm very fond of that,
> But I'd rather have a
> Bow-wow-wow.'

He knew, of course, where the dog was: the dog was sitting curled up at Florence's feet, but he was buggered if he knew where her place was, and even more buggered if he was going looking. That was her affair. One cold afternoon, he did follow her towards the rock pools, but his heart wasn't in it. The point was, she didn't want him. He'd tried, hadn't he? And anyway, she couldn't paint. She could paint a bit, but not really paint. Painting should be left to the painters. He picked up his wide brush. The truth was, he rarely thought of his wife and when he did he ravaged the picture forming and framing in his mind's eye. He could go on without her. And he would! He thought only of his art and his next drink and his stack of horse paintings and the prices they fetched and the dog who'd deserted him.

The cushions had made a difference. And the rug.

'Florence?'

'Mmm?' Her eyes were closed, her voice calm.

'I had a lovely letter from Joey today. What a brother you have! It brought tears to my eyes.'

'I know . . . he wrote to tell me . . . I suspect he might know.'

'About us?'

'Yes.'

'And another thing.'

'Mmm?'

The February light was fading in the window. He spoke into the crook of her neck, his mouth in her hair, his mouth on her neck, his mouth near her ear.

'Your photograph. May I have it?'

'Yes,' she said sadly. 'If you want it. Of course you can.'

'You do look a little severe . . . but then, you are . . . a little severe.'

'We could have one taken together.'

'How?'

'In Chapel Street, if you wish. After lunch next Wednesday. Alfred's going away again on Wednesday.'

He squeezed her.

'Yes, let's. I'll carry yours everywhere . . . always. I promise.'

'Everywhere? Is Africa part of everywhere? Is Lagos?'

'Part of, yes. So is Lamorna.'

'Harold Knight has just finished another portrait of me. It took him five months.'

'The profile one? In his studio?'

'Yes. Five months, imagine.'

'Do you like it?'

'Yes, yes, I do. It's very . . . different. It's peaceful to look at. He allows me to be alone in his room, and in his portrait. It has that feeling. Of being alone. Of being left to oneself.'

'So you'll be hung in the Royal Academy again?'

'He's going to submit it, he says.'

'You'll never be forgotten. Not now.'

She doubted it and kissed him again. She spoke quietly and evenly to his mouth, looking at the little lines on his lips.

'Laura's asked me to . . . ask you. And Alfred has . . . of course . . .'

'Mmm?'

'Did you have to accept the post? They've begged me to ask you to withdraw. But you've made up your mind, haven't you?'

He breathed out and nodded, unable to trust his voice. She felt his head nodding on her shoulder, and she said:

'I'll never mention it again.'

He squeezed his thanks. She went on:

'This place . . . this place is all I ever want. This place, and you.'

'It's a bit on the cold side,' he said, wrapping the rug round her.

'Not with you here. Tell me about rock pools.'

'Rock pools? What do you mean?'

'Tell me what's in them.'

'Joey's the one to ask, he really is.'

'But he's not here,' she said sharply, 'and I want to hear *you* describe it, I want to see what you see. Please.'

'Why this sudden interest?'

'Please! If I hear your voice I feel calmer.'

He spoke to her closed eyes.

'Well, limpets . . . obelia . . . green weed . . . shore crabs, blennies, they're wonderful at changing colour, and . . . fiddler crabs sometimes. They're bright blue under their arms, with brilliant red eyes . . . sea snails . . . Is that enough?'

'No. Keep going.'

'Starfish . . . and anemones of course. But Joey told you all about those.'

'I'm so blind . . . I've wasted so much, I've missed so much. Why are they called fiddler crabs?'

'Because if you try to pick them up they make fiddling movements . . . like this . . .'

He moved his fingers in and out of her hair. She relaxed in his hands. Outside the wind was blowing up.

'Should we go back?'

'Is the Colonel very upset you're leaving? I'm sure he must be.'

'Yes, a bit, but at least I'm going out with the Royal Engineers. He approves of that.'

'I'm sure he won't miss you at half past four on a dark afternoon like this . . . will he?'

'You're probably right . . . no. Even so, I ought to get back.'

'Stay for a bit longer. Please. Just keep stroking my hair.'

'There it is. And the Cameroons.'

'There!'

Her fingers followed his to West Africa. Coming down to Lamorna from London was one thing, going up to the Lakes from London was another, but this! She shook her head. He could not want to go there. And the names of the places, you had to say them slowly, you had to speak each syllable so carefully, as if to a child.

Oyo . . . Oshogbo . . . Maiduguri . . .

She spoke the words to herself, wanting to laugh but fearful she would cry. She put her hand to her lips to stop the twitching and the trembling. He did not notice her hand move. He was speaking to the Atlas. She pushed her elbow into his side, to be sure, to be really sure, he was still there, sitting next to her, in the next chair, in the Morrab Library in Penzance, alive, next to her, in Cornwall ... In February, on the Wednesday. Their Wednesday in Penzance.

'The river Niger is huge, of course. Everywhere is hot, goes without saying. And plenty of bush, hundreds of miles, very rainy too ... even rainier than Cornwall ... and some wonderful mountains. And mosquitoes. Have to say, plenty of those little blighters. They made quite a joke of it at the interview.'

'Mosquitoes!'

'You get used to them, you get used to anything.'

'Do you?'

'Even the white ants.'

'The white ants!' She shuddered.

'And going back to the rivers, the rivers do flood. Imagine something terribly wide ... wider than the whole of Boskenna. I'm serious ... that's how big the rivers swell.'

Mosquitoes, white ants, black faces, Kano, Zungeru, Kaduna, Jos, Bauchi, and Oshogbo again. How could he carry her photograph through all that? Would it survive white ants and big floods? No, she could not imagine any of this! She looked at his face peering over the open map: she looked at his skin, still shiny from shaving. She looked at his hair, his ears, his nose, the shape of his lips. No! She could not imagine him there. In a flood of terrible fear she imagined she could not imagine him at all! Once he had gone to Oyo and Oshogbo there would be no trace, nothing left, nothing but wet sands, no body, nobody. Only her and Alfred. She gripped the table, her skin draining to a white-bluish tint.

She closed her eyes and talked sternly to herself. She opened her eyes and stood up.

'Shall we go?'

'What?'

'I don't want to see any more about Nigeria.'

'Oh, sorry.'

'We'll miss the photographers.'

'Oh yes, yes, the photographers.'

A butterfly landed on the rock. Florence, watching its random flight, said:

'Tell me about these rocks.'

'These rocks?'

'Yes, I want to know. And don't tell me to ask Joey, he's not here.'

'They're granite . . . there are granite rocks here . . . and in Brittany, and the Ardennes. It's part of the Cornwall-Ardennes massif. And look . . . that's quartz there, in the veins. Can you see . . . running along, we're talking about 250 million years, something like that, and the sedimentary rock has eroded and the granite has protruded. We're sitting on 250 millon years.'

'Are we?' she said dreamily, glad of his shoulder. 'How wonderful!'

It was Sunday 22 February, 1914, and sitting very close together on the rock, the granite rock on which Laura Knight had painted Dolly, Gilbert and Florence exchanged photographs. They told each other they loved each other and that no partings and no packings, no floods and no fare-wells could or would ever change that. They lounged back on the rock, high above the sea's perpetual unrest. It was so hot they both wished they were not so heavily dressed.

'This is for ever,' Florence said. 'For 250 million years. At least.'

'It's like a summer's day, isn't it?'

'Yes . . . who would believe it's February?'

Africa's a Fair Old Way

'The old pictur' is goin' a bit better, today, A.J.'

With Shrimp's words in his ears, with freezing fingers, he took the brush from his mouth, and put down his palette. He scrutinised his work. Yes. He nodded Yes to himself, took off his painting coat, wiped his hands on his rag and spat. He carried in his painting. Before leaving he went to see Grey Tick and Merrilegs. Then, with his steel-tipped shoes clipping the stones, he strode up to the hotel, feeling like a coiled spring, and longing to transmit some of his energy and pain to others, he stood in the bedroom door, hands on hips, and announced that, sad though the loss was, the loss of his dear friend Gilbert, he would be providing the best food and the best drink, the best songs and the best poems at a big party in his studio, just as in the old days, the jolliest gathering of all time, it would indeed be the party of parties.

Florence looked at the pillow and said no.

'No? What do you mean?'

'No.'

'You're telling me no?'

'Yes.'

Though fearing a terrible scene she quietly told her husband that she was sure, whatever polite answer Gilbert might give, he would much prefer something . . . individual. She was sure Gilbert wanted to leave Lamorna quietly, as quietly as possible.

'And you know that?' he said. 'You do *know* that, do you?'

'Yes, I do,' she said.

Rebuffed, Alfred headed off for The Wink, reciting as he went:

> '"Sir," said I, "or Madam, truly your forgiveness I
>   implore:
> But the fact is I was napping, and so gently you came
>   rapping,
> And so faintly you came tapping, tapping at my
>   chamber door,
> That I scarce was sure I heard you – here I opened
>   wide the door—
> Darkness there and nothing more."'

Ten yards before he reached the bar door, Munnings stopped. Drawn though he was by the smoke and the flagstones, the smell of the soil and the smell of the beer, he could not face Jory and the others and their inevitable questions about Gilbert's departure and who would be the Colonel's next agent and where exactly was it in Africa the Captain was going and how would they ever get on without him.

Munnings stood at a loss in the lane.

'NO!' he shouted.

But where could he go? He did not want to be alone, not tonight. That left only Laura. When all else failed, there was always Laura at the top of the lane.

'Laura Knight!' he said as she opened the door.

'Alfred Munnings,' she replied.

Laura often said, in later years, that she 'should have known'. Delighted though she was to hear his abrupt knocking – it was so long since last he'd called – the Alfred who came in and stretched out, legs apart, on her comfiest chair was not the same man she first saw surrounded by a bevy of girls. Not the same man at all.

Although he had been away from Lamorna he had none of his usual stories on the tip of his tongue, no news of Bond Street deals, no fresh insults to throw at the critics, no challenge to throw at the world. Above all, he had no energy. Even if she had wanted to offer him a drink, Harold would keep none in the house, nor did Alfred ask for one. Without any focus in his eyes, he stared.

'Are you all right, Alfred?'

It took him a while to answer, and when he did it was with a short bark.

'Me? Yes. Yes!'

'You're not yourself.'

'Not myself? Good point!'

He twisted and turned in his seat. He fumbled with the cuff of his shirt.

'You and Blote must come for supper soon. Shall we arrange a—'

'Do you think I could have a word with Knightie?'

He had never asked such a thing before. Laura wanted to hug him.

'But of course. Go on up. He'd love to see you.'

She opened the door at the bottom of the stairs and called up:

'Harold . . . It's Alfred to see you.'

She heard Harold pad across his studio. She stood at the bottom, half listening, wondering what the two men were saying to each other.

In fact few words were spoken. Alfred did not look at Harold. He looked at the floorboards and asked if he might be allowed to see Harold's most recent portrait of the seated Florence. With it placed before him, he sat down. Munnings could find nothing to say. It was Harold Knight who confided:

'She is a most beautiful woman.'

'It is the most beautiful picture.'

'Thank you. Thank you, Alfred.'

At that Alfred got noisily to his feet, moved as if to shake Harold by the hand, but at the very moment Harold was least expecting it. With some clattering Munnings went towards the top of the stairs. He missed the first step but managed to catch his balance.

'That's about it, I think, more or less,' Gilbert said, folding his ties neatly, then pushed his handkerchiefs deep down the right-hand side. It was like being back in his dorm at school, except that at school no one ever helped him to pack. His new brown trunk, with his name freshly printed on the side, sat foursquare and heavily on his narrow bed. If he couldn't close the lid properly he might have to sit on it to make the catch go into the lock, but he'd rather not do that: quite apart from anything else the birds' eggs and the exercise book were carefully cushioned between his cardigans and his dressing-gown.

All Florence could see was the trunk. The trunk and his name.

'One more check, shall we?' he said, looking round and opening the doors of the hollow wardrobe. Taffy, encouraged by Gilbert's tone, scrambled under the bed, coming up with a missing sock and a wagging tail.

'*There* it is, *good* dog,' Gilbert said, 'what a help you both are.'

Florence looked up, smiled a small determined-to-please smile, then smiled no more.

'Gilbert?'

'Yes.'

'Before you go over to Boskenna . . .'

'What is it?'

'I want to show you something.'

'Of course.'

'It's in my bedroom.'

She led the way. He, less confidently, followed. He had no wish to go in there.

'Yes?'

Inside her bedroom, a room he had not before seen, she held the door for him and pointed to the mahogany chest of drawers which stood facing the foot of the bed. On it there was a large oriental bowl full of rose leaves and, next to it, and even larger, a horse's white skull. In that confined setting the head seemed huge. The hollow eye sockets were darkened by shadow. Gilbert stepped forward, put his fingers in the cavities and ran his hand along the row of grinders.

'Do you see? Do you see now?'

'Yes.'

'Could you look at that all night?'

He tried to laugh lightly.

'It's bad enough by day, I agree.'

'But it's more alive than I am.'

'Don't be silly.'

'To him. Much more.'

'If it disturbs you, couldn't you just get rid of it? It could go on the landing, couldn't it? Why not ask Mrs Jory if she'd like it?'

'If she'd *like* it!'

'Yes. Or you could drape something over it.'

'Anyway, you mustn't say a word to anyone . . . ever. Swear to me you won't.'

He took her hand. Her body was rigid.

'I won't. Of course I won't. Anyway, it's too late now, isn't it?'

'Yes.'

'And I can hardly tell anyone I've been in here.'

'Sit next to me for a moment.'

'Where?'

'Here. Please.'

She pointed to the bed. Ill at ease, he did. He looked at her pillow, her bedspread. He shook his head: their bedspread. And which pillow was hers?

'If I can think, "Gilbert's been here with me" . . . I can do it.'

'I'll always be with you.'

'But don't kiss me. Not here.'

'I won't . . . I wouldn't.'

They sat side by side, rather formally, looking at the skull and the bowl of roses. Florence showed no inclination to move. Gilbert listened for a sound on the stairs.

'Where's my . . . photograph?'

'Here.' He pointed to his breast pocket.

'And which is your pillow?' he asked.

'I sleep on the right.'

He leant over and kissed that pillow. Through quiet tears she asked:

'Which train . . . is . . . it?'

'Tomorrow?'

'Yes.'

He told her.

It took Gilbert the rest of the day to say his farewells. Having sold his bicycle he had to walk the estate briskly from the cove to the mill, from the farms to The Wink. He left no one out. At Boskenna, standing as upright as an officer on parade, he said goodbye to Colonel and Mrs Paynter and the men. The speeches were simple and heartfelt. Wherever he might find himself in the future, he said, in whatever far-flung land, daffodils would always be his favourite flowers and he would always treasure the silver cigarette case and matchbox. As for Jory and all those in the bar, he shook their hands too, one by one. He told them he sailed from Liverpool, in a few days, for Lagos. They wished him safe journey by land and by sea ('twas a fair old way, Africa), as did every cottage dweller and every artist.

At the top of the hill, late that night, he said goodbye to Laura and Harold Knight; and at the hotel early next morning, with Jory waiting outside with his pony and trap, Gilbert said goodbye to Alfred and Florence Munnings.

Part Five

A Letter to Africa

Cliff House Temperance Hotel,
Lamorna Cove
Penzance
(HOOT of an address, eh?)

Dear Ev,

This will be the very first letter you will receive in West Africa. It must be! First ever! It will await your arrival, and you will read it to the sound of distant drums. If, that is, I copied down your Godforsaken address correctly, and you remain uneaten.

Now, as I write, you of course will be somewhere in the Irish Sea, with the spray hitting your face. Have to say I prefer dry land, even in the rain, if you get my slant.

I did not say this to you, Ev, when we made our goodbyes (morning is no kind of time for a proper man-to-man), so I'll say it now: I think you have been wise to make the move you did. Very wise. This last year this place has become limited and dull, VERY DULL. We're stuck, I feel, in an old fusty groove, I was saying this to Laura only the other day, and we agreed, you're a cheerful chap and you and your shifting cargo will, by the time you unseal this, have seen new seas and new lands and new people. All colours. Quite right too. And well done! It'll put a spring in your step.

We all miss you of course and I miss you TERRI-BLY, but I go along as usual, feeling very humdrum, painting or picking up all those bits of paper and orange peel and matchboxes strewn all over the clifftop. What awful people trippers are.

Even so, once the fog cleared this morning, and the heavy dew gave way to sun and sharp outlines, I had a gorgeous metallic light. I went over to Carn Barges and set up shop on the rocks and thoroughly enjoyed it all. A big ship was being towed round from The Lizard to Land's End by a small tug which left a trail of smoke, and I did a nice sketch which I can use, and later a big ironclad appeared round and steamed past, plus lots of those little white birds which fly low to the surface like a silver chain, all making for the Scillies I suppose. A good day, with all the hallmarks of useful indolence, which is a phrase I have been determined to use all evening.

Yesterday, by way of contrast, was the last day of the hunt, with big banks, damned big banks. But Grey Tick, on top form, flew over wall and bank. By the way, I've been forgiven for the fox affair, you may remember it, well, they've let the renegade dauber back into the club. I got back to Jory's as happy as the day is long, though damned tired, and slept like a top.

But what am I saying? Only just now I said how dull everything is!

Blote, I'm glad to say, has been to tea with the

Knights – she needed something to pick her up – yeast splits and jam and Cornish cream apparently. She's been a touch off her food these last few days and painting too long hours. That may sound a bit steep coming from me but she's only a filly and not too sprightly. Got to be careful what I write, she's next door, dressing for dinner. She came through not five minutes ago looking very pale and very ordinary in blouse and skirt so I suggested she had another shot and gave her startling blue dress an airing. ('Startling blue' was how she described her dress as depicted in Harold Knight's latest portrait, now en route for the R.A.)

General news: no news of your successor though Jory assures me over the bar the Colonel did briskly interview some chap yesterday who turned up out of the blue at Boskenna and the Colonel threw a box of flowers at him which he missed so that was the end of him.

As for my work, I've finished six horse paintings, let's call them a SERIES, eh, and sell 'em for even more, the dealers are that daft, still, as long as the commissions keep coming in, who cares? And I'm off to Suffolk soon. Wish you were joining me.

Funny thing about letters, when you write you see the person you're talking to, in my case my dear friend Gilbert of the Royal Engineers Survey Party, but he can't reply, though he's standing there clear as day.

Am I talking rot?

Anyway, never regret going from here but LOOK FORWARD TO THE WORLD. You are greatly missed.

> Your great friend,
> A.J.

A Walk in the Park

Gilbert was not pacing the deck in the Irish Sea. The SS *Dundas*, due to sail from Liverpool at 8 a.m. on Tuesday 21st, was delayed for five days while some last-minute fittings were made. With profound apologies all the passengers were requested by the Elder Dempster Line to reassemble at the dock the following Sunday morning.

Gilbert stood becalmed, looking blankly at the huge grey ship and the fog just beyond. He turned round slowly, wondering which way to go. Five days. That was long enough to do something, albeit long enough to become thoroughly unsettled again. He reviewed the alternatives.

He could not go back to Lamorna.

He could, at a pinch, go back to Cardiff for the remaining days but he'd only just said his goodbyes to Mother, Lionel and Maud. That painful break had been made. To arrive on the doorstep again so soon would feel silly and uncomfortable, if not false.

He could book into the Adelphi Hotel, but what would he do in a foggy city he did not know, with that idle ship mocking him at the docks?

His cabin companion, a Captain Sinclair, a pleasant

enough chap to whom he had just been introduced, said, 'Well, it's London for me, what about you?' so London it was for Gilbert. Exactly what he would do there, travelling light and aimless, he did not know, beyond the feeling that the London bustle might, far more than any other place, sweep him along, as it did so many aimless others.

On the journey down, once Sinclair had settled to his newspaper, Gilbert started a letter to Florence; in fact he started and screwed up a few letters to Florence, with Sinclair's saucer eyes peering over the top of his paper and the rhythm and sway of the train making his writing irregular and messy, much in the way his mind felt. Nagging at the back of every clumsy sentence was 'How do I address the envelope?' Could he write a letter only to her, a letter addressed to 'Mrs Alfred Munnings'? How could that possibly work? A.J. would go off like a bomb. As for Mrs Jory . . .

The train jerked.

Damnation!

Why hadn't he thought straight? Surely they should, in those final days together, have agreed on some plan, some collecting place, Penzance Post Office, *some*where, some-where.

The frustration of it made him seethe.

Long before they arrived in London he had given up: he would have to write to them both from the ship and from Nigeria, knowing that she would read between the lines, knowing she would know all that was being left unsaid. Such as:

I love you, he whispered to the window.

Better to leave things unsaid on paper than try to say the impossible and make, as he was now making, a bad mess worse.

Damnation!

'Sorry?' Sinclair said.

'Nothing . . . I do apologise.'

'It's frustrating, I agree, but what can one do? We'll have a bit of fun in London, eh? Final fling?'

'Yes . . . let's.'

Gilbert strangled a yawn and stared out of the window. England rushed past. Or he ran over England. Whichever. He looked glumly at it, the England he would soon be leaving, but he felt only the loss of Florence. He felt guilty. Her loss, the loss of another man's wife, blanked out England and Wales and family and friends and all their claims. There was only Florence.

He started to feel a bilious attack coming on. All he could do was swallow hard and close his eyes, mind over matter, Gilbert, and think of her as they sat on the fallen tree.

'I say . . . Evans?'

'Yes.'

'Meant to ask you, where d'you stay in town?'

'I don't go up that often.'

'But when you do?'

'The last time . . . a friend booked me into . . . Fuller's.'

'Good spot?'

'As I remember . . . yes.'

'Fact is, I haven't the foggiest where to stay. Mind if I join you?'

'No, not at all.'

Sinclair folded his paper.

'Thanks. Thanks . . . And where have you been?'

'Been? Up to now?'

'Yes. In recent years.'

'Oh, Cornwall.'

'Cornwall.' He half laughed.

'Yes, just south of Penzance.'

'Really? Right out in the bush? Or should I say practically on the brink?'

Sinclair's mobile mouth twitched in self-congratulation.

'A bit of both, I suppose.'

Gilbert turned his shoulder away into the seat and half stretched and allowed his half-closed eyes to remain visible.

'Enjoy it? Down there?'

'Yes. Very much.'

'Good . . . good.'

Gilbert knew he should now ask some reciprocal questions, only civilised to do so, and what about you, Sinclair, what are you leaving behind, and what drew you to Nigeria, and so on and so forth, but he did not. Minutes passed. Sinclair picked up and noisily shook open his paper.

Eyes closed, Gilbert was quickly back with her, traversing the sweet distance of love, her weight nicely on his shoulder in the hut, on the fallen tree, in the carriage, but just as quickly the tree rolled away and all he could see was A.J. on Merrilegs leaning down and launching in his usual way into Laura.

'Fact is, Laura, Blote needs cheering up. Badly needs it.'

'Oh, I'm so sorry to hear that.'

'That's the top and tail of it.'

'But you're just the chap to cheer anyone up, A.J. Pop in for a cup of tea?'

And Gilbert saw Harold sharpening his pencils upstairs and heard him telling Laura to stop exaggerating about Alfred the Great and stop showing off with Alfred the Gregarious and to settle down herself to do some serious, quiet work and kindly to allow him to continue painting his Venus, she's happy enough up here with me.

'That's it, strike while the iron is hot, Harold!' Laura boomed.

Gilbert smiled, and tried again.

Florence. Not Alfred, not Laura, not Harold. Only Florence, thank you.

Yes.

Yes, she's here. She's with me.

Florence was by his side, on the cushions, her newly washed hair on his shoulder, but the picture faded as her self-dramatising garrulous husband sat opposite him in the carriage talking loudly about his native village of Mendham on the river Waveney on the Norfolk-Suffolk border, with the thatched houses and blacksmith shop and vicarage garden and the sharp corner where he had a spill on his grey, and the racing at Bungay and how he called in to the Harleston Swan (or was it the taproom at the Coach and Horses?) and picked up how to make punch and sang 'Landlord fill the flowing bowl' and patted his horse's head and Gilbert slumped into dry-mouthed half-sleep until the white skull snorted loudly and shocked him wide staring awake.

'You all right, Evans?'

'Yes, fine . . . fine. Sorry . . . Sinclair. Bit of a dream.'

'A nightmare, more like.'

Sinclair laughed very earnestly at his joke.

It was as if he had gone into church to pray, only to feel cheated. He stood in the same dark corner, but she was not there. Perhaps he had gone wrong somewhere? He swivelled and retraced his steps, scanning every wall in every gallery, giving himself the excuse that he had been disorientated the last time. He hadn't. No, with a sinking certainty he arrived back in the same dark corner. She was not there in the clearing, with the light on her coat and her back so upright. Nor were there any approaching footsteps.

How dare the Hanging Committee do it!

How dare they take it down!

He asked the attendant. The attendant had hairy hands and an obsequious smile. It was the Academy's policy, and had been for some years, to change or rotate the pictures on show quite regularly. There was a large permanent stock, and if he cared to ask in the Secretary's office on the second floor for further details . . .

Gilbert did not care to do so.

He felt a bit bovine.

He noticed a goitre on the man's throat.

She was not there.

That was all that really mattered.

Bottled up, he went heavily down the steps and outside. The fluffy cotton skies had cleared. He blinked in the brightness and put on his hat. Then he crossed the cobbled yard and turned right into Piccadilly.

Accept facts, Gilbert. Be a soldier.

Come on, Gilbert, he said. Buck up.

How about a walk?

A walk in the park is in order.

Anything to keep away from that ass Sinclair.

Sinclair all too easily thought he was on easy terms.

He turned.

And the shock he felt was unlike any other he had ever experienced, or ever would. Looking back later, looking back over his long life, although terrible things were to happen, he never doubted that this was his biggest single shock. The pavement was packed. The sun shone directly down. Ten yards away. It must be a trick of the light.

Head bowed, Florence stepped down from a cab.

His knees went.

No, it could not be her.

Other women were beautiful. Other women wore beautiful coats. Other women had hair of her colour. There were many beautiful women in London, Venuses even.

She stood, head down, listening to an unseen man.

The man inside waved a weathered hand.

Then Gilbert heard A.J. barking from the back, he heard the voice from the Norfolk-Suffolk border:

'King's Cross, driver, and hurry. I need a new suit!'

Only A.J. could speak like that. Only he threw his hands around like that.

Gilbert still did not move. A passer-by brushed into him. Excuse me. Another bumped him. I'm sorry. My fault. I do apologise.

She walked towards Burlington House.

He'd know that walk anywhere in the world.

His body now moved.

He followed her, automatic, weightless, his eyes fixed.

Along how many cliff paths had he followed those legs, that back, that hair?

He did not call.

She turned.

It took them half an hour to recover. Gilbert sat her down on the seat in the courtyard, his face as white as hers, his lips as blue. There were explanations. They touched each other's hands very tentatively, as if unsure there was a body to be touched. There was. They looked at each other and shook their heads and bit their lips.

When they stood up, arm in arm, a little colour returning to their faces, he asked her if she was all right, and she said yes she was, and he asked her if she would like to take that long-awaited walk in the park and she smiled and said yes yes she would.

They were reflected in a slow line of shop windows. They were smiling.

They walked to the park, with strength returning to their legs, they walked, happy and anonymous, and when they had tea, they sat opposite each other, their hands sliding together through the cups and spoons. She said I hope it's a good safe ship, I want you to be safe, very safe. Alfred was off to Suffolk and she would stay at her parents' but she did not mind, whatever, whatever. Whatever happens, she said, I'll never stop thanking God for this. Nor will I.

You're a windfall. A wonder.

He bought some eau-de-Cologne from a machine. It cooled his hands.

From being head down and small she felt large in spirit, warm, swept along in the certainty that she could climb any cliff, accept any fate. They drove to Fuller's, there was never any doubt they would. Going up the stairs they met Sinclair coming down and Sinclair's eyes said I say Evans you're a quick worker.

Tuesday	Liverpool. Departure delayed. Went down to London.
Wednesday	Spent day with Sinclair.
Thursday	Another day with Sinclair. (A third would be a terrible prospect.)
Friday	Met Blote! Walk in park. Had tea together, then drove to the hotel. Dinner with her.
Saturday	Met Blote at Trocadero. Went into park and sat and talked. Back to Trocadero for lunch. She

saw me off at station.
We parted at 3.15. I went
to the train, alone and
very sad.

Putting Together the Pieces

It was only when he was shot, an injury which took him back across the seas, that Gilbert was able to put the pieces together, or as many pieces as fitted. Laura Knight provided the framework. She was the only one who could, and anyway she was the only one who he could find in Lamorna that morning. Although A.J. kept his studio, not surprisingly he had moved out of his rooms and was, Mrs Jory said, rarely seen in the district these days.

As for Harold Knight, he was very ill in Penzance Hospital. It all started before the war with a mouth infection but soon his whole system was seriously affected. With the outbreak of hostilities and Harold's reaffirmation of his conscientious objection, he was put to work alone in the open fields on the coastline by Zennor, on the bleak stretch sloping down to the place where Alfred saved the fox. In the appallingly cold conditions of the 1914–15 winter, frozen to the marrow and cut to the quick, the ostracised Harold buckled and broke. Having explained all this, Laura put two more apple logs on the fire, and turned the toast on the fork.

'But that,' she said, her face red from the heat, 'is not what you came to hear.'

'I'll go to see Harold this afternoon. If I may.'

'Oh, would you? That is kind . . . would you take some more pencils in for him? You remember what he's like over his soft pencils.'

'Of course I will, Laura, anything you like.'

'He has very few visitors. Very few indeed. More tea?'

'Please.'

Laura looked at the young officer, the same old Gilbert, but not quite the same.

'It's so very good to see you, Gilbert. How long will you be here?'

'In England? I don't know. For as long as it takes.'

'No . . . in Lamorna, I mean.'

'I don't know . . . It depends.'

Laura smiled at him, and she knew it was time to talk, really to talk. Gilbert sat and listened. Behind her back the walls were covered with her lively drawings of acrobats and fairgrounds.

'I saw quite a bit of Blote that May and June: just after you left us. Quite a bit. Sometimes we painted together at my hut . . . or up here or on the rocks. She seemed very well, and much more sociable. I'd started to paint gypsies. Alfred suggested that, and then Blote and I went to the circus a few times, and when Dolly came down again from London Blote tried some larger works . . . Funny to think of it now. Whenever we saw a ship, your name came up, always, always your name, which was nice, a ship on the sea meant Gilbert and many mornings she sat upstairs for Harold. It was a happy spell . . . I think she liked all the scurrying and slapdash with me and the silence with Harold. Whatever . . . my paintings started to sell like hot cakes, so did Harold's, that explains the car outside, you saw it? . . . and Alfred started his parties again. It all seemed to fit together . . . pictures selling, cars bought, Lamorna more alive again, though it wasn't for long, I agree. Not for long. Hard to believe that now . . . is that only a year ago? A *year* ago . . . when we were all singing:

'We are wonderful people . . . we are . . . we are . . .
We are won-der-ful people we are . . .

'Oh, Gilbert, please don't look like that . . . I know. I know. Where was I? Yes, June. No. This would have been in . . . *July*. I played the piano, and Alfred had bought a gramophone. You've never seen anyone so excited with anything. There was all the usual singing and dancing but now we had an extra entertainer, the gramophone, and Alfred insisted we played it on and on . . . over and over.

'Well . . . one very hot night, only a few weeks before the war, I can see her now, with a bunch of sweet peas tucked in her grey skirt . . . and I was larking and dancing away like billy-ho with Alfred, and Blote came over, and at the end of the dance she said if nobody minded she'd be off to bed, she said she had a bit of a headache. I knew she'd been off colour for a few days, and I said no, sleep well, and see you tomorrow, come for a picnic with us if you feel up to it, and then just as she got to the door and lifted the latch A.J. shouted:

'"Yes, off you go to bed, you bloody whore!"

'It was absolutely terrible, Gilbert. By a strange quirk, no one was talking at that precise second, there was no music, and A.J. said it so loudly the whole room just . . . well, you can imagine it as well as I can explain it. We all looked at her. Blote didn't react at all, she turned and looked at him and walked slowly out . . . followed by their dog, which also walked slowly . . . as if the dog grasped it too. Oh,

I can see it now. Excuse me . . . a moment, would you? Sorry. Sorry about that. So . . .

'I told A.J. what I thought of him, of course, and so did the others, we all did. I told him that was the last party of his I'd ever attend and that remains true. To this day. After a moment or two he wandered out and sat under the trees, drinking on his own. We all drifted away . . . in a sour, sour mood. That changed everything . . .

'More tea? No? More toast? No . . . Anyway . . . the next morning I was sitting on the front porch, just enjoying the sun in my chair. I'd told Harold a bit about the night before, and he kindly agreed to come with me for a picnic. If he thinks I'm upset he'll drop whatever he's doing, he always has done, but I like to think I was thinking of him too, that the sun and the air might do him some good, he looked very peaky, nothing like as bad as now of course, but of course he agreed, so I'd just packed the cheese and onion and saffron cake when I heard the shouting and I could tell it wasn't normal shouting or horseplay, you know the difference, don't you, when you hear it, your spine goes. "Mrs Knight . . . Mrs Knight!" a young woman was bawling at me from forty or fifty yards and I could see it was Betty from the hotel, she had run all the way up the hill, she could hardly speak, and while I was asking her to sit down and get her breath back Harold came rushing downstairs, straight past and tried to start the car. Unfortunately it wouldn't start, and would you believe, it was facing the wrong way, and Betty stayed with Harold while I ran off down the hill, and I was halfway to the hotel when Harold came roaring down, going terribly fast, and I thought he would kill us all, which somehow he didn't.

'Mrs Jory was pacing outside and waved us up . . . and at the top of the staircase there was Alfred . . . completely out of control. We were too late, I knew that, Gilbert . . .

I've seen it before and I know when it's too late. I won't say much more . . . if you don't mind, the doctor eventually . . . half an hour after us . . . and I tried . . . all that time.'

Laura stopped.

How could she tell Gilbert about the enamel bucket, the penetration of the smell, that horse's head and . . . Florence's purple face? How could she tell Gilbert that Blote's tongue was sticking out, sticking right out? Laura would never forget that beautiful woman in that state . . . accusing her . . . or so it felt . . . sticking her tongue out at the world. Such details were not for Gilbert's ears, a wounded soldier and a wounded lover.

'Harold, as you'd expect, was marvellous. He took Alfred outside, they walked round and round the field, while I stayed with Blote. Poor Mrs Jory . . . she's never really recovered, everyone knows about it, people talk, and those rooms haven't been taken since. You'll stay here tonight, won't you . . . I'd appreciate it if you would, I really would.'

'Yes . . . thank you.'

Laura stared into the fire.

'Harold organised the funeral, organised everything. Jory helped a good deal . . . he's a good sort, isn't he, and we all followed behind. And then the inquest was in the paper, of course . . . very distressing. A few weeks later I did speak to Mrs Jory. Blote, she said, came down for breakfast and seemed as normal as ever. She and Alfred ate together, a full breakfast, but when he went upstairs he found her. This time she'd taken enough. To face that once is bad enough . . . isn't it, Gilbert? But twice!'

'But she prom—' Gilbert stopped, and moved his hands to say he had nothing to say. He and Laura watched the flames.

'Anyway . . . I think you should ask Harold anything

else. He spoke to A.J., comforted him for many hours . . .
I think Harold knows a bit more than I do. He hasn't told
me, he wouldn't. But I sense it. In the way one does.'

'In what way?'

'Ask him when you see him. Oh . . . and the pencils
are there, on the bookcase. And when I was . . . helping
to prepare Florence . . . I found this on her, and, well, I
thought you should have it.'

Laura handed Gilbert his photograph.

'How was he?'

'On that day? Well, I presume Laura told you I took
him off. He was much as you'd expect. Mostly incoherent.'

'What did he do?'

'Afterwards? In the following weeks? Munnings? Oh, go
on much as before . . . painting and drinking, riding off on
his own.'

Harold's arms, stick-thin, lay outside the sheets. Looking
a bit like an emaciated bishop, he sat up on his pillows with
his pince-nez on his nose and an open sketchbook on the
blanket. 'There's one good aspect to Penzance Hospital,' he
said with a cynical smile, 'it's full of interiors, and pleasantly
free of fresh air.' On the sketchbook Gilbert could see a
wickedly accurate drawing developing of the man in the
next bed.

'Laura . . . said you knew more than she did. About
Munnings.'

'Did she?'

Harold tapped his fingers slowly on the blanket. His
mouth was reluctant.

'Do you mind?'

'Mind?'

'Talking to me . . . about that day.'

'I don't mind, I just don't care for this topic ... I don't care for it at all. Well, Gilbert, if you must know, in a nutshell, Munnings said the marriage had never been consummated.'

'Oh, I see ...'

'He can't have found that easy to say, can he ... least of all Munnings ... least of all to me. At the time he was sitting on the grass, near some cows. And I wondered for quite a while why he would say that to me. I'd never have spoken to the man myself if I had not been married to Laura.'

'Why would he? Why would he say that?'

'Laura told you what he said ... at the party the night before, did she?'

'Yes.'

'I don't know with any certainty, Gilbert, but I'd painted Florence three or four days a week for those final months. I'd finished three portraits of her. Did you know?'

'She always loved being painted by you.'

'Did she? She never said that to me ... I'm so glad. Thank you. And between ourselves, again, very strictly between ourselves, I'd noticed a change, very slight at first, but if you look at someone, a woman sitting for you, as closely as I looked at Florence, well, I don't think much can remain hidden. Not if you study her from every angle, not a woman of her perfect figure.'

'I see.'

'And I don't think she could hide it. I suppose something must have been said.'

'By Florence?'

'Yes.'

'To A.J.?'

'To Munnings, yes. Don't you?'

Gilbert stood up, walked a few paces away, then returned to his seat. Harold moved a little in his bed.

'I'm sorry if all this upsets you, Gilbert.'

'It doesn't.'

'It does. I can see.'

'Harold . . . are you saying . . . how shall I put it . . . that there was a close connection between what he told you in the field and the words he shouted at Florence that night at the party?'

'That is the possibility . . . even the probability in my mind. Even in his abject despair he was trying to explain himself. There was, I think, an element of . . . self-justification there, of self-exculpation . . . which he might wish reported.'

Gilbert thought about this and then nodded.

'Laura tells me Florence is buried in Sancreed.'

'Yes, she is.'

'Where exactly?'

'Oh, you're going? Good . . . I am glad. The vicar there was first-class, by the way . . . Give credit where it is due. First-class. No one else in the whole area would allow it. That is true magnanimity to me, don't you agree? Yes, just go in by the church gate and turn right, and keep going.'

'Is there a stone?'

'Yes, we saw to that.'

'Thank you, Harold.'

'Are you going back to Laura tonight?'

'Yes.'

'Good, good. Two things, would you . . . One, give her my love. I do miss her, you know.'

'I will.'

'And second . . . Go up into my studio, and you'll find something wrapped up, with your name on it. Next to the clock, you can't miss it.'

Gilbert could see how tired Harold was.

'I hope you get better soon, Harold.'

'I hope *you* do, too. But let's be thankful it's all over for you.'

'How do you mean?'

'Your wound . . . at least you'll play no further part.'

'No, no, I'm afraid I'll be going back.'

Harold's eyes sharpened.

'You're going back!'

'Yes.'

'You want more deaths, do you! More and more? Is that what you want?'

'No . . . no, I don't.'

'Is human life so . . . pointless?'

'No . . . no, it's not.'

'You're going back to the same place?'

'Yes.'

'Is it bad there? The fighting?'

'Yes.'

'Well, come and see me before you go, won't you, because I want to ask you some more questions. Now's not the time or place.'

'I certainly will, Harold. And thank you again. For all you did . . . for all you did for her.'

'It was nothing.'

'No, you did everything you could. And more.'

Harold took off his glasses and cleaned them on the sheet. His fingers were like twigs. He said quietly:

'We both loved her, I think.'

'Yes, we did.'

'In our different ways.'

'Yes.'

'I'm so glad she allowed me to paint her for so long.'

'I am, too.'

'Goodbye, Gilbert.'

Gilbert, pale from his injury, stood at the ward door, caught the eye of his artist friend, and half waved, half saluted.

And the Raven, never flitting, still is sitting, *still*
  is sitting
On the pallid bust of Pallas just above my chamber
  door;
And his eyes have all the seeming of a demon that is
  dreaming,
And the lamplight o'er him streaming throws his
  shadow on the floor;
And my soul from out of *that* shadow that lies floating
  on the floor
    Shall be lifted – never more.

                                        Edgar Allan Poe

Sancreed

Gilbert hired a bicycle.

The tiny village of Sancreed is more or less due west of Penzance and north-west of Lamorna. The ride there from the hospital took him the best part of an hour, with a chilly breeze on his face but with his body warming up as he went. Once, forced to stop by a butcher's cart going too fast, he took the opportunity to pick some wild flowers from the hedgerows, and mixed them in with some thrift from his pocket, the pink so common on the clifftops where they walked.

Cycling, he was hit by the sweet smell of dung as he passed a farm, and the sharp sting of sea air as he made the top of a hill. He noticed the cawing crows and a flock of gulls . . . and the occasional raven. He noticed how, a little inland, the slopes were scarred by smaller rocks, so tiny after the huge granite slabs at Lamorna.

This forward motion for the best part of an hour was long enough for his mind to go back to their best days. Crows and gulls and ravens were common enough in Cornwall, as were the guillemots and razor-bills returning in March, but what about the day they climbed to a dangerous spot to see the storm petrel, a rarity hurled on to the coast by an October gale? He remembered the tiny abrasions that climb had left on Florence's ankles, and the contrast her voice made with the drowsy sound of the mill; he could see her brother's face bending over rock pools, pools glowing with urchin and sea anemones. He remembered her love of chicory and lettuce salad and her body swirling in the shed, around and around and around in his head.

Buoyed up by these memories he heard himself whistling and then he was angry that he was, and then he was even angrier because A.J. started singing at the top of his voice:

> 'You can only wear one tie
> Have one eyeglass in your eye
> One coffin when you die
> Don't you know!'

'No!' Gilbert shouted at the hedges. 'No, *not now*!'

The Sancreed sign.

His stomach in a squeeze, the strength swiftly ebbing from his legs, but with his straight mouth firmly set, he placed the bicycle against the churchyard gate. He turned right past two heavy Cornish cross heads, paced along a row of eighteenth-century stones, some as high as his shoulder, searching slowly, walking with great care until he saw the newish mound. That was it. It was right on the far edge of the consecrated ground. Perhaps the vicar felt it was a case of this far but not an inch further.

This is where she is.

He paused and took out the flowers.

He took off his hat.

He had not been to her marriage, though he had often enough painfully imagined the scene in Westminster, the guests filling up the pews, Joey smiling openly on everyone, Florence walking down the aisle on her father's arm, some flowers in her hand, as Alfred Munnings turned, eyebrows raised, his face tanned and triumphant, to claim her.

He had not been to her funeral, though he had often enough painfully imagined the wagonettes and the horse-drawn hearse, the mourners walking in pairs with black crêpe on their skirts and arms. Who were the bearers? He did not know. Did her mother and father attend? Did Joey? He did not know. He could see the flowers. There must have been flowers, boxes full of flowers from Boskenna, flowers for Florence.

He moved forward with his own. He saw:

EDITH FLORENCE
'BLOTE'
WIFE OF
A.J. MUNNINGS
SEP. 4 1888
JULY 24 1914

It was a small stone, so low and so small, Gilbert had to stoop down to read it, as if the stone knew its plain, apologetic position. He placed his bunch of wild flowers at his feet, which was where he imagined her feet would be. The mound looked as small as Sammy's. Then he knelt, and closed his eyes. He knew memory-pain.

Sammy.

How fragile birds' eggs were.

Florence.

Blote.

Edith Florence.

Wife of A.J. Munnings.

He could feel the pressure of her hand.

Yes, he could feel it.

He could see her walking, so upright, along the Penzance Promenade.

Yes, he could see her. In the Morrab Library.

He could feel her waist as she skated along.

He could hear her little murmurings as she kissed him.

Yes, if he listened, if he really listened, he could hear her . . . little murmurings.

He could see the wild look in her eyes as all her horses won, all all won.

Yes, so wild, her purple-lined eyes.

Yet so still and calm, floating, Botticelli's Venus.

Would all this go away? Would it all fade into a dull ache? Would it heal, as the bullet wound in his head was already healing? Would it? She said:

I hope you're safe, Gilbert, that's all.

I'm safe. I've survived, so far.

Was it a very long journey to Nigeria?

Yes, and back.

There and back?

But he didn't want to tell her about the terrible marches and the sickness. He would, fairly soon, go back to all that, the canoes and the mud huts and the bursts of fire from river banks; yes, he had to go back, but that was not what he came to Sancreed for. He wanted to hear her voice, though he could hear no sound now beyond the birds in the square church tower. When he opened his eyes he read the simple facts on the small stone again. Then he stood up and took two upright paces back, as an officer, before he bent his head. Below, the grass showed the patches where his feet and his knees had pressed.

Promise you'll come back.

I'll come back.

And stay alive?

I'll do my best.

Even though I broke my promise?

I'll come back.

Even though I'm useless?

I'll come back, Florence. Trust me.

Without turning for a final look, because he knew he would be back, Gilbert walked through the shadow of the tower and from the churchyard and cycled slowly back down the lanes towards the sea and Lamorna, and by the time he arrived at Laura's, with dusk falling and his face cold, he had composed himself.

All rag tag and bobtail, Laura was waiting for him with a big hug and a warm hearth, with rabbit soup and a flavouring of onion, and some home-cured ham.

In Harold's studio that night, just before he went to bed, Gilbert placed his lamp on the table. The room was full of the familiar smell of oil paint. There was an old cot, full of unused canvases, and the parcel left for him had a familiar shape too. It was large and flat. An envelope was glued to the brown wrapping and the writing on the envelope was in a familiar hand.

Captain C.G. Evans

Gilbert sat on Harold's wooden chair, next to his easel, and opened the envelope.

Dear Ev,

I know you will come back to Lamorna and, when you do, I hope you will accept this.

A.J.M.

Gilbert took off the brown paper, making sure his fingers kept well clear of the surface. In his hands he held, close to the lamp, *Morning Ride*, the portrait of Florence on Merrilegs.

The Future and the Past

Dame Laura Knight (1877–1972) was only the second woman to be elected a full Royal Academician (1936). When the President addressed the Academy he began not with 'Ladies and Gentlemen' but with 'Gentlemen . . . Laura, you're one of us'.

Given all that had happened, Harold Knight (1874–1961) was not disappointed to leave Cornwall in 1920. He recovered his health and was elected to the Royal Academy one year after Laura.

Joey Carter-Wood was killed in France in 1916.

Major Gilbert Evans, Deputy Surveyor General in Nigeria, retired in 1933 to Lamorna to live in the clifftop house he started to build in 1912. He died in Penzance in 1966.

Sir Alfred Munnings (1878–1959) was elected President of the Royal Academy in 1944. In 1949, the year in which he retired from that position, he made a controversial speech.

Author's Note

Anyone who has read the autobiographies of Sir Alfred Munnings and Dame Laura Knight will know how indebted I am to them. Anyone who has read them will also know that Munnings does not say one word about the central events in Cornwall described here, while Laura Knight alludes to them only in the most tantalising way.

The two excellent biographies of Munnings, *The Englishman* (1962) by Reginald Pound and *What a Go!* (1988) by Jean Goodman, do address the years he spent in Lamorna and were of course invaluable.

When travelling and 'reading around' the period I became absorbed in, and influenced by, the work of A.C. Benson and Adrian Bell.

Winston Churchill plays a very small, non-speaking part in *Summer in February*, but the fellow commonership given to me by Churchill College, Cambridge, helped me, in a large way, to complete it.

I am very grateful to Brian Manning for encouraging me to start on this story; and above all to David Evans, the younger son of Major Gilbert Evans, without whose detailed and sympathetic co-operation this book would have been impossible.

To buy any of our books and to find out
more about Abacus and Little, Brown, our authors
and titles, as well as events and book clubs,
visit our website

www.littlebrown.co.uk

and follow us on Twitter

**@AbacusBooks
@LittleBrownUK**

To order any Abacus titles p & p free in the UK,
please contact our mail order supplier on:

+ 44 (0)1832 737525

Customers not based in the UK should contact
the same number for appropriate postage
and packing costs.